UNDERGROUND
ROYALTY

Lost Island
PRESS

UNDERGROUND
ROYALTY

BELLADONNA, BOOK 2

MEL TORREFRANCA

Lost Island
—— P R E S S ——

Underground Royalty
Copyright © 2025 Mel Torrefranca

All rights reserved. No part of this book may be reproduced or used in any manner without written permission of the copyright owner except in the case of brief quotations embodied in critical articles and reviews.

Library of Congress Control Number: 2025904853

ISBN 978-1-962876-08-7 (paperback)
ISBN 978-1-962876-07-0 (ebook)

This book is a work of fiction. Names, characters, places, and incidents either are the product of the author's imagination or are used fictitiously. Any resemblance to actual events, businesses, companies, locales or persons, living or dead, is entirely coincidental.

Cover design by MAD Book Covers
Select interior illustrations by Gonzalo Mansilla

Lost Island Press LLC
Oro Valley, AZ
lostislandpress.com

GUARDIAN DIVISIONS

RESEARCH

DEFENSE

MEDICAL

For Dad

PROLOGUE

AMONG CHERRY BLOSSOMS

Twenty-one days and fourteen hours ago...

The old man stood out like a thorny rose among cherry blossoms. He had buttoned his dress shirt in misalignment, causing one collar to droop lower than the other.

From across the crowded ballroom, Pinto squinted, catching flashes of the redhead as guardians twirled between them, stomping their feet to the melody. His unbrushed, dyed auburn hair had grown out, leaving his roots a charred gray that matched his stubble. *Why would the Force invite a sloppy man like him to our graduation?*

Perhaps the Force *hadn't* invited him. Unlike others, he didn't dance or chat. He stood still in the chaos, sipping on a glass of blood-red wine, his eyes drifting from one attendee to the next.

The bitter taste of dread coated Pinto's tongue when the man's eyes locked on him. In an instant, the air turned to ice, and the music melted into silence. Attendees vanished, one by one, until it was only Pinto and the redhead eyeing each other.

He looks at me like he knows me. Pinto gulped and adjusted his leather eyepatch. *And something about him feels familiar too.*

From behind Pinto, Vell rushed forward into the emptiness, her violet dress rippling behind her as she led Yahshi to the center of the ballroom, his hand wrapped tightly in hers. Her silky, petal-like sleeves paired nicely with Yahshi's sage green suit.

Together, they bloomed.

The warmth of attendees flooded the room again as the band's music returned, thawing the frost in Pinto's veins. He watched from afar as Vell guided Yahshi's hand to her waist and stepped closer, leaning in to whisper. The chatter kept Pinto from hearing her.

"What?" Yahshi asked. It was easy to read his lips.

Vell grinned as she placed her free hand on his shoulder. Whatever she said next made Yahshi look at the Academy guardians by the stage. They stared back, muttering under their breaths.

I bet they're concerned about his behavior earlier, Pinto deduced, recalling Yahshi's bold reaction to the announcement of Vell's Defense Division placement. *I hope they let it slide. He's been doing so much better these past few months.*

When Pinto looked back at Yahshi and Vell, they were dancing and laughing as though they hadn't been tense just seconds ago. The change in demeanor seemed to ease Roz and Embre, who turned their attention elsewhere, smiles returning.

But Blimmery didn't smile with them. His eyes drifted from Yahshi and Vell to the redhead, who raised his wine glass, acknowledging him with a crooked grin.

Pinto narrowed his eye. *Do they know each other?*

Blimmery studied the old man, holding his stern expression.

"Congratulations, Red."

It took a moment for Pinto to process that someone had spoken to him, referencing his fiery formal wear. He faced a guardian who looked a year or two older than him. She had stood next to Cal in the crowd earlier and had cheered when Roz announced Vell and Quax's unit placements.

"I like your formal wear." She tucked her hands into the pockets of her black leather jacket, which she had paired with a crimson dress.

"Because it matches yours?" Pinto asked.

"Maybe I like red."

"I don't have a preference, but my sister always called red my color." Pinto frowned at the ribbon that tied the guardian's ash-brown hair into a ponytail—its golden shade gleamed like his blazer buttons. "I assume you're one of Commander Cal's unit members."

"As of tomorrow, *ex*-unit member." She extended a hand. "Evaris Starfall. Defense."

"Starfall..." Pinto chuckled, ignoring her gesture. "You're from that City family of fashion designers. How did you end up as a guardian?"

"I have a thing for breaking codes." Evaris withdrew her unshaken hand, turning her attention to the old redhead. "But that's enough about me—I'd rather talk about you ogling Professor Ogga."

"Don't be crude. I wasn't *ogling* him."

"I know, but I couldn't resist the wordplay."

"Wait..." The band's strings swelled as Pinto followed Evaris's gaze to the man. "Did you say *Professor*?"

"He's a guardian."

"Him?"

"He's sharper than he looks. Reads a book a day, leads all the important meetings, and reports directly to Emperor Vakoi."

As a final violin note ripped through the air, Pinto smiled at Evaris. "You seem to know a lot about him."

"I notice things. Just like I noticed you." She offered a hand again, this time to dance. "How about a few songs?"

"How about *one*?" He took her hand, and with a chuckle, she yanked him into the crowd.

Together, they burned.

PART 1
REWIND

CHAPTER 1

CONTROLLED CHAOS

Thirteen days and one hour ago…

♫ HIDE IN PLAIN SIGHT · JIM JAMES ♫

"He murdered his own father."

Pinto strangled his pen, struggling to document the guardian's claim.

"Hurry," Famir said, nudging his side.

I can't lose my restraint. Pinto closed his eye and took a deep breath, reminding himself that the first forty-eight hours following Yahshi's desertion would be most crucial in the Force's effort to trace him. *If I want the truth, I need to log everything—even what I don't believe.*

So he exhaled, opened his eye, and brought his pen to the transcript.

> [LOCATION: Detainment Facility, Interrogation Room 3]
>
> ROZ: He murdered his own father.

Famir waited until Pinto completed the sentence to address their witness again. "Commander, let's rewind to your arrival. What was the first thing you saw?"

Pinto looked up as Roz leaned in, his shoulders spread, his hands interlocked on the metal table. It looked like *he* was leading this interrogation.

"What first caught my eye," Roz said, "was the white horse in Martu's yard."

Famir elbowed Pinto again, and he lowered his head, rushing to keep up with the conversation.

ROZ: I knew a guardian didn't belong there, so I untied the horse and sent it running. Then I knocked on the door, and Martu answered, his son behind him. Before I could say a word, Yahshi drew his swords, and...

FAMIR: He drew his swords, and...?

ROZ: He got angry. Furious.

Pinto glanced up to find Roz's gaze lost in the darkness of the sparsely lit interrogation room.

"And then he murdered his father right in front of me."

Pinto ducked his head, transcribing the words without thinking. His mind wandered back to eighteen months ago, during orientation at Belladonna Guardian Academy.

"I'm just worried I let my father down today," Yahshi had said. *"I'm his only family, and he has no idea when he'll see me again. He must be heartbroken."*

Pinto's jaw tightened. *Yahshi loved his father too much to kill him.*

"We engaged in a quick skirmish, but he got past the door. That's when he stole my horse and headed east, leaving me no choice but to pursue him on foot."

That's enough. Pinto slammed his pen down and glared at Roz. "Yes, we confirmed that Martu Konya was a false convert. And yes, Yahshi knew and kept it a secret. He may have breached our trust, but I refuse to blame him for a completely different crime he didn't commit. Tell me, Commander, why after breaking Protocol to protect his father, Yahshi would skip his meeting yesterday to *murder* him? How does that make sense? Why would he—"

"Pinto!" Famir's mustache twitched with every word. "Must I call in a scribe to replace you?"

He ignored his unit leader, locking his eye on Roz.

"I know it's hard to accept," Roz said with a slight pout, "but think about it—this behavior isn't out of character for Yahshi. Sometimes he acts without reason."

"He may be senseless at times, but he's not heartless," Pinto said in a softer voice.

"He injured Quax over a petty argument, abandoned you during the final filtration, and jumped off a balcony to avoid shadowing Cal," Roz argued. "That sounds pretty heartless to me. Perhaps he thought we'd kill him for his Protocol violation, so he took his rage out on his father, the cause of it all."

Pinto blinked, at a loss for words. He hadn't known that Cal had been Yahshi's initial shadow unit leader, or that he had jumped to avoid her. The shadow confidentiality rule had kept the full story behind Yahshi's outbursts concealed from him. *What made him so afraid of Cal?*

Pinto shook his head, brushing the question away. "You violated Protocol too," he said, taking the offensive role. "You traveled past the border when you should've returned to the City."

"On a technical basis, yes, I made a minor Protocol violation that warrants a few months of community service. What you need to understand, though, is that I entered Eastern Territory hoping to stop Yahshi while I was right on his tail. I searched all night and all day. Even now, I still haven't slept. If my effort for the Force is a crime, then I will gladly spend a week pruning flowers in the parks."

As Pinto clenched his teeth, Famir forced a chuckle. "I-I apologize for my unit member's behavior, Commander. He's not himself today."

"Oh, it's understandable, considering his connection to Yahshi. You know the saying—final five, side by side." Roz stood and dusted his pants—dirtied from his night of searching. "If you need anything else, I'll be counting sheep in Room 17."

Famir grinned. "I appreciate your time, Commander."

As Roz left, Pinto fought the urge to follow him. *He wouldn't cut this interrogation short unless he was hiding something.*

"He's right." Famir plucked the pen and transcript out of Pinto's grip. "You're not in the right state of mind to investigate Yahshi's crimes—plus, I'm sure you're exhausted after staying up all night. Why don't you rest for now, and return once you wake?"

Pinto's face ran hot. He almost protested, but with a glance at a clock on the wall, he shut his mouth. While sleep didn't call him, he could use the extra time to speak with Vell. *She'll be leaving any minute now.*

Pinto nodded, stood, and left the room. The chilling corridors of the Detainment Facility greeted him on his way to the front door, torchlights flickering.

In the foyer, Roz stood in the vast emptiness, his arms crossed. "Planning to see Vell?"

Pinto ignored him, speed-walking toward the door.

"Do me a favor. See if she knew about Yahshi leaving."

"I'm not doing you any favors," Pinto muttered as he passed him.

Roz swerved, snatching his shoulder. "Drop the attitude," he whispered, his deep voice rumbling in Pinto's ear. "We're not at the Academy anymore."

Goosebumps sprang over Pinto's neck as Roz let go.

He straightened and continued walking, slow and steady, but when he reached the metal door, his hands fumbled with the bar.

Dammit. His act of calm crumbled as he skidded onto the grass outside. It took both arms to shut the heavy door behind him, and he half believed Roz was pushing the other side.

"Hey, Red."

Pinto turned to Evaris Starfall of the Defense Division, posted at the Facility entrance.

Red? He grazed a hand against his cheek, wondering if he appeared flustered—but then he remembered when she'd called him *Red* at the graduation ball, referencing his formal wear.

"What's wrong?"

"Uh... nothing." Pinto dropped his arm and looked back at the door. Roz could exit any moment now. "Shouldn't you be at the Hospital?"

"My unit's staying behind to manage the Facility." With a sigh, she reached out for him. "Look, I can't imagine—"

He stepped back, dodging her attempt at comfort. "Sorry, Commander, I..."

She tilted her head with a frown.

"I have to go," he said, already darting across the clearing.

"Where?" Evaris shouted.

It took Pinto a solid minute after reaching the stable to catch his breath. He secured a saddle and bridle on his white horse, leading it outside in record time. Only then did Roz leave the Facility—their gazes locked from opposite ends of the clearing.

He's framing Yahshi, and I'm gonna find out why.

Pinto stopped his horse by Vakoi City Hospital and scowled at the line of shimmering vaults disappearing eastward. Scanning the remaining guardians, he snapped his head left and right. His grip on the reins loosened at the sight of Quax and Cal packing tools into a passenger box. *Thank the stars. Vell's still here.*

Pinto secured his horse and dove headfirst into the chaos. "Commander Cal!"

Quax and his older sister looked over as Pinto approached them, their brows rising in sync.

"Where's Vell? It's urgent." He peered into the aluminum passenger box, which they had stuffed with an absurd amount of tools.

"We're getting ready to leave," Cal said, her tone flat.

"She's in the lab." Quax pointed to the Hospital's front steps, earning a glare from his sister.

Pinto thanked him and bolted toward the building. Guardians carrying extra primary tools, wooden boxes, and white briefcases formed a whirlwind around him as he ran up the stairs into a network of stark hallways and staircases. While he'd never been inside the Hospital before, he recalled the floor plans he'd studied at the Academy and made a sharp turn, descending the nearest stairway into the basement's serum and remediation department.

The first door on the left brought him to the lab, just as he'd memorized. Across the room, Vell's black hair swayed as she packed Keiyo's vials of belladonna serum into a white briefcase.

"Vell!"

She spun around, her frown loosening. He took a few steps toward her, and she rushed forward, wrapping him in a tight hug.

"I'm glad you're here," she said.

Pinto closed his eye, tightening his arms around her. "When do you leave?"

"Any minute." She pulled away and stared up at him. "Did Commander Roz return yet?"

"Is it true?" Keiyo cut in, fidgeting with a vial. "About Yahshi's father?"

Pinto peered over Vell's shoulder, studying Keiyo's expression to gauge his level of concern. He wasn't sure if he was asking about Martu's connection to the Bayins, or about his death.

"What? Surprised to see me?" Keiyo chuckled at Pinto's silence. "Us doctors can help out during emergencies. You have *no idea* how many berries I picked this morning."

"Well, is it true or not?" Vell asked. "Is Martu a false convert?"

Pinto sighed, relieved Roz's accusation about Yahshi killing his father hadn't spread yet. He'd rather not burden Vell with the news until her return from the search.

"It's true," he confirmed. Martu hadn't genuinely pledged his loyalty to the Vakoi Empire when he'd moved west after the War. Like the Bayins, he'd likely converted to gather information as a spy for the Underground.

He thought back to Dice Bayin, a fellow Academy trainee from his hometown. As a boy, Dice once excluded Pinto from a game, claiming his parents wouldn't let him play with pirates—a jab at his eyepatch. Pinto had taken his remark as a sign that the Bayins supported the Eastern raids. And he'd been right. They were spies. Dice had vanished with his family without a trace, and for months, the Force searched with no leads—until yesterday.

"We just received an anonymous tip that Dice's father, who was a postal officer before he disappeared, had been delivering personal letters to Martu during work trips to Sitra," Pinto explained. "We called Yahshi in for a meeting to see whether he knew about it. I thought he was oblivious, but he ran, so…"

"No, Pinto, I wasn't asking about Martu being a false convert," Keiyo said. "I was asking about him being dead."

Oh, great…

"Dead?" Vell swerved, facing Keiyo with widened eyes. "Why didn't you say anything?"

"I didn't want to stress you out, alright?" He shot his palms up in surrender, dropping the belladonna vial he'd been fidgeting with. It shattered against the pearly floor, forming a red pool between their boots.

With a sigh, Vell looked back at Pinto, awaiting further clarification.

Pinto gulped. "It's true that Martu was murdered last night, and…"

Her face drained of color. "And what?"

"According to Commander Roz, it was…" He trailed off again, but Vell filled in the blanks.

"No." She frowned at the blood-like puddle of serum on the floor. "Yahshi would never."

"Something isn't adding up," Pinto said, omitting his suspicions about Roz for now—Vell had enough to stress about. "I heard another Research unit found a bag in his flat. They say he's been planning to run for a while. Maybe he feared we were getting closer to uncovering his father's secret."

"So when you called Yahshi into that meeting, he panicked and ran off," she concluded.

"Exactly."

"But why wouldn't he bring his bag?"

"Wait." Keiyo rubbed his chin. "Are you saying Yahshi could be a spy?"

"No," Pinto said without hesitation. "I think he just cared about his father more than he cared about Protocol."

"Assuming you're right"—Vell's voice was softer now—"and Yahshi knew the entire time, aren't you mad?"

"Now's not the time for that," Pinto said. Yahshi had a lot to answer for, but none of it would matter if he wasn't here to explain himself. "First, we need to focus on bringing him home."

Vell's expression lightened, and Pinto couldn't place why she looked surprised.

The door opened, drawing their eyes to Quax. "Vell, you ready?"

"Almost." She held her palm out, and Keiyo passed her a few more vials to pack into her briefcase.

Quax's gaze drifted to Pinto. "Everything okay?"

He nodded, and Quax shot Vell a concerned glance before leaving the lab.

Pinto stepped over the pool of serum and broken glass, joining Vell and Keiyo at the counter. "How long will the search last?"

"Until late tomorrow night, unless we find him sooner." She finished packing the vials, closed her briefcase, and swung it off the counter. "My unit's starting at the mid-east coastline and heading north from there, toward Atherus City."

"Could he have traveled there this quickly?"

"If he hitched a ride with traders, he could be anywhere by now." Vell's voice grew frantic and raspy. She wouldn't look him in the eye. "We're focusing on production points—they have a history of harboring criminals and passing off supplies."

"What's wrong?" Keiyo asked, stealing Pinto's question.

"If we trace him," she said, "you know what happens next."

"He'll be interrogated," Pinto stated.

"And after that?"

"Vell..."

"No, listen to me." She stared deeply into Pinto's eye, her cheeks reddening. "Do you really think the Force would allow Yahshi to walk free? After everything that's happened, and this crazy lie they believe, how can we trust them to treat him fairly?"

"She's right." Keiyo tucked his hands into his overcoat pockets. "The punishment for keeping his father's secret is death. And if he also killed him—"

"He *didn't*," Vell snapped.

"I'm not saying he did," Keiyo said. "But if they believe that—"

"Stop!" Pinto's eye hopped back and forth between them. "I promise, I'll talk to the other professors and get him pardoned."

"No disrespect, Pinto," Keiyo said, raising his voice, "but you don't have any authority in the Research Division."

Pinto held his breath, the statement piercing his lungs like an arrow.

"I don't know what to do." Vell dragged a hand down her face, muffling her voice. "None of us have control over this."

"Shut it!" Pinto shouted, making her flinch. "Of course we have control!"

She stepped back, and Keiyo sighed, shaking his head.

Pinto looked away. "Sorry," he whispered.

Quax opened the door again, singing, "Sister's getting antsy!"

Vell started for her unit member, but she stopped to look back at Pinto.

"Just focus on the search, okay?" He managed a weak grin. "I'll handle things here."

She lingered a moment, then left with Quax down the hall.

"You better stick to your word." Keiyo leaned back against the counter, his mouth forming a grim line. "I've been fighting myself all morning not to get her hopes up—to be realistic about this—but then you barged in with a crazy promise to save Yahshi's life. If they end up killing him now, it'll hurt even more. So... well done, *Professor*. I hope you have a plan."

The morning after the Defense Division left on the search, all thirty-two members of the Research Division converged in Meeting Room 1 in the Investigation Office to share evidence and discuss their next steps. They sat around a comically large, circular table—except for a man in his mid-fifties, who stood in the hollowed-out middle of the table, clutching a golden bell. By his freshly dyed hair and crooked tie, Pinto recognized him as the disheveled man from his graduation ball.

"He's sharper than he looks," Evaris had said. *"Reads a book a day, leads all the important meetings, and reports directly to Emperor Vakoi."*

Ogga rang his bell, silencing the mumbling professors. In his other hand was a hefty bag, which he plopped onto the marble floor—its contents clinked with the sound of glass.

"Yahshi Konya's getaway bag. Discovered in his flat." Ogga's voice wasn't as deep as Pinto had expected of the so-called *most important guardian in the Research Division.* There was a boyish raspiness to it.

Professors leaned in as Ogga crouched by Yahshi's bag, unbuttoned the main compartment, and pulled out its contents, narrating his findings. "Eight maintenance vials. All untaken."

Ogga chuckled as he removed a seemingly endless series of velvet pouches. "Exactly 3,198 coins, amounting to his earned bills of exchange for two weeks of service—the second of which he didn't complete, of course—minus unknown personal expenses."

Next came three daggers, sixteen throwing darts, and maps with golden-edged pages that marked them as original documents from the archives. "Border Control Towers," Ogga noted, "Eastern Officer Patrol Routes, Eastern Trade Routes..."

Pinto's eye widened as Ogga removed the last item. "The Bayin case files, assigned to Professor Pinto Dempsey of Frontal."

Famir frowned at Pinto from across the table. "Explain how Yahshi acquired your files."

The blood rushed to Pinto's head as every professor awaited his reply. With a deep breath, he folded his hands under the table. "I noticed them missing a few days ago, but I had no clue Yahshi possessed them."

Famir raised his voice. "Why didn't you tell me?"

"I thought I had a rival." Pinto lowered his gaze. "That someone was trying to crack the case before me."

One professor chuckled, then another, and soon, the tension melted into laughter. Pinto's face warmed up, but the noise halted when Ogga rang his bell again. "It's fair to assume that Professor Pinto had nothing to do with his friend obtaining the Bayin files unless proven otherwise."

Pinto smiled back at Ogga. He had spent nearly two weeks as a guardian in the Force, and he could count on one hand how many times guardians had used his honorific *Professor.*

"Now." Ogga's gaze swept over every professor in the room. "May we stay on topic?"

Everyone nodded in unison, and Ogga, pleased, stared down at the evidence. "What can we gather from this?"

Pinto studied the contents scattered across the floor. Yahshi had a motive—by taking those files, he protected Martu's secret *and* himself from getting caught for keeping it. The real question was not *why* Yahshi took the files, but *how*.

Pinto stiffened, remembering when Yahshi had knocked on his door to chat after their first day in service. He had been so excited to tell him about his assignment to the Bayin case that he'd run late for a welcoming supper with his unit.

As Pinto rushed to the door, Yahshi held his hands out. *"Here. I'll lock up for you."*

He tossed his ring of keys without a second thought.

But Yahshi couldn't have taken the files while professors were still working, Pinto thought. *He must have snuck in late at night, after returning my keys.*

That's when the last puzzle piece snapped into place—the evening before last, Pinto and his fellow graduates had shared supper at a restaurant to discuss their first week of service. He had told them about the Bayin files disappearing, to which Keiyo had responded, with an odd seriousness, *"When did those files go missing?"*

Yahshi nearly choked on his bite, and soon after, he left for the restroom. He had hardly touched his plate of fish.

In the hour I didn't have my keys, Yahshi must have tricked Keiyo into getting involved. With his crafting skills and access to Vakoi City Hospital's equipment, he could have easily made a duplicate, which Yahshi used to sneak in later, once the Office was empty.

"Alright, enough mumbling. Let's break this down step by step." Ogga tossed a coin pouch up and snatched it from the air. "We know these pouches amount to 3,198 coins, which means?"

"He spent 802 coins before his desertion," Famir said without a moment of thought.

"In just eight days?" a second guardian asked.

"He couldn't have spent it all on food," said a third.

Embre cleared her throat and stood, a stack of pages in hand. "I interrogated a convenience store clerk this morning who claims to have encountered Yahshi the night before his desertion." She circled the table, passing out copies of the interrogation transcript as she summarized the information. "He was wearing a black headband over his forehead, to cover his mark, and he overpaid for the store's entire stock of nonperishables—he spent 500 coins."

"The numbers line up," Famir said. "That leaves 302 coins for personal expenses—a reasonable spending amount to cover food outside the Palace and Complex during his time here."

"But where did the nonperishables go?" Ogga nudged the bag with his boot.

"The clerk saw Yahshi with a girl," Embre said. "She had black hair and bangs. Looked about the same age. Wore a beige trench coat."

"So the girl has the food," Ogga concluded. "They were planning to leave together."

"Commander Roz didn't mention a girl with Yahshi at his father's house," Famir countered.

"Clearly, Yahshi left the bag *and* the girl," Embre said.

"She's probably still in Vakoi City, and she may even know his destination." Ogga pointed to a scrawny older guardian around his age. "Professor Kanter, I'd like your unit to investigate Yahshi's accomplice."

Kanter nodded, maintaining his blank expression.

Embre handed Pinto the clerk's interrogation transcript, and he skimmed it over as Ogga continued to their next topic of discussion. "The Defense Division will return tonight at the latest. We need a backup plan in case Yahshi isn't with them. Ideas?"

"I know this would look bad for us"—Embre returned to her seat—"but I propose we have Doctor Blimmery publish a wanted article in *Capital Weekly* announcing Yahshi's desertion."

"There'd be an uproar," Famir said. "People will see weakness in the Force."

"Temporarily." Embre held her calm. "That's the price we pay to ensure everyone's on the lookout. Besides—after he's traced, we can publish a new article and rewrite the story."

"What kind of rewritten story could restore the people's trust?" Famir asked.

"How about this?" Embre straightened her back and spoke in a higher pitch. *"After further investigation, the Research Division uncovered that Commander Yahshi Konya of Sitra didn't know about his father's affiliation to the Underground. He killed Martu Konya after discovering the truth out of outrage and loyalty to the Force. Then he ran, fearing we wouldn't believe him."*

"That could work." Famir nodded slowly. "We can paint him as a hero in memory."

Pinto blinked. "In memory?"

The look on Embre and Famir's faces answered his question.

"We can't kill him," Pinto argued.

"Shadow, he broke Protocol," said his unit member.

Pinto pursed his lips. *I'm not your shadow anymore.*

"He kept a massive secret from us and couldn't own up to it. His fate isn't up to negotiation," Famir continued. "We'll say the Underground killed him before we could bring him home, to keep the story plausible."

Pinto shot up from his seat. How could they plan to kill Yahshi before confirming the real story? He kept his father's secret, skipped his maintenance vials, abused his friends' trust to steal important documents, and deserted the Force. However, behind his multiple violations of Protocol had to be an understandable motive. *There must be a reason to pardon him.*

"I'm sorry, Pinto," Embre replied to his outraged silence. "Yahshi brought this onto himself."

"No, he didn't." Finally, Pinto's argument came together and left his mouth in a cohesive stream. "Out of everyone here, I know Yahshi best. I shared a quarter with him at the Academy for months, and we helped each other make the final five. I think I have the best idea of what happened." He caught Ogga's gaze. "May I?"

The redhead offered a crooked grin. "The floor is yours."

Pinto walked through the table's opening, joining Ogga in the middle, and stared at Yahshi's getaway bag. "Martu was loyal to the Underground, but I doubt Yahshi was. I think he joined the Academy because he *disagreed* with his father. If Yahshi's motives were fishy, I would have known."

Embre sighed. "Pinto, you can't just assume that—"

"Please, let me finish."

She looked away with an eye-roll.

"Even if Yahshi didn't share his father's views, he likely didn't want him killed, so he broke Protocol to keep his secret. No wonder he panicked when I told him about our breakthrough in the Bayin case. He feared we'd discover the truth and wouldn't forgive him."

The guardians watched Pinto intently as he paused for a breath.

"Look at it this way. Since his father was a false convert, he might have crucial knowledge about the Underground."

Despite not believing that Yahshi had killed Martu, Pinto couldn't oppose Roz without evidence, so he went along with the story for now.

"Maybe the truth isn't too far off from Professor Embre's cover story. To me, Yahshi murdering his father proves his loyalty to us. If granted a pardon, I'm confident he would gladly share what we need to know. He's our key to ending the Underground, not a target to trace."

Some guardians tilted their heads in confusion. Others closed their eyes in thought.

"Well?" Ogga spun in place, holding his arms out. "Should we take this to the other divisions?"

It was silent for a moment longer before the frail, older guardian raised his hand. "I'll back the pardon," Kanter said, his voice stronger than Pinto had anticipated.

The guardians started mumbling, and with discussion came more raised hands.

After the meeting adjourned, the Research guardians dispersed, their discussions continuing in hushed voices. Pinto spotted Kanter gathering a stack of papers, his bony fingers methodically stacking copies of interrogation transcripts and written reports.

Pinto straightened his tie and looped around the table. "Professor Kanter?"

The older guardian looked up, his expression neutral but his eyes sharp. He said nothing as he folded his stack of papers in half. He simply waited.

"I wanted to thank you. If you didn't raise your hand, I'm not sure anyone else would've."

With a nod, Kanter tucked the folded papers into his overcoat.

"But I'm curious." Pinto leaned in, quieting his voice. "What made you back the pardon?"

Kanter's eyes darted to Ogga, who hung his meeting bell on a hook. A moment passed before he stood, gesturing for Pinto to follow. "Walk with me."

Pinto left with him, and they descended the staircase together.

"You crafted your argument well," Kanter said. "But more importantly, I find it honorable to protect guardians who clash with the wrong people. Sometimes the most dangerous are among our own."

Pinto thought of his encounter with Roz in the Detainment Facility. "Do you mean to say that guardians can't always be trusted?"

"That's not what I meant." Kanter patted Pinto's shoulder with an unsettling look on his face. His eyes seemed to say, *That's exactly what I meant.*

CHAPTER 2

NUMBER FORTY-THREE

Twelve days and two hours ago...

♫ MAPLE SAP - RIVER WHYLESS ♫

Saunti tugged his blood-orange jumpsuit on, preparing for another miserable ten-hour shift.

Is my role in the Underground nothing more than my role here?

The sound of chopping logs echoed from the workroom into the foyer as Saunti buttoned the weighted fabric over his personal clothes, cloaking himself in the bright color that marked every worker at Vakoi's production points.

Across the foyer, his reflection in the mirror scowled at him. *Am I nothing but one of many identical units? Essential, but replaceable?* He tied his hair back into a low bun and slammed his cabinet door shut, revealing the number forty-three engraved into it—the same one embroidered into the fabric over his chest.

Saunti shivered as the front door burst open, inviting a chilling breeze. He looked over as Podge rushed inside and kicked the door shut with his boot, panting heavily. He lived farther than most workers, along the City's coast, which often resulted in him literally running late.

"Well, if it isn't Saunti!" Podge exclaimed between gasps. He stumbled to cabinet forty-four, pulled his orange jumpsuit out, and slung it over his shoulder. Then, one by one, he transferred items from his cabinet onto the bench behind him, rummaging for something buried in the mess.

Saunti didn't understand why Podge kept so many items at the mill. *The more you bring to work, the more permanent your job becomes. And this can't be permanent.* He glared at the mandatory portrait of Emperor Vakoi hanging over the workroom door, but his frown loosened at an odd detail. The foyer's portrait frame had always been gold-plated, but this one was silver.

Did they replace it?

"Hello?" Podge called, still rustling through his cabinet. "Are you still there?"

"I'm still here," Saunti said. "I'm just not listening."

"I asked if you heard about the production point inspections. Apparently the Nightshades were crawling everywhere yesterday. My guys think they're looking for someone."

Saunti ignored the comment, acting oblivious—even though he *had* heard about the inspections. Like his mother always said, *Looking ignorant can only play in your favor.*

Podge flung a tattered red book onto the bench, and Saunti's eyes widened at the title—*The Force's Hidden Agenda* by Meridian Owding. While his mother would never keep an incriminating book at home, she had once outlined its contents. Published about forty years ago, the author exposed how the Force was fabricating crimes and blaming them on the Atherus Empire, just to justify Vakoi's eventual seizure of its land. The Nightshades executed the author shortly after its release—before most people even read it.

"What the hell?" Saunti whispered fiercely. "You brought that thing *here*?"

"Oh, relax."

"How the hell did you even *get* the Meridian book? I thought the Nightshades burned them all ages ago."

"Sure, in the West. But they didn't have power over our land back then, and by the time they won the War, they forgot about it. There are more of those bad boys circling around than you think."

"Doesn't mean you can lug one to work. The Nightshades would kill you." He wasn't exaggerating—just possessing a banned book warranted the death penalty.

"*Easy*, now."

Saunti shook his head with a sigh. He had known that Podge's family shared rebel beliefs for years—mainly because Podge had a hard time hiding it. *One of these days, he'll get himself killed.*

"Oh, and a little word of advice?" Podge pulled a few candy wrappers out of his cabinet and searched their insides for leftover pieces. "Next time, don't say anything. Recognizing the title makes you look just as guilty, you know?"

Saunti scoffed, but Podge had a point. He'd failed to follow his own mother's advice.

"Ah, bullseye! I knew I had one left." Podge swiped a package from the back of his cabinet, popped it open, and shoved a handful of peanuts into his mouth. "Listen, friend..." he said as he chewed.

"We're not friends."

"Listen, *coworker*. You free tomorrow night?"

"No."

"Me and my guys are heading to the Palace ruins. You should come."

Saunti rolled his eyes. "The ruins? Really?"

"What? It's cool."

"It's not cool. It's historic." The word lodged in his throat. He'd never told Podge, but his father had died there thirteen years ago, defending the Atherus Royal Family against the Nightshades' final assault of fire and poison.

"*It's not cool. It's historic*," Podge echoed in a mocking tone. "Gosh, you're such a Vakoi boy!"

Saunti stiffened at the label. People like Podge used it to mock officers, teachers, production point bosses, and anyone else deemed *too loyal* to Vakoi's regime. He was *not* a Vakoi boy; he was a member of the Underground.

"Get rid of that book," he snapped, pointing at Podge on his way to the workroom.

"Hey, wait." Podge rushed after him. "Tomorrow night's gonna be a big thing for us, okay? Months of work, finally coming together."

"Congratulations," Saunti said, continuing to walk. He knew better than to get involved in the mysterious project Podge and *his guys*—whoever they were—had been working on. Unlike the Underground smuggling network, which took great precautions to appear obedient on the surface, Podge's group was likely full of reckless teenage boys begging to be called rebels.

"You remember Kwinnie, right?"

Saunti stopped in his tracks and looked back at him. "Caught-the-biggest-salmon-Kwinnie? Doesn't she make traps at the fishing plant now?"

"That's the Kwinnie."

"Well, what about her?"

"She's gonna be there tomorrow at midnight."

After a moment of pause, Saunti chuckled. He hadn't spoken to Kwinn since they were fourteen at their Atherus City Primary graduation. He had no clue Podge had kept in touch with her over the past two years.

"Ah, a smile! Number forty-three, finally curious."

"Just a bit." Saunti crossed his arms. "I didn't know Kwinn was one of *your guys*. I don't even think I've seen you talk to her before."

"Oh, but we talk. Our project's been over a year in the making." Podge nudged Saunti's shoulder. "We're gonna turn our lives around and get out of working in shitholes like this."

Saunti turned his back on him again. "Have fun with that."

"Oh, come on. Hey, hey!" He grabbed Saunti's shoulder and spun him around.

Saunti forced an agitated look. The truth was that he *did* want to know how Podge's guys planned to get out of working in shitholes like this. *But my role is with the Underground, not with them.*

Podge's lips smiled, but his eyes didn't. "I just don't get you, man. You always claimed to be busy with homework after school, but now we're sixteen, part of the stupid workforce! We don't *have* homework anymore."

There was an undertone of concern in his expression. "I mean, what are you doing with all your time after work? Do you have fun, *ever*, or is your mother your only friend?"

"My mother's my only friend," Saunti said in a monotone voice. Even before he had started assisting her as a courier, she had always stressed the importance of keeping people at arm's length. To protect the Underground, and themselves, they needed to maintain a perfect act as loyal residents. *And the thing about an act*, she'd say, *is that if someone gets to know you too well, they'll see right through it.*

"Saunti, my man..."

"No."

"Come to the ruins tomorrow."

"Like you said, I'm always busy." Saunti removed Podge's crumb-infested palm from his shoulder and turned around again. A wave of sawing and chopping noises flooded the foyer when he opened the door.

"Busy with what?" Podge shouted over the noise.

Saunti ignored him, entering the mill's vast workroom, where sawdust snuck into every breath. He coughed as he dragged himself to his workbench, following the same route through the aisles he took every day, greeting each coworker as he passed them. He knew most not by name, or even face, but by number.

"Hi, forty-one," he mumbled. "Morning, forty-two."

Saunti slipped his gloves and goggles on, grabbed a log, and pushed it across his workbench into a water-powered saw, slicing out a plank. He tossed it aside to start his first plank pile of the day, then pulled the log back, readjusted it, and pushed it forward to cut another, and another, and another. With every push, pull, and plop, he watched his plank pile grow. But for what?

Push, pull, plop. Worker sixty-seven collected Saunti's pile, so he started a new one and repeated the steps all over again. *Push, pull, plop, push, pull, plop...*

Podge entered the room a few minutes late, as usual, finally wearing orange. Once he reached his workbench and donned his identical gloves and goggles, the motions of every worker in the room fell in sync as their boss, in his hideous neon green jumpsuit, watched from the corner.

A few minutes passed before the door reopened, halting every saw in the room. Podge, number forty-four, was always the last to enter. That door wasn't supposed to open again.

The workroom turned cold as a Nightshade with a slick bun marched in from the foyer. Saunti recognized her almost instantly as Cal Avarium of Sitra. He had seen far too many portraits in *Capital Weekly* articles to forget her, despite wanting to. His mother theorized the Force wanted a pretty face—a mascot—and so Cal had become their *Belladonna Prodigy*.

Saunti chucked a plank onto his pile, breaking the silence. *What is she doing here?*

The Nightshade scanned the room with her chin high, searching for their boss. As soon as she made eye contact, the man in the neon green jumpsuit rushed over.

"Good morning, Commander Cal," he said, eyeing the bandolier of throwing blades across her chest. "It's an honor to meet you."

"I'm here for a routine inspection of this production point," Cal claimed.

Saunti and Podge exchanged a glance.

"Of course." Their boss rubbed his sweaty palms against his jumpsuit. "What do you need?"

"Let's speak in private."

The man in green nodded and faced the workers. "Back at it!"

The workroom filled with motion again as their boss led Cal toward his private office, but Saunti didn't grab another log. In his two years of working at the lumber mill, he hadn't once witnessed a *routine inspection*.

Like Podge said, they're probably looking for someone. He'd heard stories about traitors receiving support—either in shelter or supplies—from rebel production point workers.

A second Nightshade entered from the foyer, distracting Saunti once more. He looked young enough to have graduated in the recent cycle from Nightshade Academy, and his uncanny resemblance to Cal made it easy for Saunti to identify him as Quax Avarium of Sitra, her little brother.

Quax planted himself by the door, his eyes hopping from one worker to the next.

Saunti lowered his head to keep a low profile. The last thing he needed was for an unrelated investigation to expose him as part of the Underground, a role he'd kept secret since he was twelve. Being caught would mean certain death at the hands of the Force, who had no mercy for smugglers like him—he'd heard too many stories. Worse, if the Force targeted his mother next, thousands of hiders would lose access to vital supplies sourced from Atherus City. Only the two of them had the knowledge necessary to transport those goods.

Saunti froze at the memory of the banned Meridian book stashed in Podge's cabinet. He peeked at the workbench next to his, where Podge cut another plank without a care in the world.

If the Nightshade siblings search the mill, they'll kill him.

He stared intently at Podge, who still wouldn't look at him.

Great. To walk over and whisper might draw attention.

With a sigh, Saunti's eyes drifted to the restroom pass on the corner of his workbench—a necklace with a ridiculous neon green tree pendant. He snatched it and headed for the door. Forty-one and forty-two sent him concerned glances as he passed.

Quax met eyes with him. "Where are you going?"

"Restroom." Saunti held up the pass, and Quax nodded, allowing him into the foyer.

He shut the door behind him and let out a soft breath. *I need to be quick.*

With sloppy footsteps, he marched to the front door, opened it, and slammed it. Only after faking his departure did he creep toward the wall of cabinets and open the one labeled forty-four.

His heart skipped a beat as a heap of items threatened to pour out. With a step forward, he shoved his abdomen against the cabinet, blocking the items from tumbling onto the floor.

You owe me one, Podge.

With his body pressed against the cabinet, he reached in from the top and dug gently through the items, searching for the book. Several seconds passed before he gave up and grabbed the contents, pulling the mess out and setting it on the floor. The items scattered quietly, and among the snack wrappers, extra clothes, and unused ration tickets, he spotted the Meridian book.

Saunti glanced at the workroom door before kneeling and swiping the book from the ground. Only then did he realize he didn't know where to put it.

I don't have time for this. He crossed the foyer, swung the front door open, and chucked the book toward the surrounding trees. His heart raced at the thought of the junk he needed to scoop back into Podge's cabinet before returning to the workroom. *Hopefully the brother won't notice the pause in my footsteps.*

He was about to close the door when he spotted a Nightshade standing by a shimmering vault parked in the trees. She was young too—perhaps a fellow graduate of Quax's—with tan skin, long black hair, and spotless boots.

And by her boots rested the book he had just thrown.

Saunti froze as the Nightshade leaned over and took *The Force's Hidden Agenda* into her hands. Her icy-blue eyes scanned the title before darting to the number on Saunti's jumpsuit.

He let out a breath and slammed the door.

Shit.

Work ended around 6:00, when traders arrived at the mill to pack lumber into their carriages. They would transport a portion to other production points for construction, or for parts and fuel, and send the rest to shelves in the Vakoi Empire's Saver Stores. The only lumber left behind were unusable scraps—offcuts, splintered pieces, and wood covered in too much bark and moss.

After stashing his orange jumpsuit in cabinet forty-three, Saunti sifted through scraps allotted for production point workers outside, behind the building. Given the Meridian book incident, he'd rather not stay at the lumber mill longer than necessary, but he always took scraps after work— not doing so would draw extra attention to himself.

I cut it way too close today. Saunti pushed a few logs aside, his pulse quickening. After the Nightshade had tucked the Meridian book into her overcoat, he had rushed to re-stuff Podge's cabinet and return to his workbench. Thankfully, he hadn't drawn suspicion from Quax, and he made it back just in time for Cal to summon a worker into their boss's office for questioning. She only spoke with a dozen of them during the so-called *inspection*, Saunti and Podge not included.

That Nightshade who saw me outside could still get me killed, though. He selected a suitable piece for carving and added it to the growing pile in his arms.

"Saunti." Podge turned the corner, stomping after him. "Did you take my book?"

"Not me." Saunti plopped his scraps aside and stood to face Podge. "It was one of the Nightshades."

"*What?*"

"Don't panic. She doesn't know it's yours. I thought they might search the cabinets, so I took the restroom pass and threw the book outside. I didn't expect there to be another one... standing there." He averted his gaze. "Sorry."

"I don't care about the book, man," Podge whispered, briefly peering over his shoulder. "What the hell were you thinking? You're lucky you weren't questioned."

"Yeah, I know. Let's just forget it, okay?" Saunti knelt to pick up his scraps and took off for the main road.

"I can't believe you did that to protect me." Podge caught up to him and smirked. "I always thought if I were starving, you wouldn't spare me a single ration ticket."

"Shut it. I'm in danger here."

"You *were* in danger. Not anymore. She probably thinks you're too attractive to kill."

"Not funny."

"Oh, cheer up! She was nice to you. Just be grateful and get on with your day."

"She can't be *nice*."

"Why? Cause she's a Nightshade? Hate the organization, not the people."

"The people *are* the organization," Saunti whispered. He caught Podge frowning at him and sighed. *Dammit. It slipped out.* Twice in one day, he had failed to be cautious.

"Saunti," Podge said, his tone serious again. "Tomorrow at midnight. It's the last time I'll say it."

Saunti strolled down the cobblestone roads, bundles of scrap wood in his arms. Residents flew in and out of shops, tossing gold coins around as though they were mere rocks from the roadside. He was lucky to have grown up in Atherus City, which had once been the Atherus Empire's wealthy capital. Even after the War, residents here were much better off than in other Eastern towns.

He stopped by an *OPEN* sign hanging from a butcher shop window. Through the glass, he watched a man swing his knife through a thick cut of meat. Running his own shop meant he had enough money to live without working for ration tickets at one of Vakoi's production points. *I bet it's nice to be an exception.*

The butcher made eye contact with him through the window and gestured welcomingly. Saunti tightened his grip on his scraps and turned to leave. He didn't have enough coins to buy meat anyway.

After walking a few more minutes down the road, he stepped aside for a trader's carriage to pass him. It was likely heading for the same destination—Atherus City Market, the place Saunti walked to after work every evening. His mother believed he left the lumber mill at 7:00 instead of 6:00, a lie he'd planted to have a bit of time to himself every day.

"Saunti, Saunti!" a young girl called as he neared the market. She disappeared from the glassless window and ran through the door, which she held open for him. "Hurry!"

Saunti entered with a chuckle, and a piece of wood slipped from his pile when a black dog ran between his legs, breaking his balance.

"Wow." Saunti made eye contact with the dog. "I appreciate that."

The dog barked back as the young girl picked up the scrap Saunti had dropped.

"Must be my lucky piece." She skipped to her group of friends chatting by a window—fellow students from Atherus City Primary. Their parents worked at the market, so they often spent time together here after school.

As Saunti approached them, they jumped to their feet, pocket knives in hand. He plopped the wooden scraps down, and the chaos began. Some dove at the pile while others pulled at Saunti's shirt, urging him to see what they'd made of the wood he'd brought them yesterday.

"Look, Saunti, it's a fish!" said a young boy with a choppy haircut. He held his figurine up with so much excitement that he nearly took his eye with his knife.

Saunti guided the boy's arm down. "Careful."

"And look at mine, Saunti! I carved *you!*" The young girl who'd opened the door for him raised a blob that resembled a fictional ogre more than a human.

Saunti leaned toward her, hands on his knees, studying the piece. "It's perfect," he said, prompting a few muffled laughs from the older children.

The parents, from their stands, watched the scene with wide grins. They waved at Saunti whenever he looked their way and mouthed *thank you.*

Stand owners at the market weren't fortunate enough to own shops in the City center, but they *were* stubborn enough to work for themselves. Making a living independently was far more challenging than working at a production point, but it gave them a sense of freedom from Vakoi's rule, and Saunti respected that.

On the flip side, they seemed to respect him for providing their kids with a distraction from their propaganda-riddled curriculum. Vakoi had eradicated secondary schools after the War, converting them into officer posts. Saunti knew from personal experience that the primary school in Atherus City only taught basic reading and arithmetic—everything else focused on logging, milling, and fishing to mold them into skilled members of the local production system.

Saunti smiled at a child struggling to carve into the wood with his pocket knife. "Let me sharpen that for you." He took the knife and scraped it along one of their shared whetstones, nearly finishing by the time boots echoed from outside the door. He paused and peered at the window to spot brown horses out front.

Saunti sighed. *Oh great...*

"Vakoi boys," a man grumbled from behind his stand.

The door opened, and the black dog ran circles around the floor, barking wildly. The officers seemed apprehensive about taking another step inside until a child rushed over to pet the dog, calming it down.

She should have let it keep barking, Saunti thought.

"What are they doing here?" the choppy-haired boy whispered.

"I don't know," Saunti whispered back. They weren't on patrol—he'd memorized their routes. Officers wouldn't be around the market this time of the day unless something unusual was going on. *Could it have to do with the inspection earlier?* His face heated up. *Could it have to do with the Meridian book?*

He relaxed when a third and final officer entered with a framed portrait of Vakoi's despicable face—a replacement for the market. Saunti hadn't even noticed the old one gone from its spot above the door.

"They were missing at school too," the boy told Saunti.

"Missing?" he asked.

"The teachers are going crazy," a teenage boy chimed in, crouching next to Saunti. "They can't figure out who's doing it."

Saunti scowled as an officer stood to the side, using hand signals to help the other two align the portrait straight. Hanging it crooked was a crime.

When they finished, the black dog sniffed its way to the boots of an officer. He leaned over to rub the dog's ear, and a few students approached him to admire his navy-blue uniform and question the badges on his sleeves. Their parents struggled to hide their disapproval, as did Saunti. Easterners could never be Nightshades, but they could be officers, and to him, that was just as unforgivable.

The officers smirked at the children on their way out.

"Maybe if you study instead of whittling," one said, "you can be an officer someday too."

Saunti gripped the knife and whetstone harder. "They're just kids. Mind your own business."

The officer scoffed at him before leaving the market. It wasn't against the law to insult an officer like it was to insult a Nightshade, but Saunti could tell that the man wished it was so.

"Watch your mouth," said the second, who slammed the door behind them.

Saunti leaned over to finish sharpening the younger boy's knife. The teenager next to him waited until the trotting of the officers' horses disappeared before whispering, "There's a rumor that the Underground has been taking Vakoi's portraits."

"Hmm..." Saunti hummed, faking disinterest. If the Underground were doing something like that, he'd know. *I wonder who's actually behind this.*

He returned the young boy's pocket knife, encouraged the other kids to keep practicing, and left them to browse a jewelry stand he'd been eyeing the past week.

I don't even know if Aero likes jewelry. He'd never seen her wear any, and he couldn't be sure if that was because she preferred not to, or because Underground hiders didn't have access to items like that. It was a risky gift, sure, but it wasn't like he had any better ideas.

"Are you looking for something in particular?" asked one of the children's mothers, the woman responsible for the jewelry-making. Months ago, she'd told Saunti that she sourced her chains from a neighbor and business partner who had been a silversmith before the Vakoi War, while she collected stones and shells for the pendants herself.

"Not exactly. Maybe you can help me out." Saunti smiled. "I need something for a girl."

"Someone special?"

"Not exactly." Aero hardly spoke about herself or her life in the hideout, despite Saunti's persistent curiosity during the four years he'd known her. Allegedly, someone had forbidden her from revealing anything about Headquarters to him—most likely his own mother.

"So you want something generic, then," the woman said, scanning her pieces. Her eyes brightened as she raised a necklace and pointed to its pendant. "How about this one? You can only find these gems deep underground."

Saunti laughed, which made the woman raise a brow. "I don't think that's the right move."

"Shells, then?"

He recalled the questions Aero had asked him about the ocean. *What color is the water? Are there waves all the time? How deep is it? Do you think it's anything like the Waterway?*

For the millionth time, Saunti wondered, *What the hell is the Waterway?*

The woman took his silence as a *yes* and introduced him to necklaces with shell pendants, explaining the story behind each piece. Saunti gravitated toward a sea snail shell she'd found along Atherus City's coastline. The tiny beads decorating its swirling spiral strangely held Saunti's gaze longer than the others, and he took that as a positive sign.

"How much?" he asked, reaching into his pocket for a velvet pouch.

She offered it to him in exchange for twenty gold coins. "I hope she likes it."

"Me too," Saunti said, turning to leave.

The children called out their parting goodbyes as he left the market.

"Thanks, Saunti!"

"Bye, Saunti!"

"See you tomorrow, Saunti!"

He realized, as he left with Aero's necklace in his pocket, that he would miss Atherus City Market the most. The noises, the smell of fresh bread, the kids tugging at his sleeves for extra lumber scraps—he'd look back on these memories fondly. It was the one sliver of his life above ground that seemed real, where he didn't feel pressured to play a role.

Saunti reached into his pocket, wrapping his fingers around the necklace. *Everything changes tonight.*

CHAPTER 3

ANYTHING FOR YOU

Eleven days and twenty-three hours ago...

♫ NIGHT AND DAY · LEE DEWYZE ♫

After his shift at the Investigation Office, Pinto rode by horseback across the city, racing against the last traces of sunlight beneath the flickering glow of elevated oil lamps along the roadsides. At last, he spotted the Academy guardian through the window of Brackle Beans, a quaint tea shop just north of Vakoi City Hospital.

He rushed inside and slapped the *Capital Weekly* article on Blimmery's table, making his teacup rattle.

"I know you wrote this." He tapped the page with his pointer finger, and his stern tone caught the attention of patrons enjoying their evening tea. They peered up from their novels, sketchbooks, and bite-sized pastries, muttering amongst themselves.

"It's about the news."

"The Belladonna Traitor?"

"I heard every commander is out looking for him."

Blimmery glanced around at the staring customers, and they turned away, shutting their mouths. The trickling indoor fountain and the faint harp notes of the musician behind the counter were the only noises left in the room, and in the quiet, Pinto re-read the wanted notice, his blood boiling.

> The Force is offering a reward of 100,000 coins for information leading to the successful tracing and detainment of Yahshi Konya of Sitra, 17, a fugitive guardian wanted for desertion.

"If you want a conversation," Blimmery whispered, "lower your voice."

"Fine." Pinto took the seat across from him and leaned in. "I thought we decided on the pardon, not Professor Embre's plan."

"Nothing's decided until Defense returns from the search to vote," Blimmery said. "In the meantime, we've had our scribes working all night to get these articles ready. I know it's not the best look for us, but Embre has a point—painting Yahshi as dangerous betters our odds of tracing him, and right now, that's our priority."

"I don't recall voting on that."

"It didn't need votes, because unlike the pardon, it didn't involve a Protocol exception. The higher-ups approved it, so now it's out of our hands."

Pinto eyed Yahshi's inky portrait. *He must be terrified.* He'd spent over twenty-four hours in a foreign land, fearing for his life and grieving his father. Thanks to the article, he likely believed his closest friends had turned against him too.

"We could have waited an extra day so we could publish news of his pardon instead."

"That would muddy the narrative too soon and give enemies the incentive to kill him." Blimmery continued writing in a leather journal. "Research and Medical already voted in his favor, so I'm sure the pardon will clear. As soon as he's traced, he'll find out that he's safe."

Pinto set his elbow on the table, biting his nails as he watched Blimmery write. He couldn't shake the feeling that the Force was blundering.

"Do you ever think before you write?" he asked. "Or do you just do what you're told?"

Blimmery's face reddened. With a sharp exhale, he slammed his pencil down, snatched the article, and offered it to Pinto as though telling him to take his things and go.

"Congratulations, Pinto. You found a way to save your friend." The tremor in his voice signaled his struggle not to speak any louder. "In the end, he'll be okay, so there's absolutely no reason for you to disrupt me in my favorite tea shop to call me a stooge."

Pinto leaned back. "I'm not calling you a *stooge*, Doctor. I'm just wondering if—"

"Leave," Blimmery snapped, baring his teeth. His grip on the article tightened as he shook the page, motioning for Pinto to bring it with him. "You've ruined my tea."

Pinto pulled his horse to a stop at the Detainment Facility stable, his stomach sinking at the sight of Evaris by the front door. They hadn't spoken since their awkward parting after Roz's interrogation—he'd brushed off her attempt to talk in his rush to leave. *I hope she doesn't remember that.*

After securing his horse, Pinto started across the clearing. Evaris locked onto him like a hawk spotting prey, and in an instant, the grassy distance between them seemed to stretch. He glanced away, pretending to take an interest in the surrounding trees. *Could this walk be any longer?*

Finally, as he neared the door, he looked at Evaris again, and she chuckled. Clearly, his walk from the stable amused her, though she didn't say. "Professor Famir isn't in."

"Actually, I'm here for Commander Roz," Pinto said. He'd asked around for his whereabouts once he caught word that he hadn't left on the search— the Force granted him a brief respite to *recover* from his earlier efforts to trace Yahshi.

"He's likely in Watchtower 5," a doctor had told him.

Evaris leaned against the stone wall, not persuaded to open the door.

"May I see him? It's urgent."

She stared him down for a moment longer before nodding, though it was clear she wasn't convinced as she opened the front door. "In you go, Red."

Pinto stepped into the Facility foyer, and the coppery haze of the torch-lit, windowless building devoured him. His recollection of the floor plans he'd studied at the Academy led him straight to the exact ladder of Watchtower 5.

He ascended, climbing until his head popped into a small, circular room.

Roz stood on the opposite side, gazing through a window at the coast not far off from the west wing of the Facility. "I've been wondering how long you'd go before apologizing."

"Apologizing for what?" Pinto huffed as he pushed himself to his feet in the watchtower. "You're the one who killed Martu Konya."

Roz unsheathed a sword and dragged a handkerchief against the blade. "I did no such thing."

Pinto lowered his head, eye narrowed. *I'm not gullible, Commander.*

Roz peered back with one eye, giving his sword a final swipe. "I heard about your plan to get Yahshi pardoned."

He forced himself not to cringe as Roz slowly sheathed his tool, the blade scraping against its holster. After tucking his handkerchief away, he turned fully to face Pinto, his silhouette dark against the deepening blue sky, where the last remnants of sunset faded.

"I think you'll come to regret that choice."

"I doubt that," Pinto replied, his voice firm. "Yahshi deserves a chance to redeem himself, especially after what you did."

Roz stepped forward, crossing his stocky arms across his chest. "Wake up, Pinto. You don't know him as well as you believe. Even if the Defense Division votes in favor of the pardon tomorrow, he won't accept it."

"Of course he'll accept it. His best friends are here."

"In his eyes, only enemies are here. It's time you accept that. The pardon is only valid if he cooperates, which he won't."

Pinto glared as he crouched, readying to descend the ladder. Roz's attempt to sow doubts was clearly a deflection, and he wouldn't fall for it. As soon as Yahshi accepted the pardon, he would expose Roz, and everyone would learn the truth.

For now, I shouldn't push him. Pinto remembered the advice Kanter had given him. Perhaps this impulsive visit hadn't been the smartest idea. The last thing he needed was for Roz to consider him a genuine threat—there was no telling what he might do.

Pinto dropped his legs through the ladderway, catching the reflection of Roz's smile on the window as he made his way down.

It was around 11:00 when Pinto trekked downstairs to the front of Complex, where he found a guardian with shoulder-length hair sitting on the front steps, gazing at the stars with a glowing cigarette in hand. He coughed a few times before taking another drag.

Typical Keiyo. Irresponsible as ever. Pinto marched over and plucked the cigarette from his mouth.

"Hey!" Keiyo shouted. "What the hell?"

"You made a vow to maintain optimal health, remember?" Pinto narrowed his eye at the stream of smoke before tossing the cigarette down. "And you're a doctor. You're better than this."

"But all the cool guardians are doing it," Keiyo whined sarcastically. "And it's not like there's a rule against it in *The Guardian Handbook.*"

"It's not like there's a rule against cutting off your toes. Have you done that too?"

"Okay, smartass." Keiyo scoffed and looked back at the sky, but it didn't take long for his lips to form a subtle curve. "What does it matter if I smoke now, anyway? I eat more vegetables than you, so it balances out."

"That's not how it works."

"I'm the doctor here, aren't I?"

A smile broke through Pinto's stern expression. With a shake of his head, he took a seat next to Keiyo, tracing his gaze to the stars.

"It's almost midnight, and they're still not back," Keiyo said. Vaults had trickled in earlier that night—all without Yahshi—but Commander Cal's unit was among the few that hadn't returned yet.

"I don't think that's a good sign," Pinto said. "If they traced him, they would have returned earlier." He flinched at a *click* and looked over to see Keiyo holding up a glowing match.

"I don't want him to die, you know." Keiyo brought the match closer to his face, watching its flame flicker in the gentle wind. "I only came at you so harshly yesterday morning because you didn't see how stressed Vell was before you arrived. I didn't want to risk getting her hopes up, only for the Force to kill him anyway."

"I get it. You were being realistic."

"And yet, somehow, you delivered on your promise." Keiyo waved his match, extinguishing the flame. "If you hadn't vouched for Yahshi in the Research Division, pardoning him wouldn't even be an option. Thanks to you, we actually have a shot at bringing him home, and keeping him alive."

"I have you to thank for that too," Pinto said. "I know you did the heavy lifting to get the Medical Division on board. They supported the pardon because of you."

"Now it's all down to Quax and Vell. I'm sure that together, they can get Defense on board."

They sat in the stillness for a while, waiting for the faint sound of Commander Cal's vault approaching in the distance. The longer they waited, the more they felt it would never come.

"So, talk to me," Keiyo said, breaking the silence. "I'm way out of the loop. You've been to all these cool meetings and interrogations and stuff, but what do I get? Oh yeah, more tools to lace, berries to harvest, and medicine to deliver. Now, don't get me wrong—I love my tools and berries and medicine. But not right now. Not in the middle of... *this*."

Pinto mulled over the evidence, wondering where to begin. Roz's suspicious interrogation, and the threat he'd made to Pinto? His knowledge that Keiyo had been involved in Yahshi accessing the archives? The mysterious girl Yahshi had supposedly been planning to leave with?

"She had black hair and bangs. Looked about the same age."

Pinto frowned, recalling the store clerk's interrogation transcript. His description of Yahshi's accomplice was awfully vague, but it matched—

"Oh no..." Keiyo's eyes searched Pinto's face. "What is it?"

"The Research Division believes there's a girl involved. She was seen with Yahshi at a convenience store the night before he left, and the clerk described her as having black hair and bangs—around the same age as him. I'm just now wondering if it might have been..." He trailed off, and it took Keiyo a moment to reply.

"You know, I've been wondering for a while if there might be something going on between them." Keiyo paused, his brows inching toward each other. "Yesterday morning, when Vell panicked at the Hospital, I really started to think I might be right. It was almost like she was—"

"Left behind?"

"Maybe that too." Keiyo paused. "I was gonna say something else."

"What else could possibly be going on between them?"

He lowered his chin, urging Pinto to think harder.

"No..." His brows knitted together. "You don't mean..."

"I do."

"What makes you think *that*?"

"Well, they're awfully close."

"I'm close to them too."

"Yeah, but..." Keiyo rocked back and forth, deciding whether to finish his sentence.

"But *what*?"

"Does Vell ever hold your hand?"

Pinto went silent.

"During the branding ceremony, Yahshi tried to avoid saying the Vows," Keiyo said. "He fought back against the Academy guardians time after time. I wouldn't be surprised if he—"

"Yahshi moved on from that. He wouldn't break the rules, and neither would Vell."

"Or they're good actors." Keiyo hesitated before adding, "Some people know how to hide."

Pinto nodded. "I'm going to ask her."

"Pinto. Don't."

"I'm asking *tonight*. If Vell was more involved in Yahshi's desertion than she's letting on, I deserve to know. I'm the one who started the fight for his pardon."

"She'll be exhausted from the expedition. I don't think it's a—"

The distant rumbling of a vault interrupted them, and they stood in unison, making brief eye contact. Together, they rushed down the stairs and planted themselves by the Complex stable, close to the main road, watching the distant aluminum approach.

After standing there for a few minutes, Keiyo cleared his throat. "I never said thank you."

"For what?" Pinto asked.

"For not telling anyone about the key."

He chuckled. "How did you know I found out?"

"You're smart. I figured you put the pieces together."

The vault was much closer now, and Pinto squinted to see Cal smiling from the driver's seat, waving with one hand on the reins. She parked the vault by the stable and hopped down. "Couldn't wait to see me?"

"Why *wouldn't* we stay up to see a pretty face like yours?" Keiyo asked.

Pinto glared at him, and Keiyo tilted his head as if to say, *What did I do wrong?*

"We're here!" Cal shouted to her unit members, hands cupped around her mouth.

Pinto heard the door burst open, followed by Vell's and Quax's boots hitting the ground. They emerged from around the passenger box, their pants dirtied and their hair disheveled.

"We didn't trace him," Vell said in a monotone voice, wrapping a tense arm around her waist.

"That's okay," Keiyo said. "We have wanted articles going up in Eastern Territory by morning, and with everyone looking, we'll find him eventually." He elbowed Pinto's side a few times. "Plus, thanks to this guy, we've almost secured Yahshi's pardon! The Defense Division takes the final vote tomorrow morning."

Cal frowned, but her little brother smiled.

"You really managed that?" Quax asked.

Pinto nodded, but his eyes were on Vell—she stared blankly at the Complex, strangely unmoved by the good news.

"Vell," he said, eyeing the tight grip around herself. "Are you hurt?"

"No." Vell hastily released her abdomen. "I'm gonna shower. Will you be up?"

"I'll be in my flat."

She offered a faint smile and headed for the front steps, her paces short. It was like she feared moving too quickly would cause something heavy to slip from an interior pocket of her overcoat. *She's hiding something.*

"They're considering a pardon?" Cal asked, recapturing Pinto's attention. "All because of you?"

Pinto couldn't believe the bitterness seeping into her voice. How could the Belladonna Prodigy, the youngest unit member in guardian history, be jealous of Yahshi? Did she not believe that he deserved the same second chance the Force had given her years ago, after she'd murdered Chima Fernis?

"I only pitched the idea," Pinto said, aiming to downplay his efforts. "It was over half the Research Division that agreed to escalate it."

Cal cleared her throat, breaking eye contact. "Well, that's quite the feat. He better appreciate it."

A few blocks from the Complex, Pinto and Vell strolled down the north wing of Vakoi Square, a road lined with a lively array of restaurants, bars, and live music. The various genres from all directions blended together terribly.

"You *like* this place?" Pinto resisted the urge to cover his ears with his palms, but only because he seemed to be the center of attention. With every step he took, another pair of eyes landed on his uniform.

Vell ran her hands through her damp hair. "I don't mind it."

A Medical guardian walked past them, his cheeks bright red. At his sides were two attractive Vakoi City women, laughing at something he'd said. Pinto looked over his shoulder as they passed, seeing the doctor snake his arms around both women's waists.

His lips parted as he faced forward again. *I could report him, but he's my superior, and I don't have any evidence.* Plus, he couldn't report a potential violation of *that* Vow when it was the exact one he intended to discuss with Vell tonight.

"Want a drink?" Vell asked, stopping at the entrance to an open-air bar with only a few available seats. By the entrance, a man in a clown outfit played an obnoxious tune on a violin—Pinto couldn't tell if his purpose was to attract prospective customers or scare them away.

A bar. How ridiculous. If people want to have a good time, what's so hard about doing that sober?

"We can get juice," Vell said. "I just wanna sit."

Pinto glanced down the bench-less road and shrugged. "Okay."

They took the open seats at the bar, catching a few eyes and nods of acknowledgment of their service. Pinto ordered two fruit juices and bit his nails, formulating how to ask the dreaded question.

"Are you sure you're not too tired for this?"

"What?" Vell shouted over the violin music.

"Are you tired?" he yelled.

"Yeah!"

"Sorry!" Pinto glared at the violinist, who eased the volume down a little. "Should we go back?"

Vell shook her head as the bartender slid two iced juices down the bar, which stopped directly in front of them.

"So..." Pinto paused and took a sip. "How was the expedition?"

"Tiring." Vell raised her glass but hesitated to drink from it. "Actually, the reason we took so long was because I convinced Commander Cal to make a detour through Frontal."

Pinto's eye widened. He had passed his journal from the Academy off to Vell earlier that week, hoping she could find an opportunity to deliver it to his little sister during one of her expeditions. He still hadn't received a visitation right.

"The truth is, we could have stopped in Frontal a few days ago, but I was too scared to ask Commander Cal for a personal favor. With everything going on, though, it could take even longer for you to get a visitation right, so it was now or never. She wasn't happy about it, but she agreed."

Pinto took another sip, bracing himself. "Was Perma there when you delivered it?"

Vell nodded.

"What was she like?"

"Surprised to see a guardian, but happy to see your journal."

Pinto had a million more questions. *Was she still mad at me for leaving her? Did she look healthy? How does she style her hair now? Was she wearing her Frontal Secondary uniform?*

But he kept those questions to himself. He'd visit Perma eventually, and a reunion in person would be better than one through Vell's recollection.

"Thank you for doing that."

Vell took a sip. "Anything for you."

They sat in the noise for a while longer.

"Vell, you trust me, right?"

"Of course I do."

"Then can you tell me what you were hiding in your overcoat?" he asked, recalling how she'd left the vault with an arm wrapped around herself. "Whatever it is, I won't make a fuss."

Vell stared at him for a moment, her expression lightening. The loose gold coins in her pocket rattled as she grabbed a handful of them.

"Follow me."

She scattered the coins onto the bar and left her seat behind.

"So the worker threw it outside, and out of all the things you could have done, you *took it with you*?" Pinto exclaimed, pacing Vell's flat.

Vell crossed her arms. "You said you wouldn't make a fuss."

Pinto halted, glaring at the book on Vell's bed—*The Force's Hidden Agenda* by Meridian Owding. The Force had banned it decades ago, rounding up existing copies for a massive bonfire. "There shouldn't be any left."

"I figured it might be a banned book, but I wasn't sure," Vell said. "I only brought it with me because I recognized the name *Owding*. That's Doctor Blimmery's family name."

"I remember the story." Pinto recalled an old *Capital Weekly* article he'd read. "When Doctor Blimmery was young, his uncle was executed for writing that book. That's the reason he became a guardian in the first place—he needed to prove his family wasn't treasonous like his uncle and redeem the Owding name."

"Really?" Vell peered down at the book. "Do you know anything about its contents?"

"Only that it's dangerous." Pinto reached for the cover but withdrew his hand. He couldn't touch it. It was filled with propaganda and false information the Force had worked tirelessly to eliminate. The fact that it had made its way into the Complex sent a chill down his spine.

He turned to Vell. "Did you read it?"

"No."

"Good." With a wince, Pinto snatched the book and stuffed it into his overcoat, making a beeline for Vell's door. "We need to get rid of it."

Vell didn't bother to lock her flat as she rushed to catch up to him down the hallway.

"How?" she asked.

"I know a place," he whispered back.

It was nearly 1:00 in the morning when they left the Complex on their white horses and galloped toward the outskirts of Vakoi City, where ocean waves crashed against the shore of a desolate beach. The moonlight illuminated every ripple of water in view.

"Are you sure we shouldn't read it first?" Vell stared at the horizon. "It's short."

Pinto tossed the book onto the sand, and its title glowed tauntingly in the moonlight. What kind of agenda could the Force have, apart from protecting the Empire?

Kanter's warning echoed in the wind that rustled his curls. *"Sometimes the most dangerous are among our own."*

He shook the idea away. Even entertaining the thought of reading it felt criminal.

"You shouldn't have brought it with you, Vell." The words came out sharper than he'd meant, and in a rush to move on, he reached into his overcoat for a matchbox—but he didn't have one.

Dammit.

Vell offered hers without hesitation. "Here."

"Thank you." Pinto sighed as he took the matchbox. "And... sorry."

With a *flick*, he knelt and brought the flame to the book. It took several seconds for the heat to grab hold of the pages, warming his hands as it nibbled on the words inside. He stood and stepped back, returning Vell's matchbox as she joined his side.

They stared down at the burning Meridian book, shivering as another chilly ocean breeze washed over them. Pinto yawned, and Vell rubbed her eyes. It had been a long two days, and the night was coming to a close.

It was time.

"I really hate to say this," Pinto muttered, eye on the fire, "but was there something going on between you and Yahshi?"

The question came out painfully blunt.

"Of course not," Vell said, her voice as calm as ever. "Why do you ask?"

Pinto figured it was best not to mention the girl in the convenience store or the comment Keiyo had made about them holding hands. He settled on saying, "You were the last person to see him before he ran."

"Pinto..."

He turned to look her in the eye.

"I'm not keeping any secrets." With a tired smile, she stepped closer and took his hand in hers. It was like she'd read his mind.

Pinto smiled back. "Forget I asked."

CHAPTER 4

DOOM AND GLOOM

Eleven days and five hours ago...

♫ CASTLES · LEE DEWYZE ♫

"Considering all these *inspections*, I bet the Nightshades are up to some-thing shady." Noris jammed a crowbar between two wooden wall panels. "Be careful tonight."

"I'm always careful," Saunti said.

"Be *extra* careful then." Noris narrowed his eyes, applying *just* enough pressure to prop a panel free with his crowbar. The wood landed in his hand, revealing a hidden compartment with a single stack of papers smuggled from the production point he worked at.

"More paper?" Saunti swung his empty rucksack off his shoulders and crouched by the hole in the wall. "When supplies are low, writing isn't a priority. It's about time you cut into your rations. You obviously get more than enough food anyway."

"It's not *my* fault supplies are low." He rubbed his round belly. "Why should my stomach pay?"

Saunti scoffed and slipped the hoarded goods into his rucksack. The *click* of the wooden panel popping back into place made Noris gasp.

"Quiet. Someone could hear." He crept to the window and peered between the curtains, then at Saunti, then between the curtains again. He might as well have said, *Grab the papers and scram, boy!*

"What was that?" Saunti projected his voice, despite having heard him just fine. "Sorry, Noris, I left my bat ears at home."

"Saunti," Noris scolded.

With a sigh, he stopped and faced the middle-aged collector.

"You'll be extra careful, right?" Noris offered a warm smile, but his lazy eye and balding hair detracted from the otherwise charming expression.

"Fine. I'll be *extra* careful, Noris," Saunti said, exaggerating his concern. He swung the door open, and the sky seemed to mock him as he stepped out into the alleyway, Noris's hanging lantern illuminating his face. Saunti's mother always told him that their ancestors lived in the stars, watching over them—which wasn't as comforting as intended. If that were true, then his father was up there, scowling at him for being nothing but a measly delivery boy.

"One mistake of yours, and it'll be all of us up there," Noris said from inside the house. "Every one of us, twinkling in that sky, watching the misery—"

Saunti shut the door behind him, muting Noris. He already knew how much responsibility he held as a courier. *Mother and I are the only people in the City who know the nearest access point's location. If I get caught, she'd be at risk, which would put the entire rebellion at risk.*

He pulled his coat hood over his hair and exhaled, his white breath melting into the darkness. *But unlike what Noris thinks, it's easy not to get caught.*

Saunti set into motion, following a route his legs had memorized on their own. There were fifteen collectors in Atherus City, each offering different supplies. A few, like Noris, stored goods in their homes, requiring Saunti to knock on their doors. Most, however, left their supplies at discreet outdoor drop-off points.

He fished for five pouches of crushed charcoal hidden in an overgrown bush.

He hauled a bag containing three jars of fish oil out of an inconspicuous alleyway barrel.

He jumped to grab the roof overhang of a short building, hoisted himself up with a boot against a window frame, and jumped back down with an armful of canned beans.

See? I'm careful, Noris. Saunti stopped and held his breath as faint footsteps echoed in the distance. Like his mother always said, *If you can hear them, they can hear you.*

Once the footsteps faded, Saunti continued to the access point, lugging his now-heavy rucksack on his back. His thoughts drifted to the inspection at the mill earlier that day, when that blue-eyed Nightshade had stared right at him.

Another reason to leave tonight and never come back. Saunti nodded, more confident in his choice than ever. *If she ever comes after me, I'll be long gone.*

The alleyways narrowed with each turn closer to the access point, the sides of his coat skimming the brick walls on either side. Finally, when he reached the designated spot, he stopped right beside a manhole cover.

Saunti looked left and right, ensuring he was alone before dropping to his knees and dragging the cover open, revealing a ladderway into Atherus City's sewer system. His nose wrinkled as he descended, reaching up to pull the cover closed above him.

The world turned black.

He struck a match from his coat, illuminating the ladder steps beneath him. With the match pinched between his fingers, he climbed to the bottom platform and stepped off the ladder.

Just ask her. He reached into his coat pocket, clutching the shell necklace he'd purchased as a peace offering, to help his case. *She'll say yes.*

Saunti exhaled, pulling his hand out of his pocket. He knocked on the space between two ladder steps. Three times. Two times. Three again.

A few seconds later, the *click* of a lock sounded from the other side of the hidden door. He grabbed the ladder step ahead of him—which also functioned as a door handle—and pulled until the hinged, concrete cutout swung toward him, revealing Aero's smiling face.

Saunti wondered if she greeted his mother with the same cheerful look whenever she handled the deliveries, or if she enjoyed interacting with someone closer to her own age.

"Well, if it isn't the Cricket." Aero leaned forward, blowing out Saunti's match, but the torches in the tunnel behind her allowed them to see—just barely.

He grinned and flicked the dead match aside. She'd been calling him *Cricket* for the past two years—ever since he'd shown up one night with, unknowingly, a few crickets clinging to his coat.

"You're not gonna be happy," Saunti said, eyeing Aero's ponytail. In the dim light, he could never tell if her hair was brown or black.

"Don't tell me Noris sent more paper…"

"Loads of paper."

"That greedy old man. We've got hungry children down here." She tossed Saunti her empty rucksack, and he caught it with a chuckle. She'd been cracking more jokes lately, likely because they'd been spending extra time together. In the past, he'd only seen her on Mondays and Wednesdays—his mother would handle the rest of the week, restricting his shifts out of caution. It was only a few months ago that she began trusting him enough to take on more nightly deliveries, and he was now nearing a one-month streak.

"Are supplies still low?" he asked, transferring the smuggled goods from his bag into hers.

"Lower than ever. I traveled down the Waterway earlier this week—"

"The *what*?" he asked, hoping she'd elaborate.

"—and according to the handlers I met with, the Nightshades have been killing off our smugglers faster than ever. Some collectors are even swapping out their lantern chains. They're scared the Nightshades will crack the code soon."

"They're giving up," Saunti paraphrased. "Right when we need them most, they're giving up."

"It'll work out." Aero shrugged and leaned against the doorway. "But enough with the doom and gloom. Give me the weather report."

"Doom and gloom," Saunti echoed. "Still winter. Cold."

"*Details*, Cricket."

"Uh, I don't know." Saunti transferred the canned beans next. "Not much wind. Just a still, dry coldness in the air. And the ocean feels like ice. Even the sand has a chill to it."

He looked over to see Aero gazing up at the manhole cover. "I don't even remember what the moon looks like."

"It's white. Sometimes round-ish, sometimes banana-like."

"Yeah, I know. But can you see those little shadows and crevices, or is it only drawn that way in children's books?"

"Never thought about it," Saunti said, completing the transfer. He slung his empty rucksack over his shoulders and passed the stuffed bag to Aero.

"You should pay more attention to life up there." She snatched her bag, slung it over her shoulder, and took a step deeper into the tunnel.

"Wait!" Saunti called, stopping her. He rustled through his coat pocket, pulling out the necklace. "This is for you."

Aero frowned, taking it. She ran her thumb over the shell.

"It's from the shore along the outskirts of Atherus City, about twenty minutes from here. The woman at the market finds stones and shells, and turns them into jewelry." Saunti babbled—he didn't know what else to say. "I don't even know if you like jewelry, but in the worst-case scenario, I figured it'd be nice to look at. Or maybe you could take the shell off the chain and do something else with it."

He was almost certain her eyes were watering, so he shut his mouth.

"No one's ever brought me a gift from the outside before." She smiled. "Thanks, Saunti."

He smiled back. "It's nothing."

Aero tucked the necklace into her pocket and stared him up and down. "So what do you want?"

He looked away. "What do you mean?"

"Oh, *come on*. I know you didn't buy me this just to be nice, so what do you want?"

"Fine." Saunti took a deep breath before saying, "I want you to take me with you."

She tilted her head, eyes narrowed. "What?"

"I want you to take me to Headquarters, so I can play a bigger role, and...

and really help the Underground, you know?"

"Oh." Aero stared back at him blankly, her cheeks slowly reddening. Before he could question her, she burst into laughter, choking on her own breaths. "Oh, shut it!"

"Aero…"

"I can't just *take you with me*!" She took a few moments to settle down. "That—that breaks *every* rule. Your mother would kill me. Scratch that—the entire Council would kill me. Plus, your disappearance would put a spotlight on your mother, and if your mother's in danger, we're all in danger."

"If anyone can handle the extra spotlight, it's my mother."

"You're being selfish. How do you expect this to go down?" The humor in Aero's voice faded. "You think you can waltz into Headquarters with me, and everyone would greet you with open arms? I guarantee the Council would send you right back up to your mother, and she'd never trust you to play delivery boy again."

Saunti glared at her, gripping the straps of his now-empty rucksack.

"Did you even bring anything with you? Spare clothes? Food?"

"You don't get what it's like, Aero." He raised his voice, shaking his head. "I work as a courier like this less than one percent of the time, and for the rest of it, I'm cashing in ration tickets and working at one of Vakoi's stupid production points. I probably help the bastard more than I help the Underground."

Aero took a deep breath, her gaze softening. "Look, I'm sure it's tough up there. I don't doubt that. But it's a different kind of tough down here. You wouldn't last a day."

"Oh? And why's that?" Saunti stepped toward her, trying to catch a glimpse down the tunnel. He knew little of the secret world she lived in, but surely the hiders were doing *more* for the cause—much more than he could accomplish in his fake life above.

Aero blocked his way. "Thank you for the necklace," she said, her voice firm.

"Wait, please, don't—"

She slammed the door and locked it, trapping Saunti in total darkness.

He set his hands on the concrete door and leaned his forehead against it. They were both members of the Underground, but their lives couldn't be further apart.

The crickets sang their nightly song as Saunti dragged himself home. *Of course she said no.* He scoffed at himself. *I can't go under without Mother's permission, and knowing her, it's more likely I'll go under in a casket first.*

He stopped near the end of an alleyway, holding his breath at the sound of boots against cobblestone. Carefully, he peered around the corner to see an officer pasting an article to a building, his open book bag displaying an entire stack of copies.

Must be news from the Nightshades.

The officer ran his hands down the paper, sealing it to the brick wall, before closing his bag and mounting his brown horse. Saunti waited for the clip-clopping to fade before releasing a heavy breath and emerging from around the corner.

The *Capital Weekly* article featured a portrait of a young Nightshade, one of the recent graduates.

> The Force is offering a reward of 100,000 coins for information leading to the successful tracing and detainment of Yahshi Konya of Sitra, 17, a fugitive guardian wanted for desertion. The Force believes him to have fled into Eastern Territory earlier this week, following the mysterious murder of his father, Martu Konya of Sitra.

Saunti frowned. *Earlier this week? That means he deserted within a few days ago.* He figured it must have taken the scribes hours to prepare so many pages for distribution—and even more hours for the messengers to deliver them to officers to put up across Eastern Territory. The Force distributing news so hastily could only mean they were desperate to find him.

Saunti peeled the article off the wall. The glue had yet to dry and stickied his fingers as he continued through the alleyways, his breaths leaving a trail of white clouds behind him.

It was 3:06 in the morning when he returned home to find his mother frying fish on the stove. She always stayed up late during his delivery days, which usually involved unnecessary activities to keep from dozing off.

Tonna looked over as Saunti closed the door, a sigh of relief escaping her.

He raised the article. "News from the Nightshades."

Tonna left the crackling pan behind, crossing the room to take the sticky page. Her grip tightened as her eyes soared over the article.

"I can't believe one of their own betrayed them," Saunti said. "That must be the real reason behind these *inspections*."

Tonna's eyes stilled, her face draining of color. She turned her back on him and paced the room, her breaths shallow. "Did anyone see you?"

"No one ever sees me."

Tonna nodded and looped around the sofa, the article wrinkling in her hands as she re-read it. The crackling of the frying fish intensified until Saunti could bear it no longer. He transferred the fish to a plate and extinguished the stove fire with an iron lid. By the time he looked back at Tonna, her hands were trembling.

"I need you to promise me something." She stopped pacing and stared from across the room.

He crossed his arms and frowned. "Okay…"

"Promise me that if you hear anything about this boy, you'll tell me immediately."

Saunti blinked. His mother had called the Nightshade a *boy*, as though Yahshi Konya were a child and not one of Vakoi's devils.

"What do you know about him?" Saunti asked.

She clenched her jaw and turned away, crumbling the article in her tense hands.

"Mother—"

"Quiet," she snapped, tossing the wadded paper into the flames. She backed up and sat on the sofa, watching the fire devour the portrait of the Belladonna Traitor. A minute of crackling passed before she patted the sofa cushion next to her. "Come here."

"Do you want your fish?"

"No, Saunti, I don't want my fish."

"It's a waste of rations."

"Come here," she repeated.

"Fine." He crossed the room, joining her on the sofa. "Are you gonna tell me what's going on?"

Tonna tugged gently at her braids, eyes locked on the fire in front of them. "All you need to know is that this boy could really help us. He's not an ordinary Nightshade. If the article really is true, and..." She trailed off, struggling to find the right words.

"If it's true, then what?"

"If it's true, then..." Her voice broke on the second attempt, and she covered her mouth with a trembling hand. For a moment, Saunti wondered if she was holding back tears.

He rested a hand on her shoulder. "Just tell me."

Tonna closed her eyes, exhaling a deep breath. "I want you to help me find him before the Nightshades do."

Saunti's eyes widened, his hand leaving her shoulder as though it burned him. "What for? The ransom?"

"Not to turn him in. Headquarters needs him."

"Why?"

"Because..." She opened her eyes and scoffed, turning to face him. "You just need to trust me."

"How do you expect me to trust you when *you* don't trust *me*?"

"I tell you what you need to know."

"Because you think I'm a child. That's why you won't let me go under."

"Going under isn't the only way to help." Tonna's brows furrowed. "You're always talking about doing more for the Underground, right? Well, here it is. Here's your chance."

Saunti clenched his fists and stood. "I'm too tired for this," he said, heading for his room.

"We're not done talking," Tonna called after him. "Saunti!"

He slammed the door.

The following day, Saunti woke up, walked to work, and slipped his orange jumpsuit on. Absolutely nothing had changed.

He cut plank, after plank, after plank.

He brought scrap wood to the kids in the market.

He showed up with an empty bag at Noris's door and raised his fist to knock—but something stopped him. His face heated up at the memory of Aero laughing at his request to join her underground, and how his mother wouldn't tell him the reason behind what she wanted him to do *above* ground. How could he keep working for an organization that didn't even seem to trust him, or want him to be anything more than a brainless pawn?

With a frown, Saunti lowered his hand and left Noris's door behind.

Moonlight streamed between branches as he weaved around the trees that separated the heart of Atherus City from the pile of rubble where his father had died. Despite having lived so close his entire life, he had only ever gone to the Palace once, during a school field class. Podge had rolled his eyes when their instructor described the day the Nightshades burned down the Palace as *glorious*—earning himself ten ruler strikes on his arm.

He may be reckless, but at least he takes action.

Eventually, Saunti crossed the greenery to enter a wide expanse of flat land with piles of rubble. His boots crunched against chipped rocks as he visualized people walking in his footsteps thirteen years ago, when the half-standing rooms overgrown with weeds once formed the walls of Atherus Palace.

I wonder what their lives were like. He would never know, because they were dead, their ashes scattered across these ruins and their stories lost in the history books Emperor Vakoi had rounded up and burned.

Saunti ran his hand along a mossy wall as he walked past it, emerging through a final structure to spot Podge and Kwinn sitting on mounds of stones.

Podge's face lit up at the sight of him. "I knew you'd show."

Kwinn raised a beer bottle in place of a wave. "Hey."

"Hi," Saunti replied, stopping in front of her. "Congratulations on catching that mega-salmon." He'd always felt a little guilty for never acknowledging how well she'd done on that school assignment, and it wasn't like he had anything else to say.

Kwinn paused for a moment, as though she thought he was joking, before letting out a chuckle. "That was, like, three years ago, Saunti."

"Be nice," Podge warned her.

"Oh, that reminds me!" Kwinn continued. "Congratulations on your first day of primary school. I bet your mommy packed you a nice snack, didn't she?"

"*Anyway*," Saunti said, eager to change the subject, "where is everyone?"

"Welcome to the club!" Podge threw his arms out. "We call ourselves the Boomers. Me, Kwinnie here, and Runner."

Saunti glanced around. He had expected more people. "And where's Runner?"

"Running," Podge and Kwinn said in unison.

"He's always on the run," Podge clarified.

"Not that he's wanted by the Nightshades or anything crazy." Kwinn took a sip of beer. "He's a trader from some southern coal town. Heston, I think. Runs all over the place with his carriage. Thanks to him, we have everything we need for tonight's test run."

"Fine, I'll bite." Saunti crossed his arms. "What are you testing?"

Podge stood from his mound of stones and walked backward, nearly stumbling over the uneven ground. "Why don't you come look?"

Kwinn stood and followed him, leaving her beer bottle behind.

Saunti quickened his pace to catch up with them. "So how exactly did you two get involved in... whatever it is you're doing?"

"I know this guy looks stupid," Kwinn said, elbowing Podge's side, "but he knows when to be careful and when to mess around."

Podge ducked his head in gratitude. "Thank you, thank you."

"And he's good at sniffing out people who think like him. Including me, and *you*—assuming you're not here to spy for the Nightshades."

"Of course I'm not," Saunti said.

"We'll explain everything else in a few minutes," Podge said. "It'll be easier to process once you see... *the thing*."

Once they'd crossed the Palace ruins, they entered a forested area separating Atherus City from the nearest town over. They didn't travel too far into it before Podge made a sharp turn east, toward the ocean. The waves crashing against the rocky shore grew louder the longer they walked, and soon their feet were breaking shells, not twigs.

Their group of three came to a stop by a suspicious pile of *something* covered with a dark red tarpaulin. Podge and Kwinn pulled the fabric aside, revealing a stack of Vakoi's mandatory portraits.

"Twenty-six of them," Kwinn said.

Atop the portraits was a box about the size of a palm—a rope stuck out of a hole in the wood.

"Introducing BPB." Podge grabbed the box and held it over his head. "Short for Black Powder Boombox."

"Ah, I should have guessed," Saunti said.

"You know how the Nightshades have their poison? I realized we should have our own special thingy too. So I teamed up with Kwinnie here, and we put together something no one's ever seen before. This thing!"

Saunti raised a brow, and Kwinn laughed.

"It's a box filled with *black powder*—Podge's invention." She pulled her sleeve back, revealing a burn across her forearm, and Saunti winced at the sight of it. "I only came up with the mechanism for using it."

"We call it a *boombox*!" Podge exclaimed.

Saunti continued studying the burn on Kwinn's arm until she pulled her sleeve back over it. "I did a lot of experimenting before I figured out the right amount of powder, how thick to make the box, and how long to make the string. Oh, and how to make the string burn slower. That was the key to everything."

"And the black powder?" Saunti asked, turning to Podge.

"I was working on it with help from my parents before I brought Kwinnie into the mix. Getting the ingredients alone took months—and it took even longer to get the right ratio, but I eventually settled on seventy-five percent saltpeter, fifteen percent charcoal, and ten percent sulfur."

Saunti could hardly believe that *ratio* and *percent* had left Podge's mouth. He'd known that his parents had been alchemists before the War, but Podge always acted as though he'd picked up on none of their knowledge. He'd never been a fan of school—but then again, he also called school *propaganda*, so maybe that's why he never tried.

"I make the charcoal at home with scraps from the mill. The saltpeter and sulfur I get from Runner. They're used to preserve canned goods, so he trades them at production points all over the East. You know, to make sure stuff lasts long enough to get to those stupid Saver Stores."

"You know about those?" Saunti asked. He'd only learned about Saver Stores in the Vakoi Empire—and how they funded the Nightshades—from his mother.

"The real question is, how do *you* know about those?" Podge smirked before continuing. "Long story short, I played around with black powder once I figured it out and quickly realized I needed help to use it efficiently. That's when I remembered how Kwinn would make those crazy-looking fish traps with all the strings and stuff. I figured she'd have some ideas."

"And the portraits?"

"It was a group effort. Kwinn and I have been sneaking into places for the past week."

Saunti scoffed in disbelief as he scanned the tall pile.

"Up until tonight, it's all been preparation, all talk. But we're *finally* taking action. We're going to get these portraits boomed as a test run. And you're lucky you showed up just in time to witness it. You get all the benefits and none of the work. Good for you."

"Why *are* you here, anyway?" Kwinn asked. "I thought you only made time for your mommy."

Saunti sighed and looked away, his cheeks warming up at the realization that he was quite literally here because he resented his mother.

"So, are you gonna tell us why you decided to show up?" Podge asked.

"No," Saunti said. "Tell me how the boombox works."

"We just light the string, and... *boom!*" Kwinn clapped in Saunti's face. "Just a warning—it's pretty loud. Could be *too* loud. We've never boomed this much before."

"And if people hear?"

"Oh, we're counting on it," Podge said.

"Don't worry. We've had tons of smaller test runs." Kwinn turned to Podge. "How many, you think? Like, a million?"

"A billion," Podge corrected.

"Yeah, a billion test runs." Kwinn smiled. "That's why this time, we'll have an audience."

Saunti's eyes widened. "What?"

"Shh…" Kwinn held a finger to her lips. "You hear that?"

His blood ran cold as he heard horses galloping their way.

"Perfect timing." Kwinn returned Podge's high-five and leaned toward Saunti, lowering her voice. "I left an anonymous tip at the officer post to report suspicious activity in this area." She pulled a matchbox out of her coat pocket, and Saunti's stomach dropped as he pieced together their plan.

"Wait," he said—but the fuse was already burning.

"Run!" Podge yelled.

As the galloping grew louder, their group of three raced back into the woods. Branches whipped past as Saunti imagined the end of his story—the boombox would obliterate the portraits, the officers would send them to Vakoi City for questioning, and by the morning, all three of them would have belladonna serum pumping through their veins.

"Saunti! Saunti! Right here!"

He scuffled to a stop, and Kwinn gestured for him to join their hiding spot.

"Right here!" she called again from behind a cluster of trees. The trunks offered little protection, but he had no better place to hide, so he scurried to join them.

Peering through the gaps between branches, Saunti spotted an officer on horseback approaching the pile of portraits. He shut his eyes, inhaling a shaky breath. *This is crazy.*

Podge nudged his shoulder. "Relax. We know what we're doing."

Slowly, Saunti opened his eyes to see the officer motioning for the others to join him. Their group of six dismounted their horses and formed a circle around the suspicious mound.

Saunti gulped. "How long until it—"

"Shh!" Kwinn said, watching with a smile.

One officer pointed to the boombox while taking a step back, as though he dreaded something horrible was about to happen.

Podge and Kwinn covered their ears in unison, and Saunti followed suit. His pulse quickened as they waited in the silence.

"Three," said Kwinn.

"Two," said Podge.

A deep rumbling filled the air, and Saunti flinched as the ground shook beneath his feet. The stolen portraits grew an instant fire, blooming into a flower-like bulb with a force that threw the officers off their feet. They scrambled, crawling on all fours to escape the heat and flying debris.

The boom slightly scorched Saunti's face, even from his distance. He couldn't imagine how painful it must have been up close.

Smoke rose like a gray cloud in the night sky as a few officers flung themselves into the ocean, desperately attempting to soothe their burns.

"The real Vakoi's next." Kwinn faced Saunti, her smile widening, her eyes reflecting the flames. "Him and his whole family."

Saunti smiled back as Podge hopped up and down, mouthing shouts of excitement.

CHAPTER 5

ULTIMATUM

Two days and twenty-two hours ago…

♫ BRIDGE - HIGH HIGHS ♫

Two weeks had passed since Yahshi's desertion, and while the Defense Division had voted in favor of pardoning him, the Force's decision meant nothing if they couldn't trace him first. Even with wanted articles distributed island-wide, there were hardly any new leads on his whereabouts. Defense units left and returned on perpetual expeditions, their hope waning with each trip east and back.

It was time for a special operation.

To prepare for such, nearly the entire Force met in the Complex to discuss the game plan, chatting amongst each other as they waited for the meeting leader to arrive. Pinto scanned the common room for Vell as he sat on a sofa, but he couldn't find her. She'd hardly been in the City lately, often leaving on consecutive expeditions with little rest in between.

"Vell and Quax left yesterday afternoon," Keiyo said, joining Pinto on the sofa. "Hopefully they'll make it back in time to rest before the operation."

He reached into his overcoat for a notebook and pen, which made Keiyo chuckle.

"What?" Pinto asked.

"You're taking meeting notes for them. That's such a professor thing to do."

They shared a smile, and the surrounding chatter intensified as Ogga entered through the front door, carrying a map of the island pinned to a board. He planted it on a stand in the middle of the common room.

Pinto leaned in, studying the harsh red line dividing the Vakoi Empire from Eastern Territory. It always baffled him how small the West looked compared to the East. *It's not always strength in numbers. Emperor Vakoi's rule is proof that we can't underestimate the Underground.*

"Alright, quiet down!" Embre's voice cut through the murmurs, instantly silencing the common room. "Let's listen respectfully to Professor Ogga."

Keiyo leaned toward Pinto and whispered, "She still acts like she's our instructor."

Pinto concealed a grin as the redhead reached into his wrinkled overcoat for a tin of golden pins.

"Professor Famir," Ogga said, pushing a pin into the map. "You'll take Commander Evaris and Commander Galler to be stationed in Erenford, a few towns south of Atherus City."

"G-Got it." Galler smiled at the ex-unit member next to him. "Just like o-old times, right?"

Evaris smiled back at the twenty-five-year-old with a nod, but her gaze drifted to Pinto. She held her palm up in a subtle wave. He turned away.

"Doctor Blimmery," Ogga announced, placing a pin to mark Vori. "You'll take Professor Kanter and Commander Lim to be stationed in Vori, where Yahshi Konya was first sighted. It's farther from Atherus City, but he could have gone backward to throw us off his trail."

Pinto spotted Blimmery and Kanter leaning against the wall beside each other. Kanter nodded with a blank expression, and Blimmery glanced at his operative unit member with a faint smile.

Keiyo piped up, catching Pinto by surprise as attention turned their way. "Is there a reason we keep using Atherus City as an anchor point?"

Embre smirked at Keiyo's observation. "We have a feeling the former capital is Yahshi's final destination. Reported sightings note him moving north."

The front door opened, drawing eyes to Quax and his precocious older sister. Most guardians smiled at Cal, though some—including Evaris—turned their heads away as though they wished to ignore her entrance. Pinto couldn't help but remember what Roz had revealed during his interrogation about Yahshi having shadowed Cal once at the Academy. *Is she not as admired in the Force as Capital Weekly makes it seem?*

Pinto's curiosity faded as Vell entered behind the siblings, her hair slicked back into a tight bun. He exchanged a glance with Keiyo.

"Bet it won't be long before Vell starts wearing her hair in a slick bun like my sister," Quax had predicted the day before Yahshi's desertion. Pinto hadn't believed it—she rarely put her hair up. Yet here she was, proving Quax right.

"Commander Cal!" Ogga exclaimed. "Great timing. I'd like you stationed in the woods between Thornwick and Grimward. It's located along the path to Atherus City from his last reported sighting location, so there's a high chance you'll intercept him."

"Oh, jumping right into it," Cal said, sparking a few laughs. She noticed a strand of hair poking out of her bun and frowned, pushing it back into place.

When Vell shut the door behind them, Pinto waited for her to look at him and Keiyo, but she didn't. Her eyes were on Ogga as he announced Cal's operative unit members.

"More than anyone, Yahshi would trust his fellow graduates with the pardon, so we've assigned Professor Pinto, Commander Vell, Commander Quax, and Doctor Keiyo to be stationed with you."

"That's quite the plan." Cal grinned and scanned the room, making eye contact with each of them. When her gray eyes landed on Pinto, a chill ran down his spine. He didn't know if it was something she had done that had made Yahshi jump from that balcony, but either way, Pinto couldn't deny that the Belladonna Prodigy left him with an unsettling feeling.

"Professor Embre," Ogga called next.

She stepped forward as though accepting a badge on graduation day.

"Pass out the pardons for me, will you?" He handed her a stack of golden slips from his overcoat, each about the size of a palm.

"Of course, Professor." Embre ducked her head as she took them.

"Each of you will bring a pardon with you, just in case you run into Yahshi alone," Ogga explained as Embre passed out the slips. "They are each signed by Emperor Vakoi and marked with the Imperial stamp."

When Pinto received his shiny slip, he ran his fingers over Emperor Vakoi's signature. Each loop and flourish of the dark red ink radiated authority in a way that inspired him to practice his penmanship. *What a perfect name...*

For about an hour longer, the meeting continued. Ogga announced the remaining placements and explained how to handle Yahshi based on various scenarios.

"If he runs, aim to capture him without inflicting major injuries. If he fights, don't be afraid to respond with force, but remember—our primary goal is to present the pardon." It was Ogga's last scenario that left goosebumps on Pinto's arms. "If he doesn't cooperate with our terms, you have the authority to kill."

He better not encounter Yahshi. Pinto's eye darted to Roz, who was engrossed in a stack of pages unrelated to the special operation—likely documents for the next cycle of Academy trainees, judging by the familiar look of the exam score sheets. Pinto knew for certain that if given the opportunity to kill Yahshi without even presenting the pardon, Roz wouldn't hesitate.

"We'll meet in front of the Complex tomorrow night at 10:30," Embre said. "Be punctual. We leave at 11:00."

Famir cupped his hands around his mouth and shouted, "What do we do?"

"Bring! Him! Home!" Pinto chanted with the others.

As the Force cheered, he glanced at Vell, who stood by the door with her lips pursed. She tightened her bun as Pinto faced Keiyo next to him—he leaned back with his arms crossed.

Neither of them had said a word.

The following evening, Pinto woke to a knock on his door.

"It's me," Vell said. "We leave in an hour."

"One minute," he grumbled, stirring in bed and wiping a bead of sweat from his forehead. *No wonder it's so hot. I'm still in uniform.* It took a minute for him to remember that it was the night of the special operation, and that he'd fallen asleep in the afternoon to squeeze some rest in before the trip. He reached for the eyepatch on his nightstand and slipped it over his head as he rose. It felt odd to get ready for service when the clock read 9:26, with moonlight slipping in between his curtains.

Vell knocked again as Pinto pulled his heavy overcoat on. "You're not sleeping, are you?"

"I'll be right there." He adjusted his eyepatch, laced his boots, and slung his bow and a quiver of arrows over his back.

Vell flinched when he opened the door. She had slicked her hair back into a low bun again. *Maybe the new style is here to stay.*

"Your curls are all over the place." She eyed Pinto's hair just as intently. "How long have you been out?"

"Since 4:00, maybe." Pinto stepped away as he yawned, and Vell slipped past him into his flat.

He closed the door behind her. "What's wrong?"

"Nothing." Vell sat on his bed. "Why do you ask?"

"You only invite yourself over if you're in a bad mood," he said, smoothing out the wrinkles in his dress shirt. "Usually you have crackers too."

She chuckled, but the furrow in her brow told him she wasn't in a playful mood. Her eyes drifted to his primary tool as he joined her on the bed. "Are your arrows laced?"

"Not today."

"Neither are my throwing blades. And don't tell Quax, but I swapped his swords out."

Pinto managed a smile. "We're not gonna hurt him. He's pardoned."

"But you heard Professor Ogga yesterday." She met his gaze, her voice hardening. "What if he doesn't cooperate? He had a bag, Pinto. He planned to leave behind our backs. What if he hates the Force more than he loves us?"

Pinto stared at his boots, his thumbnail finding its way to his lips out of habit. He couldn't deny that Vell likely understood Yahshi more than he did.

If *she* doubted his willingness to return to Vakoi City, perhaps Roz could be right after all.

"The pardon is only valid if he cooperates, which he won't."

Pinto shook his head, refusing to consider the idea any longer. Of course Yahshi would cooperate. Vell was just second-guessing his loyalties because her role in the Defense Division had conditioned her to view every target as a criminal.

"Don't worry. We're bringing him home today," Pinto said, arguing with both Vell and Roz at once. "He's not a spy for the Underground. He's our best friend."

Vell's eyes watered. "What if he's both?"

A frown touched Pinto's lips. Such a horrible combination couldn't be possible. To get along with an Eastern convert was nothing like befriending a member of the organization that gouged out his eye. The latter was akin to a naive rabbit willingly approaching a wolf. The predator would be kind to its prey not out of friendship, but to enjoy the entertainment of playing with its supper.

"We're running out of time." Pinto stood and glanced at the clock on his way to the door, dodging her question. "Let's have a meal before we leave."

"I hate Complex food," Vell muttered, but she ate with him in the cafeteria anyway.

At 10:30, all ninety-two guardians involved in the special operation met by the stable. From there, they dispersed into their unconventional units, taking off in a trail of shiny vaults heading east.

Pinto was the last to hop into the passenger box, joining his fellow graduates right before the clock hit 10:45. He rubbed his arms in the late-night chill as he sat next to Vell, opposite Quax and Keiyo's bench.

"Be prepared for anything." Cal winked at them from the ground. "Yahshi's game of hide-and-seek ends today."

A gust of cold air brushed Pinto's face as Cal slammed the vault door shut, leaving the four recent graduates in pitch black, their hair rustling in the breeze. Had Yahshi been with them, they would have formed a complete set.

Vell struck a match to light a handheld lantern, illuminating their faces in the passenger box. Their journey tonight would be a long one, but the dense silence between their glowing faces told Pinto it would feel much longer.

After seven hours of sleepless travel, their operative unit disembarked in the woods between Thornwick and Grimward. They searched for only an hour before successfully intercepting their target at 6:40, just as the first light of dawn began threading through the branches.

Pinto couldn't believe it was him. How could Yahshi Konya, his best friend and fellow graduate of Belladonna Guardian Academy, look so unexceptional and small? Perhaps it was only because Pinto had never seen him wear anything but school uniforms, fancy silk pajamas, and his formal wear—and now, he dressed in the plain, casual attire of Eastern Territory.

On the flip side, maybe Yahshi had become weaker in actuality. Upon closer inspection, his face seemed more angular, his shoulders less broad. Two weeks on the run could have worn him down physically, though if it had, it surely didn't wound his stubborn spirit. Even with his shoulder wounded and his strength belladonna-impaired from the darts Cal had sliced him with, he stared at the pardon slip for an abnormally long time.

Pinto frowned, waiting for him to make the only valid choice.

Why isn't he moving? He exchanged concerned glances with Keiyo and Quax. *There's no complicated math involved. The answer is simple. It's time to come home.*

"Yahshi," Cal said, pressing him to make a choice.

"Accept the pardon," Pinto ordered, his pulse quickening.

"Let us fix this," offered Quax.

"Can you please come home?" asked Keiyo.

"Yahshi." Vell spoke to him for the first time since they'd surrounded him in the woods, catching his attention. "Prove me wrong."

Her words flew at him like throwing stars, and his face drained of color.

That's right. Pinto gulped hard. *Listen to her.*

"Look around." Cal gestured to the operative unit surrounding him. "Look at the mess you've made."

Yahshi's eyes hopped from Quax to Pinto to Vell to Keiyo—until finally, he returned his gaze to Cal. "How do I fix it?" he asked, his voice softer than before.

Cal pointed to the vault, and he nodded.

Thank the stars. Pinto's shoulders loosened, but his relief was short-lived.

"Pinto," Cal said, meeting his gaze, "your bow."

The last thing he wanted was to aim at Yahshi, but he couldn't deny Cal's order, and he understood why she'd made it. If Yahshi were to sprint away at the last minute, his loyalties would become crystal clear, forcing them to kill him, as Ogga had ordered.

But he won't run, so I won't have to shoot. He understands that too. I'm sure he knows I'm not trying to hurt him. Pinto raised his bow and aimed at Yahshi, pivoting so his arrow tracked him as he walked toward the vault.

The forest fell silent.

Yes, keep walking. Just get in the vault, and everything will go back to the way it used to be.

It was a lie he told himself to calm his nerves. Deep down, he knew everything wouldn't be the same. The Force would question Yahshi and likely send him to correction. It would take time for the other guardians to trust him again—including Pinto and Vell. Yahshi had so much explaining to do, and disappointments to make up for. However, eventually, life would improve.

And most importantly, he'd still be alive.

Pinto readied to lower his bow as Yahshi set one foot on the passenger box platform, only to freeze. He stood with just a single leg raised, walking the tightrope between redemption and death.

I could shoot him in his good shoulder to make him stumble right in. Pinto pulled his bowstring back tighter. *I could do it right now.*

Yahshi removed his foot from the platform first, putting Pinto's plan on hold. "I reject the pardon," he announced, turning to reveal a calm, blank expression. It was as though he knew this choice would end in his death, yet didn't care.

Pinto gritted his teeth. The sudden rustle, the distant voices, Yahshi's unexpected capture—the past ten minutes flashed through his mind in fragments. He had expected resistance leading up to presenting the pardon, but he'd never imagined Yahshi would distrust them *after* such a kind gesture. Cal had offered him a slip that would save his life. Yahshi should have been grateful for the Force, but instead, he spit on their efforts.

Vell and Roz were right—Yahshi had no intention of returning home.

Pinto opened his mouth, ready to shout about everything he'd done to keep Yahshi safe, but Cal's sniffling broke the silence first. It felt like a backward miracle to see her cry. She was the Belladonna Prodigy. She always had restraint.

"I murdered Chima Fernis," Cal said, her voice raspy. "You were there, Yahshi. You remember."

As Cal expressed her gratitude toward the Force for pardoning her, Pinto recalled the articles he'd read about her situation years ago. Cal had protected Quax from a violent school bully, attracting attention from the Force and ultimately leading to her pardon four months later. Pinto hadn't known that Yahshi had been there during Chima's murder too. In fact, Yahshi had explicitly told him once, at the Academy, that he hardly knew Cal.

He was there? Pinto's eye widened. *Why would he keep that from me?*

"...And here you are, rejecting the Force's mercy," Cal continued. "They're giving you a second chance, and you're throwing it away like it means nothing."

"Because I'd rather die on my terms than theirs," Yahshi said.

Do you realize what you're saying? Pinto stepped forward, his blood running hot. *Your life is the most valuable thing you'll ever own, and you're willing to throw it away for nothing?*

Cal echoed Pinto's thoughts, calling Yahshi ungrateful, and claiming he had no other way to survive. That's when Yahshi turned back to his friends and spouted the most ridiculous lies Pinto had ever heard—ones that made his skin crawl.

"You want the truth from me, don't you?" Yahshi asked. "Well, here it is—the Force *lies*. I didn't kill my father—Commander Roz did. Emperor Vakoi initiated the Eastern raids to give him an excuse to control both sides of the island. This entire time, we've been the bad guys. We've been the monsters. Maelin Vandros of Frontal saw that, and the Force killed her for it."

"No, Yahshi. No." Pinto lowered his bow, shaking his head. He didn't doubt that Roz killed Martu Konya, but Pinto had seen portraits of Maelin's face hanging in his hometown, along with articles about her heroic death framed on school walls. She had been an inspiration to many, including him. *The Belladonna Savior.* He knew her story inside and out.

"The *Underground* killed Doctor Maelin," Pinto corrected. "I'm from Frontal. I would know."

"Look in the archives," Yahshi said. "It's all there."

Pinto shook his head as Quax spoke up again. "Commander Roz would never do that. He would never kill Martu and blame it on you. He would have no incentive."

"The Force killed Doctor Maelin? Emperor Vakoi initiated the raids?" Pinto scoffed. "Who's telling you these things? What kind of propaganda have you been exposed to?"

"Yahshi, stop this, please," Keiyo said, his lips downturned. "Save yourself. You deserve it."

Pinto raised a hand, trailing a finger along his leather eyepatch. *How cruel could the Underground possibly be, to take away not only my eye, but my closest friend?*

"I've had enough!" Cal shouted, turning to Pinto. "Finish him."

He lowered his hand from his eyepatch. "Finish?"

"You know what I mean."

He gulped, his arm shaking as he aimed at Yahshi again. "Don't make me do this."

"You have a choice," Yahshi said. "Don't be blind."

"Hurry up," Cal ordered.

Yahshi stepped toward the horses leading the vault, and Pinto drew his bowstring tighter, stopping him.

"Move again," he warned, "and I'll shoot."

"You're shooting regardless," Cal reminded him.

Vell aimed her star at Yahshi too.

"How could you do this to us?" Pinto asked. "You made a Vow to support your fellow guardians."

"I'm not a guardian, Pinto," Yahshi replied. "Don't you get it?"

Pinto's eye watered, because despite Yahshi saying all the wrong things, he still couldn't bring himself to hurt him. The Underground might have brainwashed him, but surely the real Yahshi was still in there. Why should the Force require that he walk into the vault upon his own will? They should capture him and drag him home. They could force him to face the falsities of his new beliefs, and once he'd wake up to reality, he'd thank them for it.

He can still be of value. He can still be saved.

"Shoot him!" Cal yelled. "Shoot him now!"

I need to think of something. Pinto narrowed his eye, formulating an argument against killing Yahshi that Cal might consider. His pulse quickened when Yahshi shuffled, preparing to run. *I need to say something!*

But before he could, something struck the tip of Pinto's drawn arrow. He flinched as his bow jolted aside against his will, the arrow shooting off in a different direction.

A throwing star landed near his boots.

Pinto craned his head to see Vell in the final position of her throwing form, her face bright red. She glared at him as though she believed he were about to murder their best friend.

I wasn't going to shoot, Pinto wanted to say, but a clot formed in his throat.

"Vell," Keiyo said weakly. "What did you do?"

Pinto's breaths raced, his head spinning as the reality of what had taken place struck him all at once. Vell had broken Protocol, but she had only done so because Pinto had resisted Cal's order by hesitating to shoot. *Does that mean I broke Protocol too? Are we both at fault?* His fingers twitched as he considered reaching for another arrow. *Should I still shoot Yahshi? Would that fix this? If I don't shoot him, does that make me even more guilty than I already am? Perhaps I—*

Quax's piercing scream interrupted his train of thought, and Pinto looked over to see him staring at his older sister in horror.

Pinto's arrow had pierced through Cal's neck.

His arm fell limp, the bow slipping from his grip and striking the ground. He turned his back to the siblings, his lips trembling, unable to watch.

"No, you're okay," Quax cried out. "It's not that bad. You'll be fine. You're okay."

What if Cal dies? Pinto leaned over, the panicked voices swirling around him into a blur. *Would I take the fall for it?*

The muffled voices behind him cleared as he gripped his stomach, trying to settle his nausea. *Have some restraint. You can salvage this.* He tuned out Quax's sobbing and Cal's gasps enough to hear Vell speak.

"You made me a promise, Yahshi, and you broke it." She was crying, joining in Quax's tears. "You left me alone in the capital. And the things Cal made me do…"

"Get away from my sister!" Quax yelled at her.

"Promise?" Pinto inhaled a shaky breath and forced himself to turn around. He gulped at the sight of Quax leaning over Cal as blood streamed down her neck from the puncture point. Next, he noticed a dagger on the dirt nearby, Yahshi gripping Vell's wrist above it, as though he had just stopped her from…

She tried to kill Cal. Pinto's breath hitched as he met eyes with Vell. *She hadn't struck my arrow out of impulse. She wanted Cal dead. She's a traitor, just like him. That's why she knew he wouldn't want to come home. Was she in on this? Had she known all along?*

"What promise, Vell?" Pinto asked.

With his hand still wrapped around her wrist, Yahshi pulled her toward the vault.

Pinto picked up his bow and sprinted after them. "Stop!"

Yahshi and Vell mounted two of the horses, and Pinto reached them just as Vell used a dart to cut the ropes binding them to the driver's seat. The horses trotted out of Pinto's reach just in time.

He shot an arrow, purposefully grazing Yahshi's horse as they galloped away. It barely skimmed the animal, failing to spook it as intended.

He shot another arrow, perfectly aiming to pierce deeper this time, but Yahshi's horse swerved, evading the shot completely. The arrow pierced a tree instead.

Dammit. Pinto's next shot missed too. He drew his bow a fourth time, aiming directly at Yahshi's horse and hoping the fall wouldn't be too dangerous.

Right before shooting, a force struck his shoulder, and his feet slipped out from under him. His arrow shot feebly into the air before dropping onto the dirt, and he fell next to it, finding Keiyo pinning him down.

"What the hell are you doing?" Pinto yelled. He tried to push himself up, but Keiyo shoved him down again.

"I don't know," Keiyo said, his voice hardly more than a whisper.

CHAPTER 6

GOING UNDER

One hour ago...

♫ THE VIEW BETWEEN VILLAGES - NOAH KAHAN ♫

Saunti returned home around 6:30 in the morning after spending another night with Podge and Kwinn at the Palace ruins. They had discussed the results of the portrait booming—which no one had linked them to—and had brainstormed ideas for their next big scheme. *Maybe their calculated risks are exactly what the Underground lacks.*

He crept into the main room and sighed, relieved his mother hadn't woken up for work yet. Her door was slightly ajar, so he peered through the crack to find her curled up in bed, sound asleep.

Instead of waking her, he returned to the main room and cooked her breakfast. It wouldn't hurt to butter her up before breaking the news, he figured, and perhaps it'd help him feel less guilty too.

As he brought a plate into her room, his approaching footsteps sent her jolting up with a gasp.

"Oh, it's you." Tonna settled down, eyeing the plate of fried fish and canned vegetables. "What's this?"

"Breakfast."

She squinted at a stream of light slipping between a gap in the curtains, her jaw dropping at the realization that they were running late for work.

"We don't have time." She attempted to get out of bed. "We need to—"

"Mother," Saunti interrupted, forcing the plate into her hands. "It's okay. One day off won't be suspicious. I'll say you gave me your cough."

Tonna stared back at him, her frown loosening. With a sigh, she stared down at the plate in her hands and picked up her spoon. "I suppose one day off won't hurt."

Saunti smiled back, urging himself to confess that he wouldn't be helping her as a courier anymore—at least, not until she was ready to be honest with him.

He had just opened his mouth when someone knocked on the front door.

Tonna swallowed her bite and nearly got up, but Saunti left the room first, gesturing for her to stay in bed. "I've got it."

As soon as he left his mother's room, his eyes widened, thinking back to the fire at the shore. Were local officers finally closing in on him?

Saunti stopped at the door and took a deep breath, regaining composure. *If they were onto me, I would have known by now.*

He opened the door to find two teenagers—one of whom was the boy from the wanted articles, the Belladonna Traitor his mother had asked him to help her find. Minus the thin cuts on his face, he perfectly resembled the portraits. *He lost the bandana, but he's clearly covering that mark under his hair.*

Saunti's eyes darted to the girl next, his lips parting in disbelief. She looked almost identical to the Nightshade in Cal's unit who had inspected his lumber mill a little over a week ago.

"The... sky weeps with us?" Yahshi said, his voice shaky.

"Oh yeah?" Saunti broke a grin, his eyes darting to the girl's boots, which confirmed his suspicion—those were the same shiny black shoes he'd seen the Meridian book land by.

The girl took a step back.

The wanted articles only mentioned one traitor—Yahshi Konya. Considering the girl wasn't included in the story, Saunti figured the Force had set this up as a trap. *What if they conjured this story to lure couriers like us into exposing the hideout? They must be targeting me because of the Meridian book. They think I know something. Oh, I see through your scheme, Vakoi, and I'm not falling for it.*

"We're looking for Tonna," the boy said, bringing Saunti's attention back to him.

"To what? Poison her?" Saunti leaned against the doorframe, making a statement that they weren't welcome here. With their training, they could easily kill him, but even knowing so, he refused to bend his will. He wouldn't stab his dignity to step aside and say, *Come in, Nightshades. Raid my house. Kill my mother. Blackmail me into showing you where Aero lives so you can kill thousands of innocent people.*

So instead, he called their bluff. "I know you're with the Force. That's why you're with *her*. What is she? Your unit member?"

"Saunti?" Tonna called from her room. "Who is it?"

"No one!" he yelled back. "Just a—"

"Are you Tonna?" Yahshi shouted. "I'm your—"

With a scoff, Saunti slammed the door and locked it shut. He didn't know how Yahshi and his mother were connected, but the fact that his wanted articles left her in such intense distress didn't sit right with him. He headed for Tonna's room to explain the situation, but she reached him first, eyeing the door.

"Who's here?" she whispered.

"Just Noris, being Noris."

She glared. "*Saunti.*"

"Fine," he said, glancing at the door. "It's the boy from the articles."

Her eyes widened into moons. "Why would you lock him out?"

"Why would you *let him in*? He's a Nightshade."

Tonna nearly argued but stopped herself and hastily rushed to the door. Saunti leaned against the bookshelf as his mother greeted the Nightshades, confirming her name. She welcomed them in, and he crossed his arms. "Mother, do you really think—"

"Quiet." Tonna shut the door behind them.

Yahshi faced Saunti, studying him up and down.

"Why are you staring?" Saunti asked.

He glanced between him and Tonna. "She's your mother?"

"No, she's my father. What the hell do you think?"

Tonna studied Yahshi intently, and he gulped as she approached him. The room fell silent, and Yahshi's accomplice seemed to stiffen as Tonna, smiling, reached for his face.

The girl stepped forward, and Saunti snapped at her.

"If you touch my mother, I'll kill you. I know you're a filthy Night..." He trailed off as Tonna wrapped her arms around the Belladonna Traitor as though she'd been waiting for this moment her entire life.

"It's really you," she muttered.

Yahshi closed his eyes, relishing her embrace like he'd been waiting for this moment too.

"Okay, what the hell?" Saunti said. "How do you know him?"

Tonna pulled away with a sniffle, finally meeting Saunti's gaze. "There's no time to explain." She walked to the bookshelf he was leaning against and shooed him away.

"Who is he?" Saunti asked, stepping aside.

Tonna held a book out for him. "It's time."

Saunti looked back at Yahshi and the other Nightshade, shaking his head. "No..." How could it be that after months of her telling him he wasn't ready to go under, this Belladonna Traitor had changed her mind?

"Deliver this book to Noris," Tonna instructed, holding it out for him. "Letters are circled to form the name of the nearest courier. He's to seek him for instructions on how to reach the access point."

Saunti snatched the book. "Noris won't fit in the access point."

"I need you to be serious, Saunti."

"You're the one who can't be serious. You're about to compromise Headquarters to a pair of Nightshade *spies*."

"Go. Tell Noris that his first assignment as a courier begins one week from today. Take no longer than three minutes, and meet us at the access point using Route B. I'll explain everything once we're safe."

Saunti thought of Podge and Kwinn, and how thrilled they were to have him on board. While he'd enjoyed his time with them, he could tell by the urgency in his mother's voice that something serious was happening with the Underground, and it had something to do with Yahshi Konya. If this was his chance to join Headquarters, and finally enter Aero's world to serve the cause directly, he couldn't pass this off for anything else.

"Whatever. I had a feeling I'd die this week anyway." Saunti sent Yahshi and his accomplice a scowl before leaving, slamming the front door behind him.

"What are you doing here?" Noris asked, eyeing the alleyway left and right.

Saunti raised the book in his hands. "Special delivery."

Noris ushered Saunti in, shut the door behind him, and drew every curtain shut. "I don't like you coming here unannounced like this."

"Well, lucky for you, it's the last time. Mother and I are leaving," Saunti said. While he would have liked to enjoy Noris's confusion, he had three minutes, so he cut to the chase. "We're moving to the hideout, and you're assigned to take over as courier."

"*What?*" Noris faced him in an instant. "You'll go missing! It'll draw unnecessary attention to the City!"

"Quiet," Saunti mocked. "Someone could hear."

Noris shook his head, lowering his voice. "As much as I respect your mother, choosing me to replace the two of you is a grave mistake. I've always been a collector, and I'm damn great at it. I've got the best hiding spot in the City." He gestured to his wooden-paneled walls. "But me, sneaking around at night? No. That's ridiculous."

"Oh, I agree. Completely." Saunti set the coded book on Noris's dining room table. "But unfortunately, it's not my decision."

Noris took a deep breath, exhaling as he took a seat. He gestured for Saunti to join him at the table, but he didn't. *How ironic that the first and only time I'm actually in a hurry is the same time Noris wants me to take my time.* The doorknob was looking shinier than ever.

Noris glanced at the clock, as though he suddenly understood that time was of utmost importance.

"What's the book for?" he asked, dragging it in front of him.

Saunti set his hand on the table and leaned forward, explaining the instructions Tonna had told him to pass along.

Noris flipped through the first few pages, searching for the circled letters.

"First one is *O*," he said, jotting it down on a spare page.

"Burn the book and your notes when you're done," Saunti whispered, and Noris nodded.

He lingered, watching Noris decode the book with an odd sense of concern. Tonna had taught everything to Saunti firsthand, even accompanying him on his first few deliveries, but Noris would have to figure everything out with instructions from a stranger. He wouldn't have the privilege of trial and error, and if he were to mess up, the blood of thousands in Headquarters would be on his hands.

While Saunti had an easy time trusting himself as a courier, passing such a role onto someone else made his stomach churn. He finally understood why Tonna had been so hesitant to give him the responsibility in the first place, and why Noris always warned him to stay safe.

Being a courier isn't the challenging part. Trusting someone to be a courier is.

Saunti leaned back as the sound of another flipped page filled the room. He made his way to the front door, leaving Noris to handle the rest of the work on his own.

"Wait," Noris called.

Saunti looked back at Noris, his gaze loosening at the warmth in the man's eyes.

"Stay safe, Saunti." Noris offered a smile.

For the first time, Saunti smiled back. "Take care, Noris." He waved as he left the man's house, his feet moving on their own to take Route B.

As he walked, he realized how much he was about to leave behind. Atherus City had always felt like a prison to him, but there was something beautiful about it this morning. Despite its imperfections and the looming knowledge of Vakoi's control, Atherus City was home.

Maybe I could stay behind to help Podge and Kwinn. I could even offer to help Noris, if he needs it. The mere idea, which had seemed like a valid option just seconds ago, suddenly made him chuckle. The Underground was where he belonged now, and if he were to stay behind, officers would question him about his mother's disappearance. Going under was his only right choice.

Staying isn't an option anymore, but I wish you the best, Podge. Please be careful.

He entered the access point alleyway to spot his mother coming from the opposite side. They met in the middle and stopped.

"You're not thinking straight," Saunti said, eyes on Yahshi and the other Nightshade. He still didn't agree with bringing them under, but at the same time, they were the reason his mother had finally decided to move, so perhaps he shouldn't be *too* resistant.

"Did you do it?" Tonna asked, referring to the book delivery.

"Reluctantly."

"Good." She turned to Yahshi and the other Nightshade. "Listen, we need to enter fast. If anyone spots us, *thousands* will die."

Saunti offered a mocking grin. "No pressure."

Tonna dropped to her knees and gripped the manhole cover at their feet. After watching her fail to tug it out of place a few times, Saunti rubbed the frown from his face and sighed, kneeling to help her. Together they dragged the cover aside, revealing a ladder descending into the access point.

"You'll go first," Tonna said, peering up at Yahshi. "Then me, then"—her gaze drifted to the Nightshade—"*you*. And Saunti?"

"Yeah?"

"You're last. Don't let her run."

Saunti nodded, glad that Tonna was at least taking *some* precautions.

Yahshi peered down into the dark abyss, squinting, perhaps hoping to spot something at the bottom.

"You heard her," Saunti said. "Down the rabbit hole you go..."

Yahshi lowered his feet onto the ladder steps, beginning his descent. Next went Tonna, then the Nightshade. She had slipped her legs through when she stopped to meet Saunti's gaze. Her icy blue eyes sent a chill down his spine as she leaned toward him, staring a moment longer despite his hand motions to hurry.

"I never turned you in," the Nightshade whispered. "Don't make me regret that."

Saunti held her gaze, fighting the urge to look away and give in to her empty threat. She was bluffing because she didn't trust him, and Yahshi meant something to her—but she was no threat. Not for now, at least. She didn't have her overcoat, meaning she didn't have her weapons.

Still, I'm keeping my eye on her.

The Nightshade finally broke eye contact, slipping her feet through the opening. She climbed down the ladder so quietly that Saunti nearly believed she'd allowed herself to free fall. He half-expected her to splat onto the concrete slab at the bottom, but when he peered down, she was standing next to Yahshi, staring up with her fingers pinching her nose.

Saunti descended last, dragging the cover over his head to conceal everyone in the darkness. He struck a match and used the dull orange glow to guide him down, joining them at the bottom. They stood so close together that their shoulders touched.

Tonna knocked on the door in a three-two-three pattern, which was soon followed by a *click* from the other side. Yahshi and the Nightshade shuffled in place, searching for the sound's unknown source.

"Stop squirming," Saunti muttered.

The pair stilled as Tonna gripped the third ladder step from the floor, and with a yank, the hinged block of concrete swung toward her to reveal a secret entryway.

Standing in the shadows was Aero. Saunti hadn't spoken to her since she'd laughed at his request and slammed the door in his face. He wasn't necessarily excited to see her, but regardless, he found his eyes searching for the necklace he'd gifted her. *Of course. She's not even wearing it.*

"Tonna!" Aero shouted. "Long time no see." Her eyes trailed over Yahshi and the Nightshade. "Who are the kids, Cricket?"

Saunti nearly replied, but Tonna held her palm up, muting him. "Step aside, Aero. It's time."

Her eyes darted back to the Belladonna Traitor with an open-mouth grin. "Holy shit. It's *him*, isn't it?"

Saunti paused for a moment, wondering who *him* referred to. Did Aero somehow know about Yahshi? Had another courier in some other town delivered the latest issue of *Capital Weekly* to the hideout? He turned to Tonna, wondering how she'd reply, but she said nothing.

Realizing that Tonna didn't intend to answer, Aero stepped aside, and they filed into a tunnel lined with torches. Saunti closed the secret door behind everyone and fumbled with a small metal block.

"Wow." Aero reached past him and twisted it. "You don't even know how our locks work."

Saunti huffed. "How would you expect me to—"

She blew his match out with a chuckle.

"Aero," Tonna said, "as a handler, I assume you have direct access to the inventory room?"

She retrieved a ring of keys from her pocket and jingled them. "Indeed I do."

"Not many people inside, right?" Tonna asked.

"Only handlers have access."

"And you know how to get there without being seen?"

"'Course." Aero skipped to the front of the group, passing Tonna to lead the way. "Follow me."

She guided them to a ladder at the end of the tunnel, and they descended into a network of interconnected passages. The twists and turns were natural for Aero, but Saunti found his shoulders skimming the walls during unexpected bends, and he occasionally pressed his hands against the coarse rocks to balance himself.

About ten minutes later, Aero stopped to unlock a metal door. Saunti estimated they were under the outskirts of Atherus City now, closer to the shore, but they'd taken too many turns for him to be confident in his sense of direction.

Aero swung the door open to reveal a room filled with coal, canned fish, oil, matchboxes, blankets, and other supplies that Underground collectors across Eastern Territory had smuggled into the hideout.

The Belladonna Traitor and the Nightshade entered after Tonna and Saunti, but Aero lingered in the doorway with her hands in her pockets, awaiting further instructions.

Saunti watched the Yahshi carefully as he reached for a can of beans. He studied it like it was the most fascinating item he'd ever seen.

"Leave us locked in here for now, and don't announce our arrival publicly," Tonna said. "I want you to deliver a message directly to the Provisional Council members."

"Got it," Aero said. "What's the message?"

Despite opening her mouth, no words came out. Tonna's eyes watered as she looked over her shoulder, locking eyes with the Belladonna Traitor.

Saunti's cheeks ran hot with impatience. *Just say it, Mother. Who is this boy, and why have we brought him here?*

"Tonna?" Aero prodded. "What do I tell the Council?"

Yahshi's grip on the can of beans tightened when Tonna smiled at him. Her eyes overflowed, and silent tears spilled down her cheeks.

"Prince Runix has returned."

PART 2
DIVIDE

CHAPTER 7

RUNIX RETURNS

Day 1 Underground | Clocks Read 07:34

♫ CONSPIRACY OF SILENCE · THE SWOONS ♫

The can of beans tumbled out of Yahshi's hands, clattering onto the stone floor of the inventory room. Saunti watched it jump and roll as he recalled the wanted articles he'd read about the Belladonna Traitor. *How could Yahshi be Prince Runix, as well as a Nightshade?*

When the can hit the base of a storage shelf and rolled to a stop, the inventory room fell silent.

Aero cleared her throat, bringing everyone's attention back to where she stood in the doorway. Tonna quickly wiped the tears from her cheek.

"I'll... uh..." Aero forced a grin. "I'll let the Council know." She stepped back into the tunnel and closed the metal door, locking the inventory room from outside.

Yahshi's accomplice sprang into action, snatching another can of beans and clutching it closely. "You have the wrong person," she said, eyeing Saunti and Tonna. "Runix Atherus died in the fire."

Beside her, Yahshi stood petrified—his eyes were marbles, his body stone. *Him? The last of the Atherus bloodline?* Saunti squinted at Yahshi's paling face and shook his head. Even if Runix had survived the Nightshades' attack on Atherus Palace, how could he have grown up in the enemy's land without knowing his true identity, only to work for the same organization that had nearly killed him?

The girl tightened her grip on the can of beans when Saunti met her gaze. He chuckled and nearly spoke, but Tonna snatched his arm, stopping him. His mother seemed to fear offending the Nightshade, considering they were now locked in a room with her.

"This is ridiculous. He's not the Prince, Mother." Saunti ripped his arm free, pointing to Yahshi. "He's the Belladonna Traitor."

"They're the same," she whispered.

"And *you*." Saunti pivoted, pointing to the Nightshade next. "You're seriously threatening me with a can of beans?"

"It's heavy." She reeled her arm back a little. "With a metal shell."

The sharpness of her tone made Saunti chuckle again, and before he could stop himself, he was laughing. *Only a Nightshade could look at beans and see a weapon!*

"Saunti," Tonna snapped.

He tried to settle down. He really did. But his efforts failed.

Tonna raised her voice, overpowering his laughter. "Please, put the can down," she said to the girl. "I'll explain everything."

The Nightshade didn't budge.

Saunti calmed himself just as the supposed *Prince* came to his senses. Yahshi side-eyed the Nightshade girl and muttered, "Vell."

So that's her name.

Vell looked back at Yahshi, who gestured to the shelf with his eyes, urging her to appease Tonna. She shot Tonna and Saunti a final glare before placing the can back.

Tonna faced her son first. "Saunti, your father worked as a guard for the Royal Family."

"Right." He nodded with a smirk. *I've heard the story a million times.*

"But he didn't die in the fire," she added.

"Oh yeah?" Saunti crossed his arms, still unconvinced.

"He was there when the Nightshades attacked—that part was true,"

Tonna continued. "But he didn't fight them. He knew it'd be a losing battle, so he evacuated Prince Runix instead. Then, after seizing control of our land, Vakoi allowed a single migration of our people to pledge their allegiance to him and move to his side of the island. Your father converted to the Vakoi Empire and took the Prince with him, changing his name to Martu Konya and Runix's to Yahshi. We sent the Bayins to join him and live nearby as a protective measure—hoping their son, Dice, would someday infiltrate the Academy too."

Saunti's jaw tightened, and a sickening feeling settled in his stomach, as though his body refused to process his mother's words. If the Nightshades hadn't killed his father during the Atherus Palace raid, that meant he'd abandoned Saunti to raise the Prince. That meant he'd been alive this entire time, making no effort to connect with his *real* son. That meant he had died in the Vakoi Empire, and that his ashes didn't rest in the Palace ruins. No, it had to be a lie. Those realities were too cruel, too unthinkable.

"Are you saying," Yahshi muttered, eyes on the floor, "that my father wasn't really my father? That he was actually your husband, and an Atherus Palace guard? Is that why he knew how to fight?"

He looked up at Tonna, and her light smile confirmed it all.

The look of realization that crossed Yahshi's face twisted a knife in Saunti's gut. If Tonna's long-winded story made sense to him, maybe it really was true. This revelation called everything he knew about his father into question, and his own mother was to blame for the wounds it caused. *Why would she lie to me about this?*

"That night two weeks ago," Yahshi continued, "Father told me he'd explain everything, and take me home. He was talking about Headquarters."

Saunti's eyes darted to his mother. *Look at me. Apologize.*

Tonna nodded back at Yahshi. "It was always the plan for him to return with you a few years from now, once you turned eighteen."

"A few years?" Yahshi's voice was stronger now, laced with skepticism, as though her statement had thrown him out of an engaging story. "But I'm *seventeen*. The Prince would have been fifteen…"

Vell shot him a questioning look, and Yahshi lowered his head with a gasp.

"I was never a late bloomer," he whispered to himself. "Father lied about my birthday."

"It must have been an extra precaution," Tonna said. "You couldn't be linked to the Prince if you were older than him, so he changed your birthday."

"That's why I don't remember anything from the War," Yahshi concluded. "I was only two."

"That's ridiculous," Vell said. "You're not *fifteen*."

"*Mother*," Saunti cut in, his blood boiling.

Tonna hesitated, her gaze lingering on the Nightshades before slowly turning to face her son.

"You always told me Father died for the cause, but he left *us* to raise *him*." Saunti glared at the monster his father had raised. "Even if he's related to Emperor Atherus, he doesn't belong here. He graduated from Nightshade Academy. Royalty or not, he's one of *them* now. For all we know, he really *did* murder—"

"I didn't kill my father!" Yahshi yelled, his voice cracking under the strain.

"He wasn't *your father*," Saunti spat, "and even if you didn't kill him, it's *your* fault he's dead!"

Yahshi turned his head away, his lips twitching as he struggled to hold back his rebuttal.

"I'm sorry, Saunti," Tonna said, her voice hardly more than a whisper. She tried to offer a hug, but he stepped out of reach. Was that really the best apology she could manage?

"Don't touch me."

She stepped back with a sigh. "Just know that your father and I did what we needed to protect both of you, and to honor Emperor Atherus."

Saunti shook his head, chuckling bitterly. Of course she didn't grasp the real root of his anger. Perhaps if she had been honest with him from the start, he could have understood, or even justified, his parents' actions—but now, steeped in lies, he only felt betrayal. Where was her apology for deceiving him all these years?

"Please don't blame the Prince for this," Tonna added.

"The *Prince*? For the millionth time, he's a *Nightshade*, Mother." Saunti stepped toward Yahshi, reaching for his head. "Just pull his hair back and look at his—"

"Shut it!" Vell stepped between them, voice low but firm. "We're *guardians*."

"You don't guard *shit*."

As he glared back into the Nightshade's chilling blue eyes, he thought about that morning at the lumber mill nearly two weeks ago, and how she had slipped the Meridian book into her overcoat without reporting him. *I wonder why she didn't.*

He flinched when someone unlocked the door from outside, and they all turned to face a towering, bald man. He seemed to be around the same age as Tonna, and his broad shoulders skimmed the sides of the doorway as he entered the inventory room.

"Rimoso," Tonna acknowledged, stepping forward to offer a hand. "You've aged well."

"Oh, don't give me that." He pushed her hand aside and wrapped Tonna in a tight hug. "How long has it been? Thirteen years?"

As soon as they pulled away from each other, Rimoso offered Saunti a smile, approaching him next. "Long hair and freckles. You must be Cricket."

Aero must have mentioned me. He forced a smile. *Could Rimoso be her father?*

A frail woman entered the inventory room next, and Tonna's face lit up. "Lira!" she called.

Saunti recognized that name. His mother had mentioned Lira occasionally—over a decade ago, they had both worked together as personal attendants to the late Empress at Atherus Palace.

Lira rushed after Tonna with open arms, but a coughing fit stopped her before they could embrace. Turning away, she pulled a sage green handkerchief out of her coat and pressed it to her mouth.

A deep frown crossed Tonna's forehead as she rushed to her friend's side.

"I'm fine," Lira assured her in a deep, hoarse voice.

Saunti spotted a twinge of blood on her handkerchief as she tucked it away.

"So, which one is he?" Lira asked, her eyes hopping back and forth between Saunti and Yahshi.

"The shorter one," Tonna said.

Lira coughed into her fist as she locked eyes with Yahshi, but she only stared for a moment before her attention turned to Vell.

"And you are?" Lira asked, approaching the Nightshade.

The girl faced Yahshi, who nodded, but she still hesitated before saying, "Vell."

Lira reached out, and Vell flinched as the woman pushed her bangs aside, revealing the four-petaled flower emblem branded on her forehead. It was the first time Saunti had seen such a mark up close, and the raised skin made him cringe. *That must have hurt.*

"A Nightshade," Lira said, her raspy voice tense.

Yahshi pulled his hair aside to reveal a matching mark. "She's with me."

Lira's jaw dropped, allowing another cough to escape her. She turned her back on the Nightshades, taking a few steps away and grasping for her handkerchief again.

"It's just like the Bayins claimed," Rimoso muttered, eyeing the Nightshades' marks. "The Prince ended up in the system."

The Bayins...

Saunti stared at his boots, struggling to remember why the name sounded familiar. It took a moment to recall the family of three on the run who had stayed the night with him and his mother over a year ago. Tonna had brought them to Headquarters, where they'd be safe from the Nightshades searching for them. *The Bayins must have told Mother about how the Prince ended up at the Academy. But of course, she excluded me from that conversation to cover up her lies!*

"I had no line of communication with my husband," Tonna told Rimoso, "but when I brought the Bayins to safety, they assured me he did everything he could to keep the Prince out of the Academy."

"That shouldn't have been a challenge. It's not easy to get *into* the Academy." Rimoso raised his voice, gesturing to Yahshi. "What is this boy? A genius? A killer? What caught the enemy's eye?"

Tonna went quiet, and Saunti wondered the same thing.

Rimoso faced Yahshi as Lira coughed even louder, and he raised his voice to speak over her like it was normal. "We're planning an immediate gathering to announce the truth, including your history as a Nightshade," he said, addressing Yahshi directly for the first time. "There's no hiding that mark for long, so it's better people hear it from us upfront. The Council won't be pleased to have the Bayins' rumor confirmed, though."

"Let them complain," Tonna said firmly. Her eyes drifted to Lira, who waved her handkerchief in response, as though saying, *Don't mind me.*

Saunti frowned. It didn't seem like his mother was used to Lira's sickness, meaning it must have been a development after moving to Headquarters. *I wonder what caused it.*

Rimoso's gaze lingered on Vell for a moment before he turned and held the door open for everyone. "Let's break the news."

Their group of six passed through several interconnected tunnels, each wider and better-lit than the last. The distant murmuring grew louder until they emerged into a vast chamber with a ceiling at least three times higher than the tunnels they'd been walking through. Saunti's eyes darted around, taking in the sight of people bustling about their tasks. Some carried supplies while others huddled in quiet conversation around stone tables. Everyone seemed to act with a purpose.

To Saunti's right walked Vell, who cast wary glances around the tunnels as she fiddled with her bangs, ensuring they concealed her mark—though the secret wouldn't last long.

Next to her, Yahshi's face was pale, his eyes distant. While he was younger than he thought, and the man who had raised him wasn't his actual father, at least he had grown up *with* a father! At least he hadn't burned to death in Atherus Palace with his family years ago. Yahshi had life to be grateful for—who did he think he was to look so horrified?

Rimoso and Lira led them into a chamber larger than any room Saunti had entered before. It was cylinder-shaped with two rows of torches lining the curved walls, placed only an arm's length away from each other. There must have been hundreds of them, and their flames flickered upon his entrance, as though greeting him. Saunti had always imagined Aero's world as a grim, dark place, but this chamber radiated with a golden glow akin to a beam of sunlight piercing a hole in the clouds.

It didn't take long for the hiders rushing in and out of the chamber to realize that something odd was happening. Their tasks slowed, and fingers pointed at the newcomers, whispers scattering as Rimoso and Lira led their group to the stage across the chamber, upon which stood nearly a dozen muttering individuals. *The Provisional Council.*

A crowd gathered, and it became apparent to Saunti that hiders didn't wear colors—in retrospect, Aero had always dressed in shades of brown. The more striking detail he noticed, however, was the dullness of their skin. Even those with darker complexions lacked healthy saturation. It was hard to believe they hadn't seen daylight for the past thirteen years—and the children a few years younger than Saunti had never seen daylight *ever.*

As they cut through the crowd, Saunti's eyes locked on the familiar face of Dice Bayin. Like he remembered, he still wore a bandana around his head.

Dice waved, recognizing him too, but his smile vanished when he spotted Vell in the group of newcomers. Saunti realized they had spent a month or two together as fellow Nightshades-in-training. *I wonder how well they know each other.*

Tonna leaned over Saunti's shoulder. "Look out for the Nightshade," she whispered. "I don't trust her, but if she gets hurt, the Prince won't trust us, and that'd be an even bigger problem."

Saunti stared straight ahead, pretending not to hear her.

The chamber fell silent as they joined the Provisional Council on stage. One of them, an older man with a pointy beard, pulled a rope attached to a brass bell hanging from the ceiling that Saunti hadn't noticed until now. It rang so loudly that its vibrations shook the air—and he resisted the urge to cover his ears with his palms.

The resonating bell lured additional hiders into the chamber in an endless stream. He estimated that a few thousand people lived here—and even more hiders dwelled in their sister bases farther south.

Rimoso raised his hand, and the room fell silent. He accepted a cone-shaped stone from a fellow Council member and spoke through it to amplify his voice. "We have a significant development to share," he said, his voice echoing off the chamber walls.

Chatter filled the room again as Saunti spotted Aero in the crowd. She stood among a group of teenagers around his age. Their gazes met. He smiled.

Rimoso waited until the crowd settled before raising the amplifier again. It was so quiet that Saunti could hear his own heartbeat.

The Council member took a deep breath before adding, "Prince Runix has returned."

A collective gasp rippled through the crowd. Hiders looked back and forth between Saunti and Yahshi, muttering amongst themselves.

"There are two boys."

"Which one is he?"

"And what's with the girl?"

"I thought he was returning at eighteen."

"Shouldn't he be *fifteen* right now?"

"If he's here early, that can't be good."

Yahshi shriveled under the weight of their attention, and next to him, Tonna raised her chin as though she'd been waiting for this moment forever.

Saunti thought back to the truth about his father, his fingers rolling into fists. *You died to raise a Nightshade, Father. How could you?*

Rimoso handed the amplifier to Tonna, and she continued from where he left off.

"As many of you know, we knew it'd be safest for Prince Runix to live in plain sight, without knowing his true identity, so my husband falsely converted and raised him in the Vakoi Empire. As an added safety measure, the Bayins moved nearby to keep Martu informed. They also planned to raise their son, Dice, to infiltrate the Academy.

"Unfortunately, the Force selected Prince Runix to join the Academy as well. Without knowing of his role in the Underground, he signed the contract, and my husband could do nothing to stop him. Dice tried to convince him to return home from inside the Academy, but in the process, his identity was blown. The Bayins fled to Headquarters, and the Prince ended up graduating."

Eyes drifted to Yahshi's forehead, searching for his mark.

"After a Nightshade murdered Martu, the Prince abandoned his role in the Force and survived on the run with help from our overground smuggling network. As of today, he's joining us earlier than planned with his fellow Academy graduate"—Tonna gestured to Vell—"to join the Provisional Council in preparation for his future role as Emperor Atherus."

Saunti's jaw dropped. *Emperor Atherus?*

The name, once neutral to him—nothing but a historical identity—now reeked of a bitter smell. The Prince was a Nightshade. How could the Council be willing to give up their power to a boy who once devoted his life to the enemy? Why did Tonna so easily assume that Yahshi wasn't the one to kill her husband? Did they not care that Yahshi might have murdered members of the Underground network he later sought help from? They were making reckless assumptions about his values and ability to lead.

Slowly, the room picked up with noise again. Saunti scanned the crowd, searching for a hint of shared opposition—but instead, a few people threw their fists into the air and cheered. Aero joined in, clapping with a smile, and a teenage boy next to her hollered between cupped palms. The chamber filled with laughter and chants as they welcomed Runix, the so-called *Prince* who had returned to reclaim his father's throne.

Saunti didn't applaud, and when he looked over at the Council members, he noticed that Rimoso didn't either. With a cough, Lira elbowed his side, prompting him to offer a few solid claps.

The cheering settled into a loud chattering, the crowd discussing the news together. Tonna passed the amplifier to Lira and turned to face Yahshi.

"Prince Runix," Tonna said, quietly enough for the crowd not to hear. "The Provisional Council would like to meet with you in private." Her eyes darted to Vell.

"I'm not leaving her," Yahshi said, his voice firm. "If they wanna talk to me, then—"

"We have a lot to discuss, and they won't talk with a Nightshade around."

"I was a Nightshade too," Yahshi muttered.

That we can agree on, Saunti thought to himself.

"Yahshi," Vell said, stealing his gaze. "Go with them. I'll be fine."

He stared back at her, clearly unsure of whether that would be true.

"In the meantime, Saunti can look after her," Tonna said.

Saunti scoffed, still refusing to look at her. After all of her lies, how could she ask for a favor?

"Attention!" Lira's raspy voice roared through the amplifier, cutting through the chattering. "Please exit the chamber and—" Her own cough interrupted her, and she rubbed her throat before restarting. "Please exit the chamber and resume your work. We ask that you give our newcomers space during this adjustment period."

As hiders dispersed through the various connected tunnels, Tonna locked eyes with Aero. She smiled, rushing up to the stage without further prompting.

"I'd like you to show Saunti and Vell around," Tonna said.

Typical. Not even a smile.

"Will do." Aero tucked her hands into her coat pockets, meeting eyes with Saunti. "Well, hop down."

Saunti looked over at Yahshi, who engaged in a parting, whispered conversation with Vell. He didn't bother even glancing at his mother before hopping from the stage. Vell followed, her boots meeting the stone floor with a *click* that Saunti had always linked to the Nightshades. He froze and held his breath, his heart skipping a beat.

I'm not afraid of her, he assured himself. *It's just a habit.*

"You okay, Cricket?" Aero asked.

Saunti nodded, turning to see Yahshi, Tonna, and the Provisional Council members disappear into a tunnel connected to the stage—all except Rimoso. The stocky man locked eyes with Saunti, offering a slight upward nod of his head before leaving through a different tunnel alone.

"Where is he going?" Saunti and Vell asked in unison. They frowned at each other, and Aero chuckled.

"Guild training," she said. "My father leads the Underground's military."

Saunti frowned, taking a step toward the tunnel Rimoso had entered. The man had looked him right in the eye—there was no denying it. Did he expect Saunti to follow him?

"I'm gonna watch." Saunti shot Aero a quick glance as he headed toward the tunnel. "You can handle the Nightshade."

"But Tonna said—"

"I don't care what she said!" Saunti yelled without looking back. While he had joined his mother in Headquarters, he hadn't chosen to continue playing her pawn. Plus, Vell appeared to be protective of Yahshi—at this point, he doubted she would attempt to flee.

He disappeared into the tunnel Rimoso had entered before Aero could argue, his pace slowing at the sight of an abundance of clocks. With every few steps, he encountered another pair, mirroring each other from opposite walls. Their numbers marked the time from hour zero-zero to hour twenty-four.

Are the days considered twice as long here?

A clicking noise farther down the tunnel caught his attention, and Saunti squinted, spotting an open metal door. When he reached it, he peered inside to spot Rimoso in a cramped chamber packed with swords, bows, daggers, and various other weapons. Perhaps he was gathering supplies for Guild training.

"Cricket," Rimoso said, glancing back at the doorway. "I was hoping you'd find me."

Saunti stepped into the armory, spotting a rusty dagger on a shelf, its handle beaten, its blade dull.

"These are your best weapons?" he asked.

"Is there a problem with them?" Rimoso fired back.

"They just... look weaker than what the Nightshades use."

"I *remember* what the Nightshades use." Bitterness seeped into his voice, but he attempted to cloak it with a short laugh. "We work with what we have, right?"

Saunti glued his lips together. He knew better than to antagonize members of the Council on his first day here. However, he silently hoped that the Guild's skills—or their number of fighters—could compensate for their poor weaponry.

"I saw the look on your face during the announcement earlier." Rimoso selected the crossbow he'd been studying and slung it over his shoulder, turning to face Saunti. "I can imagine it's difficult, discovering how that Nightshade boy took everything from you."

Saunti furrowed his brow, unsure of where Rimoso was going with this. It would be a lie to say he felt no resentment for Yahshi, but more than anything, it was his mother that deserved his frustration.

"My daughter told me about your little request the other day—how you wanted to play a bigger role in the Underground, and move to Headquarters against your mother's word." Rimoso stepped toward him, his lips spreading into a smile. The dim light cast shadows that made his teeth appear unnaturally sharp.

Saunti gulped, fighting the urge to step back into a shelving unit.

"You'll notice quickly that moving here isn't enough to make a splash. We have lots of different roles, some more important than others. To get involved in the real action, you need connections—that's where I come in. I happen to have a very important job that would suit you perfectly, and it'll open the door to so many future opportunities."

His expression softened. "What kind of job?"

The Council member leaned in, his eyes catching the reddish torchlight that shone in from the connected tunnel.

"I need your help," he whispered, "to kill the so-called *Prince*."

CHAPTER 8

SHARKS IN THE WATER

Day 1 Underground | Clocks Read 08:21

What Vell noticed first were the clocks. They were everywhere—in every chamber, above every entryway, and on every hider's wrist. As she followed Aero through the maze-like tunnels, no more than ten seconds would pass before she'd spot another clock between torches. The mechanical *tick, tock, tick* echoed in the air as a never-ending background song.

In a long, quiet tunnel, she slowed to a stop, falling behind Aero to observe a clock crafted out of metal scraps. Its numbers, painted with ink, ranged from zero-zero to twenty-three instead of the usual twelve. *Without sunlight,* she realized, *these clocks must be the only way to know whether it's morning or night.*

It was 08:21, over an hour since she and Yahshi had escaped her operative unit in the woods.

Tick. She thought of the moment her throwing dart redirected Pinto's arrow. She hadn't planned to injure her unit leader and join the Underground, but to protect a friend, she had done so, and now there was no turning back time.

Tock. Cal would likely die soon if she hadn't already, and Quax would blame Vell for his sister's death.

Tick. The Force would punish Keiyo for helping her escape, and to cope, he would resent her for it.

Tock. Pinto would realize she had lied to him at the beach on the night they burned the Meridian book—she *had* been keeping secrets from him.

Tick. She had lied, betrayed, and fled.

Tock. There was no pardon awaiting her in Vakoi City.

Tick—

"Are you okay?" Aero asked, coaxing Vell out of her thoughts.

Vell faced her but couldn't formulate a cohesive response. Of course she wasn't okay! She had traded *everything* for Yahshi Konya, only to discover that Yahshi Konya wasn't even his real name. How could he be Prince Runix, the boy who had died in the Atherus Palace fire? How could he be the special figure thousands had been waiting for in Headquarters? How could he be *fifteen*?

She had wished Yahshi happy birthday twice, on his sixteenth and seventeenth days. She had learned about his modest past as a baker's son in Sitra, getting to know him as a fellow trainee, graduate, and friend. She had always seen him as one of her own kind—not someone cut of the same cloth as Kodo and Kia Vakoi.

Aero tilted her head with a frown, but Vell still couldn't decide what to say. She had seen in the eyes of the handful of hiders they'd passed in the tunnels so far that no one trusted her. They viewed her as an enemy, not a welcomed figure like Yahshi. So long as they didn't trust her, she couldn't trust them either.

"Let's go somewhere quiet," Aero said, offering a smile. She continued with a spring in her step, gesturing for her to follow.

The tunnel soon merged into a chamber with seven students who looked to be about thirteen. They sat in alcoves carved deeper underground, allowing them to use the floor itself as desks. The wall ahead of them was a flat stone surface, and a middle-aged woman dragged a stick of soft limestone across it, leaving behind powdery mathematical equations.

They're a few years behind Vakoi Empire standards, Vell noted.

The students shuffled in their dug-out seats to face the newcomer. Their gazes seemed to drift right above Vell's eyes, as though searching for the mark hidden under her bangs. One of them whispered, "Nightshade."

A few students' eyes widened at the word, sparking more whispers that spread like a wave through the chamber. One boy stood from his desk, preparing to run if needed.

"Eyes on the stoneboard," their teacher snapped, tapping her limestone against the wall.

As they left the classroom, Vell caught Aero scanning her forehead too, though she had enough shame to look away when caught.

She doesn't seem afraid of me. Vell's gaze dropped, observing Aero's body language—she wasn't tense. *I wonder why.*

They continued walking in silence, and Vell's mind drifted to Yahshi again. The Council wouldn't hurt him—if they had planned to, they would have done so in the inventory room without publicly announcing his return. He was safe, but she hoped he was managing everything okay. She couldn't imagine what it felt like to learn that his father had kept the truth from him for all those years.

Her thoughts shifted to Saunti next. His mother had lied to him too. Perhaps he and Yahshi hadn't grown up too differently after all, despite being raised on opposite sides of the island. Even their names sounded similar. *Was that intentional?*

Aero shuffled to a stop, waking Vell from her daze. Ten minutes had passed since leaving the classroom—she had checked the clocks.

"Most of us sleep in bunker rooms like these." Aero grabbed the handle of a flat, circular stone and turned it, rolling the door aside. "It's not glamorous, but it does the job."

Vell's eyes widened as she entered one of the women's bunker rooms. The walls included hundreds of narrow slots, each just wide enough for one person to slide into. Ladders between columns allowed for access to the higher bunks, some of which nearly reached the ceiling.

"Dangerous," Vell said. "Someone could roll off."

Aero laughed, approaching a mound of head-sized rocks near the door. "That's what these are for. We call 'em *roll stoppers*. You just put one next to you when you sleep, and it'll keep you from falling." She selected a rock and carried it over to Vell. "Here."

Vell took the heavy rock, and for the first time since entering Headquarters, she grinned. What a ridiculous place this was.

Aero smiled too, shook the dust off her hands, and led Vell to her designated bunker. "You know," she said, drawing out her words, "you don't seem like a Nightshade."

"Why?" Vell asked, following her.

"To be fair, I don't remember seeing any Nightshades. I was just four when I moved here."

That makes her seventeen too.

"But I've always heard people describe them as buff guys in fancy clothes," Aero finished.

"There's all kinds of us," Vell said, her smile fading as the faces of everyone she'd left flashed through her mind—her fellow graduates, her unit members, her superiors...

I might not see them for a long time.

"This one's yours." Aero stopped and pointed to a bunker labeled with the number forty-three, which was thankfully in the lowest row.

Vell recalled the number on Saunti's orange jumpsuit, and a smile tugged at the corner of her lips. *What are the odds?*

"It's been vacant for a while." Aero's voice was softer now. "The poor woman died."

Vell tightened her grip on the roll stopper. "How?"

"She was caught in a cave-in. Sometimes the ground shifts, and certain walls collapse."

Swallowing hard, Vell approached the bunk and set her roll stopper on the stone bed. Tucked at the end was a pillow—a few dove feathers poking through the fabric—and a single wool blanket. She hoped they hadn't belonged to the dead woman too.

"Can I ask you a question?" Aero added.

Vell locked her eyes on the bed. "I'm not a spy."

She laughed. "I was gonna ask why you joined the Prince."

"I didn't know he was the Prince."

Aero leaned against the wall of bunkers. "Well, now I'm even more curious."

Vell looked over at her, struggling to find the right words again. What was safe to say? Which words would paint a bigger target on her back, and which wouldn't? Anyone could be an enemy here, even another seventeen-year-old girl who had been nothing but welcoming.

Without warning, Aero stepped toward her, and Vell backed away, her eyes widening.

Aero took another step. "You're afraid of me." Something had shifted about her voice. It was richer and smoother now.

Vell sharpened her gaze, fighting the urge to raise her hands in a defensive stance. Considering how Aero's father led the Underground's military, how could she trust that she hadn't brought her to this empty bunker room to kill?

"You're careful," Aero added, nodding to herself. "That's good."

Vell took another step back, and Aero halted. She looked around at the bunkers carved into the walls, as though she were saying, *A lot of people sleep here at night.*

"Why is it good?" Vell asked. *I want to hear you warn me aloud.*

Aero hesitated, her eyes drifting back to bunker forty-three. "I lied. It wasn't a cave-in."

Vell raised her brows.

"Some people go crazy, being cooped up here for too long. Maybe it's the lack of sunlight, or all the canned food—I don't know. Whatever the reason, she tried to leave. My father killed her. Can't have loose ends, he said."

She couldn't place why Aero would tell her such a thing. Was she making up this story to discourage her from leaving, or did she actually want to warn her?

"There's a lot of crime down here. Thieves, predators, murderers—I've seen 'em all, and I know what to look for. Bad things happen when supplies are low." Aero offered her hand. "I'll have your back, and you'll have mine, yeah?"

She blinked. "Why me? I'm a Nightshade."

"Exactly."

Aero didn't leverage her fear for much in return, and that had to be worth at least a pinch of trust. She took Aero's hand with a shake.

"Now come on!" Aero called out, suddenly back to her usual cheerfulness. "You've gotta see the arena! But first, I guess we should get you some normal clothes..."

As Aero turned for the door, Vell crouched and pulled two vials of belladonna serum out of her boot. She had relocated them from her overcoat earlier—while mending Yahshi's shoulder—already anticipating that he'd ask her to ditch her tools.

I'm sorry, Yahshi, but I don't trust these people yet.

She slid the vials under her pillow and followed Aero out.

According to Aero, the restrooms connected directly to Atherus City's sewer system, just as the water tanks linked to the City's supply lines. The hiders were leeches, mooching food, resources, and utilities from both allies and non-allies alike. Vell couldn't decide if she found them clever or greedy. What made these people deserving of such a safe haven? How had they ended up here in the first place? She could only guess that most were of nobility.

While Aero waited in the tunnel outside, Vell slipped into a stall—a stone cutout in the wall—and locked its wooden door. The clothes Aero had loaned were loose and practical, stitched from undyed, coarse fabric that chafed slightly against her skin. They reminded her of her clothes she had worn back home in Miranda, but despite their nostalgia, her eyes watered as she held up the perfectly tailored button-up from her guardian uniform. *Will I ever wear clothes like these again?*

She left the stall and tossed the soft fabric into a trash bin, her reflection in a cracked mirror catching her eye. For the first time since orientation at the Academy, she saw herself dressed in clothes the Force hadn't assigned her. She didn't feel lighter, like Yahshi had described. She felt *smaller*. She had earned that uniform, and now it was gone.

Vell brushed her bangs aside and stared at the four-petaled flower emblem on her forehead. It was the only proof that she had ever set foot in Vakoi City and worked as a guardian in the Force. She had literally shed blood, sweat, and tears for this mark—yet now she felt the need to hide it.

At that restaurant, when Yahshi had made her a promise to figure out the next phase of life together, she had imagined that it would take place in Vakoi City. Not a world like this. She had not found fulfillment as a guardian, but at least she had a sense of pride. At least she had a community and knew who she was, and didn't have to hide.

"I hope I don't regret this," she whispered to her reflection, the words tasting like betrayal. To regret the sacrifice she had made would be the same as wishing that Pinto had killed Yahshi instead. No, this was the only choice she could have made.

"Pair nine!"

Rimoso's booming voice echoed through the chamber as two children, both around the age of twelve, approached a raised square platform. The poles at its four corners connected ropes to form a webbed fence around what Vell assumed to be the Guild's version of a sparring range.

The children climbed over the ropes and faced each other, preparing to fight in front of about three hundred spectators. Vell and Aero had slipped into the crowd a moment ago, and only a few people seemed to recognize her now—a tremendous improvement compared to earlier in the tunnels.

The new clothes helped. She glanced at Aero, who mouthed *you're welcome* as though she could read her mind.

"Three!" Rimoso yelled, drawing their eyes back to the sparring range.

The young girl held up her hands, eyes narrowed, shoulders tense.

"Two!"

The boy made a point not to mirror her, as though to say, *I'm not afraid.*

"One!"

The arena fell silent, waiting for Rimoso's cue.

"Go!"

The spectating Guild members clapped and cheered as the pair circled each other in the sparring range.

"Hurry up, Flaire," the boy teased, hopping around as though ready to spring out of reach at any moment. His arms flopped at his sides, leaving him defenseless.

The spectators *oohed*, feeding into his prodding. Just seconds in, and Vell concluded that the Guild took training far less seriously than trainees at the Academy did.

"Mont," Rimoso warned. "Be serious."

Mont ignored him, tucking his hands into his pockets to make an even bolder statement.

Flaire shook her head, a smile meeting her lips. She stepped forward with a snapping jab to his face.

Mont leaned back, dodging her strike. He threw his leg forward as Flaire reeled her arm back, his boot meeting her stomach first. She stumbled back, nearly hitting the ropes behind her, but she regained balance just in time.

Mont laughed, and Vell's frown deepened when Flaire laughed too.

It's like it's a game to them.

Based on their ages, they had likely never seen daylight before. This underground world was all they knew, and they had no clue what they were up against.

Someone in the crowd moved toward them, and Vell looked over to see Saunti briefly catch her gaze. He stationed himself on the other side of Aero and leaned toward her.

"Aren't they too young for this?" he whispered.

"My father rarely allows kids in the Guild," Aero explained, "but he added them to the waiting list a couple years ago. He's taken a liking to those two—they dreamed about being Guildies and made sure he knew it."

Vell frowned. *Why would there be a waiting list?*

"Why would there be a waiting list?" Saunti asked. They seemed to share many questions. "Shouldn't the Guild take all the help they can get?"

A young man, likely a few years older than Vell, scoffed and looked over his shoulder at Saunti. "We're running a civilization down here. If everyone's training, who's gonna cook? Who's gonna teach? Who's gonna keep the time? And even with that aside, not everyone wants to fight."

"I certainly don't," Aero agreed, bobbing her head.

"So Rimoso can afford to be picky." His voice told Vell that he was awfully prideful of making the pick. "In fact, Rimoso *needs* to be picky. So if I were you, I wouldn't get your hopes up about joining us."

Saunti laughed as the man's eyes studied him up and down. "Nice to meet you too." He crossed his arms, grinning even wider. "I'm Tonna Suvo's son."

"As if we need another Council baby." He snorted. "Piggybacking on your parent's status will make you friends down here *real* quick. Ask Aero— she'd know."

Aero faked a smile back. "You're an ass, Varin."

Varin smirked and faced the sparring range again.

"Don't tell me that guy's your friend," Saunti muttered.

"Oh, he's all talk," Aero replied.

In the sparring range, Mont rushed after Flaire again. She ducked under his punch and popped back up, right in front of him. Her hands snaked around his neck, and she yanked his upper body into her knee.

The crowd clapped and whistled as Mont grunted, trying to land a punch to Flaire's abdomen. She dodged him, her hands falling back into their original position. Mont smirked anyway. It seemed his plan wasn't to actually strike her, but to increase their distance. Flaire had lost her lead.

They fought more seriously now, their chain of back-and-forth attacks continuing, though they still broke into a laugh every so often.

"They're good," whispered Saunti.

"They wouldn't stand a chance," muttered Vell.

A few nearby Guild members frowned in her direction, their gazes lingering as they seemed to recognize her despite the new clothes.

Varin turned around, his face reddening. He hadn't even looked at her earlier, in his discussion with Aero and Saunti, and it seemed he felt cheated to not have known that a Nightshade had been standing right behind him.

"What was that?" Varin asked, looking Vell dead in the eye.

She continued focusing on the sparring range.

"Say it again," he pried.

Vell exhaled a deep breath. Ignoring him did the opposite of diffusing the situation, so she settled on saying, "Those kids couldn't fight the Nightshades. That's all I meant."

Varin stepped toward her, but Aero caught him by the shoulder, shaking her head. "Leave her alone."

He yanked his shoulder free. "She's the one with an opinion to share, and I wanna hear it."

Doesn't seem like it, Vell thought.

Aero clenched her jaw as Varin stepped past her, forcing Vell to look at him again.

"Go on. Tell us why our Guild couldn't take on the Nightshades."

Vell remembered Aero's warning in the bunkers. The last thing she wanted to do was make an enemy out of Varin. Being a Nightshade made her enough of a target already, so she decided to share the facts behind her claims—hopefully they would help him realize that she hadn't meant to insult him.

"We have officers all over the island," she explained. "It's not just the guardians your Guild would be up against. It'd be the entire Vakoi Empire military. Plus, I assume you know about the poison on our tools. Just one cut is fatal."

"*Tools*?" Varin scoffed at her word choice. "Is that what you Nightshades call *weapons*?"

"Yes. Tools." She didn't see the problem with it.

Varin took another step toward her, and this time, she stepped back. "Just because you went to some fancy school, you think you could take on anyone in the Guild?"

"I never said that." Vell stepped back again. He closed the distance.

From across the chamber, Rimoso shouted, "A win for Mont!"

The crowd clapped as Mont helped Flaire to her feet. She winced, but the pain didn't stop her from giggling as she flicked her opponent's forehead.

"Hey, I'm talking to you," Varin said, drawing Vell's eyes back to him.

"Varin, that's enough!" Aero's yell drew attention from the crowd—

nearby Guildies stopped clapping and turned to watch as Varin closed in on Vell. Their whispers weaved through the crowd, carrying weighted words past her ears.

Nightshade. Spy. Trouble.

"You think you're *so* sly, huh?" He lurched, throwing his hands forward to shove her back.

Vell stepped aside just in time—his palms met nothing but air.

Varin threw a punch next, and Vell dodged it too. "You spend five minutes in the arena and think you can predict the outcome of a war?"

His moves were sloppy and predictable, corrupted by rage. He fought even worse than the giggling children in the sparring range, as though he were a trainee on his first day in the program, trying to prove himself through aggression because he knew no other way to appear strong.

"How much do you enjoy doing Vakoi's dirty work?" Varin failed to land another strike. "*Killing* people like us?"

He circled her, forcing Vell to spin to keep her eye on him. He was the shark; she was the fish.

"If it weren't for Nightshades like you, my—" His voice clotted in his throat.

Vell's eyes widened as she dodged his next attack.

"My brother—"

"Varin!" Rimoso yelled, his voice striking from across the chamber.

In an instant, Varin dropped his guard, backing from Vell like a fearful dog that had done wrong and knew it.

"What do you aim to accomplish by harassing our newcomer?" Rimoso spoke to Varin, but his eyes were on Vell. She studied him back, questions itching to leave her mouth. *Why are you the only Council member who isn't at the meeting with Yahshi? Why didn't you clap during the announcement earlier? Did you really murder that woman for trying to leave, and if so, how?*

Varin lowered his head, refusing to respond, and all eyes turned to Vell. The chamber fell silent, as though they expected her to speak, but she would rather not make any more enemies. She turned and marched toward the nearest exit.

I don't care if I get lost. Vell quickened her pace down the tunnel. *I need to find a place to think.*

When a set of footsteps trailed after her, Vell's heart rate picked up. She peered over her shoulder, expecting Varin, but it was Saunti.

"You don't have to follow me." Vell stared directly ahead. "I'm not planning my escape."

"Wait, Vell!" Saunti jogged to catch up to her, and she sped up even more. "Wait. I-I just... please..." He grabbed her arm, urging her to stop.

With a sharp exhale, Vell halted, but she didn't look at him.

Saunti stepped back and peered down both ends of the tunnel, ensuring they were alone. "The way you just—Varin was coming after you so fast, but you—I mean, it was like..." He trailed off with a sigh, and it took him a second to gather his thoughts. "I've just... never seen anything like it."

She finally met his gaze. "Are you complimenting me?"

For the first time, it seemed he looked at her with something akin to trust. "I'm trying to ask you something." He peered down the tunnel ends again before leaning toward her. "Are they all as skilled as you? The Nightshades?"

"You've never seen one fight?"

"I hide from the Nightshades. I've only ever *heard* of their fights." He shook his head, a flicker of disgust crossing his face. "Just answer the question."

"Most guardians are better than me," Vell said. "The training's intense. The standards—"

"Oh, wonderful!" Saunti paced between the tunnel walls, rubbing his temple.

"What's wrong?"

He paused to make eye contact, shaking his head in disbelief. "My mother's been talking about Headquarters like it's this powerful place, but in reality, it's an actual death hole." He continued pacing. "If the Guild can't beat the Nightshades, we're *dead*. Everyone here, including their *beloved Prince*—"

"Stop." Vell didn't like how angry he sounded when he talked about Yahshi. "We don't know everything about this place yet."

"At least we don't have to worry about digging our own graves." Saunti ran his hands down his face. "We're already living in them!"

A faint shuffle echoed down the tunnel.

What was that?

Vell stood straighter, peering past Saunti.

In the distance, someone peeked at them from around a corner, but as soon as Vell squinted, the figure ran off.

CHAPTER 9

GREEN BLOOD

Day 1 Underground | Clocks Read 11:04

♫ FLICKERS IN THE FLAMES - DAVE THOMAS JUNIOR ♫

"Why this room?" Saunti asked, following Vell into the stuffy chamber she had insisted on. Inside were nothing but three clocks and a massive, imposing metal water tank in the corner.

When a droplet struck the top of his head, he stopped and looked up. A blanket of pipes crisscrossed the ceiling, creaking and trembling as water coursed through them. Drops fell from leaks he couldn't pinpoint, forming puddles on the floor—Vell's boots splashed in one as she sat at the base of the water tank.

"Why are we here?" Saunti asked again, keeping his distance. Earlier, he had convinced himself that Vell couldn't be a spy because she cared too much for Yahshi—but after his encounter with Rimoso, he couldn't be sure anymore. If a Council member wanted Yahshi dead, how could he predict the intentions of *anyone* in Headquarters, especially a Nightshade like Vell?

She leaned back against the tank and closed her eyes, exhaling a steady breath. "No one can eavesdrop," she finally answered. "The water's too loud."

Her paranoia about being spied on proved that the untrusting stares and her clash with Varin had shaken her more than she let on—and realizing that she wasn't fearless eased Saunti's nerves. He approached the tank and rounded the curve to sit on the opposite side, close enough to see Vell around the bend but far enough to give himself a running start if threatened.

"They're a bit off," she said, her voice softer now.

"What?"

"The clocks." Vell pointed. Their second hands were a few *ticks* out of sync.

They watched time pass together, until Saunti said, "Why don't we start with why you're here?"

"I care about Yahshi." Her reply was instantaneous. He wondered if she had rehearsed it.

"Am I really supposed to believe you betrayed the Nightshades *just* for him? That you committed *treason* for him, with no other motive?"

"Believe what you want."

"So you're on our side now?" Saunti asked.

"I'm on Yahshi's side. And he's with the Underground."

"It's not that simple."

"It's not simple for you either. You may be on the Underground's side, but you're not on Yahshi's. Clearly, you think he has no right to be here."

Even in the chamber's chilly, damp air, Saunti couldn't stop his face from steaming. Why were both Rimoso and Vell so quick to assume that he would draw Yahshi's blood to spite his history? Yes, Yahshi had broken up his family, and it had upset him in the inventory room, but he knew, deep down, that it wasn't *actually* Yahshi's fault. Just because he didn't believe that he deserved special treatment for being royalty didn't mean that he wanted to kill him!

"Can I trust you with him?" she asked.

His scowl deepened with a scoff. "I may be angry, Vell, but I'm not vengeful."

"Anger can do nasty things to a person." Even such a bold sentence left her mouth calmly. "But I'm not saying it's wrong to be angry. You have every reason to be."

"I'm angry at my *mother*," he clarified. "You would think that if someone loves you, they'd tell you the truth."

"Sometimes you lie *because* you love them."

"No." He shook his head. "Trust and love go hand in hand."

A chuckle escaped her.

"What?" he asked.

"You're an idealist."

"And that's funny?"

"Yahshi's an idealist too," she said.

Saunti cracked a grin. Perhaps she had a point. He wanted to believe he could forgive his mother, keep Yahshi alive without pissing off Rimoso, and also help strengthen the Guild—but clearly, this would not be an easy mess of problems to fix. He would have to address them according to urgency, and it all started with Rimoso.

How could he request such a cold task so casually? And if I refuse, then what?

Vell adjusted her position beside him, and it caught Saunti by surprise when he didn't flinch. Never in his life would he have thought that one day, he would sit by a Nightshade and feel *less* alert.

"Why didn't you report me?" he blurted out, remembering the cold eyes that darted to the number on his jumpsuit. He'd been so anxious in the days after Vell had caught him with the Meridian book, certain she'd come after him.

"I'd be a hypocrite to report you, Forty-three."

"Why's that?"

"I kept the book because I wanted to read it."

He pushed himself to his feet and curved around the water tank, heading in Vell's direction.

She looked up at him as he sat beside her and gestured. "Go on..."

With a light nod, Vell broke eye contact. "I was curious about the Meridian book because the author's nephew helped me in the past." She told him about how she'd worked with belladonna illegally for her ill mother, and how a Nightshade who she called *Doctor Blimmery* could have reported her for doing so but selected her for the program instead. "...He knew my mother needed the family pension for her medicine. If it weren't for him, she likely would have died."

Saunti had assumed that Nightshades were Nightshades because they wanted to be. He had never known about the family pensions, the infrastructure bonuses, and the societal pressures to accept one's selection. He had never thought there were Nightshades like Vell and Blimmery—ones who didn't always follow the codes expected of them.

"So did you end up reading it?" he asked.

"I burned it. A friend convinced me to."

"Another Nightshade?"

She nodded, and while he might have been imagining it, he sensed regret. Her interest in a treasonous book and her choice not to report him suggested that she wasn't entirely aligned with the Nightshades' rules. Maybe she had the potential to not only be on Yahshi's side but also the Underground's. With her knowledge, she could be valuable. Perhaps confiding in her, and pitching in a little trust, would help her trust him in return.

"Vell," Saunti said. "Earlier, I—"

The words caught in his throat as a figure appeared in the entryway.

Vell stood to her feet swiftly; Saunti stumbled to follow suit.

"Get away from him." Dice narrowed his eyes on Vell as he whipped two vials of red fluid out of his coat pocket.

She rolled her eyes, her jaw tight.

"Yeah, that's right. I found them under the pillow of your assigned bunker." He took a step forward, his boot splashing in a puddle. "What were you planning to do with them?"

Vell faced Saunti as though she wanted to assure *him* of her intentions, not Dice. "I didn't want a reason to use them."

He stared back, unsure of how to read her. On one hand, he understood Dice's frustration with the contents under her pillow—but on the other, with the reputation of Nightshades among members of the Underground, could he really blame her?

Then again, what if her story was a lie? What if she never cared about the Meridian book at all? How could he be certain he could trust her?

He *couldn't* be certain—that was the blunt truth.

Dice huffed, shoving the vials back into his pocket. "Saunti, I want to show you something." He made eye contact before leaving the chamber, and the water noises drowned out his footsteps. It was like he'd vanished into thin air.

Vell caught Saunti's gaze, her eyes lingering with a silent question.

Will you stay?

He sensed her subtle fear of being left alone in this maze, but he followed Dice anyway.

From Saunti's observation, most entryways in Headquarters didn't have doors. Only important ones did—like the inventory room, Rimoso's armory, and the one Dice had just unlocked, which supposedly led to his private lab.

"These are bioluminescent fungi." He swung the door open, leading Saunti into a chamber bathed in green light. Inside, thousands of glowing mushrooms grew from tall plant beds along the walls, jagged mirrors behind them directing their glow to shorter beds in the middle of the room.

"I get them from the Waterway," Dice added, locking the door behind them.

Saunti's eyes widened. "What *is* the Waterway?"

"So essentially, the mushrooms turn dead plants, animals, and waste into energy, and create light from it." He hurried past Saunti to a plant bed containing flowers. Their outstretching white petals boasted light pink and purple dots. "These are toad lilies—also from the Waterway. They don't have much of a purpose, but they're the only flowers that grow here naturally."

"Again, the Waterway is..."

Dice pulled out one of Vell's vials and waved it in front of Saunti's face. "And *this* is belladonna, also known as nightshade. Slick. Red. Lethal. One cut from a belladonna-laced weapon"—Dice popped the cork stopper off, making Saunti flinch—"and you're dead."

He turned and tilted the vial over a toad lily. One drop landed on a petal, but nothing happened.

"What are you—"

"Shh!" Dice pointed at the flower. "Watch."

With a sigh, Saunti squinted at the toad lily. The ticking of clocks filled the chamber as the flower stood unaffected. Dice tapped his boot against the floor, growing impatient—but soon after, the petals shriveled, their pink and purple dots fading to brown.

"Look," Dice ordered.

"What do you think I'm doing?" Saunti muttered.

Within seconds, the stem curled over until the petals—now brown—collided with the dirt. Dice's second drop of poison drained its last bits of life, turning even the stems and leaves brown. The flower coiled into itself as though it were in pain, then stopped moving, resting as a crumbly dead mess.

Dice pushed the cork stopper back into the vial and faced Saunti, his eyes darkening. "Imagine if Vell had emptied this poison into our water tanks."

Saunti gulped. *One drop killed a flower. What could it do to a person?*

Dice headed for another entryway across the room, and Saunti followed him into a smaller connected chamber lined with more mirrors and mushrooms. One wall included a carved-in bookshelf and a desk covered in papers from the production point Noris worked at. *I guess the hiders have a use for his paper after all.*

"Not many people know this, but Nightshades build immunity to belladonna during training—that way they won't die if they're cut by their own weapons." Dice approached a single plant bed in the middle of the chamber and gestured to its three bushes. "Calabar, the Nightshades' antidote. It's used for emergencies while they're building a tolerance to their poison. If the belladonna in their system surpasses their immunity level, they can use calabar to reverse the effects."

"So?"

Dice let out a sharp sigh. "What I'm saying is that calabar is just as poisonous to them as belladonna is to us. I went to the Academy for key intel that would level out the playing field, and this is it." He gestured to the bushes again. "*This* is why Rimoso trusted me with a lab and the freedom to work alone. I'm cultivating concentrated calabar serum for the Guild."

Saunti paused, thrown out of the science lesson. "*Rimoso* gave you this lab? Does he have access to it?"

"Of course he has access to it. He leads the Guild, and teaches them how to lace weapons now and then."

"So the Guild plans to fight poison with poison?" Saunti asked, knowing better than to ask too many questions about Rimoso in a row.

"Exactly." Dice pulled out a ring of keys, used one to open a lockbox on his desk, and stored the vials of belladonna inside. "And just so you know, I don't show many people my lab. I only brought you here to prove that Vell's a shark. She's had Prince Runix wrapped around her finger since day one, and just because *he* trusts her doesn't mean *we* should. For all we know, the Nightshades planned her betrayal so she could infiltrate Headquarters."

"Maybe," Saunti said. *But that's not my biggest concern right now.*

Rimoso had access to this lab, which gave him a direct supply of calabar. He likely had an easy assassination plan in mind for Yahshi—something involving Dice's poison. *I imagine it wouldn't be difficult to add a drop to a bowl of food or a glass of water.*

A quarter-day bell shook the air, washing out the *tick, tock, tick* of the Underground clocks. Saunti followed Dice through the tunnels toward the canteen, where the cooks served meals.

"Here, this way." Dice made another sharp turn. "Shortcut."

"What's the hurry?"

"Prince Runix could be back from the meeting by now!"

Saunti frowned as he raced after him, catching up to his side and matching his pace. While he didn't care to *kill* Yahshi, he understood Rimoso's motive. How could hiders like Dice so naively welcome a boy to power who had murdered their own?

"Watch it!" Dice shoved his arm against Saunti's abdomen. "Ventilation."

The sharp blow momentarily took his breath away, and peering down didn't help him catch it. Through a hole in the floor that he'd nearly stepped into, he spotted a level below with another hole in the same spot—and a third below that. Falling would have sent him splatting to his death on the Underground's literal rock-bottom.

"Why aren't they staggered?" Saunti focused on steadying his breaths as he crept around the ventilation shaft. "There are children down here. It's dangerous."

Dice hopped over the shaft. "Unlike you, most kids are smart enough to avoid them. Now hurry up."

Wait a minute. Saunti shuffled to a stop and peered back at the hole he'd nearly fallen through, tracing his eyes up to the ceiling to find another hole right above it. His brows drew closer as he caught up to Dice again. "Do those go to the surface?"

He nodded. "They're mostly connected to out-of-service wells and hidden air ducts in town markets."

"You're kidding. What if someone discovers one?"

"They fall and die."

"*Or* they climb down with a rope and peg, discover Headquarters, and go back up to report us to the Vakoi boys."

"It's a risk we need to take to... you know... *breathe.*"

That same pit in his stomach from earlier—when he had watched Vell evade Varin's attacks—returned once more. Where was everyone's sense of urgency? Every day they wasted in preparation was another day they risked the Force discovering and slaughtering them. Rimoso wanted to assassinate Yahshi as though there was even a throne to be taken. It was all theory, all delusion. *If we don't act soon, the Nightshades could find us before we take them on.*

Dice turned down another tunnel, and soon enough, Saunti heard voices emanating from the canteen's entryway. They followed the noise into a vast room nearly as massive as the one the Council had announced Yahshi's return in. Like some rooms Saunti had glimpsed earlier, everyone sat in alcoves, allowing them to use the floor itself as tables.

"Behold—the canteen!" Dice said, gesturing to the room.

There must have been hundreds of people in the chamber, but Saunti didn't spot any Council members. *No Mother. No Rimoso. No Lira.*

"How often is food served?" Saunti asked.

"Every quarter-day bell, give or take half an hour. The cooks aren't timekeepers, after all."

"Timekeepers?"

"This way," Dice said, leading him across the canteen to a hole in the wall—it seemed to be connected to a kitchen on the other side. "Two please."

The server lowered her head and smiled up at them through the hole—Saunti recognized her as Flaire, one of the youngest Guild members.

"Hi there," Flaire chirped.

She disappeared from view, and soon after, slid her arms through the hole, holding two chipped bowls. Lunch consisted of rice porridge stuffed with tuna, carrots, corn, and peas—the most common canned fish and vegetables that Saunti had delivered to Aero as a courier over the past four years. A few fruit flies also swirled in the mix, but his stomach still grumbled—he hadn't eaten since breakfast yesterday.

"Thanks." Saunti cringed as he took his bowl.

"I know. It's gross," Dice said, noticing his expression as he led him to a table. "You should've seen the meals at the Academy. They were over-the-top fancy."

"Sounds nice."

"Yeah, but that was about the only nice part." Dice crouched with his bowl, taking a floor seat at a table with Aero and Varin.

"Hey, Cricket," Aero said as Saunti sat beside her.

He set his bowl on the table. "Why are so many chairs carved into the ground like this?"

"Low wood supply," Aero explained. "Our carventers make use of the environment."

"Carpenters?"

"*Carventers.* They work with stone."

"That's cool." Saunti chuckled. "I've never cared much for wood."

Aero blinked a few times, frowned, and looked around. "I thought Vell was with you."

"Yeah, the two of you ran out of the arena earlier." Varin narrowed his eyes at Saunti, his tone accusatory. "Don't tell me you left the Nightshade alone."

"It's fine, Varin." Dice reached up, tightening his bandana. "She hid two vials of poison in her bunker, but I already confiscated them. Plus, everyone has their eyes on her, and the access point is being guarded. There's nothing she can get away with."

Aero frowned. "You can't just go into the women's bunkers."

"*Poison*, Aero," Dice repeated. "*Poison*."

"*Great.* More creepy stuff for your creepy mushroom lair." She took a few hasty bites, then shoved her hands against the table to push herself up. "Now, if you'll excuse me..."

"Where are you going?" Saunti asked.

She grinned as she backed away from the table, holding her hands out. "To find that girl you boys are *so* obsessed with." With a turn, she left for the closest exit, waving at friends at distant tables.

Varin chuckled to himself. "Aero's a chore."

Saunti glared at him and took his first bite. The porridge was a nasty, pasty thing, and he smacked his lips together a few times, hoping to rid his tongue of its lingering taste. Varin asked something about Vell, but he tuned him out.

"Hello?" Varin asked, waving his hand. "Did you hear me?"

"I zone out when people babble," Saunti mumbled.

Dice stifled a chuckle, and Varin scoffed.

As a wave of hiders swept into the chamber, the canteen grew louder, and the supply of empty tables ran low. Curious bystanders stood along the perimeter of the room, eyeing the many entryways in anticipation of which one Runix Atherus would enter through—assuming he'd even show. Judging by the lack of bowls in their hands, they weren't even hungry. Being Emperor Atherus's secretly surviving son was enough to win over most people's hearts, despite his past as a Nightshade.

While Saunti didn't understand their unconditional love for Yahshi, killing him would devastate the hiders. They didn't *need* Underground royalty, but the vast majority *wanted* it.

He braced himself for another bite, the room falling silent. Flaire peeked through the serving slot from the kitchen, and some people stood from their tables to get a better view, forcing those behind them to do the same. It looked as though half the canteen was preparing for a standing ovation.

From one of the canteen entryways, Yahshi forced a smile, eyeing the many silent faces staring back at him. The noisy room that had awaited his presence didn't seem to know how to act upon his arrival—especially with Vell at his side. They both wore new clothes that matched the baggy, undyed style of Headquarters, perhaps to blend in. *At least the Council didn't dress him like royalty.*

However, the four-petaled flower marks peeking out between gaps in their striking black hair kept them from blending in completely. Even with the outfit change, hiders of all ages recognized Yahshi and Vell, offering their tables as the pair stepped deeper into the canteen. Yahshi peered past them, waving his hand to signal that he didn't need their tables. He seemed more interested in finding *someone* than finding a place to sit.

Saunti froze when Yahshi halted and locked eyes with him, raising his hand in a wave. Thousands of eyes turned to him next, expecting him to reciprocate the gesture.

Before he could, Yahshi broke eye contact, his smile fading.

Well, it's too late now. Saunti took a bite as the storm of curious eyes turned to glares.

Yahshi and Vell sat at a nearby table, which a group had fled from just a moment ago. He expected hiders to flock to them like hungry birds, but it seemed the Prince attracted people just as much as his fellow graduate repulsed them, balancing the energy.

Soon enough, a soft chatter filled the room again, and most non-hungry bystanders walked out with lowered heads, as though Yahshi's entrance had disappointed them.

Saunti chuckled to himself. *Were they expecting him to dance and sing?*

"Hey," Dice snapped, catching his gaze. "Why did you ignore him?"

He shrugged. "I hardly know him."

"But he's practically your brother."

"Not at all, actually."

"Well, at the very least, he's the Prince."

As if that should dictate how nice I act.

Saunti tilted his head, and through the corner of his eye, he saw Yahshi hunch over, shriveling in the aftermath of attention like the poisoned toad lily in Dice's lab. With his spoon, he poked at his porridge, fished out the chunks of tuna, and added them to Vell's bowl.

Is that supposed to be some kind of gesture?

"I heard rumors from couriers at our sister bases," Dice said, his eyes on the pair too. "During Prince Runix's time on the run, a couple of collectors he stayed with—the ones who recognized him, at least—claimed that he refused to eat meat."

"He can hardly stomach death," Varin concluded, watching Yahshi pick out another chunk of tuna from his bowl. "Now he chooses not to."

"Very poetic," Saunti muttered, resisting the urge to highlight that Yahshi was a Nightshade just like Vell, the girl he had attempted to pick a fight with in the arena. How could Varin admire one Nightshade and hate the other?

Dice pointed to Saunti's porridge, his own already eaten. "Are you gonna finish that?"

He slid his bowl in front of Dice. "All yours."

"Well, if you're done here, you might as well head to the kitchen," Varin added. "Rimoso wants you on dish duty. Told me to pass the word."

Saunti scoffed. *I abandoned my life to join Headquarters,* he wanted to say, *and he expects me to do dishes?*

But he *didn't* say it, because he knew it was exactly the response Rimoso hoped to elicit. This was part of his bait, a way to say, *Do my bidding, and I'll give you a tolerable job instead.*

"Yeah, sure." Saunti wouldn't fall for Rimoso's trap. He stood from the table and looked around. "Where do I go?"

Saunti lugged the porcelain bowl out of the sink and scrubbed his sponge against it in rhythm with the ticking of the kitchen's clocks. He had discovered that if he focused hard enough, and pretended he was wearing his orange jumpsuit, he could think more clearly—and there was a lot to think about.

Rimoso. Yahshi. Vell. The Guild versus the Nightshades. Ventilation shafts.

Bubbles climbed up his arms, tickling his elbows as he scoured his sponge against a stubborn bowl. A spatula helped him scrape the hardest bits off before he scrub-attacked with the sponge again and hit the bowl with a spray of water. It took several rounds before he felt a sense of progress.

Scrape. He needed to keep Yahshi alive.

Scrub. But if he didn't kill Yahshi, Rimoso might find another way to get the job done.

Spray. He needed to uncover Rimoso's full intentions—that was the missing piece.

Saunti scraped the spatula against the next bowl until the porcelain squealed.

From across the kitchen, Flaire yelped, nearly dropping the next round of dirty dishes she'd brought back from the now-vacant canteen.

"You scared me!" she exclaimed.

"Good!"

They'd been working for the past hour, tasked with cleaning as many dishes as possible before the next pair of dishwashers would arrive. Saunti figured that post-meal clean-ups would be much more efficient if they had over two sinks in the kitchen, but unfortunately, they did not.

Flaire rushed to set the dirty dishes by Saunti's sink. "You really don't have to be frustrated. I know it's not a fun job, but I'm sure Rimoso will let you join his Guild eventually."

Saunti concealed a grin. Flaire had no comprehension of the actual source of his frustration, and she didn't seem to realize how embarrassing it felt to be consoled by one of the youngest Guild members. He pulled his hand out of the sink and flicked a lump of bubbles at her face.

"Hey!"

He laughed as she wiped her face down with a wet rag, revealing her wide grin.

The door creaked open, and they turned to see Tonna enter the kitchen. Saunti dropped his smile.

"Sweetie, could you give us a minute?" Tonna asked, smiling at Flaire.

With a giggle, Flaire tossed her wet rag at Saunti's face and bolted for the door. Tonna stepped aside just in time for her energized exit.

Saunti stopped the sink's running water and wiped his hands off with the rag Flaire had thrown. It was just him and his mother now, alone in the kitchen, surrounded by dirty bowls and the scent of soap, canned vegetables, and tuna—a nauseating combination.

"I'm sorry you couldn't be at the meeting," Tonna said. "The Council has strict policies."

Typical. Saunti looked away. *It's the rules. You just have to trust me. Blah, blah, blah...*

"I know this kind of role isn't what you expected either." His mother's eyes drifted to the many piles of clean bowls stacked to Saunti's left. "So I talked to Rimoso, and he agreed to let you join Aero on her next trip down the Waterway."

"Speaking of which, what—"

"She usually travels with Varin, but he's been extra busy with the Guild lately, so they're seeking a replacement with boating experience. I said you'd be the perfect fit."

"When?" Saunti asked. *How does this play into Rimoso's plan?*

"About a week from now," Tonna said. "He asked me to bring you to his chamber to go over the details in advance."

Saunti met his mother's gaze again, his eyes widening. Rimoso was pressuring him into helping before having the proper time to think everything through.

"I'll show you there," Tonna said, gesturing for him to follow her out.

Saunti took a deep breath and tossed the rag aside, torn between telling his mother the truth or staying silent. While he liked the idea of passing the information about Rimoso's plan to the Council, would they believe his word over Rimoso's? Given his mother's track record of struggling to trust him, she couldn't be sure if she would take him seriously.

He caught up to her in the connected tunnel, and as she led him toward the Provisional Council's quarters, Saunti pried for a sign as to whose side she would take.

"It's nice of Rimoso to consider bringing me on board for the trip," he said, forcing a cheerful tone. "I'm sure he has a lot on his plate already. It seems like he runs *everything* down here." This wasn't an exaggerated observation—Varin and Flaire's assumption that Saunti wanted to join the Guild without him saying so confirmed that impressing Rimoso was key to perceived success in the Underground.

"Oh, you can't even imagine, Saunti," Tonna said, making yet another turn. "He holds this place together. He always has."

She admires him.

"You know, Rimoso and your father were good friends. They both worked at Atherus Palace together."

She shares an emotional connection with him.

"If Rimoso weren't with us, I'm not sure we'd even have a military."

She trusts him.

Those three facts were more than he could claim about Tonna's view of himself. He knew then that he couldn't take the risk of hoping that she would trust him. No, she would most likely take Rimoso's side, and there would be no predicting his retaliation.

I need to fix this alone.

"He's down there. You'll see his name on the door." Tonna halted and pointed down the tunnel labeled with a sign that read, *PROVISIONAL COUNCIL MEMBERS*. "I need to get back to the Prince now, okay? We have so much work to do to bring him up to speed."

Saunti nodded, and his mother vanished the same way she'd come.

As he entered the tunnel, he scanned the metal doors to his left and right, each containing the engraving of a Council member's first name. The door labeled *RUNIX* made him chuckle. *Of course he doesn't need to sleep in a cramped bunker like the one Rimoso assigned me to!*

He stopped at Rimoso's door and raised his hand to knock, but a muffled voice through the metal made him pause.

"I'll kill you," Rimoso said, hardly loud enough for Saunti to hear.

He pressed his ear to the door and listened closely.

"You slimy bastard," Rimoso continued. "I'll crush that nasty head of yours and split you open 'til your guts spill out."

Saunti flinched at the sound of a blunt force—a *clang* like metal against stone. His eyes widened when Rimoso grunted, followed by a second clash. He took a few steps back and looked around, trying to decide what to do, but he must have been too loud, because footsteps headed toward the door next.

He knows I'm here. Saunti straightened his back, wiped the shocked look off his face, and approached the door, raising his fist as though he were just approaching now.

Rimoso opened the door before he could knock, his face lighting up. He held a rusty hammer, and thankfully, there was no blood on its head.

"Finally." He stepped aside, gesturing for Saunti to enter. "Hurry in!"

As soon as Saunti entered, Rimoso slammed the door shut and gripped the handle of his hammer tighter. He scanned his chamber with sporadic jolts of his head and lowered his body, creeping like a predator stalking an invisible prey.

Rimoso's tense posture deterred Saunti from asking questions, so he watched silently as the man surveyed every nook and cranny from the floor to the ceiling.

"We're having the *Prince* propose his new war strategy in about a week." Rimoso ducked under his wooden desk, surveying the floor beneath it. "He doesn't seem to like the one we've been developing for *thirteen years*. Too much violence, he says. The Council's still eating out of his hand, but all the better. The night after his proposal will be the perfect time to strike, right when they wake up and see him for what he is—just a scared little pacifist."

Rimoso reemerged from under his desk with a disappointed huff. "You'll get in, get out, and immediately leave down the Waterway with my daughter to pick up supplies from our sister bases. No one will suspect your involvement, and once you're back, you'll have a spot in my Guild waiting for you."

Saunti's jaw tightened. *As if that would motivate me to kill!*

Rimoso dropped to his knees and peered under his bed in one swift motion, but nothing was there. He stood with a growl and made his way to his dresser.

"Actually," Saunti said, choosing his next words carefully, "I was wondering if you could explain your reasoning behind this. I mean, it's kind of... a big decision. Killing someone."

"Oh, it's simple, really. He's a freeloading distraction." Rimoso opened each drawer of clothes to ransack, one at a time. "He thinks he can crawl into my space unannounced, and I'll let him stay? I built this home of mine, and somehow, he's entitled to it?"

Rimoso tossed a pile of shirts onto his bed and sifted through them. "He doesn't understand our system, our culture, our plans for the future. He's a vermin, is what he is."

A smile spread across Rimoso's face as he froze, his eyes locking on his target. Saunti followed the man's gaze to a bright green gecko that had crawled out from under his laundry basket.

The gecko lay still as Rimoso edged toward it, raising his hammer.

"The thought of him keeps me up at night," he whispered. "Exhausts me. Infuriates me."

He leaped forward and swung the hammer down. The metal struck the stone floor, but the gecko escaped unscathed, scurrying across the room and halfway up the dresser.

"Can't we just open the door and scare him out?" Saunti offered. "He probably doesn't even realize that he's intruded. We just need to make that clear to him."

Rimoso laughed. "And let him remember me as weak? No, that's just treating the symptom. If we scare him out, he'll come back, maybe even better prepared."

It was only then when Saunti understood why Rimoso had ushered him inside and shut the door so quickly. He wanted to contain the gecko because it had already wronged him. It presented itself as a problem that needed a permanent fix.

Saunti's pulse quickened as the man and the gecko ran in mismatching circles around the chamber. *Rimoso won't stop until Yahshi is dead.*

He recalled how Yahshi had picked the tuna out of his porridge, his own way of rejecting the bloody life he'd led. Perhaps it was time for Saunti to stop judging the Nightshades so harshly. Everyone had a reason to kill. Even himself.

His entire family had sacrificed for the Underground. His father had left to raise Yahshi. His mother had dedicated herself to being Atherus City's courier. Now it was his turn. He had been searching for a more valuable role to play in the Underground, and this was it.

It wasn't flashy. It wouldn't gain the Council's respect. But it would change everything.

A squishing noise brought Saunti's eyes to the corner of the room, where Rimoso's hammer pierced through the gecko's body. Its lime-green blood oozed out, forming a sticky pool.

"Disgusting," Rimoso murmured, dropping his hammer to the floor. He snatched a shirt from his bed and tossed it over the gecko, cloaking the mess with a sigh.

"So," he said, peering back at Saunti, "have you decided?"

Saunti glared at the green blood soaking through the shirt on the floor. "Yeah, sure." He nodded. "I'll help you."

CHAPTER 10

BAD ONE

Prepare for flood season at your local Saver Store.
Sandbags are fifty percent off!

♫ FOOL OF ME · SAY LOU LOU, CHET FAKER ♫

Evaris Starfall once thought he was a good one. There was a gentle boldness to Yahshi that she'd trusted since meeting him on his first shadow assignment nearly a year ago, when she was still nineteen. His eyes held an irresistible promise to help shoulder the weight of any secret, and he had a talent for asking questions in a way that made even the most guarded people *want* to open up. *I even told him the truth about my friendship with Cal.*

But in the end, Yahshi had let her down. He was a bad one, and the look on Pinto's face proved it. After everything the poor professor had done to grant his best friend a pardon, Yahshi had denied it—and in doing so, denied their friendship.

Evaris's mind wandered back to her early days at the Academy. The boys in the program mocked her privileged Vakoi City roots, but she quickly gained their respect by denouncing the Starfalls and stressing how hard she'd worked to leave her family of fashion designers behind. Her roommate, Cal, didn't have such an easy time forming alliances—the boys kept their distance from the quiet, odd trainee who had murdered Chima Fernis.

As the only two girls, Evaris figured they should stick together, so she had taken it upon herself to befriend Cal and help her fit in. Thanks to her efforts, the boys eventually warmed up to her too.

It was only during Cal's promotion, over a year ago, when it finally clicked to Evaris that their friendship had never been real. Cal had only kept her around because calling her a friend made life easier—it cheated people into liking her by piggybacking off of Evaris's social standing. Any kindness Cal had shown was solely to keep her around, like throwing bones to a hungry dog.

"Of course you're joining my unit," Cal had said during her promotion ceremony.

"Because you can't get enough of me?" Evaris teased. She figured Cal had requested her as a unit member to keep a close friend around.

"Because I get the job done faster, silly."

The words had cut through Evaris like a dagger, and she figured Yahshi's rejection of the pardon had cut Pinto even deeper.

As Evaris ran her fingers down her horse's mane, she studied Pinto's tense expression. He stood several paces away, his eye locked on the gentle creek their horses drank from.

"It's not fun to realize that you've never really known someone. That they've played you for a fool," Evaris said, finally breaking the silence regarding the tragedy of their special operation. They had been traveling for nearly six hours, only exchanging brief words about their route home.

Pinto gripped his horse's lead rope tighter, and his lack of a verbal response made Evaris think of the dagger in her overcoat. She had danced with him once at his graduation and had spoken with him a handful of other times during active service, but she didn't really *know* him. If he had attacked Cal, there was no knowing whether he'd attack her too.

Calm down, Evaris told herself, resisting the urge to reach for her dagger. Famir had already confiscated Pinto's tools. If he had planned to fight without them, he would have done so hours ago.

You have him under control.

They waited a few more minutes for their horses to finish drinking, then began the last hour of their trip back to Vakoi City. Pinto lagged slightly behind, perhaps to deter further conversation, but Evaris ignored the message and slowed down, their horses falling in sync again.

"Why did you shoot her?"

"I *didn't*," Pinto snapped.

"You were the only one there with a bow," Evaris countered, recalling the moment her operative unit had intercepted his. Famir, Galler, and she had reached the outskirts of Grimward to find Keiyo checking Cal's vitals while Pinto dodged Quax's swinging swords. It didn't take a genius to put the pieces together—Yahshi had denied the pardon, Vell had turned sides, and Pinto had shot Cal to allow the pair to get away.

"Don't let him out of your sight until I'm back," Famir had whispered to Evaris. He cut two horses free from the vault and sent her to escort Pinto home.

"Yes, it was *my* arrow"—he faced Evaris with a whip of his head—"but it wasn't my fault."

"Quax seemed to think it was your fault," Evaris said, fishing for the full story.

"He just needed someone to blame. It was Vell who..." Pinto stopped himself and swallowed hard. "I was trying to find a way out of killing Yahshi when her throwing star hit my arrow. It threw my aim off-target, and..."

He trailed off again, and a tightness pulled at Evaris's chest. It sounded like Vell only had the opportunity to intervene because Pinto had hesitated to follow Cal's order. The accounts of Quax and Keiyo would likely back up that assumption. *His plan to blame Vell won't save him, but I can't let him know that. I need to keep him calm until his interrogation.*

"I had my back turned for a while." Pinto's voice quaked. "Vell said something about a promise Yahshi made to her, and when I finally faced them, her dagger was on the ground. Yahshi was holding her wrist as if he—as if he'd stopped her from finishing off Commander Cal. That's when they ran."

"Well, I guess it's not your fault, Red," Evaris said—though she knew the Force would blame him. She quickened her horse's pace, and this time, Pinto kept up with her.

The silence between them returned, but it weighed less on her shoulders than before. Now that she felt more confident that he wouldn't stray, she allowed her mind to rest and focused solely on weathering the trip. Never before had she traveled from Eastern Territory back to Vakoi City without a vault. It was a strenuous task—one that left her lower back sore, her legs constantly falling asleep, and her stomach biting itself in search of food. She and Pinto had stopped at least once an hour to stretch their legs and allow their horses to refresh themselves.

They had nearly reached the outskirts of Vakoi City when a bolt of lightning sliced the air. Evaris looked up as rain pelted down from the dark clouds overhead, meeting her cheeks in a sudden storm. She and Pinto occasionally exchanged glances of discomfort as they rode their horses side by side, water dripping down their faces and drenching their uniforms.

At their next stopping point, Evaris pulled out her pocket watch to check the time. It was 1:22 in the afternoon, over six hours since her operative unit had discovered Cal lifeless on the forest floor, bleeding out from her neck.

"She's unconscious, but I found a position that allows her to breathe," Keiyo had said, his fingers pressed to Cal's wrist. *"Her pulse is weak but steady. We need to get her to the nearest hospital. She can't survive a trip back to Vakoi City."*

Evaris wondered if Cal had even survived the trip to Grimward Hospital, and her eyes burned despite the cold water running down her face. *Why do I feel this way? It's not like she treated me well.*

"Commander." It was Pinto's turn to break the silence. "I'm really sorry."

Evaris hadn't realized how emotional she must have looked until she heard Pinto's apology. She abandoned her frown and rubbed the wet hair out of her eyes.

"I know you're close to Commander Cal. If I could go back and change how I—"

"Stop," Evaris said through clenched teeth. The word came out harsher than she'd meant. *Why does everyone so easily believe that we're best friends, simply because the Belladonna Prodigy says so?*

The rain soaked through her boots and socks, leaving her toes numb.

Oh, look at me! She mocked Cal's voice in her head. *I'm friends with Evaris, the rich City girl who joined the Force to piss off her family of fashion designers. How rebellious! Aren't I cool too?*

"Do you think she'll be okay?" Pinto asked.

The Force will punish you either way, Evaris thought. But instead, she muttered, "I don't know." *And I'm trying not to care.*

"What about Yahshi and Vell?"

"I'm sure they've been caught and killed by now," Evaris lied again. It was more likely they had only killed Yahshi—the Force would bring Vell back for questioning.

"And me?" Pinto asked.

Evaris pressed her lips together, and his face contorted—he seemed to realize she'd been lying.

"What's going to happen to me?" he asked again, his words nearly indiscernible.

She ignored him.

"Commander," he pressed.

Evaris gripped her reins tighter, thinking of the guardians she knew who the Force had sent to correction for much smaller altercations. Whatever horrors had taken place behind locked Detainment Facility doors had changed them.

"They won't kill you," she replied.

Another bolt of lightning struck the sky as Pinto wiped his eye with his wet sleeve, his lip trembling. He had read between the lines.

The rain fell even harder in Vakoi City. Residents went about their business, umbrellas in hand, smiling as though there was no storm at all—most were oblivious to the special operation underway.

Evaris chuckled at the realization that every Starfall except her was likely designing formal wear for the next masquerade ball at Pandora's Hall. Meanwhile, she was babysitting a one-eyed raid victim who had accidentally shot a superior. *It must be so boring to be a Starfall. Sewing and dancing while we guardians do the important work.*

As they neared the Guardian Complex, Pinto slowed his horse, likely eager to rest. Evaris couldn't blame him. She yearned to shower and sleep—but Famir was a unit leader, a superior, and he had given her orders.

"We have errands to run," Evaris said, stopping her horse beside his.

"Can't we take a break first?" He didn't question why she insisted he join her on the errands.

"We'll be quick." She urged her horse to move faster, and with a sigh, Pinto caught up.

Their first stop was at Vakoi City Hospital. Evaris alerted the Medical guardians who had stayed behind about Cal's condition. Two of them rushed off to Grimward to assist in case she'd survived this long. *We likely won't have an update until tomorrow morning.*

Next, they stopped at the Detainment Facility. Evaris had Pinto stand a safe distance from the door so he wouldn't hear her tell the guard to prepare for Vell's detainment. When Pinto questioned her afterward, she claimed that Famir just wanted the Facility unit to have an estimated time of his arrival.

Their third and final stop was at Vakoi Palace. They left their horses with the Defense guardian who opened the gate for them and made their way down the garden, their uniforms sloshing with every step.

As they approached the stairs leading to the grand entrance, a pink umbrella whirled out from around a tree, halting them. The fifteen-year-old girl beneath it wore a silky sage green dress that Evaris recognized as one of her great aunt Cove's designs.

"It's pretty, right?" Kia offered a smug grin as she ran her hands over her waistline. "Your grandmother mentioned you during my fitting for this piece."

"She's not my grandmother." Evaris frowned. How many times did she have to clarify such a simple fact? Surely Kia remembered and just wanted to annoy her—the Princess had always been a nuisance during her guard shifts at the Palace gate. Once, Kia even threatened to use her *secret method* to escape through the Wall and pin the blame on Evaris, just to get the guardian's heart rate up.

"Right. My *dearest* apologies." Kia reached into her white coat, pulling out a palm-sized package of dried fruits. "Your *great aunt* told me your next visit will probably be at her grave."

"That's an exaggeration. She's a drama fanatic."

"She's dying, Commander."

Evaris froze. She could hear her own heartbeat as she tried to recall the last time she'd visited her great aunt. Blimmery, Cove's cousin, had invited her countless times to join them for supper, but she'd always declined. The last thing she needed was to stay close to family members who would rather see her collecting needles and spools of thread instead of daggers.

Kia fidgeted with her package of dried fruit. "So, did you find Commander Yahshi yet?"

"No," Evaris said.

"Shame." Kia's eyes darted to Pinto for the first time, and her smile widened as she tossed him the package.

He caught it with furrowed brows. "Dried mangoes?"

"You look hungry, Professor." Kia winked and twirled around, heading toward a weeping cherry tree with her umbrella swirling above her.

"She can't possibly be the Princess," Pinto muttered.

"She's definitely a handful, and not very popular among guardians."

A moment passed before Pinto said, "I'm... I'm sorry about your great aunt."

Evaris faced him, clearing her throat. "Wait out here. I need to update Emperor Vakoi on the special operation."

His face lit up. "Could I join you?"

"Sorry, Red." She shook her head, turning to scale the steps alone. "This one's all mine."

As Evaris reached the front door, she glanced over her shoulder. Kia plucked a cherry blossom from a tree—its pink petals complemented her dress and umbrella beautifully. Just like the Starfalls, Kia belonged among cherry blossoms. Had Evaris rejected her selection three-and-a-half years ago, perhaps she would have worked with Cove on that dress.

Evaris peered down at her sloshing uniform and dirtied boots. She had made a choice at sixteen to leave her life of luxury behind, and now she could never go back.

She swung the door open. *I hate cherry blossoms.*

As Evaris and Pinto scaled the staircase of the deserted Guardian Complex, their steps echoed through the building in a haunting song. Throughout her past two years of service, she had never seen the Complex this empty before. Even the common room lacked the light smell of food wafting from the adjacent cafeteria. The cooks must have had the day off.

Evaris stepped onto the fifteenth floor but lingered by the staircase, listening to Pinto ascend to the highest one without her. She waited until she heard his door close before finally entering her own flat down the hallway. *I can't let him leave until Famir gets back.*

While her bed called out for her sore body, Evaris ignored her exhaustion and rushed to the restroom. She dried off quickly—throwing her soaking uniforms into the shower to deal with later—and pulled her hair into a . tight bun, squeezing out the excess water.

When the distant, muffled splashes confirmed Pinto was showering up above, she sighed in relief, changed into a fresh uniform, and jogged back to the common room to guard the exit.

The rain had stopped, but the lingering gloominess made the early afternoon feel like the evening. She lit a few lanterns and plopped herself onto a sofa, kicking her boots up onto the low table ahead. Someone had left behind a novel on the seat cushion beside her, which she attempted to read, but the story was too slow to keep her eyes from drooping. She was running on just two hours of sleep that she'd squeezed in the night before, on the way to Erenford, thanks to Galler offering his shoulder to rest on in the vault.

Stay awake, Starfall. She slammed the book shut. *You have a job to do.*

Gazing out at the dark clouds proved to be a better strategy for staying alert, so she tossed the book onto the table and stared through the window. It didn't take long for her thoughts to drift back to the fact that Cal and Yahshi were surely dead by now. Her eyes watered, and she scowled as she wiped them dry. *I have no reason to cry.* Cal had hurt her countless times, and she had hardly known Yahshi.

Keep drying your tears, silly. Evaris imagined what Cal's ghost would say, had she been sitting on the sofa next to her. *Don't cry over my death. Grab your dagger and do something about it!*

Evaris stopped wiping her eyes, shaking her head at how far her mind had wandered. She wouldn't let some ghostly Cal of her imagination sway her into harming Pinto in vengeance. *Why would I even think of such a thing?*

She distracted herself by imagining Yahshi next to her instead. She realized he had sat by her on this very sofa just two weeks ago on the very day he'd left.

"You don't miss your old unit?" Yahshi asked. *"Cal says you're best friends."*

It had taken little prying from him for Evaris to open up about her relationship with Cal. She couldn't remember the last time anyone had drawn the truth out of her like that, and it stung to realize she might never experience it again.

I wish I was right about you, Shadow. A few tears finally trailed down her cheek, and she rubbed them with her sleeve. *I wish you were a good one. I'm starting to think they aren't real.*

"Are you okay?"

Evaris froze at the sound of Pinto's voice. She peered over her shoulder as he emerged from the staircase, his heavy locks dripping after his shower.

"I'm exhausted." Evaris gave her eyes a final rub, selling her cover story. "Can hardly keep my eyes open." The last thing she needed was a guardian catching her on the brink of tears.

Pinto scoffed in response, and Evaris frowned as he crossed the common room, stomping his way to the door. Although he hadn't slung another bow and quiver over his back, the way his fresh overcoat draped heavily as he walked told her he carried concealed tools from his flat. *I'm sure he has a dagger in there.*

"Hey," Evaris scolded, her voice firm enough to stop him in his tracks.

"If you were *that* exhausted, Commander, you'd be upstairs sleeping, not playing guard." Pinto turned to face her, his cheeks bright red. "I know

Professor Famir asked you to keep me on a leash."

Evaris blinked a few times, calculating how to handle him. Considering his intensified rage and his new set of tools, it would be difficult to contain him in the Complex. Perhaps she needed to adjust her plan.

"Where do you wanna go?" Evaris stood from the sofa. "I'll join you."

Pinto looked away with a shake of his head. "So you won't even admit it?"

"It's simple, Red." She took a step toward him and crossed her arms. "Either you leave with me, or you don't leave at all."

They stood at the front door to the Investigation Office with no way in—Famir had confiscated Pinto's keys, minus the one to his flat. She figured they had both forgotten, but when she turned to insist that they head back to the Complex, Pinto was biting his lip, flipping through the ring of keys that she had clearly seen Famir confiscate.

Evaris frowned. "How the hell did you get those back?"

Pinto winced, almost too subtly for her to notice. "I had duplicates made," he admitted—likely because her assumption that he'd pickpocketed his unit leader could have landed him in greater trouble.

She tilted her head, studying the keys in his hands. Upon closer inspection, they were far cleaner than any guardians' keys she had seen, confirming that they were new. While there was technically no rule against making duplicates in *The Guardian Handbook*, Pinto surely knew that it would look suspicious, because he unlocked the Office door and rushed inside.

Someone's in a hurry.

Evaris followed and shut the door behind them, blocking out their sole light source. Professors had drawn the curtains the evening before leaving to prepare for the special operation.

"Why did you make duplicates?" she called into the darkness.

Only silence replied. She couldn't see Pinto, but it was not *hearing* him that sent a chill down her spine. Creeping forward blindly, she reached into her overcoat and gripped the handle of her dagger.

With a *flick*, Pinto's face appeared, catching the glow of a match in his hands. He used it to light the candle of a handheld lantern.

Evaris released her dagger just before he met her gaze.

"Could you bring an extra to the archives?" Pinto gestured to another lantern on a nearby table.

"Uh... sure." Evaris pulled out her own matchbox to light it. Pinto had likely asked for the favor to distract her from the question he still hadn't answered, but she decided not to pry. *If I need to play stupid to keep him calm, I will. It's not my job to interrogate him.*

As they headed for the staircase, lanterns in hand, Evaris snatched a few novels on the way. Hopefully, they would be less boring than the one she had found in the Complex common room earlier. It'd be easy to monitor Pinto in the archives—the real challenge was staying awake.

They scaled the staircase to the second floor, which Evaris had only seen in passing once before, when a Research unit had called her in for a meeting regarding a traitor that she, Cal, and Galler had traced. The Detainment Facility's chilling corridors could never compete with the warmth of a room filled with overflowing file cabinets, beautifully crafted wooden desks, and rolling chairs with velvet cushions. *Makes me wish I could change my division.*

She plopped the novels onto a nearby desk and looked around, basking in the presence of documented history. Drawers of cases, both solved and not. *So many stories...*

Pinto marched by, breaking her attention. He made a beeline for a file cabinet across the room and rustled through its contents, holding up his lantern to illuminate their titles. She joined him and opened the curtains nearby, letting in a dull gray light from the windows.

"What are you looking for?" Evaris asked.

Once again, he acted as though he hadn't heard her.

"I'm not trying to set you up. My ears don't belong to Professor Famir."

"You think I'm naive, don't you?" His arm tensed up, and he flipped through the files with jagged flicks of his wrist. "If I say the wrong thing, you'll tell him, and use my downfall to get a promotion."

"What are we? Primary schoolers?" Evaris chuckled. "If I was *that* desperate for a promotion, I could just lie about you, and Professor Famir would take my word over yours any day. But I *won't* do that, because I play fair." *And more importantly, I don't want the responsibilities that a promotion entails.*

Pinto slammed the drawer shut and swiftly faced her. "Commander, I might have killed a guardian, my best friends might be dead, and the Force might punish me for a crime I technically didn't commit. What I need right now are certainties." He leaned toward her, his voice deepening. "You've done nothing but lie."

As Pinto turned his back to her and rustled through the next drawer, a sickening feeling burrowed into her gut. No one had seen through her so easily before.

She stood there, speechless, as Pinto brought a file labeled *Fernis* to a nearby desk. He set his lantern down, sat with a heavy sigh, and began sorting the file's contents into four stacks of pages. Unable to bite his nails, he tapped his boot on the floor instead, his movements quick as he flipped through pages and slammed them down into his piles.

"I'm not good with coddling," Evaris muttered. It was the closest thing to an apology that she could offer.

"I don't need coddling. I need answers." Pinto grabbed the first stack to read through, not bothering to spare her a glance. "If you can't help with that, then get some rest. You don't have to worry about me running off. I know that would only make things worse."

Evaris gulped. *The least I can do is help him find what he's looking for.*

He didn't acknowledge her presence as she dragged a chair to the other side of his desk, grabbing another stack of papers to read. It was a collection of transcribed reports between guardians and witnesses of Chima Fernis's murder. The other two stacks on the desk contained general information about the investigation and transcripts of Cal's interrogations at the Detainment Facility.

Evaris started reading the first witness report between a Research guardian and thirteen-year-old Quax Avarium. She had nearly finished it when Pinto broke the silence.

"I won't run," he repeated.

"I believe you," Evaris replied, and she meant it. "I'm just... not sleepy anymore."

Pinto's shoulders loosened slightly as he turned a page. "We are looking through the Fernis files because Commander Cal mentioned the incident after Yahshi rejected the pardon. She said he was there when she murdered Chima." His softer tone and choice of the word *we* told Evaris that he appreciated her help.

No problem, she thought to herself, finishing off Quax's transcript. *It's not like there's a more interesting way for me to kill time here anyway.*

Evaris flipped to the next transcript, her eyes widening at the sight of Yahshi's name. "Yeah, looks like he was there." She stood and walked to Pinto's side of the desk, spreading the pages out in front of him. "He never mentioned being a witness?"

Pinto shook his head, taking the transcript from her with a firm grip. "I asked him once if he knew Cal, considering they were from the same town, and he said *hardly*."

Evaris leaned over Pinto's shoulder, and they read the transcript together.

[LOCATION: Sitra Secondary School, Main Office]

PROFESSOR: Thank you for being brave, and having this conversation—

YAHSHI KONYA: Everyone has it wrong. Cal doesn't care about her brother.

PROFESSOR: Why do you say that?

YAHSHI KONYA: She ignores him all the time.

PROFESSOR: Sibling relationships are never perfect. Clearly, she loved him enough to kill for him, though she hated doing it. Another classmate of yours said that she wouldn't stop crying.

> YAHSHI KONYA: I don't think she cried because she killed him.
>
> PROFESSOR: Why else would she cry?
>
> YAHSHI KONYA: Because she knew you'd lock her up.

Pinto nearly turned the page but hesitated, looking back at Evaris. "Were you ever told the reason why Yahshi stopped shadowing your ex-unit?"

"I heard he broke his leg in training."

"He jumped off his balcony, Commander. And after that, he started acting out against the guardians. It took a few months for him to get back on track." He nodded to himself, putting the pieces together. "It all makes sense now—he's *always* been scared of Commander Cal."

"It probably didn't help that she gave him a hard time on his assignment," Evaris added, breaking the shadow confidentiality rule. If Pinto were to turn her in, no one would believe him anyway. "She made him kill our target—a smuggler—and he couldn't stomach it."

Pinto's eye widened. At first, Evaris thought she'd shocked him by breaking the shadow confidentiality rule, but after a moment, she caught on to his train of thought. *If Yahshi was a spy for the Underground, that would explain his spirited reaction to his first assignment. What if he was angry at himself after killing an ally to keep his cover?*

"I don't know," Pinto said, his look of surprise fading. "I doubt he spied for the Underground. He's the one who outed Dice. Why would he do that if they were allies?"

"Let's keep reading," Evaris said, reaching past him to turn the page. She swore she could hear Yahshi's voice in her head as they finished the transcript, his rage seeping into every word.

Pinto thought to himself for a minute before leaving the desk and approaching a drawer labeled *Correctional Profiles*. "Yahshi said something else that was strange earlier too. He brought up Maelin Vandros, a war hero from my hometown. We had her portrait up in almost every room at Frontal Primary."

"I've heard the story." Evaris joined him, and he opened the drawer to reveal a lonely file inside.

"Yahshi told me that the Force lied—that they executed her for being a traitor but didn't want to taint the public's image of the guardians." He grabbed the file and sat on the floor, Evaris following suit. "He told me the truth is all here in the archives."

The file disclosed that everything Yahshi claimed had been true. After attempting to save the life of a traitor, Maelin had resisted correctional meetings, resulting in her insanity and eventual execution. A final note contained Blimmery's justification for lying to the public about her death in *Capital Weekly.*

While it sounded unjust, Evaris understood why the Force had done so. *News of Maelin's execution would have devastated the residents of Frontal, but calling her a hero allows them to fondly remember her and put up portraits in her honor.*

"This doesn't make the Force evil." Evaris set a hand on Pinto's shoulder as the color drained from his face. "They're not even lying to us. The truth is right here, free for any guardian to access."

"That's not it." Pinto rubbed his temple. "It's the other claim he made that worries me—he thinks that Emperor Vakoi initiated the raids, not the Underground."

"You don't possibly believe that, do you?"

Pinto looked at her, his eye containing a storm that only answers could tame.

Evaris squeezed his shoulder tighter. "He could have mentioned the story about Maelin to make his claim about the raids seem more plausible."

"Maybe," Pinto said softly, but he didn't seem convinced. She didn't blame him for being confused. The evidence, on the surface, pointed to Yahshi being a traitor, but the story had to be more complicated than that. Yahshi had told some truths—along with some lies. He had been a friend to Pinto and a listening ear to Evaris, but he had also killed his own father. Whatever he was—good or bad—had drawn Vell in enough for her to turn sides. There was clearly so much that they didn't understand.

Evaris took Maelin's file from Pinto's shaky grip. "Read what you need to, okay? I'll pick up some food."

Pinto raised his brows as Evaris returned the file to its assigned drawer.

She left him alone in the archives despite Famir's order to watch him, and nearly an hour later, when she returned, he was still there, back to flipping through the Fernis pages he hadn't finished reading earlier.

They wolfed down a takeout meal as they read through transcripts, meeting notes, and witness reports, only sharing an occasional word. She wanted him to savor this moment of solitude, because as soon as the guardians arrived, he might not have such a luxury for a long time.

It was in the early evening when Pinto's head began to droop, his eyelid heavy. Evaris watched as he drifted off, a stack of pages serving as a pillow.

"Red?" she whispered.

Pinto snored in response.

She chuckled, setting her pages down to watch him. As a guardian, she spent every night lying alone in her flat, again and again, every time the same.

Today was different. She reached out and flicked one of his curls. *It was nice.*

As the clocks ticked, the air grew colder, a chill sweeping through the archives. Pinto shivered and stirred, so Evaris stripped her overcoat of its tools and draped the weighted fabric over his back. He settled down, and her smile faded at the sight of his leather eyepatch. *What does it look like underneath?*

She reached out but retracted her hand. *No, I shouldn't.* Other guardians in the Force had rumored that Pinto never took his eyepatch off. To remove it without asking would violate his privacy.

A knot of guilt twisted inside her as she opened her notepad. *If I'm gonna do this, I should pay my dues first.* She jotted a letter *O* and took a deep breath, the guilt slowly fading.

Pinto's nose twitched when she gripped the edge of his black patch. She froze, waiting ten seconds for another reaction, but he didn't budge. Deeming it safe, she gently tugged the leather aside and rested it on his forehead. His eyelid, scarred and pale, was sunken into the crevice where his eyeball should have been. It was no battle scar; it was just sad.

Evaris gulped and moved his patch back into place. She would not lie and say he looked better without it.

CHAPTER 11

JUST A TOAD LILY

Day 1 Underground | Clocks Read 23:21

♫ RIVERSIDE · AGNES OBEL ♫

Vell entered her assigned bunker room with a handful of wrinkly pages. She'd spent the last six hours wandering through Headquarters, sketching floor plans to make sense of the place. Tunnels merged into chambers that didn't exist before, entryways appearing where there used to be dead ends. Every new iteration contradicted the last, nearly convincing her the walls could shift.

Accurate floor plan or not, she had hoped to at least run into Yahshi again. She had shared a brief half-hour meal with him, but there had been too many watching eyes and listening ears to discuss anything important. And before Vell could even finish her bowl, Tonna had whisked Yahshi away for another Council obligation. *What could they possibly be doing with him during all this time?*

The bunker room was darker than earlier, most of the torches snuffed out. The only light source was the brazier—a wide, shallow dugout in the middle of the room filled with burning coal.

Ignoring the surrounding women's stares and whispers, Vell held the floor plans to her chest and made a beeline for bunker forty-three. She hadn't slept since the night before last, and her exhaustion made a dead person's hole in the wall sound just as comfortable as a proper bed. *Hopefully I'll have a chance to talk with Yahshi tomorrow.*

Vell slipped her sketches under her pillow, her hand grazing something cold. *Steel.* She peeled the pillow back to reveal a dagger in place of the poison vials Dice had confiscated.

A whooshing noise caught Vell's attention. She covered the dagger with her pillow and whipped around, raising her hands. A wad of fabric landed right into them. It was another set of clothes for the morning.

Aero chuckled. "You're fast."

"Thanks," Vell muttered, looking up at her with a slight smile. It wasn't just the clothes—Aero had made everything about her first day in Headquarters easier. She had eaten supper with her in the canteen when Yahshi didn't show, fetched papers and pencils for her pointless floor plans, and now she had placed a dagger beneath her pillow. *She must have heard that Dice took my belladonna serum.*

"No problem." Aero winked and climbed up a ladder to reach her bunker.

As Vell lay in her suffocating slot that night, she shuffled, trying to find a more comfortable position, the floor plans crinkling under her pillow. Even wrapping herself in the tattered quilt didn't help her relax. How could she sleep in a room with hundreds of women who feared her? *Fear makes people violent. Fear is why Rimoso killed the last woman in bunker forty-three.*

The longer she stayed in her stone box, the smaller it felt. The wall above her—only a forearm's distance from her nose—bounced her breaths back at her face, drying her eyes, which, despite their heaviness, refused to shut.

Maybe Saunti's right. Vell tried to turn onto her side, but the low roof caught her shoulder. She pressed her cheek against the stone instead and stared out at the glowing brazier. *This sure feels like a casket.*

From her bunker, she couldn't see any clocks, but she was certain over an hour had passed, because she didn't hear as much fabric rustling. Headquarters was falling asleep, and she wished to fall too, but she found her fingers wiggling under her pillow, reaching for the dagger.

Staring through the slot of her bunker, her eyes locked on the door. *I'm sure there are multiple people here who want me dead.*

In perfect timing, the stone door rolled—so slowly that it hardly made a noise, causing only a few people to shuffle. Vell tightened her grip around the handle of her dagger and narrowed her eyes barely enough to see through them, pretending to be asleep.

For the first time that night, she lay perfectly still. The stone door stopped a little over halfway open, revealing someone in the connected tunnel.

Vell's eyes widened as the figure crossed the room, each step faster than the last—though not louder. Only a guardian could move that swiftly.

"Yahshi?" she whispered.

The silhouette halted by the brazier, and in the dull light of the fire, Vell recognized her fellow graduate's face. Now that the chaos of their escape had settled down, she wanted to run after him and wrap him in a suffocating hug, but then she remembered the past two weeks she'd gone without knowing where he was, why he'd left, or how long he'd survive.

Vell released the dagger and slipped out of her bunker to approach him. Hundreds of women slept around them, oblivious to their presence in the middle of the room because they were silent—because they were guardians.

It was likely too dark for him to see Vell's guarded expression, because he swooped forward and wrapped his arms around her. He was so warm.

Vell left her hands at her sides. The day's chaos had kept her too focused on survival to let her resentment settle.

"You shouldn't be in here," she whispered.

Yahshi stiffened, noticing her hesitation, and pulled away. The warmth between them faded.

"I just... I had to find you," he whispered back. "I couldn't sleep."

Vell hesitated to admit the same, and Yahshi frowned, studying her face. She had betrayed the Force for him, but that didn't mean she would forgive him without an explanation.

After a moment of tense silence, Yahshi nodded to himself and gestured for her to follow. It didn't take long for him to lead her through the tunnels and down a few ladders to an underground riverbank. The inky water stretched through a long, narrow cave lined with endless glowing mushrooms and toad lilies.

"They call it the Waterway," Yahshi said, sitting down by a cluster of fungi. They sprouted from the soil at the cave's base—this was the only part of Headquarters where Vell recalled seeing dirt.

She sat beside him, her eyes widening at the river. The mushrooms' green light illuminated the water in a hue that made it look not sickly, but magical.

"Tonna told me it's connected to the ocean," he continued, his speech quickening. "The current's direction changes based on the tides, so you could travel to sister bases farther south and even make your way back to Headquarters."

Vell could tell he was nervous by the way he threw words into the air, but she refused to be the one to lead this conversation in a serious direction. She touched the dotted petals of a toad lily, ignoring his gaze, her thoughts drifting to a memory from long before her mother had fallen sick.

"What do these do?" Vell had asked, holding out a few flowers she'd picked in the woods.

"Oh, these are toad lilies," her mother had said, taking the flowers with a warm smile. *"They don't do anything. They're just pretty."*

"What's the point in that?" She had always believed plants ought to have a purpose—whether it be to harm or cure. Without one, it was no better than a glorified weed.

"They're toad lilies. That is the point."

Vell didn't understand her mother's answer until now, as she sat by the Waterway in baggy clothes instead of her guardian uniform. There was something hypnotizing about admiring a flower just because it was pretty, but she still struggled to believe that a toad lily was all it needed to be.

"Vell?" Yahshi set a hand on her shoulder, and she brushed it away.

You know why I didn't hug you back.

He sighed. "I tried to tell you I was leaving."

"But you *didn't* tell me."

"I know. I'm sorry." He plucked a toad lily from its root and fidgeted with the flower. "I can't imagine how frustrating it must be for me to... break your trust a second time."

It took her a moment to realize he was referencing the final filtration, the time he'd plucked her feather to increase his odds of making the final five. She had forgiven him months ago—they all knew, deep down, that it was every trainee for themselves. However, this situation was different. Yahshi didn't *need* to betray her to save himself. He had *chosen* to.

"I didn't forget my promise, Vell. Leaving you in the dark has been one of my biggest regrets," Yahshi said, his voice breaking. "For the past two weeks, I was sure you hated me, and it *killed* me. I know I hurt you—but still, you saved me this morning, and now you're paying the price for it."

Vell gulped, her eyes watering. Though her mind told her to stay angry, the guilt in Yahshi's voice chipped away at her barrier. He was apologizing for everything she'd lost in joining him, but it was *he* who had lost the most—his uniform, his father, his identity—and he was far too desperate not to lose her too.

I'm being cruel, she realized. *He doesn't deserve another stressor.*

"There won't be a third time, Vell." He held the toad lily out for her, his arm shaking, weakened by his shoulder wound. "I'll make it up to you, not because I owe you my life, but because I *want* to fix this. I'm not the same person I was when I left."

Vell stared at the flower, her stomach twisting into a knot. He spoke as though he'd done nothing but wrong her, time and time again. *I've wronged you too. I ignored you when you broke your leg at the Academy, when you needed me most.*

"Please," Yahshi said. "You're the only part of my old life that I want to keep."

"Why?" She looked up from the toad lily, meeting Yahshi's gaze with a shrug. "I'm not this hero you're making me out to be. I don't even have my uniform."

He frowned, his grip on the flower tightening. "You don't need that bloody uniform."

"I needed it to save my mother," Vell muttered. "I needed it to save you."

He chuckled lightly. "That wasn't your uniform. You did that yourself."

"How?" she asked.

"Because you're Vell," he said simply, as though that answered everything.

Her gaze drifted back to the toad lily in his outstretched hand. He hadn't lowered it.

Maybe a toad lily really can be... just a toad lily.

She reached for it, her fingers grazing his as she took the toad lily into her grasp. Its petals glowed in the mushroom light, standing out as the only flower capable of surviving in the harsh botanical conditions of Headquarters—with scant light and sparse soil. It was a beautiful flower, but also a strong flower. With hope, it grew.

Vell set the toad lily aside and wrapped Yahshi in a hug, careful not to agitate his shoulder.

"Thank you," he whispered into her ear.

They embraced for a while as the waves splashed gently against the cave walls.

"I'm sorry too," Vell said, pulling away. "I mean, this whole situation has been a lot."

"You know what the craziest part is?"

"What?"

He smirked. "Turns out, you're older than me."

Vell laughed.

"Did you know that my actual birthday is next month?" He shook his head in amused disbelief. "Next month, Vell. On the twenty-sixth. It's ridiculous."

She made a mental note as Yahshi's smile faded, his gaze finding its way to the water.

"But to be honest, I think I have more closure now that I know the truth. Even if we're not related by blood, my father will always be family to me. I just hope Saunti doesn't hate me forever. I'd like to get to know my father's..." He trailed off, unsure of which words to use. "My father's *first* son."

Vell thought back to her conversation with Saunti in the water tank room.

"He'll warm up to you," she assured him.

As they sat on the riverbank that night, immersed in the hazy green light of fungi, they caught each other up on the past two weeks. Yahshi told her everything about his plans with Kia, how Roz had murdered Martu, and the highlights of his time on the run. In turn, Vell told him everything Pinto had done to grant him a pardon, the various expeditions she'd been on to trace him, and her choice not to report Saunti's copy of the Meridian book.

"I can't believe Pinto did all that for me," Yahshi said. "If only he read the book with you instead of burning it."

"Have *you* read it?"

"Not all of it, but I have a copy. Lira dropped off a stack of banned books earlier. There's a lot of Atherus history the Provisional Council wants me to learn—or *unlearn*, rather. I only had time to read a few sections, but so far, everything tracks with what Princess Kia and the smugglers told me."

"What's it about?" Vell asked. "I only kept it because I recognized the author's last name. Pinto said Doctor Blimmery's uncle wrote it."

"Meridian Owding," Yahshi confirmed. "He was a messenger who delivered *Capital Weekly* articles across the Vakoi Empire. Being so involved in the press, he did some digging and discovered that the Underground never existed—it was just a name for key players in the Force to commit crimes under. *Capital Weekly* claimed Eastern rebels led it so they could pin the blame on Emperor Atherus's inability to manage his people. The book documents his entire investigation."

"Did they kill him for it?"

"Almost immediately. The Force rounded up his books and burned them."

Vell frowned as Yahshi's earlier claims in the woods echoed through her head.

"Emperor Vakoi initiated the Eastern raids to give him an excuse to control both sides of the island. This entire time, we've been the bad guys. We've been the monsters."

His tone of voice had proved that he believed what he claimed—but Vell grasped every reason not to. If the Force had initiated the raids and committed the various crimes leading up to them, that would invalidate Pinto's motive to become a guardian.

"That doesn't make sense," Vell countered. "You're saying the Force committed crimes—including the raids—and blamed them on the Underground, a fake organization led by rebels from the Atherus Empire."

He nodded. "Exactly."

"But these people call themselves the Underground too." She gestured to the cave walls surrounding them. "How could the Force make up an organization if it's right here?"

"That's exactly what worries me." Yahshi leaned toward her. "At the meeting earlier, after lunch, I asked the same question. Rimoso told me, *If the Force wants a violent enemy, we'll give them one. We'll become exactly what they want their people to fear.*"

Vell froze. Whether the Underground or the Force started the raids wasn't the real problem—based on what the Provisional Council had told Yahshi, they were capable of just as much evil. They had named themselves the Underground, taking on the image the Force had given them.

"What are they planning?" she asked.

Yahshi broke eye contact. "The Provisional Council is *provisional*— meaning, they've been waiting for me to return and lead in their place someday."

"Lead the Underground?"

"Lead the Empire."

Vell's heart skipped a beat, and she leaned toward him. "What?"

"They're planning something called *the siege*. Rimoso wants his Guild to raid Vakoi City and burn down Vakoi Palace just like Emperor Vakoi did to my"—the next words seemed to get caught in his throat—"original family."

Vell shook her head. "He won't succeed. I've seen his Guild."

"His Guild is three times the size of the Force."

"But the officers in Eastern Territory outnumber the Guild by *fifty*. They'll die before they even reach Border Control."

"They won't have to go through Border Control." Yahshi pointed west. "They're building a tunnel, Vell. It'll go right under the towers, all the way to the opposite coast. The Guild could bypass general officers and strike the Force directly, without warning."

"No..."

"Thanks to Dice, they have calabar to lace their tools with too," Yahshi added. "I tried to convince them to use less violence, but they won't consider it unless I have an actionable plan. They're letting me make a proposal next week."

Vell lowered her head. While she hated the idea of the Guild striking the Force, she knew that Yahshi's efforts to stop Rimoso would be risky. The Underground might have welcomed their Prince home with open arms, but he had been a guardian too. Perhaps there were skeptics who secretly saw Yahshi the way Varin saw Vell—watching from the sidelines, waiting for a reason to discard a Prince they didn't need.

"Be careful," she warned.

"I don't care if I upset them." Yahshi raised his voice. "If I can prevent innocent people from dying on both sides, I'm gonna do it. Think of our friends!"

Vell gulped as the faces of Pinto, Quax, and Keiyo flashed through her head. She had watched them train and fight for eighteen months at the Academy, defeating challenge after challenge. They were nonperishable guardians. Indestructible.

"Tunnel or not, the Guild won't win."

"Do you really want to take that chance?" Yahshi asked, his tone fierce. "You and I have one foot in both worlds. We see the full picture. We can stop this before it escalates."

The Waterway seemed to roar as Yahshi reached out, taking her hands in his. Unlike earlier, she didn't brush his grip away. What he sought to do was hopeless, but he had already survived the impossible. Perhaps he had a chance, and perhaps she could help him, even without her uniform.

"Please, Vell." He squeezed her hands tighter. "There's no need for another war, right?"

A few hours later, the clocks read 03:06. They sat across from each other at a table in a library they'd found, flipping through a stack of old books Lira had assigned Yahshi to finish within the week. The more Vell read, the clearer it became that the Vakoi Empire's banning of these titles had less to do with safety and more to do with concealing what key players in the Force didn't want the public to know.

The Force's Hidden Agenda tied all the pieces together, detailing a story about the guardians that she never could have imagined. For decades, the father of the current Emperor Vakoi had orchestrated chaos in the Underground's name, so his son could take over both sides someday. As Blimmery's uncle had expected, these crimes soon escalated into violence once his son took over, leading to the eye-gouging raids that officially ignited the Atherus War.

Despite Vell's desire to deny them, the facts laid out before her were challenging to dispute. *Assuming this is true*, she thought as she turned a page, her grip on the Meridian book tightening, *then Yahshi asks for too much. This conflict runs deep. There are too many lies to unravel. The Underground can't defeat the Force without harming innocent guardians. There is no peaceful remedy.*

"What if we distribute these banned books to the guardians?" Yahshi asked—his fourth suggested solution that night.

Like the others, Vell easily knocked it down. "Pinto was terrified to *touch* this one." She looked up from the Meridian book with a shake of her head. "We'd be lucky to convince even a few guardians to read one, and even if they *did*, the Force could lie and call it propaganda."

To prevent a war with books? I'm sorry, Yahshi, but that won't do.

"We could start our own news outlet like *Capital Weekly*," Yahshi proposed next. "There are enough people down here to work as scribes. We could have our smuggling network distribute the truth across Eastern Territory."

"And get them killed, cutting off our supplies?"

The spark in his eyes died out. He leaned over the stone table and grasped his hair, clenching his eyes shut as he racked his brain for another solution.

Vell spotted a dot of red on Yahshi's shoulder, seeping through the brown shirt the Council had supplied him with. She set the Meridian book down and joined his side of the table, rolling back his sleeve to survey the arrow wound. Someone in Headquarters had wrapped his shoulder with fresh bandages, but had done a poor job at it. The blood had already seeped through.

"I should clean it again," Vell said.

"I can do it myself in the morning."

"Yahshi…"

"Really, you said it yourself earlier—it's not deep."

Vell stepped back, but she still intended to fetch medical supplies in a moment. First, though, she couldn't resist the urge for the full story behind his injury. When she previously tended to his shoulder upon their arrival in Atherus City, Yahshi only told her that Evaris had shot him, and she didn't have time to ask follow-up questions.

"What happened before we intercepted you?"

Yahshi glanced at his shoulder wound. "Professor Famir, Commander Galler, and Commander Evaris found me first, back in Erenford. They tried to present the pardon to me, but I kept running. I wouldn't listen to them. I assume Commander Evaris tried to injure me mildly so she could explain the situation."

"How did you get away from her?"

"I tipped over a barrel of apples to slow her down."

Vell laughed. "Really?"

"And in Erenford, people keep shoes on their front doorsteps, just out in the open." Yahshi chuckled. "So I started grabbing the shoes and tossing them onto rooftops to create a diversion."

"You're making this up."

"I'm not!" He nearly doubled over. "I swear!"

She settled down and lit a lantern on the desk, preparing to look for the infirmary. "You're lucky you're alive," she muttered. What she really meant was, *I'm glad you're still here.*

"I'm lucky you're here," he replied, as though he'd read between the lines.

Their eyes met, and they smiled together. Maybe they could figure out what life would look like down here, in this Underground world, under such ridiculous circumstances.

"I'll be right back," Vell said, leaving with the lantern.

The clocks told her it took seven minutes to find the closest infirmary. Supplies were scarce, so she only took what she needed—a few long strips of clean cloth and a can of saltwater. There wasn't much of anything else, anyway.

By the time she made it back to the library, fifteen minutes had passed, and Yahshi had already fallen asleep, his cheek glued to the table, his hand on a book. The sight brought a smile to her face as she set the lantern and medical supplies on the table. It reminded her of the many late nights they had spent studying at the Academy. No matter how tired he was, she always had to fight him to get him to sleep. If he had done so accidentally, she couldn't imagine how exhausted he had been. Sleep was more important—his wound could wait until morning.

Vell leaned toward him and reached out, gently brushing the hair away from his forehead to reveal the mark he had been hiding for the past two weeks. The thought of the branding ceremony left a metallic taste on her tongue, and she could almost feel the heat against her head. It had not been pleasant to earn such a mark, yet looking at Yahshi's now, it was beautiful because it matched her own. They were the only two people in Headquarters with the Belladonna Guardian Academy emblem branded onto their foreheads, and no one could take that away.

Vell took her seat across from Yahshi again and continued reading the Meridian book. She turned a page. Then another. She finished one section and moved onto the second. Then the third. She couldn't stomach the thought of sleeping in the bunkers, nor did she want to leave Yahshi here alone, so she read, read, and read.

The next thing she knew, she woke to her face in the open book, struggling to remember how she'd fallen asleep.

"Morning, Vell," Yahshi muttered. "Tonna's calling, but I'll find you as soon as I can, okay?"

Her eyes were too heavy to look up from the pages—all she offered was a half-asleep nod. It must have been earlier than the first bell, which rang at 08:00.

Yahshi set a hand on her shoulder before leaving the library. She could still feel the warmth of his grip as his footsteps disappeared down the adjacent tunnel, and she wished she had called after him, *Please, stay a moment longer! I can't keep losing you like this.*

But she was too tired, so she fell back asleep.

CHAPTER 12

JUDGMENT DAY

Apples are going out of season.
Stock up at your local Saver Store before it's too late!

♫ SURVEILLANCE - GEORGE OGILVIE ♫

As the sun broke over the horizon, golden light shone into the Investigation Office, stirring Pinto from slumber. He found himself hunched over in a cushioned chair, his cheek glued to a desk in the archives. The glare from a nearby window nearly blinded his good eye.

How did I end up here?

Perhaps it was a dream. Yahshi hadn't deserted the Force two weeks ago, and Vell hadn't run off with him yesterday. Pinto had simply fallen asleep after a late night helping Famir with a case.

He peeled his cheek free and sat up, Evaris's piercing gaze proving that his nightmare had been real.

"About time, Red." She peeked at her golden pocket watch before tucking it back into her overcoat. "It's nearly 7:00."

Pinto's head swayed as he reached for his eyepatch, ensuring it hadn't slipped off in his sleep. Only his family had ever seen his bad eye—he hadn't even looked in a mirror without his patch on in years. Luckily, his fingers met the leather over his eye, and his dizziness faded.

Evaris raised a brow as Pinto stood, rushing to the nearest window. A few blocks down by the Complex, vaults lined the road, clusters of guardians waiting outside for the last few units to return from Eastern Territory. The special operation had officially come to an end—and he'd slept right through the finale.

He spun around, his cheeks hot. "Why didn't you wake me?"

"You were out cold," Evaris said, seemingly unfazed by his accusatory tone. "Has anyone told you that you snore like an old man?"

He faced the window again. "I'm not in the mood, Commander."

"It's your judgment day. I don't blame you."

As he heard Evaris head for the door, Pinto squinted at the guardians in the distance, trying to make out their faces. The Force had surely killed Yahshi and Vell by now, but the childish optimist in him searched for their faces anyway.

They're dead, Pinto told himself, killing the child in him that believed otherwise. *That's the way it needs to be. They lied to you—why should they deserve your pity?*

His eyes watered as he gulped down the clot in his throat, his grief kicking the anger away just as soon as it'd come. He deserved a chance to speak with Yahshi and Vell one last time, to confront them with rage, to say goodbye—but the Force had denied him such an opportunity.

They probably think I was conspiring with them too. Pinto forced his tears away, taking deep breaths to calm himself. Now wasn't the time to grieve. *They're going to interrogate me soon, and I need to be prepared.*

"Hey," Evaris called from the staircase. "I've stalled for you long enough!"

Pinto turned his back to the window and headed toward her, taking in the grandness of the archives for what could be the last time.

It only took a few minutes for them to ride their horses to the Guardian Complex, where they joined the crowd of grumbling guardians with dark bags under their eyes. Pinto had expected them to be exhausted after a day and night of tracing and traveling, but he hadn't expected to see them *restless*. It was almost like the special operation had never come to a close—like they were all still in Eastern Territory, following Yahshi's tracks.

Pinto's eye widened as he led his horse between guardians, catching scattered snippets of conversations. He had always admired the Force's level of organization and order, but that morning, no one seemed to be on the same page.

"Commander Cal's injured?"

"Someone told me she died."

"*Died*?"

"I thought she was at Thornwick Hospital."

"That was *yesterday*. She could be long gone by now."

"How did Yahshi get a bow?"

"Maybe someone else shot her."

"I heard Commander Vell helped him."

"That girl from his cycle?"

"You didn't hear? We're supposed to be tracing her too."

Pinto shot Evaris a confused glance as they broke free from the crowd and entered the Complex stable. Inside, Galler was securing his horse, and his face lit up at the sight of Evaris.

"W-We couldn't t-trace them!" he shouted over the noise seeping inside. "W-We think they made it to—to wherever the hiders are."

Pinto's eye widened as he shut the door behind them, blocking most of the muffled chatter from outside. He found his heart torn between relief and justice. While Yahshi and Vell deserved death, he also wanted his friends to be safe—and they would never again be safe in the hands of the Force.

"You're kidding," Evaris muttered, securing her horse in a stall.

Pinto nearly followed suit, but Galler met his gaze. "You n-need to get going, Professor. You were c-called to the Facility half an hour ago."

My interrogation. Pinto took a deep breath, his grip on his horse's lead rope tightening.

Before he could even make his way to the door, Famir burst into the stable.

"Commander Evaris," he called from the doorway, his mustache twitching. "Where the hell have you been?"

Evaris crossed her arms, leaning back against a stall door. "Just wandering."

Famir's eyes darted to Pinto for just a moment, perhaps hoping he would offer a more specific answer, but he knew better than to speak. Surely Famir would be furious if he were to learn that he had made duplicates of his keys, including one to the Investigation Office.

Thankfully, Famir turned back to Evaris, his eyes narrowed. "A word alone, please?" He turned to leave the stable, expecting her to follow, which she did.

I shouldn't have been so harsh on her this morning, Pinto realized as Evaris passed him. She had been kind enough to let him sleep through the night—buying him a few extra hours of freedom—and had even lied to Famir to keep his duplicates a secret. He wondered why she had done him such favors. Was it because they were close in age that she didn't look at him like someone beneath her? Having graduated just two years before him, she had recently been in his shoes—new to the Force, still figuring out who to trust. Maybe there was a bond in that.

As soon as Evaris and Famir left the stable, Pinto froze, remembering where he was supposed to go. The thought of entering the Detainment Facility without knowing how long he'd be there left his boots glued to the straw-covered floor, his lips trembling.

"If you w-want my advice"—Galler inched toward Pinto, his voice nearly a whisper—"y-you should put yourself first."

The Defense guardian stationed at the door perked up as Pinto approached the Facility.

"Tools," he ordered, holding out his palm.

Pinto resisted the urge to roll his eye as he removed the daggers he'd slipped into his fresh overcoat the day before. The guardian had likely sensed, by the way the fabric draped, that he had replaced the one Famir confiscated.

"Just following Protocol," the guardian said, stashing Pinto's tools. He swung the door open and gestured to the darkness. "You're all set."

Pinto stared through the doorway at the void awaiting him. With a deep breath, he stepped into the darkness of the foyer and flinched as the guard slammed the door. The resonating *boom* rang in sync with the last bit of light disappearing from behind him.

Pinto crept forward, his steps echoing in the expanse. No one had told him which room to report to, so he made an assumption and trailed his hand along the stone walls, feeling his way to the entrance of the corridor containing the interrogation rooms.

He stepped inside and spotted Embre leaning against the wall, her arms crossed, her boot tapping the floor impatiently.

"Finally," she said, locking eyes with him. "I was starting to think you and Evaris ran off too."

Pinto cleared his throat. "I'm sorry I'm late, Professor."

Embre raised a brow before heading down the corridor, expecting him to follow. "I hope you're ready to explain yourself. Tell the truth, and maybe you'll get off easy."

He rushed to catch up to her. "Why would I lie?"

"Good answer." She stopped at a metal door and fished through her overcoat for a ring of keys.

Pinto closed his eye, inhaling what felt like his last breath. He could easily predict what the interrogator would ask him. How he would answer those questions, however, was the real challenge.

Why did you take so long to shoot Yahshi? the interrogator might ask.

If Pinto were to say that he cared for his friend more than he feared the guardians, it might sound like slander.

Did you know about Vell's plans to betray us?

If Pinto were to confess that Vell had possessed the Meridian book, and that he had burned it with her instead of turning her in, it would only reinforce the idea that *he* was treasonous too.

Why didn't you go after them when they ran?

If Pinto were to expose that Keiyo had tackled him, Keiyo would face consequences for breaking Protocol to protect his fellow graduates—for doing the same thing as Pinto when he hesitated to follow Cal's order.

With the sound of Embre's key turning in the lock, Pinto opened his eye.

I can't lie to the Force, he decided, *but maybe I can tiptoe around the truth...*

He followed Embre into a plain investigation room with nothing but a table and four chairs. Two were occupied—Ogga seated opposite Keiyo. Pinto's heart skipped a beat at the sight of the redhead. If one of the most powerful guardians in the Force would lead this interrogation, that meant they didn't plan to take the matters lightly.

Pinto took the empty seat next to Keiyo, who shot him a pleading stare. Quax had been too focused on his sister to see Keiyo help Yahshi and Vell escape, which made Pinto the only witness to his crime.

Pinto nodded subtly, assuring Keiyo that he had his back. Then they sat up straighter, bracing themselves for battle, as Embre sat next to Ogga. She wielded a pen, preparing to write on the blank pages in front of her.

"Let's start from the beginning," Ogga said, "when your operative unit arrived at the scene." His raspy voice surprised Pinto again, and for the first time, he wondered if the older guardian was a smoker. *Could a man as respected as him treat his body with such disrespect?*

"Quax was the first to find Yahshi," Keiyo said, volunteering the information—perhaps he believed doing so would make him look less suspicious. "I heard their voices and watched them from the trees. Yahshi had somehow stolen Quax's swords, so Quax armed himself with his dagger and warned Yahshi to stand down."

Ogga turned to Pinto, who admitted, "I found them later, when Yahshi was already fighting Cal. He was quickly intoxicated from the serum on her blades."

"Alright. Let's fill in the gap..." Ogga asked follow-up questions with a playful fascination, as though the tragic events were pieces of a fascinating jigsaw puzzle. Pinto didn't understand his amusement, but he didn't have time to dwell on it. He focused on answering Ogga truthfully—but more importantly, with as many words as possible to put off the part of the story that could incriminate him. Keiyo did the same.

Embre had filled several pages with the recent graduates' words before Ogga asked the first fateful question: "What happened after Yahshi rejected the pardon?"

Keiyo looked at Pinto, urging him to speak for himself.

"Cal ordered me to shoot him." Pinto folded his hands together tightly under the table, struggling to maintain an emotionless expression as he conveniently left out his hesitation. "When I drew my bow, Vell threw a star and redirected my arrow. It went right through Cal's throat."

Embre cringed as she jotted down his words.

"Hmm..." Ogga tapped his fingers against the table and leaned in, studying Pinto's stoic expression. After a moment, a grin tugged at the corners of his lips. "It's understandable that you'd struggle with such an order. Fellow graduates always have a special closeness to each other. The Academy bonds us. Final five, side by side—that's the saying, after all."

Pinto's fingers numbed from his own tight grip. How had Ogga pieced together his hesitation so quickly?

"What were you thinking," Ogga continued, "as you drew your bow?"

In the split second before answering, Pinto decided to focus on his confusion, rather than highlighting his hesitation. "I wasn't sure *what* to think. Yahshi rejected the pardon I worked so hard to get, and he was making ridiculous claims about the Force—saying *we* initiated the raids, and that *we* were the bad guys."

"Were you planning to shoot?"

"I drew my bow," Pinto replied, dodging the question.

Ogga nodded. "And what were you thinking, after Vell redirected your arrow?"

Looking him in the eye, Pinto infused his voice with as much sincerity as he could muster. "I was horrified to see my arrow in Commander Cal's neck. I turned around. I just... I couldn't look."

"What about you, Doctor Keiyo?"

"I couldn't believe Vell would interfere like that." Keiyo shook his head, his voice trembling. "I tried to talk to her, but she..."

Pinto's eye widened as a look of regret crossed Keiyo's face.

"She *what*?" Ogga leaned in, his reddish-brown eyes pressing him to continue.

Keiyo looked away, crumbling under the weight of the professor's stare. "Vell tried to stab Commander Cal."

"After she was already shot?"

"She wanted to finish her off," Keiyo confirmed, "but for some reason,

Yahshi stopped her."

Pinto's jaw dropped, his brows furrowed. He had already suspected Vell's attempted murder, but hearing Keiyo say the truth aloud left his arms covered in goosebumps. *Why would Vell try to kill her own unit leader?*

"Professor, you look pale," Ogga noted.

"I'm just..." Pinto hesitated. "I'm thinking of what Vell said after Yahshi stopped her. She mentioned something about a broken promise."

Ogga and Embre made eye contact.

"The accomplice," Embre whispered, and Ogga nodded. Pinto recalled the meeting about Yahshi's getaway, and how he had been planning to leave with a girl who matched Vell's description.

Is it really true? Pinto wondered. *Did she know about his plan to leave and keep it from me? Did she lie to me that night on the beach, after we burned the Meridian book, when she held my hand by the burning pages?*

"I asked about the promise," Pinto muttered, more to himself than to Ogga. "That's when they stole two horses from the vault and headed north."

"Did you go after them?" Ogga asked.

"Of course I did." Pinto's words came out sharper than intended. "I couldn't reach them on foot, so I tried to shoot their horses down before they could get far. Unfortunately, I missed."

"That's when Quax started taking his anger out on Pinto," Keiyo added, rushing to move the story along. "Meanwhile, I tried to help Commander Cal, and Professor Famir's operative unit arrived a few minutes later."

"There's just one problem with your story, boys." Ogga went quiet, as though giving them a last chance to correct their mistakes.

Something about being referred to as a *boy* instead of a *professor* sent a shiver down Pinto's spine.

"Professor Pinto," Ogga finally continued, breaking the silence, "I've heard that people with missing senses compensate in other areas. Such as the deaf being more in tune with their vision. One could argue that losing your right eye has made your left one stronger."

"I suppose that's plausible," Pinto replied.

"It tracks with what the Academy guardians have told me. They say you're a natural with the bow."

"It's true," Embre said as she wrote.

Pinto pursed his lips, unsure of where Ogga was going with this.

"I have a hard time believing that you didn't land a single shot at Yahshi and Vell—or their horses," the redhead revealed.

Pinto nearly gasped. "I may have an easy time with a bow, Professor, but I was under a lot of stress, and they were using a formation—weaving between trees."

"You see, I might have believed you, had you actually tried. But according to Professor Famir, the quiver he confiscated from you was missing five arrows—one that hit Commander Cal's neck, and just four from your attempts to shoot Yahshi and Vell. Why is it that you gave up so quickly?"

The room went cold as Pinto stared at the redhead, stone-faced. Ogga had backed him into a corner—he couldn't skirt the truth when his interrogator already smelled something amiss.

His heart struck his chest with fury. *If I don't tell him that Keiyo tackled me, I'll be the only guardian to blame for the special operation's failure. Professor Ogga will think that I allowed Yahshi and Vell to get away on purpose—or even worse, that I was working in cahoots with them.*

Ogga leaned in. "Spit it out, Professor."

It was only now that Pinto understood the advice Galler had given him in the stable. If he were to lie, he could end up getting killed or sent to correction—all to protect Keiyo from the consequences of his own actions.

Pinto turned to Keiyo, guilt sinking its claws into his face.

Keiyo's jaw stiffened, his gaze sharp. It seemed he heard Pinto's silent apology loud and clear.

Pinto faced Ogga, forcing the words out. "Keiyo tackled me before I could shoot any more arrows. He helped them escape."

"That's not true," Keiyo snapped. "I was trying to cut the last horse free from the vault when *he* tackled *me*."

Pinto scoffed. He could understand Keiyo's desperation to protect himself, but to lie to the Force about what Pinto had done was unacceptable.

"He's the one lying." Pinto raised his voice. "If I wanted to help them get away, why would I have shot any arrows at all?"

Ogga looked back and forth between Pinto and Keiyo, his gaze struggling to settle on either of them. It was Pinto's word against Keiyo's, and he realized that for Ogga to believe him over his fellow graduate, he needed more evidence.

"There's more," Pinto said.

Keiyo nudged his boot under the table, warning him to keep quiet, but Pinto ignored him.

"I know how Yahshi broke into the Investigation Office. He stole my key and had Keiyo duplicate it, that way he could put the original back in place before I'd notice."

Keiyo's face reddened as an angry chuckle escaped him. "Are you kidding me? There's no way I'd help Yahshi steal files from the archives. That's ridiculous!"

Ogga frowned at Keiyo. "How do you know this, Professor Pinto?"

"Keiyo seemed angry about something after the Bayin files went missing," Pinto said, his voice shaky. "I already had my suspicions, but after Yahshi went missing, Keiyo thanked me for not telling anyone about *the key*. That's when I knew for certain."

"Oh, shut it," Keiyo spat, facing Pinto with a jerk of his head. "Even if I duplicated that key—which I *didn't*—there's no way I'd openly confess to you."

"So you're saying that you'd keep your treasonous activity a secret?" Ogga asked.

"That's not at all what I'm saying!" Keiyo argued. "Plus, even if Pinto's claim is true—which again, it's *not*—shouldn't you be mad at *him* for keeping the same secret? For knowing I duplicated the key but not telling anyone about it?"

"Drop the act, Keiyo," Ogga said, his voice stern. "Lying in an official interrogation will only make the consequences worse for you."

He sprang to his feet. "Pinto's the one who killed a guardian!"

"You're losing restraint," Ogga warned.

"If you want the truth—*fine*." Keiyo leaned over the table. His voice was quieter and deeper now, but it somehow sounded as though he'd lost *more* control of himself. "I *did* duplicate that key, but only because Yahshi tricked me into it. I didn't confess because I knew how it'd look, and Pinto didn't report me because he trusted me. We're both equally guilty for keeping that secret, so why am *I* to blame for all of it? And at the end of the day, I tackled Pinto for the same reason he hesitated to follow Commander Cal's order— we're all fellow graduates, and we care about each other, just like you said."

Ogga smiled, as though he'd found the missing piece to his puzzle. "*You're* to blame, because you're the one who lied to me." He gestured to the metal door. "Professor Pinto, you're free to leave."

"That's not fair," Keiyo said through gritted teeth.

Pinto struggled to stand, the weight of Keiyo's rage pulling him down. He was right that they both deserved at least *some* blame. *Why did Ogga need to pit us against each other like this?*

"You've been dismissed," Embre said, urging him to comply.

As Pinto stood, Keiyo's hand caught his wrist, pulling him back down. He gripped Pinto by the shoulders and forced him to make eye contact, muttering, "I'll never forgive you for this."

"Let him go," Ogga demanded.

Keiyo shoved Pinto aside, sending him and his chair to the floor. The wooden legs cracked as Pinto's face hit the stone. He rolled onto his back, his cheek throbbing, his vision blurry. He caught a brief glimpse of Keiyo charging after him before he disappeared from view—Ogga had snatched him from behind, pulling him back.

Pinto staggered to his feet, the room spinning, almost throwing him down again. He ran for the exit, glancing back once to see Keiyo thrashing in Ogga's grip.

With a gasp, he fled into the corridor and slammed the door behind him. His breath came in rapid pants as he leaned against the wall, the floor falling under his feet, the torches spinning into blurs of light. All he could hear was the crackling of fire and the screams of his fellow graduate, muffled through the metal door.

As Pinto rode to the Complex on horseback, Keiyo's words echoed in his head.

"I'll never forgive you for this."

Surely he couldn't mean that. Had Keiyo been in Pinto's shoes, he would've made the same choice. Whatever the consequences for his fellow graduate, Pinto hoped he'd understand that he never intended for him to suffer. He had only followed Galler's advice and put himself first.

I'll talk to him later, Pinto decided. *He'll understand that I didn't have a choice.*

The abandoned Complex ahead pulled him from his thoughts. The crowd of guardians out front had vanished, and not a single silhouette appeared in the windows of over one hundred guardian flats. He dismounted his horse and swung open the stable door to find nearly every stall empty.

Where is everyone?

The sound of laughter lured Pinto back outside. Three guardians with Medical badges on their shoulders walked down the road that lined the Complex, chatting together. He mounted his horse again and trotted to catch up.

They halted, their smiles fading upon his approach.

Pinto stopped his horse beside them and peered down at the identical golden tickets in their hands. "What are those for?"

The guardians looked at each other, silently deciding who would answer. Eventually, one of them said, "An Office meeting."

"When?"

"Soon," another said, and Pinto frowned.

"*Soon* isn't a time."

"It's not mandatory," said the third—a horrible liar.

Pinto whipped the reins and galloped to the Investigation Office. Horses occupied every stall in the stable—guardians had even tied a few to extra posts nearby. With the special operation now at a close, the Force had likely called a meeting to plan their next steps.

Pinto secured his horse to a post and rushed to join a group of guardians heading up the front steps to the Office.

Roz slowed, his steps falling in sync with him. "You're not supposed to be here."

Only then did Pinto realize why the three doctors near the Complex had lied to him.

"I'm not invited?" he asked as they entered the common room. "But I was there when everything happened."

"That's exactly why you need time off."

Pinto stopped, his jaw dropping. Despite his attempt to cue a conversation, Roz continued toward the staircase, leaving him behind.

Pinto rushed to catch up and lowered his voice. "So you expect us to be strong at the Academy, but the moment we face a problem as a guardian, you want us to cry about it?"

"It wasn't my call, Pinto."

"Commander!"

Roz stopped before entering the staircase, looking back at Pinto with an impatient glare.

Pinto gulped, remembering the claim Roz had made in Watchtower 5. *"Wake up, Pinto. You don't know him as well as you believe. Even if the Defense Division votes in favor of the pardon tomorrow, he won't accept it."*

While Pinto hadn't believed Roz, he had turned out to be right.

"Do you really believe Yahshi was a spy, all this time?" Pinto asked.

Roz stared back, and despite his blank expression, Pinto could tell he was thinking. He normally didn't hesitate to reply.

"I believe his *father* was a spy," Roz finally answered. "And if there's one thing I've learned from my time in service, Pinto, it's that insanity spreads like the plague. One rotten apple can spoil the whole bunch, but if you remove that spoiled one in time, the others can be saved." He spoke in cryptic words that wouldn't alarm the guardians passing by, but Pinto grasped what he really meant.

Martu had been the rotten apple, feeding his son propaganda about the Force. Even if it meant breaking Protocol, Roz had killed him to save Yahshi, the boy he had always seen promise in. He didn't want him to go bad.

Roz smiled, sensing that Pinto understood his choice. Then he turned up the staircase—and just as Pinto tried to follow again, someone else clutched his arm.

"Shadow!" Famir yelled, dragging him aside.

Pinto tugged himself free. "I'm not your shadow anymore," he snapped. It felt nice to finally say it.

Famir's tone sharpened. "I know you're upset about your exclusion from this meeting, but that's no excuse for sneaking in and mouthing off to your superiors."

Pinto's gaze hardened. "I'm the Force's best chance of finding them, and you know it."

"You have too many emotions tied to this case. Your involvement would destroy you."

"I bet Quax is here, though."

"No, he's still at Thornwick Hospital, with the doctors you and Commander Evaris sent back." Famir took a deep breath before reaching into his pocket and pulling out a golden ticket. "I think it's best if you take some time off service."

Pinto snatched the ticket from his unit leader's outstretched hand. *Respite Granted for the Preservation of Morale*, it read. *Valid until granted clearance to return to service.*

"Why does it say *Respite Granted*?" Pinto scoffed. "You can't grant something that was never requested!"

"Shadow…"

"And why doesn't it have a date for returning to service? Do you expect me to move east while I'm at it? Become a farmer? Grow out my hair?"

"You'll return to service when you're ready."

"And who decides that?"

"Commander Evaris."

Pinto took a step away, rubbing his temple. "You're giving me a babysitter?"

"Listen," Famir said, his voice calmer now, "you're lucky the Force trusts you enough to spare you from correctional meetings. The least you can do is allow Commander Evaris to oversee your progress and help you move on."

Pinto scowled at him.

"And once you do," Famir continued, leaning in, "we'll have a spot for you at the table."

Pinto returned to the desolate Guardian Complex and shut himself away in his flat. For the first time since the special operation had begun, he was completely alone.

More alone than he'd ever been.

He flung off his boots and overcoat, the pockets nearly empty except for duplicate keys and *The Guardian Handbook*. Quickly, he unstrapped his armored vest and kicked it aside, then loosened the top buttons of his shirt. Flopping backward onto his bed, he stared up at the ceiling, his eye tracing the four-petaled flower designs.

Without his overcoat, his vest, and his tools, he didn't feel like a professor anymore. He felt like a boy—the same boy who had spent eighteen months with Yahshi and Vell at the Academy, laughing at silly jokes they'd never again share. He covered his mouth with his palm, fighting off tears. They had hurt him, but amidst the pain of losing them, he still wanted their comfort—their friendship. He knew of no one to turn to but the very people who had ruined him.

He couldn't help but wish that he had done something differently. Maybe if he had been a better friend—more open about his feelings—they would have trusted him more. They might have confided in him about whatever was going on, and he could have talked sense into them to prevent this disaster. Everything could have turned out okay. He would be suffering over some other irrelevant drama, like a more unfit professor getting promoted first, and they would have been here to comfort him. He would not be in his flat alone, tracing the petals on his ceiling because he knew of no other way to calm himself.

Someone knocked on the door, interrupting his train of thought. It took him a moment to gather himself before asking, "Who is it?"

He wished he had waited longer to speak, because his voice came out shakily. Pathetically. *No wonder the guardians don't want me in service. I really have lost my restraint.*

The person at the door knocked again instead of answering him. He tried to push himself out of bed, but his body seemed to double in weight, forcing him back down. It took all of his energy to finally stand, and once he did, his vision tilted. He placed a hand against the wall to balance himself and rubbed his face—despite having not cried, he was paranoid it looked like he had. With a glance in the mirror, he brushed some curls back into place, took a deep breath, and opened the door.

It was Evaris. His blood simmered as he slammed the door.

Her palm blocked it from closing, just in time. "Are you okay?"

"I'm fine," he said, his jaw tense as he tried to overpower her.

"Here's the thing, Red..." Evaris said, her voice tense as she fought to keep the door open. "I don't believe you."

Pinto's grip on the door loosened, and through the gap, he finally looked her in the eye. He knew her empathy was nothing but an act. Famir had ordered her to look after him yesterday, to keep him under control, and it was no different now.

"Hey," Evaris said, her voice softer, "can I come in?"

Pinto stared at her for a while. He wasn't sure how long. It was stupid of him—he knew that—but he wanted to pretend that she had lied to him yesterday because she wanted to cheer him up, that she had gone to the archives because she wanted to help him research, and that she hadn't woken him up because she wanted him to go into his interrogation with a well-rested mind.

He chose to believe that she had agreed to oversee his progress because she *wanted* to.

Pinto stepped aside, allowing Evaris into his flat. In a single, fluid motion, she closed the door behind her and wrapped her arms around him.

He was silent, his breaths shallow, as he leaned into her. But then the reality of their positions and his responsibilities snuck up on him again, and the warmth of her embrace felt criminal. He shouldn't have indulged in the lie that she cared for him, or saw him as anything other than a work assignment.

"Evaris," he muttered, pulling away. "You should—"

She stopped him with a gentle squeeze, pulling him closer to whisper, "I could be your friend."

Pinto's eye watered, and his thoughts finally quieted. He raised his arms, hugging her back.

As they stood there, by the door to his flat, breathing into each other's ears, he wondered if Evaris had a friend herself.

CHAPTER 13

THORNY ROSES

Craving homemade cookies?
Grab a bag of baking flour at your local Saver Store!

♫ SET FREE - KATIE GRAY ♫

Evaris marched down the hallway, her boots clicking the concrete floor with every step. Most students had already made it to their classes, but the few who lingered behind froze to gawk at her uniform.

Ignoring them, Evaris stopped at a jammed door and fiddled with its rusty handle. It took some wiggling and a bit of force to pop it open.

Whispers filled the classroom as she entered, students turning in their seats to face her. A handful of them smiled too, and she forced herself to return the gesture. In Vakoi City, where she'd grown up, people lived amongst the Force and the Royal Family, so while they respected the guardians, they never saw them as *other*. Not like people in towns like Sitra.

Envy and admiration? Her eyes trailed over the star-struck secondary students. *That's new.*

A woman by the blackboard cleared her throat. "Good morning, Commander."

"I'm here for Alora Valentine," Evaris announced, skipping the small talk.

More whispers. Eyes jumped from the guardian to a girl in the middle of the room, who had her hair tied back in a single braid. Like her classmates, she wore khaki pants and a sage green shirt—both oversized. The school uniform was so casual compared to the one Evaris had worn back in Vakoi City Secondary that the designer's daughter in her nearly felt sorry for Alora.

The girl stood slowly, ignoring her classmates' gossip as she packed her book bag.

"What if they're selecting her late?"

"I heard they need replacements for Yahshi and Commander Vell."

"But the Academy's not in session. How would she train?"

Clutching her book bag at her side, Alora rushed to Evaris, who held the door open for her. She followed the girl out, chuckling as she shoved the door back into a closed position.

As they walked to the school office, Evaris could hear how tense Alora was through her heavy, uneven footsteps. While she might have shared the same uniform as her classmates, she didn't seem to share their sense of admiration for Evaris.

Strange. She opened the office door and gestured for Alora to enter first.

The final-year student walked in, halting at the sight of a guardian sitting at a desk. Evaris could understand why Pinto's eyepatch, especially paired with his uniform, made him look intimidating even without his confiscated bow.

Evaris shook her head. She had urged him to take advantage of his respite by purchasing some interesting clothes in Vakoi City—guardians could rarely dress out of uniform—but he clung to his disarmed overcoat like a lifeline.

After a brief pause, Alora gulped and crossed the room, taking a seat at the desk. Evaris closed the door behind her and followed, dragging an extra chair to Pinto's side, where she sat facing Alora.

"Can we make this quick, Commander?" Pinto asked, his eye on Yahshi's ex-classmate.

"You can brood after we're done here." Evaris handed him a notebook from her overcoat, but Pinto didn't take it. She leaned in to whisper, "The sooner you finish your assigned meetings, the sooner I can clear you to get back to work."

"How many meetings?"

"Three."

"Can we finish them all today?"

Evaris chuckled. "Trust me. You wouldn't want to."

Pinto flared his nostrils and snatched the notebook. After grabbing a stray pen, he flipped loudly to the first empty page, making Alora flinch as he prepared to transcribe the meeting.

She looked back and forth between them, her breath hitching, her face pale.

The poor thing is terrified. Evaris took a deep breath, making a conscious effort to soften her voice. "I'm Evaris Starfall of Vakoi City, and this is Professor Pinto Dempsey of Frontal, a fellow graduate of Yahshi's. We recently discovered that you were a friend of his."

"He's dead?" Alora asked.

Pinto frowned as he transcribed her question.

"You're talking about him like he's dead," she added.

"He's not dead, but he will be." Evaris pulled three pouches out of her pocket and plopped them in front of Alora, who froze at the sound of clinking coins. "Go ahead. Open them."

After shooting Pinto a cautious glance, Alora opened a pouch and pulled out a handful of gold.

"Fifteen hundred coins," Evaris stated. The money could temporarily ease her financial stress, considering how Alora's father, recently unemployed, had been struggling to find work. Famir had given Evaris a full run-down on the Valentines' situation earlier that morning.

"My family doesn't take charity," Alora muttered, dropping the coins back into the bag.

"Then consider it financial aid for your apprenticeship."

Alora looked up from the bag of coins, her brows knitting together. "Apprenticeship?"

"You're top of the class, so you've earned yourself a break." Evaris offered four envelopes addressed to a man named Marin Sorvak from Alora Valentine. "The Force is offering you an apprenticeship with the cartographer in Miranda you've been harassing by mail."

"You intercepted my letters?"

"According to the postal officer, Marin refused to take them. With the best students at Miranda Secondary fighting to work under his wing, why consider students from Sitra, with its track record of low scores and violence?"

Alora's eyes drifted somewhere else, a solemn haze marking her face.

"But we can ensure that spot is yours despite that," Evaris continued. "And we can throw in the money as part of the deal. Your family won't even know about this conversation."

Her eyes sharpened again, and Evaris smiled, knowing she'd finally earned her consideration. Working as a cartographer required significant trust from the Vakoi Empire, given the sensitive nature of the work. It involved unrestricted travel past the border to map trade routes from Eastern production points to Western Saver Stores. Such freedom was limited to trusted individuals who had trained under Empire-approved mentors like Marin.

With a sigh, Alora faced Evaris again. "What do you want from me?"

"Now that's the spirit." Evaris leaned in, propping her chin up on her fist. "Considering how you were friends with Yahshi, we're hoping you could tell us what he was like before joining the Academy."

"Well, we weren't exactly friends. We hardly spoke in the couple years leading up to his selection."

"Why's that?"

Alora's mouth opened, but she stopped herself from speaking. Her eyes darted to Pinto, then to the coin pouches in front of her. "What are you planning to do with this information?"

Evaris could read her like a book. "I understand that you want to protect him, Alora. Let's make this easier for you."

She stiffened at the sound of her name.

"I'm sure you know that Yahshi will face harsh consequences once we trace him. Nothing you say can save or harm him," Evaris explained. "His fate is sealed. He's already dug his own grave."

"Then why are you here?"

"It's strictly a personal matter." Evaris nudged Pinto's arm, and his pen splattered ink across his notebook page. "Help me out here, Red."

Pinto gritted his teeth as he looked up, meeting Alora's gaze. "I need to know," he said, his voice breaking, "if the best friend I met in the program was real."

A few hours after returning from Sitra, waves washed over the island's west coast, brewing fizzy bubbles under the glow of the setting sun. With Yahshi's files in hand, Evaris trudged along the vacant beach, her boots sinking into the sand with every step. She hadn't seen the gentle tides near Vakoi City since her last visit to her great aunt Cove's cabin. *Back when I disappointed her with my dark, boring clothes—before the Force gave me a heavy uniform that disappointed her even more.*

According to the Princess, Cove was dying, but she was still in her sixties—how could that be? An illness? An accident? Considering she didn't live too far from this beach, Evaris could easily break the rules and stop by without a visitation right to find out for certain.

She shook her head, memories of Cove's disapproval squandering her curiosity. She could never forget her great aunt's sharp words when she'd chosen the Force's training over playing with needles and colorful threads.

"You'll regret this, Evaris."

As the most successful designer among the Starfalls, Cove's disappointment spread like the plague. That same pit in her stomach returned as she recalled sitting at the table over supper, ignoring her parents as they brought Cove's judgment into their own home.

"We're going to Pandora's Ball," her mother had said. *"Go put on a dress."*

"Can't have you upsetting Aunt Cove in public and making a scene," added her father.

Vakoi City's flamboyance had never suited Evaris. It was too grand and theatrical. She much preferred the Force's muted colors, and the simplicity of owning just one piece of formal wear. In the Force, her fellow guardians never judged her for requesting a simple red dress without the bells and whistles expected of the Starfalls.

She shivered as a chilly wind whipped her hair, snapping her out of her daze. It all came back to her now—she had come to the beach to find someone, not to mope. There was something frustratingly trance-like about the ocean.

When Evaris spotted a dot of scarlet in the distance, she quickened her pace until the dot grew into the head of a red-haired professor. Ogga sat under the shade of the forest that separated the beach from the bustling City center, a bottle of beer in hand, his eyes on the horizon with a few books scattered on the surrounding sand.

"Professor Ogga," Evaris addressed him, halting by his side. "I was told to return these to you." She leaned over, holding out Yahshi's selection file, which Famir had given her that morning.

Ogga didn't even look at it. He took another swig of beer. "Come sit with me."

Evaris straightened and frowned. She had not come here expecting a conversation, nor did she want one, but she took a seat beside him nonetheless. He was her superior. What else could she do?

"I don't really need that file." Ogga jammed his beer bottle into the sand to hold it upright and leaned back, propping himself up with his palms. His eyes reflected the waves, tinted with a hint of red. They seemed more violent now, crashing against the shore with a fury. "You can ask Boa to store it in the archives for you."

She refused to beat around the bush. "Then why am I here, Professor?"

He chuckled and finally met her gaze. "I'm curious how the one-eyed guardian handled his first assignment."

Evaris thought back to the story Yahshi's former classmate had shared about his downward spiral after Chima's murder. According to Alora, he couldn't understand why the guardians selected Cal for the Academy instead of punishing her for killing a fellow student—even if she'd done it to protect her little brother. In response, Yahshi began collecting and studying *Capital Weekly* articles, desperate to make sense of Cal, the Force, and her selection. His grades and social life crumbled under the weight of his obsession.

"Pinto thought she was lying—said that if Yahshi distrusted the Force so much, they wouldn't have selected him." She peered down at the file, which outlined why the Academy guardians had chosen him anyway—if they could win his trust, they could harness his all-consuming drive *for* the Force rather than against it. "So I showed him this file to confirm Alora's story, but I'm worried he's more confused now than before."

Ogga pointed at her. "That's exactly what he needs. If we confuse him enough, he'll give up on trying to understand them. He'll finally move on, and the sooner the better. We can't let the whole bunch go bad."

Evaris raised her brows.

"Yahshi and Vell are traitors, Quax is an emotional wreck, and Keiyo has proven to be an unexpected difficulty," Ogga said. "If we lose Pinto too, the entire graduating class will have been a waste. People are already second-guessing our judgment. We can't afford another mistake."

Evaris sat in silence for a while, listening to the waves. She couldn't be sure whether Ogga's strategy to *fix* Pinto was the right move.

"You can go now." Ogga pushed himself upright and pulled his bottle out of the sand. "I'm not holding you hostage here."

Evaris stood, taking Yahshi's file with her, and turned to leave.

"Oh, and Commander."

She halted but didn't look back.

"The two of you should dress in your formal wear tomorrow. It shows more humanity than a uniform, and people absolutely adore that."

"Yes, Professor."

"And bring some roses too. It's hard to say no to pretty things."

Pinto stood on the front deck of a modest home, scowling at his red roses. "Isn't this a bit much?" he asked in a hushed voice, pointing his bouquet at the door. "Compared to them, I'm sure we're brutally overdressed."

"Overdressing shows that we care." Evaris tucked her hands into her leather jacket and leaned toward him. "It's a sensitive time right now, okay? They can either blame the Underground or blame the Force. But if we show up with pretty roses, who do you think they'll side with?"

Pinto winced as a trail of blood dripped down his thumb. "You didn't cut off the thorns?"

Evaris tilted her head. "Is that something you're supposed to do?"

He wiped the blood on his blazer. "You're lucky I'm wearing red. It blends right in."

She chuckled and stepped past him, raising her arm to knock, but Pinto grabbed her wrist.

"Commander," he warned, his gaze sharpening as he released her. "I can't do this."

"It's just like I said. You couldn't have completed all three assignments yesterday. Just wait 'til you see who's next."

"Can you be serious? Just for a minute?" Pinto's eye darted to the front door, and he lowered his voice to a whisper. "This is wrong. How could we lie to them like this?"

Evaris's smile faded. She'd known as soon as Famir had laid out the details that Pinto would hate every aspect of his second assignment. Vell was not dead to him, but for Pinto to be welcomed back into the Force, she needed to be.

"Once we find her, you know what happens next, right?"

"Of course I do," Pinto muttered, "but—"

"You're not getting her back. If you want to regain the Force's trust, you need to prove that you've accepted that. You need to let yourself grieve."

"Grieve?" His jaw dropped, and with a scoff, he raised his arm. "Fine. I'll do it. It's not like I have a choice."

Evaris cringed as he pounded on the front door, gripping his bouquet as if it were a dagger.

"Calm down," she warned.

He stepped back, his grip relaxing slightly before a woman with bloodshot eyes appeared in the doorway. Evaris peered past the woman to see two young girls and an older boy huddled at the far end of the room, accompanied by their father. They stared back at Evaris with wide eyes.

Evaris subtly nudged Pinto's arm, and he cleared his throat.

"Good morning, Mrs. Patura. I'm Pinto Dempsey of Frontal, a friend of your daughter's."

Vell's mother studied the patch over Pinto's eye as she took the bouquet from his outstretched arm. A thorn pricked her when she grabbed them, but she didn't make a sound.

"Sorry!" Pinto exclaimed, freezing as a droplet of blood trailed down the woman's finger. By the panic in his voice, Evaris could tell he was sorry for much more. She grabbed the handkerchief from his breast pocket and offered it to Vell's mother, since he was too shaken to do it himself.

"It's *my* fault, Mrs. Patura," Evaris said. "I should have removed the thorns."

"Oh, I don't mind them," she choked out, wiping her finger clean with the handkerchief. "Roses have thorns for a reason—keeps the danger away."

Evaris smiled and offered her hand. "I'm Evaris Starfall of Vakoi City. While I didn't have the privilege of knowing Vell personally, I've only heard the best about her from my fellow guardians."

Vell's mother smiled weakly and shook her hand. "Please, come in."

Evaris had conducted a few damage control trips like this before, as the Force actively worked to console those grieving the shocking deaths of loved ones. However, she had never visited a family whose loved one had been a guardian. She had worried the Paturas would blame the Force for not protecting Vell during the special operation, but it seemed they had already pinpointed the cause of their daughter's *death*. Just as *Capital Weekly* urged readers to believe, the Belladonna Traitor was solely to blame.

Mr. and Mrs. Patura sat Evaris and Pinto at a mahogany table with Vell's siblings while they brewed a pot of tea, prepared a glass platter of cookies, and found a vase for Pinto's thorny roses. Evaris couldn't help but notice the sharp contrast to the few times she had visited her own parents in Vakoi City. *I land the most competitive job in the Empire, and the Starfalls see me as a disappointment.*

When Vell's parents finished, they joined the table, bringing with them the hot pot of tea and the glass platter of cookies. The youngest daughter volunteered to fill everyone's cups, and her little hands shook as she set one in front of Evaris.

The room fell painfully quiet. The only sounds were that of pouring tea, breathing, and Pinto's foot tapping the floor repeatedly. Evaris kicked his boot under the table, urging him to settle down, but all he did was replace his tapping with nail-biting. The last thing the Paturas needed was to grow suspicious of the story published in *Capital Weekly*. For their own sakes, they needed to believe that Vell had died at the hands of the Underground rebels who had tried to prevent Yahshi's capture, so Evaris broke the silence herself.

"We're truly sorry for your loss," she said. "The entire Force is in a state of disbelief. I can't even imagine what you're feeling."

The youngest girl handed a cup to her father last, who took it with a tight grip. His eyes shimmered, his lips twitching as though he wanted to say something, but couldn't.

"She's—uhh—" The words hitched in Pinto's throat, so he paused to inhale a shaky breath. "She was one of my best friends. If it weren't for her help, I wouldn't have graduated. I wouldn't be wearing this uniform."

Pinto's confession seemed to lure the words out of Vell's father. "What was she like at the Academy?" the man asked, his voice hoarse.

Pinto gulped, looking around at the different family members, who stared back at him with wide eyes. He was silent for longer than comfortable, and Evaris couldn't fathom the pressure he felt to find the right combination of words to lessen their pain.

"Well, she—she missed all of you a lot."

The Paturas continued staring, awaiting more.

Pinto took a sip of tea, trying to buy himself time to think of more to say.

Now it was Evaris tapping her foot. *You can do this, Red.*

"One night," he muttered, staring at the tea in his cup, "Vell broke under the pressure and cut her hair. She was worried she couldn't handle the Academy, and that's when she told me why she needed to win." Pinto looked over at Vell's mother, his voice strengthening. "She was fighting for *you.*"

"She was always fighting for me, more than a child should." Vell's mother smiled, a glaze of sadness in her eyes. "I don't know if she told you this, but before I got sick, I worked as a botanist. My knowledge always seemed to fascinate her. She would bring plants back from the woods, just so I could identify them and discuss their properties. Her obsession only grew stronger once I fell sick. She pretended like she was studying plants for fun, but I knew she was doing it for me, hoping she could help me get better." She met her husband's gaze. "Even when we judged her unfairly, she never stopped fighting for us. Everything she did—it was always for our family."

Evaris reached for a sugar cookie and took a bite. It was stale, probably a few days too old.

"I suppose that explains how she understood belladonna so quickly," Pinto said. "In the program, we were served beet juice with our lunch every day, and sometimes it was laced with the plant's toxins to build our tolerance to it. My body had a hard time with that, so Vell was clever enough to lace my beet juice with belladonna on the days it wasn't served. She somehow knew the perfect dosage to help me adjust."

Evaris gulped down her hot tea to wash the crumbs stuck to the roof of her mouth. Once again, she found herself surprised that Pinto had broken the rules—surely the Academy guardians would not have allowed Vell to lace his juice with serum.

"That sounds like her," Vell's father said. "She was always good at math."

"When it comes to medicine, a poorly calculated dose can be fatal." Vell's mother smiled to herself. "If she weren't good at math, I wouldn't have let her administer potential remedies to me."

"Belladonna," the older daughter said, speaking up for the first time. "Big Sister studied that one a lot."

Pinto raised his brows at her. "What?"

Her mother chuckled awkwardly. "No, sweetie, you're confusing that with *buddleia*. Of course she didn't study belladonna." She turned to Evaris and Pinto with a strangely wide smile. "Her siblings didn't exactly get *the itch for plants*, as I like to call it."

"Nerds, those two," her husband chimed in.

Evaris nibbled on stale cookies as Pinto spoke with the Paturas for about an hour longer, exchanging stories about a dead girl who wasn't actually dead. Pinto seemed to come out of his shell as he shared the challenges he and Vell faced at the Academy, conveniently leaving Yahshi out of every story. For all the Paturas knew, it might as well have just been the two of them.

"Was she your girlfriend?" Vell's teen brother asked.

"Of course not," Pinto snapped, his cheeks reddening.

The boy laughed, as though he weren't convinced, and Evaris found herself wondering if something might have been going on between them after all. She had heard rumors of guardians breaking *that* Vow before—going to parties and mysteriously not returning to their flats for the night, or getting caught pressing their faces against famous Pandora's Box actors during afterparties.

Evaris had never believed the rumors to be true until a few months after Cal's promotion, during an expedition into Eastern Territory. She was nineteen at the time, and Galler, at twenty-four, should have known better. While Cal drove, they sat alone in the vault, and he slid closer until their thighs touched. Naturally, Evaris scooted away, thinking it must have been an accident, but the guilty look on his face suggested otherwise.

Since he never tried anything like that with her again, she kept silent. It was something else entirely—something she only heard whispers of—that landed Galler in correction a few months later.

"I'll walk you out," Vell's mother offered once the time came to leave. She waited until they reached the door, and were out of her family's sight, before leaning toward Pinto with eyes even sharper than thorns. "Please, Professor. I beg you to find... *him*, and make him pay."

It took Evaris a second to realize that she was referring to Yahshi Konya. The poor woman couldn't even say his name.

Just a few minutes on horseback from the Patura household, Pinto and Evaris strolled down the aisles of Miranda's local Saver Store. Preserved food, packaged coal, firewood, and other home essentials imported from production points in Eastern Territory overflowed shelves that stretched from the dusty concrete floor to the ceiling.

After passing a few sneezing customers—who seemed to inhabit every Saver Store—they turned a corner to enter an aisle stocked with canned beans. Each featured a classic yellow label with scarlet text that read, *Saver*

Store: Live for Less!

Evaris plucked one from the shelf, chuckling at the label's stamped image of smiling beans with arms and legs. She'd always found Saver Stores ugly in a respectable kind of way. They weren't trying to be anything else.

Pinto eyed his dress shoes as they walked. "Are we here for my last assignment?"

"No." Evaris slipped the can of kidney beans into an empty spot on the shelf. "That's tomorrow morning."

"Who am I meeting with?"

"You'll find out *tomorrow morning.*"

Pinto scoffed and kicked a stray stone on the floor, rooting up a little cloud of dust. In an eerily fast manner, an employee in a yellow jumpsuit arrived to sweep the area, offering a quick, "Apologies for the mess, guardian, sir!" before fleeing the scene.

Pinto peered down at his formal wear. "How does he know I'm a guardian?"

Evaris gestured around. "Do you see anyone else dressed for a ballroom here?"

His lips twitched upward a bit, but then he seemed to force a frown. He crossed his arms and raised his head. "If not for an assignment, then why are we here?"

She shrugged. "I've made a habit of visiting Saver Stores whenever I have the chance. They're much more fascinating than the tiny convenience stores I grew up around in the City."

"I shopped at Saver Stores all the time growing up." Pinto scoffed as they entered another aisle stocked with bottled oil and matchboxes. "Trust me, they're nothing special."

"You should appreciate them more. They're your livelihood."

"I know they fund the Force. Doesn't mean I need to worship their yellow labels."

They turned a corner into a new aisle. Evaris swerved as they walked, pretending to observe the stocked goods.

"How are you feeling?"

"Better." Pinto had said the word so quickly that she almost missed it.

Evaris turned her head slightly away, releasing a soft sigh of relief. She didn't want to think of what would happen to Pinto if the Force's plan to help him move on didn't work.

"I think I get it now." He looked around, ensuring there were no shoppers nearby, and leaned toward her to whisper, "If we told the Paturas the truth, we'd crush them. Instead, we gave them closure."

Evaris nodded. "Handling external threats isn't our only job. We have to prevent internal ones too. That means keeping people happy. Making them feel safe."

"That sounds rather altruistic coming from you."

"I can care about people. I care about *you*, don't I?"

"Maybe. Hard to tell."

"I think I've proven that."

He tilted his head, thinking. "Maybe."

Evaris looked away, her face running hot. Ever since she'd escorted Pinto back from the special operation, she had done nothing but help him, but he clearly didn't appreciate it. *Why am I trying so hard to be nice to someone who wants nothing to do with me?*

Perhaps it was because Pinto was eighteen, just two years younger than herself, making him one of the few guardians close to her age. She had learned quickly after graduation how isolating it was to almost always be the youngest in the room. It was hard to make friends in the Force when superiors only saw her as a recent graduate, hardly more than a shadow—but maybe Pinto, now in her shoes, didn't hate the loneliness as much as she did.

"Sorry," he muttered. "I'm not trying to be rude, Commander. I just have a lot on my mind."

Evaris ran her hands along the shelf next to her, studying the labels as they walked. "What are you thinking about?"

"Buddleia."

She dropped her arm and faced him again. "What?"

"Mrs. Patura claimed that Vell studied buddleia, not belladonna." Pinto stopped, and Evaris followed suit, frowning. "Vell told me once that she only studied *medicinal* plants, which buddleia isn't. It doesn't have healing properties. It's just a bush that looks pretty. My little sister always loved them because their flowers attract butterflies."

"So... you think Vell studied belladonna illegally, before she joined the Academy?"

"It would explain why she had such a strong tolerance to it—prior exposure would have raised her baseline immunity." He paused for a moment. "Plus, she always dodged my questions about her knowledge. I remember once, I pressed her too hard for answers, and she snapped—said she knew about belladonna because she stumbled upon the information in a medical book."

"You bought that?"

"I trusted her," Pinto said, shaking his head. "Just like I trusted Yahshi."

Evaris raised a brow. Perhaps he was finally opening up to the idea that Yahshi wasn't the victim in the Force's story.

He leaned against a shelf. "I've been searching for some kind of explanation behind his behavior, and why Vell would join him, but now I only have *more* questions."

Evaris walked to his side of the aisle and leaned against the shelf too.

"All I can think about now are all the times they dodged my questions or came up with excuses that I stupidly believed." He hunched over and rubbed his temple. "I trusted them, but they never trusted me, and that's the only certainty I've found. They hid their pasts from me, and now it's like... it's like I don't even know who they are anymore. Maybe I never did."

Evaris inched toward him, but as soon as their shoulders touched, he stepped away.

She could hear her own heartbeat as her body stiffened. Of course Pinto wouldn't trust her. His best friends had betrayed him, and she was acting as though she could waltz in as a replacement. If he really wanted her comfort, he would have said something back when she'd hugged him in his flat and offered to be his friend, but he hadn't.

They stood in silence until Pinto cleared his throat. "Thanks for listening, Commander."

She faced him with a jolt of her head, her jaw tense. *Do you want my company or not?*

This time, it was Pinto who stepped closer, meeting her gaze. "If I can ask—what do *you* think about all of this?"

Evaris softened her gaze. She recalled her time at the Academy, and how much she had helped Cal, only to graduate and work for her with no appreciation in return.

"I think you're waking up to the truth, Red. As much as it hurts, it's better to cut your losses than to live in denial. Yahshi and Vell may have played you for a fool, but you don't have to let them fool you any longer."

Pinto broke eye contact, muttering, "I still miss them."

"That's okay. Don't fight it." Evaris rested her hand on his shoulder, squeezing it gently. "Longing is a part of grief. You need to miss them before you can let them go."

CHAPTER 14

MAKE ME LOSE

Hearty canned soup for your sick loved one—
now half-price at a Saver Store near you!

♫ ALL ALONE · DAVID O'DOWDA ♫

"This one's all yours, Red."

Pinto frowned as Evaris sat on the front steps of Vakoi City Hospital, her eyes locked on the horizon as the sun rose, tinting the clouds light pink and orange.

"You're not coming in?" She had accompanied him to Sitra Secondary two days prior, and had shared tea with him and the Paturas just yesterday.

Evaris pulled a novel out of her overcoat, her hands shaking as she turned to the first page. "I'll wait here," she mumbled.

"You know, there's a lobby inside. It's warmer in there."

Evaris looked up from the pages at him, her eyes sharp. She didn't need to speak for Pinto to know that he'd pushed her patience. As she turned back to her book, he shivered in the breeze and ascended the remaining steps alone.

Entering the Hospital reminded him of the morning after Yahshi's disappearance, when he'd rushed inside searching for Vell. Realizing that

190

she would never enter this building again made him feel as though he'd walked into the afterlife. The white walls and floors seemed to close in from all six directions, and he looked around frantically, almost expecting to see her rushing past him with a white briefcase.

"Hello? Professor?"

His focus locked on a woman in a golden gown who stood behind the front desk.

"I was informed of your assignment yesterday, and you've since been added to the patient's whitelist," the receptionist said, stepping out from behind the desk. "Please, follow me."

Pinto caught glimpses of different rooms as he followed her to the third floor. Vakoi City Hospital was brighter than the local one in Frontal where he received treatment after the raid. He still remembered the room his five-year-old self had lain in, the scent of alcohol, and the mold spots on the ceiling he'd complained to the medics about, only for them to laugh at how observant he was.

"You've got a sharp eye," one of them had said. It was the first time someone used the singular word *eye* in conversation with him. It made him cry—and although gauze packed the hollow, soaking up the blood, his socket still burned.

The receptionist stopped at a door, and through its little glass window, Pinto glimpsed Quax's gray eyes glaring back at him. Instead of his guardian uniform, he wore a plain shirt and pants topped with a white fur coat.

Was he granted respite too? Pinto gulped and stepped back. *How did he end up in the Hospital?*

He hadn't seen Quax since Famir's operative unit had arrived in the woods between Thornwick and Grimward to find him swinging his dual swords at the guardian whose arrow had pierced his sister. Pinto didn't want to think about what Quax would have done if Galler hadn't disarmed him in time.

The receptionist opened the door before he could theorize further, and Pinto's throat tightened at the realization that Quax wasn't a patient, but a fellow visitor. Lying in the bed next to him was his older sister, Cal Avarium. Her eyes were open, as alert as ever, tracking Pinto as he stepped deeper into the room.

It's your last assignment, Pinto told himself, taking another step forward. *Once you get through this, you can return to Professor Famir's unit and get back to work.*

The receptionist closed the door behind him, and he froze, his blood running cold. Could this be a trap? Is that why Evaris was waiting outside? Had the receptionist locked him in? Did Quax have a dagger hidden in his fur coat?

A voice in his head shouted, *Run! Get out of here!*

But Pinto stayed, because he deserved whatever was coming. He had selfishly assumed Cal dead for his own convenience. It was easier to prepare for her funeral than to prepare an apology.

As he racked his brain for the right words to express his remorse, he studied the white bandages around Cal's neck, covering the arrow wound. Apart from that, she looked healthy. The sickest thing about her wasn't her body, but the hospital gown that covered it. Without her guardian uniform, she looked like a normal twenty-year-old woman, not the Belladonna Prodigy.

She looks... fragile.

Pinto lost himself in a train of thought, questioning whether he should even feel remorse. After all, it was Vell who had made him injure Cal. She had redirected his arrow. It was *her* fault, wasn't it?

Finally, Quax stood from his chair, his head turned low, heavy lines marking his brow. "You're supposed to be blacklisted."

The calm coldness of his voice somehow frightened Pinto more than his shouting would have. He took a few steps away, his back hitting the door that he'd hardly walked away from.

Quax crossed the room and pressed a palm against Pinto's chest—he wasn't pinning him to the door, but it was certainly a threat to.

Pinto peered over Quax's shoulder, glimpsing Cal staring back at him before meeting Quax's gaze again. Despite the urge to stick up for himself, he didn't fight back. It was Vell who had injured Cal, but with her gone, Quax needed someone to blame, and he deserved one.

"Don't give me that look. Like you're doing me a favor." Quax's face reddened, his fingers curling until he had an unbreakable grip around the top of Pinto's armored vest. "I know you think Vell deserves the blame, but it was *your arrow*. If you didn't hesitate to follow orders, my sister wouldn't be here. It's *all* your fault, and just yours."

His eyes raged with a flame that even a million apologies couldn't extinguish, so Pinto tried to reason with him instead.

"You grew up with Yahshi, remember?" he said. "If you were ordered to kill him, you wouldn't have been so quick to do it either."

He knew instantly that he'd said the wrong thing, because Quax's expression darkened. He pried Pinto off the door and shoved him back against it.

"Yahshi and his father lied to me for years." Quax leaned in and spoke in a low, rumbly voice, baring his teeth with every word. "When kids teased him for being a convert, I stood up for him. But all this time, those bullies in Sitra were right—he *was* a false convert, and he couldn't be trusted. We gave him grace, and he shoved it in our faces. So no, Pinto, you're wrong. If my sister had ordered me to kill him, I wouldn't have wasted a second."

They both flinched when a glass cup struck the wall. Its shards scattered across the marble floor, and Pinto and Quax looked back at Cal. She reached for a notepad and pencil on her bedside and scribbled something down.

Pinto frowned as she turned the page to face them.

I ADDED HIM TO THE WHITELIST, BROTHER

Quax looked back at Pinto, hesitating before releasing his vest. "Why?" he asked.

She flipped to a new page, continued writing, and turned the notepad to face them again.

TAKE A WALK, GIVE US A MINUTE

Quax furrowed his upper lip in disgust as he pivoted, heading for the exit.

Pinto shuffled aside to give him way, and Quax shot him one last glare before leaving the room and slamming the door. His steps were so loud that Pinto could still hear him storming down the hallway from inside the hospital room.

At the sound of pencil meeting paper, Pinto looked back at Cal to see her leaned over, writing another message for him. The realization struck him that while his arrow hadn't killed her, it had taken away more than imaginable.

I CAN'T MOVE MY LEGS

MY VOICE IS GONE

I'M NO GUARDIAN ANYMORE

Pinto's eye watered. Maybe Quax had a point. If he had just acted faster, Cal wouldn't have lost her career. His hesitation had ruined the Belladonna Prodigy, and there was no way he could make it up to her.

"I'm so sorry, Commander." Pinto rushed to her bedside, his voice breaking as remorse sunk its teeth into his heart. "If I had known that Vell would interfere, I would have acted sooner. I would have killed him. I never intended for this to happen." However, despite his guilt, he struggled to believe his own words.

Cal stared back at him, her lips sealed.

"Y-You believe me, right?" Maybe if *she* believed him, he would too.

With a disappointed look, Cal dragged her shaky hand across the next empty page. Pinto gulped when she turned the notepad around.

STOP WASTING TIME

"What do you mean?"

BY SHOOTING ME, YOU RUINED YOUR REPUTATION

THE FORCE BARELY TRUSTS YOU

LITTLE BROTHER SAYS THEY GAVE YOU A BABYSITTER

WHAT ARE YOU GOING TO DO ABOUT THAT?

Pinto bit his trembling lip. "I don't know what you want me to say." Cal narrowed her eyes as though he were stupid.

REMEMBER WHY YOU JOINED THE FORCE

CLOSE YOUR EYE

DO IT

Pinto hesitated, and she nodded her head, urging him to follow through. With a deep breath, he closed his eye, thinking back to what had first driven him to train for his selection. He had always wanted to protect people from the Underground in the way no one had protected him as a boy, when the rebels raided his home and gouged out his eye. The Underground had landed a fatal blow to his confidence growing up, and now it had done so again. The same organization was distracting him from the job he had worked so hard to earn, and he hadn't even realized it.

After graduation, he had made it his goal to get promoted at a younger age than Cal. He had been working hard on the Bayin case to accomplish that—until Yahshi stole the files to sabotage him and protect his father. Pinto had lost his drive ever since then. No wonder the Force put him on respite.

Pinto opened his eye. "Do you hate me?" he asked, his voice breaking. "I need to know."

Cal's silence cut through him as she blinked, thinking. It felt like hours had passed before she finally picked up her notepad again.

THAT'S THE WRONG QUESTION

Pinto inhaled a shaky breath. "What do you want me to do?"

She smiled as she wrote her final line, and turned the notepad around.

MAKE ME LOSE

About a dozen guardians fell quiet as Pinto entered the Complex common room. He could see it in their eyes—the truth had settled in, replacing rumors. The Force knew of Cal's condition with certainty now, and they had made up their minds about who deserved the blame.

As he headed for the staircase, he scanned their faces for a glint of understanding. He'd known from the moment he'd stepped into the Academy that he was the most loyal to the Vakoi Empire among his peers and had made no efforts to hide such a fact. He was not blind to his fellow trainees rolling their eyes at his political opinions and relentless ambition—but now, his fellow guardians looked at him with blatant distrust. They scowled and stepped back with twitching fingers, as though they wouldn't hesitate to draw their tools on him if threatened.

Pinto halted in the middle of the room, his face stiffening as he spun, facing each one of them.

"What did you hear?" he yelled.

If they looked at him as though he were *disloyal* to the Empire, they had heard the wrong story. He had not shot Cal intentionally. He was still the same young man who would give up his life to protect the Vakoi Empire.

"We heard the truth," answered twenty-year-old Boa, a fellow member of Famir's unit. He'd been nothing but a menace to Pinto since his first day in service—seemingly fearing that Famir would come to favor Pinto over him. Now, he finally had a reason to act like a superior and keep Pinto in his place.

"Commander Cal may be dead to the world," Boa continued, "but not to us. As far as we're concerned, you should have ended up in correction like Keiyo."

Keiyo's been sent to correction? Pinto frowned. *What does he mean by dead to the world?*

Seeing his confusion, Boa motioned to Galler, who pulled a crinkly *Capital Weekly* article out of his overcoat and held it up. Pinto had avoided reading it, knowing it announced Vell's false death—but he hadn't expected to see Cal's portrait on it too.

His jaw dropped, but he stifled his gasp.

"Oh, d-don't look so surprised," Galler said. "C-Commander Cal deserves a heroic end to her st-story. We can't just tell p-people that she's rotting in the Hospital."

The front door opened again, and everyone turned to see Keiyo enter. His overcoat, stripped of its tools, flitted awkwardly behind him as he stormed across the common room.

Do I look that silly too? Pinto wondered.

The point of attention shifted instantly. Guardians whispered as they watched Keiyo with the same look of distrust they'd given Pinto moments ago, theorizing how his correctional meeting had gone. Pinto couldn't shake the feeling that this was all his fault. He fished for Keiyo's gaze, but he ignored him, rushing past Galler and up the staircase before anyone could speak a word.

Pinto darted up next. "Hey!"

Keiyo's boots slammed against the steps as he quickened his pace to a jog.

"Are you okay?" Pinto yelled, without response. "Keiyo!"

Now Keiyo was sprinting, trying to outrun him and get to his flat as quickly as possible—so Pinto started running too. He needed to know they could work through this. Keiyo was the last of his fellow graduates who he had even a chance of maintaining a friendship with.

Please, tell me there's one person who doesn't hate me.

He reached the sixteenth floor just a few seconds after Keiyo, whose hands shook as he struggled to unlock the door to his flat.

"Keiyo."

He stopped fidgeting with the key and glared in Pinto's direction. "Stop chasing me."

Pinto halted at the far end of the hallway, holding his palms up as though to say, *Fine. I'll stop right here.*

Keiyo's face hardened as he rolled back his overcoat sleeve, revealing a dark, circular bruise around his wrist. It was about the size of a watch.

Pinto could hardly comprehend what he was seeing before Keiyo pulled his sleeve back down, muttering, "I hope you're happy."

He stood frozen as Keiyo finally unlocked his flat and vanished from the hallway.

I was wrong, Pinto realized. *I didn't leave the interrogation unscathed.*

While he might have escaped correctional meetings, there was no avoiding the damage his actions had left on his reputation. He had no friends in the Force anymore.

Pinto shut himself in his flat, removed his overcoat, and threw himself onto his bed. He stared at the four-petaled flower designs on the ceiling and thought of all the times Yahshi and Vell had lied to him. He had been digging through the evidence, yearning to understand them, but had only found himself deeper in the dark. He had become more confused, more lost—so he kept digging, digging, digging. And now he had dug his own grave.

Everyone hates me.

Pinto clenched his eyes shut and willed the questions away. He had talked to Alora Valentine, the Paturas, and Cal Avarium. Their stories came together to form a half-baked, confusing picture of Yahshi and Vell, the traitors he had once called friends. There was only one fact he knew for sure—they had never been fully honest with him, and yet they had encouraged him to pour his soul out. He had accepted Vell's shoulder to cry on and had answered Yahshi's questions about his past, believing they cared.

Pinto thought of the little boy in Frontal who the others teased for the patch on his eye, and that parents teared up at the sight of. He had always been a target for ridicule and a magnet for sympathy. He had trained to prove that he was more than a victim of war—that he could play a role in avenging himself, his little sister, and everyone else who had suffered from the Underground's crimes.

He had worked harder than anyone else to get selected, and from there, he had made the final five and had joined the Force as a guardian, a fighter, a *winner*. If it weren't for Yahshi and Vell, he would still be those things.

Instead, he had ruined his reputation to protect them when they would have never done the same in return.

They were traitors to the Empire, and they were traitors to him. There was no gray area. Pinto had been living in denial because he didn't want to accept that they had played him for a fool, but Evaris was right—the sooner he accepted reality, the better. Yahshi and Vell were on the enemy's side now, and for him to have a happy end to his story, they needed a disastrous one.

I won't let them fool me any longer.

Finally, he understood why Cal had told him to make her lose. It was time to redeem himself and continue toward his goal of becoming the youngest unit leader in guardian history, beating Cal by a matter of months. His biggest hurdle was that the Force didn't trust him anymore. If he were to rejoin Famir's unit now, he'd hardly have a say in the case, Boa would make every day a misery, and he'd fade into obscurity for the rest of his career as the guardian who had ruined the Belladonna Prodigy.

I need to prove that the Force can trust me. Pinto shot up into a seated position. *To do that, I need to accomplish something grand on my own.*

Famir's voice echoed in his head. *"You'll return to service when you're ready."*

"And who decides that?" Pinto had asked.

He burst out of his flat, ran down the staircase, and pounded on Evaris's door until she finally opened it.

"Red?"

"Commander!" Pinto couldn't contain his smile. "I have an idea."

CHAPTER 15

GHOST HOMES

Buy one bag of Saver Store coal and get the second free.
Keep your stove going for less!

♫ HORSE TO WATER · TALL HEIGHTS ♫

Evaris emerged from the staircase to find havoc unleashed in the archives. About twenty professors had shown up for the same shift that morning, rustling through files, zipping between desks, and slamming drawers like Academy trainees studying for a filtration exam.

Evaris spotted Famir by his curled mustache and dodged three darting professors just to get to him. He was too immersed in an interrogation transcript to look up as she cast a shadow over his desk.

"Who is it?" Famir turned a page.

"Your favorite commander."

"Name," he stated, clearly not in the mood.

"Evaris Starfall. Boa let me in."

Sitting nearby, Boa looked up from his notes. "She told me she had a meeting with you, Professor. If I had known she'd bother you, I wouldn't have let her in."

Evaris glared at him. *Snitch.*

Famir shot Boa a stern look before turning back to his pages. "If you're having trouble with Pinto, that's not my problem. The point of delegating his recovery to you is so I can focus on what's most essential."

"I'm not having trouble at all. In fact, I'm here to tell you that he completed the assignments."

"All three?"

"One per day, over three days. He would have done them faster too, had I not forced him to pace himself. You won't believe how eager he is to get back to work."

That seemed to catch his attention. He leaned back in his seat and crossed his arms, a slight upward curve to his lips. "That's great."

"No, I'm afraid not," she replied, recalling the lines Pinto had made her rehearse the night before. "The plan overcorrected. He hates Yahshi and Vell so much that he's determined to find them faster than the Force."

Famir frowned, squandering any chance of a smile. "What does he think we're doing?" He gestured to the room of bustling, overworked guardians. "Sleeping while he mopes?"

Evaris faked a sigh. "I know. I'm worried that if he returns to work now, he'll be a constant distraction. I wouldn't be surprised if he tries to micromanage the case."

"Well, that's just splendid news, Evaris." Famir's lower lip dropped, a bitter chuckle escaping him. "I have enough on my plate as is."

She looked away with a contemplative stare. "Well, I do have an idea, but I'm not sure you'd like it."

"Just spit it out."

She looked back at him, her gaze focused. "What if I take him on a final assignment, this time into Eastern Territory? We could give him a chance to find Yahshi and Vell on his own."

A moment passed, followed by a brief laugh. "That's ridiculous."

"Just hear me out, Professor. It won't take him long to realize that he can't trace them without the Force's help, and once he's back, he'll be ready to work for you again." Evaris shrugged. "Plus, it's not like I'll be less useful with him than I would be now. Ever since I was reassigned from Cal's unit, I've been spending most of my shifts guarding the Detainment Facility, and nothing ever happens there."

Famir stared at the papers on his desk, his smile replaced by a look of impatient pondering. He pulled a notebook out of his overcoat and wrote a few lines, followed by his signature.

"You have one week," he said, holding the note out. "Take this to Professor Kanter in the Complex, third floor. He'll prepare your clearance for Border Control."

Evaris took the note with a smile.

"Boa?" Famir called.

"Yes, Professor?"

"Lock the door behind Commander Evaris, please. And don't let anyone from Defense or Medical in without the explicit permission of a superior."

Boa sighed. "Yes, Professor." He stubbornly walked with Evaris down the staircase, his arms crossed and eyes averted.

"Why so dramatic?" Evaris asked, a hint of humor in her voice. She had tricked him into opening the door for her, but Famir's response—merely instructing Boa not to do it again—was lenient, even by his standards.

"You like him, don't you?" Boa asked.

She smiled. "Excuse me?"

"I don't know if you've noticed, Evaris, but everyone's pissed at Pinto right now. Everyone except you." They halted at the base of the staircase, and he finally met her gaze. "You know what happens when guardians get caught breaking *that* Vow. Galler didn't always stutter."

Evaris laughed, nudging his shoulder. It had taken far less than eighteen months in the program for her to notice how much paranoia Boa fostered. She figured his brain was exhausting. He had always trained and studied more than anyone else, counting the days until the next filtration in an effort to decipher a pattern, theorizing about the various ways the guardians might test them. The other boys called him *Brooding Boa*. Cal called him *weak*.

"I'm just looking out for you. Don't get carried away."

"I could never. You know me, Boa." She pointed to her heart as she walked backward toward the door. "It's all black in here."

He sighed, seemingly disappointed, but didn't press further. The last she heard of him was the *click* of the door as he locked it behind her.

Dropping her smile, she headed for the Office stable, lines creasing her forehead. *Why would he assume such a thing?*

Pinto must have heard her approaching footsteps, because he stepped out from his hiding spot behind the stable, his hands folded together in front of him.

"Did he go for my plan?" he asked, his voice tight with anticipation.

Evaris brushed off Boa's wild assumption and offered Pinto a smile. "Pack your bags, Red."

He chuckled through an exhale. "We're going to Atherus City?"

She raised the note Famir had given her, and Pinto practically leaped into the air as he snatched it.

"You're kidding!"

When Pinto had knocked on Evaris's door the day before, she hadn't expected him to look so lively. His face had been bright, his eye wide. It was like he'd taken medicine to cure a sickness he didn't know he'd been living with.

"The Research Division is going about this all wrong. Finding the hideout is jumping one step ahead. What we need to do first is crack the code."

"Fine, I'll bite," Evaris replied. *"What code?"*

"Just think about it, Commander. While Yahshi was on the run, there had to be a way he discerned allies from enemies. Like the way they dressed, or something about their homes."

Evaris figured that if such a code existed, the Force would have discovered it by now, but she chose to humor him. The prior few days had been a pleasant change of routine, and it wouldn't be so bad, she figured, to stretch it a little longer.

So she agreed to pitch his idea to Famir, claiming it as her own, and successfully gained approval. While Pinto packed his bags, she knocked on the door to Kanter's flat and presented Famir's signed note. She had only spoken to the quiet, scrawny old guardian a few times before, but she knew he was a friend and fellow graduate of Blimmery's. She had seen them sharing tea on multiple occasions—it wouldn't surprise her if Blimmery had gossiped to him about family drama. Part of her feared Kanter would shut the plan down and tell her, *Listen to Blimmery and go visit your great aunt Cove.*

Instead, Kanter walked to his desk, drew up a clearance document for Border Control, and handed it over without a word.

The longest leg of their trip took place first thing the following morning. They needed to travel by horseback from Vakoi City, along the western coast, to the inland town of Sitra. What had taken Yahshi nearly two hours of travel during his runaway had to be stretched out to three and a half, ensuring their horses could make the full trip to Heston in one go.

They spent most of the journey to Yahshi's hometown deciding on their strategy. Pinto wanted to investigate Underground smugglers the Defense Division had recently executed to search for commonalities in their clothes, behaviors, or residences—but such accounts were numerous. To limit their stops, Evaris suggested they focus on the criminals who lived along Yahshi's predicted route from Sitra to Atherus City.

"I like how you think, Commander," Pinto said.

From what the Research Division assumed about the beginning of Yahshi's time as a fugitive, he had passed the Border Control tower nearest to Nominner, making his way straight to the Eastern town of Heston. From there, he had likely hitched a carriage ride to Arinoma.

So it was decided. They would spend their first day in Heston, their second day in Arinoma, and all the days that followed working their way north to Atherus City.

Pinto's beaming and chattering trickled off the more they neared Sitra, and by the time they entered the town limits, he had drifted into his own world. With one hand on the reins, he bit his free hand's nails, answering Evaris's questions with one- or two-word responses. His restlessness was grossing her out.

"Can you stop that?" Evaris snapped. "You're even more anxious than Boa."

"I am *nothing* like Professor Boa," Pinto replied, forcing his hand down.

"There's no reason to be nervous. You've been to Eastern Territory before."

"*Once*, during the special operation—and that whole time, I was only in the woods. I've never actually seen... the people there."

Her blood simmered, and it took every ounce of willpower not to shame him further. Two to three years ago, when she was in the middle of the Academy program, she had been terrified to enter Eastern Territory during her first shadow assignment. However, she was leaving the Vakoi Empire to kill a traitor for the first time, while Pinto was leaving to learn about dead ones. He had nothing to be afraid of.

After another stop for their horses to rehydrate, it took over an hour to pass through Nominner and reach the very Border Control tower Yahshi had tricked his way through. Evaris presented her documentation from Kanter, but the officer seemed hesitant.

"Is he okay?" the man asked, gesturing to Pinto's pale face.

"He's fine," Evaris snapped, taking her document back. "Can we pass now?"

The Border Control officer nodded and stepped aside, gesturing for them to continue into another stretch of trees and greenery.

Pinto gulped and tightened his grip on the reins, his hands shaking as he urged his horse forward into the occupied land.

I didn't sign up to deal with his drama. Evaris shook her head and pulled a notebook out of her overcoat. As frustrated as she was, she knew she was being unfairly impatient with him, so she scribbled down a letter *O* and took a deep breath to calm herself.

The first town they passed through in Eastern Territory was Vori. Pinto eyed every Easterner in sight as though they were plotting to jump at him and take his good eye. At one point, he even asked Evaris to lend him her dagger, just so he could have *something to hold*—Famir still hadn't allowed him his tools back.

"Fine," Evaris said, handing him her dagger. He didn't notice that the same people he feared were quickening their footsteps and drawing their curtains shut at the sight of their white horses. If guardians were around, blood was usually bound to spill. He was not the victim here.

Pinto finally settled when they reached Heston, the next town over.

"Thanks for coming with me," Pinto said, glancing at Evaris. "I wouldn't be able to do this alone."

"Frankly, you wouldn't have been *allowed* to do this alone," she teased, but in truth, she appreciated his gratitude.

"Here." He offered her dagger back. "Please don't tell Professor Famir that I asked for it."

"I would never." She tucked it into her overcoat.

"So... how do we find the first house on our list?"

"Don't worry. I know where it is."

"You do?"

Evaris gripped the reins tighter, her horse taking a slight lead. "I was there, Red."

She never forgot the homes she killed in.

When they reached the house of their first deceased target, Evaris finally learned what local officers did to the homes where she made ghosts. She had always assumed they simply dealt with the bodies, but apparently, they also blocked the windows with wood and marked the doors with words in blood-red paint. The notice on this one read, *CLEARANCE UNDER WAY*, followed by *HESTON OFFICER DEPARTMENT.*

Evaris dismounted her horse and looped its lead rope around the porch railing, securing it with a quick-release knot. As Pinto dealt with his own horse, she headed up the porch steps and pulled out her lock busters at the front door.

"What happens during clearance?" Pinto called from behind her.

Evaris tuned him out, gritting her teeth as she tinkered with her tools in the lock. She had always hated lock busters—they called for too much focused precision. In her last unit, Galler usually busted locks, and she hadn't had a reason to use the tools since Vell and Quax graduated, pushing her to a new unit that mainly guarded the Facility. *I don't think I've picked a lock since the Academy.*

"Commander?" Pinto asked, climbing the steps to reach her.

She continued messing with the tension wrench and pick, but she couldn't identify the lock's binding pin. She'd only just found it when Pinto appeared at her side, which shocked her into losing it.

"Here," he offered, his hands skimming her as he took the tools.

Evaris frowned as she stepped back. "I almost had it."

With a few subtle twists of his fingers, the door unlocked and creaked open. He glanced over his shoulder at her. "Are you okay?"

Evaris's cheeks ran hot. In the two years since her graduation, she hadn't worked as hard as her fellow graduates like Cal and Boa to maintain every skill she'd learned in the program. She coasted, and every once in a while, she paid the price.

"I'm fine," she forced out, stepping past him to enter the ghost home.

The main room looked exactly as it had five weeks ago, though it smelled faintly of dust. The quaint, old furniture was still in place, along with the whittled animal figurines, which brought a charming liveliness to the boring home.

Evaris picked up a wooden rabbit sitting on a small table by the sofa, twirling it between her thumb and index finger. Had the siblings been born in Vakoi City, they could have thrived by selling their crafts as art, but here, in Eastern Territory, they were just pathetic knick-knacks.

A lump formed in her throat when she noticed blood marks on the floorboards that the local officers hadn't scrubbed completely clean. She set the rabbit down, visualizing the scene that had taken place in this room. Her arrow had struck the bushy-haired sister's heart, while Galler had knocked the brother unconscious with the blunt handle of his swords.

Stop being so emotional. They were traitors, remember?

She swallowed the lump in her throat and crossed her arms, forcing her image of the ghosts away.

Pinto didn't even notice the blood marks. He walked right over them, spinning in circles to take in every detail of the room, tapping his pencil tip against his notebook pages in an infuriating pattern. Before he had written anything, his eyebrows jumped, and he reached into his overcoat. He had accidentally placed Evaris's lock busters in one of his own interior pockets.

She held her palm up. "Keep them."

Pinto froze with his hand in his overcoat. "Really?"

Evaris nodded, unsure of why he looked so hesitant to replace one of the many tools Famir had confiscated. After all, she had recently learned that he carried key duplicates around without his unit leader's knowledge, and had likely allowed Vell to help him cheat at his tolerance training during the program. Surely he was not so inexperienced in breaking a rule now and then.

His expression lightened as he removed his hand from his overcoat, keeping her lock busters. Finally, he began taking notes, his eye hopping from one detail to the next as silence fell over the room.

Evaris soaked in the quiet, closing her eyes and taking a deep breath. She had started this trip off with a bitter attitude just because Pinto was nervous to enter Eastern Territory and could pick a lock faster than she could. She was being immature.

When she opened her eyes, she jotted down another *O* in her notepad and forced a smile.

"It starts with local officers identifying the target's family members," Evaris explained, answering his earlier question about clearance. "If they don't have adult children, the house becomes the property of the town, and usually ends up in the possession of a local officer."

"Seems like an incentive for officers to frame innocent people," Pinto said.

Evaris eyed a mandatory portrait of Emperor Vakoi across the room, which she'd opened during her expedition with Cal and Galler to find a secret compartment behind it—empty. The siblings had been astute enough to realize that it wasn't the best place to store their stash, but they had lacked the foresight to remove it once they found a better hiding place. The empty compartment hinted at their connection to the Underground, and it only took a few more minutes for Galler to find a loose board in the ceiling, which, with some pressure, opened up to a cramped attic brimming with bags of coal.

"We don't hurt innocent people," Evaris replied. "They were *definitely* smugglers."

"What else do we know about them?"

Evaris pulled their case file out of her overcoat. "Denya and Luc Parano.

They were siblings, both in their twenties. Their father worked in the Heston mines long before the Atherus War. He died when they were teenagers in an equipment accident, and according to their mother, they blamed Heston officers for it. Said conditions in the mines got worse after Emperor Vakoi occupied Eastern Territory and redefined their working conditions."

"Maybe that gave them the motive to join the Underground." He scribbled down a few notes. "Did their mother live here too?"

"No. They moved out of her home a few years ago, after an argument." Evaris flipped forward to an interrogation with their mother, led by local officers in Heston, and skimmed over the answers. "Apparently their mother disapproved of Luc's girlfriend, who was also a coworker of Denya's. Called her a bad influence, and *an alcoholic with anger issues.*"

"Did Denya and Luc's girlfriend work at the mines too?"

"Only Luc. The other two worked at a coal packaging plant."

"Interesting." Pinto made a few more rounds through the main room, then checked the bedrooms and restroom. It didn't take long for him to make a beeline for the front door, leaving it wide open. Evaris followed and joined him on the road, where he turned to face the house.

"Of course! We only need to investigate the exteriors," he said in a higher pitch, struggling to contain his excitement. "Yahshi would need to identify allies *before* entering their homes."

He flipped to an open spread in his navy-blue notebook and began sketching everything ahead of them, leaving no details spared. Evaris couldn't imagine how tiring it would be to see the world like he did—to notice everything with such intensity.

"That's quite the drawing."

"Old hobby of mine," Pinto said.

She chuckled as he drew cracks in the porch steps' wooden railing, as though that could be the code. "Do you really think Yahshi traveled from house to house, looking for a pattern of cracks? Clearly, that's natural weathering."

"I wouldn't jump to that conclusion so quickly, Commander." He looked up from his pages, meeting her gaze with a hilariously arrogant look.

"You saw the wooden figurines in there. The siblings knew how to whittle."

Evaris smiled as Pinto continued drawing, her skepticism softening. Assuming his code theory actually held water, perhaps he was the perfect guardian to decipher it.

The assembly line workers, in their bright orange jumpsuits, created packing materials, stamped labels onto bags, and loaded branded Saver Store coal into crates for transport. As Evaris and Pinto entered, their operations slowed, tense whispers filling the workroom of Heston's coal packaging plant.

Their boss, dressed in neon green, ushered the guardians into his private office and sent one worker in at a time to discuss Denya Parano, their coworker who had died five weeks ago. While they didn't know Evaris had been the one to kill her, it was better that way—the knowledge would only make them more afraid than they already were. *I don't want that kind of power.*

Pinto insisted on hosting the interrogation the *professor* way by writing a transcript, so Evaris took it upon herself to handle the questioning. It was a rather fun job, actually. As a guardian in the Defense Division, she rarely had opportunities to perform this kind of work. The questions spilled out of her naturally, thanks to her love of mystery novels with detectives who always knew the right questions to ask.

"Oh, Denya was the sweetest," answered a woman with the number twenty embroidered into her jumpsuit. "She remembered all our birthdays. I always got a sense that we were more than numbers to her—more than coworkers. I still find it hard to believe she had anything to do with the Underground."

Every worker at the production point had wonderful things to say about Denya—all except Pip, Luc's girlfriend. Her breath reeked of vodka, and she couldn't settle in her seat. She kept tapping her boot and fidgeting with her fingers, even after Evaris assured her three times that she wasn't in danger.

"Still not talking," Pip murmured. She wouldn't say more than three words at a time.

"Pip," Evaris tried, "you are legally obligated to answer our questions."

The worker leaned in, her brows raised, her words sharp. "Still. Not. Talking."

Evaris's jaw tightened as she fought the urge to wield a dagger and threaten Pip with force. It was certainly what Cal or Galler would have done.

Don't do it. Don't do it. Don't do it.

Thankfully, Pinto distracted her with a gasp, nearly dropping his pencil. He met eyes with Pip and said, "You lived with them."

Pip bared her teeth in a sneer. "What?"

"Your hairpins." He pointed to her loose, frizzy bun. "I noticed the same ones in their restroom. You lived with them, didn't you?"

For the first time since Pip entered the office, she spoke more than a few words. "I spent the night sometimes. I didn't live with them."

"You must have been around enough to know that they were hoarding coal for the Underground," Pinto said, "and yet you didn't report them."

"They weren't hoarding coal," she said. "They were framed."

"They were traitors," Pinto replied. "You're just in denial. I know what that's—"

"Shut it!" Pip shouted, despite how close they were.

He gulped under the pressure of her rage, and Pip shot Evaris a glare next. She stood slowly, showing she wasn't afraid of them retaliating, and turned to leave.

Evaris cleared her throat, lightening her tone. "I happen to know that Denya and Luc's home is unlocked right now."

Pip stopped by the door and peered back at Evaris.

"It will stay that way for at least a few hours, before the officers notice and take care of it," Evaris continued. "If there's anything small that you want to take, like some—I don't know—*wooden things*, to remember them by, now is the time. I'll talk to your boss, and get you the rest of the day off."

Pip's shoulders loosened, just slightly, and Evaris used the opportunity to make her point.

"Members of the Underground are often the epitome of perfect followers. They do everything right to avoid drawing attention to themselves. They keep their friends and family in the dark." Her next words walked the line between comforting and cold. "You didn't know Denya and Luc as well as you thought. They hid a massive part of their lives from you, and that's a hard truth to grapple with when you're also grieving them."

Evaris faced Pinto. His situation with Yahshi and Vell wasn't so different from Pip's situation with Denya and Luc. Why should she treat Pip any harsher than she'd treated him, just because she was an Easterner?

Pinto nodded and looked away, seeming to understand the same.

When Evaris turned back to Pip, the young woman looked calmer now, her face less red. She seemed closer to accepting that her boyfriend and best friend had lied to her, and that the Force had rightfully killed them. With a subtle nod, she left the room.

Evaris pulled out her notepad, but before she could add an X to her list, Pinto's whisper stole her attention.

"We need more people like her in the Force."

She looked up from the page. "You want Pip to be a guardian?"

Pinto froze, his eye widening. That's when Evaris realized he might not have been referring to Pip at all. Perhaps he appreciated how she had handled Pip's outburst without snapping back. Many guardians would have resorted to unnecessary displays of power—oblivious to how an act of kindness could disarm even the most dangerous.

"You were talking about *me*, weren't you?"

Pinto chuckled and broke eye contact, but he didn't deny it.

With a smile, Evaris ducked her head to scribble a quick X. "I try to be a good one, Red." She tucked her notepad back into her overcoat.

"What was that?" Pinto asked.

"Tic tac toe." She stood and dusted off her pants. "You ready?"

After visiting a few more ghost homes and questioning the people who had known their inhabitants, Evaris called a wrap on the day. They stopped at

Heston Officer Post to prepare for their trip to the nearest Border Control tower, where they could sleep for the night on Western soil. The local officers had offered to share their horse feed and water with the guardians—their superiors—but Pinto didn't seem to appreciate the stop.

"You've never seen a sick guardian horse before," Evaris said, assuming he was in a hurry to sleep. "It's not pretty—what happens to them when they're no longer useful. They don't get the privilege of retirement like we do."

Pinto didn't look at her. He simply watched their horses drink from a trough in the stable.

Evaris looked over at the officers' brown horses. They had shiny dark coats, unmarked by heated iron. She ran her fingertips along the brand of her white horse's shoulder—meeting a four-petaled flower mark that matched her own.

A few minutes passed before a pair of officers returned to the stable to check on them.

"Hungry?" asked the first. "We've got the best barbecued beef!"

The second officer laughed. "You can even crash here for the night, if you'd like. We've got a few extra sofas—no need to make the long trip back, just for a bed!"

Evaris smiled, intent on accepting their offers, but Pinto spoke first.

"That's against Protocol." He didn't express even a hint of appreciation.

The officers exchanged glances and chuckled, but Evaris could tell that Pinto had irked them by the briskness of their pleasantries as they left.

She glared at him in disbelief. Sure, according to *The Guardian Handbook*, they shouldn't socialize with Easterners nor sleep on Eastern soil. Guardians were to maintain a sense of elegance, but clearly, the officers didn't care whether they kept up their sterile appearance. It would be far more practical to stay the night, rather than traveling a few hours back to the border, plus a few more hours in the morning to return to the same general area.

"Why would you say no? Now we have six extra hours of travel time."

"It's not *extra* time," Pinto said. "This was our original plan."

Evaris shook her head, but she knew getting frustrated with him wouldn't change anything. Since Pinto wouldn't break Protocol, they stopped for canned supper at a ration station before making an exhausting trip to the nearest tower.

While most Border Control officers lived in nearby border towns like Nominner and Vori, they had bunk beds set up on the higher floors for them to nap between patrol shifts if needed.

"I doubt it's as fancy as whatever you have in the City." The officer opened the creaking door to reveal a room with fewer torches than the stairwell. It was dark, but once Evaris stepped inside, she identified three sets of bunk beds and grinned.

"It's perfect," she said.

As the officer descended the stairwell, she climbed a ladder to a top bunk.

"Why that one?" Pinto asked, lying down on the bottom bed of a separate bunk.

"It's something new, that's all." She took a deep breath and closed her eyes, tuning into the crackling of the room's sparse torches. Ever since graduation, she had wondered what it would be like to sleep outside her flat. Apart from one night in the archives with Pinto, this would be the only other time.

"You seem awfully thrilled to be here," Pinto noted.

"You're really embodying the detective spirit."

"Do you have an answer for me?"

Evaris opened her eyes and smiled at the ceiling. There was mold in the corner, so she turned onto her side and stared down at Pinto's bunk. He lay with his face to the wall, his back turned to her.

"Sometimes I tire of being cooped up," she answered.

"Why is that?" he asked, fishing for a better explanation.

"Well, as much as I like being a guardian, sometimes I just want to go to a park and read and forget about my responsibilities. It's just... nice to switch things up once in a while. To not have a unit leader breathing down my back."

She didn't admit it aloud, but sometimes—*sometimes*—she missed being a Starfall.

Pinto didn't reply. For a moment, Evaris wondered if he'd fallen asleep.

"I thought I enjoyed having a routine," he finally said. "But today was fun."

"It was, wasn't it?"

"It's unfortunate that as soon as the week ends, I'll go back to transcribing Famir's interrogations and taking meeting notes that no one ever reads." His voice sounded tired, as though the journey was already weighing him down. It was then that Evaris realized why he'd been so moody at Heston Officer Post earlier—he was doubting himself.

"I suppose that depends on whether you crack the code," she said.

Pinto managed a weak chuckle. "You don't seem to believe in me. I'm not blind to that."

Evaris smiled. He had seen through her lies again. "Well, maybe you'll prove me wrong, Red."

CHAPTER 16

TIMEKEEPER

Day 8 Underground | Clocks Read 06:55

As footsteps echoed from the connected tunnel, Vell glanced at the clock in the infirmary. *Five minutes.*

"Sorry!" Yahshi exclaimed, skidding to a stop in the chamber. "I-I don't know what happened. I told Lira to wake me, but she must have slept in, so I completely—"

"It's okay," Vell interrupted. "You needed the sleep."

He shook his head, guilt written across his face. They both knew she had spent nearly an hour waiting for him that morning—over the past week, they had met in this infirmary whenever the clocks struck 06:00 to talk until 07:00, when Yahshi had to rush off to spend the rest of the day with the Council.

Vell gestured to a chair. It was already 06:55. "We don't have much time."

"Sorry," he said again, taking a seat.

Her cheeks ran hot. They both knew the hour before and after Yahshi's Council meetings were the only parts of her day when she had *anything* to do. His apologies only made her feel worse. It wasn't his job to comfort her—he had enough on his plate already.

She rolled Yahshi's sleeve back to reveal the cloth strips she'd wrapped his shoulder with the night before. He could've managed his recovery on his own, but she insisted on helping—and he eventually seemed to understand it was just an excuse to be near him.

Yahshi winced as she unraveled the cloths and tossed them in a bin, exposing the wound Evaris's arrow had left behind. The hole showed signs of healing, fresh tissue bridging the edges, and the swelling had gone down. In just a month or two, he could even use his dual swords without issue—not that he still had them, or that the Council would allow him to touch a blade. They weren't guardians anymore. *Sometimes I forget.*

The clock taunted her again. *Four minutes.*

Vell tilted a can of saltwater over his shoulder, and he yelped, clutching the fabric of his pants.

"You never warn me," he said through gritted teeth.

She concealed a grin as she patted his wound dry with a rag.

He took a moment to gather his breath before speaking again. "You know, it's really not fair. The Council should appreciate you more. I mean, you saved my life, Vell, and you could really help them. If they refuse to let me near a tool, they could at least ask *you* to assist Rimoso's Guild."

"I don't want to help the Guild," Vell replied, wrapping Yahshi's shoulder with a fresh cloth. She had spent much of her endless free time reading banned books in the libraries, and while she understood the Underground's hatred for the Force, that didn't mean she would fight for their side. Why would she take an offensive role against Pinto, Quax, or Keiyo, who were just following orders?

Three minutes.

Yahshi seemed to read her mind. "The Guild won't hurt our friends. Not with our plan. But they could use better skills in case they need to fight defensively."

Assuming the Council even approves our plan, Vell wanted to argue—but Yahshi had been working far too hard on his proposal for her to cast more doubts now. This was the best idea they had, and she wouldn't be the one to crush his hopes. *The Council will do that for me tomorrow.*

Yahshi nodded to himself. "I'm going to talk to them today, and make sure you're there for my presentation."

"That's not necessary," Vell said.

"It's your idea as much as it is mine."

"Don't tell them that. Then they'll *surely* shoot it down."

"Fine—but I'm still demanding that you be there."

Vell finished wrapping his arm and rolled his sleeve back into place. The last thing she wanted was to impede on the Council's space. They clearly only tolerated her because of her connection to Yahshi. However, it was nice to know that he wanted her around for such an important occasion.

"Thanks," she muttered, offering a smile.

"It's the least I can do," Yahshi replied. "I know you're tired."

"I'm really not," Vell said. The most exciting part of her day, apart from these brief moments with Yahshi, was sitting with Aero by the access point during her three-hour morning shift as guard. It was an easy way to pass the time with no responsibilities of her own, whereas Yahshi had *no* time to himself. A few days ago, the Council had demanded that he start eating with them too, instead of in the canteen with Vell.

"Apparently, it's confusing for the people to see us together," Yahshi had told her.

Prince Runix was a concept, not a real person. Hiders only saw Yahshi wandering through tunnels with Council members at his side—never alone, never approachable. The only time he could spend with Vell came out of his sleep allotment.

"I know you're not *sleepy*," he corrected. "I meant that you're tired of this routine. And trust me—I am too."

Vell frowned. He had only told her snippets of how he spent his time with the Council, but from what she could gather, they had no respect for his schedule. They drowned him with books to read and history lessons on the Atherus Empire. His least favorite parts were the one-on-one meetings with members of the Provisional Council, where he spent an hour with each person, soaking in their governing philosophies, tasked with *absorbing their guidance.*

Yahshi stood and took her hands in his. "It won't be like this forever, okay?"

Vell found it hard to look him in the eyes. She turned her gaze to the clock. *One minute.*

He squeezed her hands tighter. "Vell?"

"Okay," she whispered, unsure of what else to say. Sometimes that happened. It never used to happen before.

Now it was his turn to look at the clock. "I should get going."

It was 07:00. He hugged her, and suddenly, the words came. They always arrived when she was just out of time.

She wished she could tell him about the feeling that haunted her after graduation—how she had wondered if she'd made a mistake trading her chance at love for a uniform and pretty tools.

She wished she could tell him how much she had missed him while he was gone—how many times she thought she saw him in a crowd, only for it to be someone else, and how that ache made her realize she didn't just grieve love. She grieved the absence of a love with him.

She wished she could ask him to skip his Council obligations for the day to spend it with her—because she had waited so long to have him back, only to keep losing him again and again.

Yahshi pulled away and smiled.

Say it.

Vell straightened her back, bracing herself—but by the time she opened her mouth, he had already turned away.

The clocks ticked louder as he vanished into the connected tunnel. *You don't have time to hesitate*, they scolded.

But she didn't listen. There was always a next time.

"You're pathetic," Aero said, standing from the floor by the access point. "We're leaving. Now." She held out her hand, offering to help Vell up.

Vell frowned. "What about your shift?"

"What about *your* shift? You've gotta do *something*, Vell." Aero grabbed her hand with force and yanked her up.

"No one will give me a job," she muttered, diverting her gaze. "They don't trust me."

"They don't trust you *because* you don't have a job." Aero dragged her down the tunnel. "Look, as much as I like the company during my boring shifts, I can't stand to watch you rot away down here like this. You were a badass, poisonous, fighter, military something-or-other, remember?"

"I was a guardian," she corrected.

Aero led her to a chamber on the highest floor of Headquarters, where Dice sat on the floor, eating spoonfuls of preserved berries from a can. Clinging to the wall opposite him was a giant clock at least three times Vell's height—its claws dug into the stone like bird talons into prey. From behind its face, gears and chains spilled out, crawling upward to a hammer waiting idly for its cue to strike the copper bell hanging beside it.

Dice looked up as they entered and hopped to his feet, frowning.

"The answer is *no*," he said, pointing his spoon at Aero.

"Oh, come on," Aero sang. "You know she needs a job! She'd be perfect as a timekeeper."

Dice's eyes drifted to Vell as he shoved another spoonful of fruit into his mouth.

"It's actually a perfect situation," Aero continued, noticing that Dice seemed to consider her offer. "You'll get to monitor her, and play *spy*. Win-win for both of you." She patted Vell on the shoulder and darted from the room, leaving the pair alone.

Vell left to run after her, but Dice's voice stopped her.

"Wait," he said, drawing her eyes back to him. He took another bite. "What do you think of Grandfather Clock?"

She turned to the clock that clung to the stone with its life. "It's... nice."

Dice set his can of fruit down, slung a bag over his shoulder, and rushed to climb the ladder next to Grandfather Clock.

"Are you gonna help me open him, or what?"

Vell walked over and stared at the clock's ticking hands, unsure of what Dice expected her to do.

"Grab his bottom," he said.

She shook her head at his word choice and gripped the clock's bottom as Dice unclasped its side. With a *click*, she felt its face come slightly loose from its body. The hinges creaked as she walked backward, pulling the clock face open to reveal the gears and levers that danced together inside, forming the rhythmic *ticks* and *tocks* that filled the air.

Dice reached from his ladder to grab a crank handle and began turning it. "How's Prince Runix's presentation coming along?"

So that's what he gets out of this. Vell smiled to herself. *He thinks I have insider information on Yahshi's plan.*

"Let me guess," Dice added. "He doesn't want to play offense."

Vell kept quiet, and Dice took her silence as a *yes*.

"We can't save both sides, Vell. He thinks he's preventing a new war, but we're still in the old one. You should save him the embarrassment and tell him to cancel his presentation. If he really wants to help us, he can't be a naive, vegetarian pacifist anymore."

Vell found her blood boiling, despite Dice's worries echoing her own. While she knew there was likely no avoiding a bloody war, she hoped Yahshi could prove her wrong, so long as she didn't get in his way. It made little sense to her—how much she believed in him, yet doubted him at the same time.

"Can we please just focus on the clock?" she asked, her tone sharp.

"Fine, but don't come crying after his presentation." Dice released the cranking rod and offered the clock's frame a solid pat. "Now listen up, Vell!"

His voice was higher now, brimming with enthusiasm, as though the conversation they'd shared hadn't existed.

"This here is the ultimate timekeeper in Headquarters, our master key. We time all our clocks to him, and he's also responsible for ringing the quarter-day bells." He pointed up to the hammer and copper bell that hung from the ceiling.

"It's automated?" Vell asked, eyeing the overflowing mechanisms that connected the clock to the hammer.

"Sure is. We used to have kids climb up here and ring it, but after Tonna brought my family to safety, I set up this mechanism myself." He leaned from the ladder, pointing out the different pieces of the clock and how they worked.

Strangely enough, Vell longed for a paper and pen so she could take notes.

Perhaps her enthusiasm came from the fact that she'd been doing absolutely nothing for the past week.

"Help me close him?" Dice asked.

Vell gripped the front face and pushed Grandfather Clock shut. As silly as the role of *timekeeper* seemed at first, Dice's seriousness made her appreciate it more. When she really thought about it, the clocks told people when to wake, eat, work, and sleep. Steady time was just one less thing for hiders to worry about, so they could focus on what mattered for survival.

After Dice secured the clasp on the clock's side, they stood at the base of Grandfather Clock together. Vell looked over to see him gazing up at the time, beaming. Her eyes watered at the memory of Keiyo. He always had that same look whenever he developed or improved a new tool. If he were here, he'd surely get a kick out of Grandfather Clock.

But he was still in Vakoi City, suffering the consequences of tackling Pinto to allow her and Yahshi to flee. *I hope the Force treats him lightly.*

Footsteps echoed from the tunnel just outside, and Dice looked over. "Saunti!"

Saunti halted by the entryway, raising his brows at the sight of Vell. They hadn't spoken since their first day here, back in that water tank room, but after every shared meal with Aero in the canteen, she'd seen him enter the kitchen. Apparently, he'd picked up the role of a dishwasher on his first day. *He's assimilated much faster than I have.*

"What do you think of Grandfather Clock?" Dice asked.

"Like I keep saying, who the hell is that?" Saunti didn't seem to make the connection.

"Never mind!" Dice laughed, and by the way he met Vell's gaze, she figured he'd stopped Saunti just so she could enjoy the humor of his obliviousness too. It reminded her of how she and her mother would fool her little siblings into believing absurd plant facts.

"So if I rub aloe vera gel on my cheeks," her little brother had said, *"she'll fall in love with me?"*

He had always been too romantic, too naive, Vell used to think. But that was before the Academy taught her she would never have love—something so simple, taken away, sealed to her fate with a mark on her forehead.

It seemed like overnight, she had come to envy her little brother. He wasn't naive for clinging to romance; she was naive for letting it slip away. She hadn't realized how much it meant to her until it was gone.

That seemed to be a pattern these days—but she brushed the thought of Yahshi away.

"Rub the aloe vera gel in your hair too," their mother had chimed in from across the room. *"It'll be fifty percent more effective."*

As her brother tore into an aloe vera leaf, her mother smirked mischievously at Vell—just as Dice did now while Saunti scanned the chamber for an old man named *Grandfather Clock*.

Vell smiled back, and for the first time, Headquarters felt a little more like home.

Late that night, at exactly 21:14, Vell entered Yahshi's private chamber for the first time. He'd never invited her before, and she'd always assumed it was because the Council's rooms lined the same tunnel—and their members had a tendency to shoot glares at her whenever she neared their beloved Prince.

Tonight, Yahshi didn't seem to care, though. He had led her straight to his chamber despite Lira and Rimoso's disapproving whispers from a few doors down.

As he flipped through his notes on the floor, Vell found herself drawn to the hanging portraits of his biological family members. Others would say that he looked like royalty, but in her eyes, it was the Atherus Royal Family that resembled *him*. She wondered what they were like—if they were even a fraction as brave and as kind.

"Hey, Vell?" Yahshi called from behind her.

"Mhm?" she asked, staring at a portrait of Yahshi's late mother. *She had his eyes.*

"On the third floor of Vakoi City Hospital, are there three doors before the supply closet or four?"

"Four," she muttered.

"And on the fifth floor, is the final room down the hallway an office, or another closet?"

She thought for a moment, then shook her head. "I forgot."

Yahshi sighed as he rustled through his stack of messy floor plans. "If only I had Pinto's memory. We haven't been tested on this stuff in months."

Vell smiled sadly at the thought of their old friend. She wondered what he was doing right now, at this very moment in time. Was he thinking about her and Yahshi, or something else entirely? Had he moved on? Would he ever?

Yahshi sighed again, and Vell looked back to see him with his knees against his chin, his face in his palms. She frowned and left his family portraits, joining him on the floor.

"I'm sorry," she said, realizing that she had hardly helped him with his presentation in the past half-hour. "I got distracted."

"It's not that. My notes are finished already." Yahshi dropped his hands, meeting her gaze with shimmering eyes. "I just feel awful. I said I'd make it up to you, and all I've done is disappear, over and over."

"It's not your fault. The Council doesn't let you rest."

"I wanna make time for you," he said. "You know that, right?"

She nodded. He *was* making time for her, and she had been keeping it, clutching it closely. Someday, they would have all the time they wanted. But until then, she would count the minutes, and savor every *tick* and *tock* they shared.

Yahshi managed a weak smile. "The Council agreed to let you join the meeting tomorrow. It'll be easier, knowing you're there."

Vell hugged him. "You'll do great."

She really wanted to believe it, but the words felt like a lie.

The following morning, at 08:18, Vell approached the apex in an off-limits part of Headquarters. The meeting room had a metal door instead of the usual arched entryways in Headquarters. In front of it stood Varin. He clutched a ring of keys in one hand and a rusty sword in the other. His face twisted into an ugly scowl as Vell approached, and she resisted the urge to snatch his keys—which would have been painfully easy to do.

"It's a joke that you're allowed in there," he grumbled, his grip on the sword tightening.

Vell fought off a grin. It was hard to take him seriously when he wasn't wearing a uniform. If she were to make the rules down here, she'd have Rimoso's Guild dress more professionally—and ideally find a less childish name for themselves than *Guildies.*

"I'm already late, Varin," Vell stated.

His face hardened, and she was certain he would have held her off longer, had someone not opened the door from inside the apex.

Yahshi's eyes widened. "There you are!" He reached past Varin and grabbed Vell's hand, pulling her in. "Where have you been?"

She didn't tell him that she had spent the last few hours huddled in her bunker, staring at the brazier as she listened to the clocks talk, losing track of time—how the tears rolled down her cheeks as she thought of her family. The feeling wasn't new, but it burrowed deeper lately. At least in the Force, there had always been a visitation right around the corner. Now she didn't know when she'd ever see them again—and she ignored the voice in her head that whispered she might not.

She wondered what they believed regarding her desertion—had the Force published lies about her, like they had for Yahshi?

In the end, it did not matter. Her family was not part of the Force, nor part of the Underground. They were safe without her. Free.

From the tunnel outside, Varin slammed the meeting room door, and Vell raised her head to see over fifty pairs of eyes staring back at her. Her lips parted in disbelief. She had expected just a handful of Council members—the ones she had seen on stage during the announcement of Prince Runix's return—but the people in this room made up at least half the size of the Force.

The Council stared at her impatiently, and her cheeks warmed up at the realization that Yahshi had likely left the room to find her, because he wouldn't give the presentation without her here.

Vell leaned toward him, whispering, "I thought there were only ten."

"Those are just the public representatives," he whispered back, guiding her to a seat near the front of the room. "You can sit here." He let go of her hand and took a deep breath, pulling a notebook out of his pocket and flipping through the pages.

Vell mindlessly sat. She knew this was her cue, in the silent moment before his presentation, when he expected her to say something encouraging. She also knew this was her only opportunity to disappoint him, and tell him to ask the Council for more time, because there was no way they would accept his plan. But she couldn't bring herself to speak.

Yahshi finished reviewing his notes and looked over at her, lingering close for a moment longer.

Say it, she told herself. *You know Dice is right. Tell him to back out.*

His eyes drooped slightly as he came to terms with the fact that she had nothing to say. He turned and walked toward the center of the room, leaving Vell with her mouth open, struggling to call him back.

She couldn't do it.

"Hi, everyone!" Yahshi said, projecting his voice loud enough for it to echo through the chamber. He scanned the group of Council members standing on the opposite side of the room, watching him with stoic faces. With another deep breath, he referred to his notes again, flipping through the pages as though he'd already forgotten what to say.

Vell gulped, crossing her hands together in her lap.

"Umm... I know I only worked for the Force for nine days," he said, looking up from his notes. "But I trained at the Academy for eighteen years—I mean, *months*—before then."

He winced, and took a breath, before continuing.

"Because of this, I know many guardians personally, and I'm familiar with just how smart and capable they are. We can't underestimate them. Every day our carventers spend on the tunnel is an extra day for them to find our hideout. By moving slowly, and overly carefully, we're risking the lives of everyone involved—all of Headquarters, hiders at our other sister bases down the Waterway, and our collectors and couriers above ground."

Vell nodded. Yahshi had said everything well so far by setting the stage with urgency—and it clearly captured the Council's attention. The apex fell quiet, still, as he turned the page and referenced his next list of bullets.

"Being a former guardian has also opened my eyes to how brainwashed they are," he continued. "Just a handful of key players control the narrative. The rest are just following orders, doing what they believe is right. They are good people who fight us because they believe us to be the enemy. And if they were to learn the truth, they would join us. I'm an example that it's possible. So is she."

He met eyes with Vell. She smiled back.

His words had stirred the Council, sparking whispers and darting eyes. Now that they were listening, he stood up straighter and spoke with more confidence.

"For starters, my friend Pinto Dempsey shared a quarter with me at the Academy for months. He lost an eye when he was young during an Eastern raid, which he believes your people are responsible for. If he were to learn that it was actually the Force that gouged out his eye, his perspective would change.

"Secondly, my friend Quax Avarium grew up with me in the town of Sitra. Even my father—well, my *adoptive* father—knew him personally, and liked him.

"Third, my friend Keiyo Pickett opened up to me once at the Academy, saying he never particularly wanted to be a Nightshade. He told me that whatever the Force is, it can't be good. He's already primed to take our side.

"And lastly," Yahshi continued, "an instructor at the Academy named Doctor Blimmery has even broken the rules to prioritize kindness. Being in his mid-fifties gives him a lot of influence in the Force—he could be a powerful ally."

"What are you suggesting?" Rimoso yelled, losing patience with his long-winded introduction.

"I want you to send me up," Yahshi replied.

"Yahshi, you can't," Vell spouted out, her eyes widening. This wasn't part of the plan they'd agreed on. As far as she knew, he wanted to send anti-propaganda posters to the surface, using the overground couriers and collectors to help distribute them westward. They also planned security measures to avoid putting their network in danger. Supplies would come down, posters would go up—no one would find out.

Yahshi looked back at Vell and lowered his voice so only she could hear him. "The idea struck me last night, and I couldn't sleep. It's the only way." He faced the Council again and raised his voice. "The Force wants *me*. So let them have me. Let me go to them, and tell them the truth."

The Council erupted with heated shouts. His presentation had not even sparked a discussion. Of course they wouldn't send him up for such a ridiculous suicide mission, and Vell internally thanked them for it.

As the shouting settled, Lira stepped forward from the group of Council members. She leaned over to cough a few times, and when she straightened up, a solemn look crossed her face.

"I'm sorry, Prince Runix," she said, her voice hoarse. "We can't blindly trust that the Nightshades will believe the truth. You and Vell are the exception to the rule."

"You don't know that for certain!" Yahshi argued.

"And besides—we can't let you go up. It's too dangerous. You're the Prince."

"I've survived them once, and I can do it again. Once I get past Border Control, I can make my way to Vakoi City on foot, undercover, and I'll only speak to the guardians I trust the most."

"They'll imprison you," Lira argued. "And then they'll kill you, like they killed your family."

From behind Lira, Rimoso smirked, and Tonna lowered her head with a sigh.

"There are too many unknowns with your plan," Lira continued. "And besides, we need you."

"I don't want the power," Yahshi stated. "I don't want to be the Prince."

"But we need you to be. You give our people hope in the Atherus Empire's restoration. It's not about power. It's about preserving morale."

"Let's take a vote!" Rimoso shouted before Yahshi could reply. "All in favor of sending Prince Runix up?"

Not a single hand.

Rimoso's gaze drifted to Vell, who sat as a silent bystander. "How about you?"

"I'm not a Council member," she replied.

"But if you were, what would your vote be?"

Vell pursed her lips, meeting Yahshi's desperate gaze. His eyes urged her to raise her hand, and prove that she believed in him.

This falsity had gone on for too long. It was time to be honest, so she kept her arm down and shook her head.

"I'm sorry, Yahshi. No."

His eyes dulled, and he shoved his notebook back into his pocket, his jaw tightening as he rushed for the door. Vell shot Rimoso a glare before following Yahshi out of the meeting room and into the hallway. She walked so fast that Varin didn't have time to taunt her as she passed.

"Wait!"

Yahshi stopped and turned around, facing her with narrowed eyes. "You don't actually believe in me, do you? No wonder you didn't show up on time. You knew I'd make a fool of myself, and you let me do it."

"No, stop. I-I *want* to believe in you. I do." Her eyes watered as she took a step toward him. "But not with this plan. I can't lose you."

He scowled at her, raising his voice. "It's the only way."

"Then send *me* up instead."

"No!" he shouted back.

Vell gulped at his sharp response, and his expression softened. It seemed he finally understood her point. His plan was so risky that he would only execute it himself.

He turned and headed down the tunnel, his head held low. "I need to think."

"Yahshi," she called.

He didn't look back.

"Thanks for helping." Aero set two wooden boxes down and unlatched them. "I've got a lot more in the other room, but we can start with these two. The left one's for the trip, and the right one's for distribution. We need to have everything packed in the next three hours, before the tides head south."

"A bit last-minute," Vell said.

"Well, I can't say I'm looking forward to leaving," Aero admitted with a guilty stare.

Vell nodded, putting the pieces together. "So this is why you got me that job."

"You can't rely on me anymore. Not while I'm traveling, at least." Aero headed to a shelf stocked with glass jars of fish oil, which Vell imagined were a great resource for medicine underground.

"Who else is going?"

"Just Saunti. Usually Varin does the boat stuff, but he's too busy with the Guild, or some stupid excuse like that, so the Council's sending Cricket instead. As if *he* can help! He doesn't even know what the Waterway *is*."

"But he lived by the ocean," Vell recalled. "Maybe he knows something about boats."

"Hopefully." Aero took a deep breath with her eyes closed, forcing her frustration away. It was something Vell caught her doing sometimes. She regulated her emotions much better than most people she had known.

Aero opened her eyes and smiled. "Alright," she said with her usual cheerfulness. "We'll fill the first one with fish oil. There's a production point in Atherus City that makes tons of it, and our sister bases are running low." She walked two jars to the cargo box on the right and set them inside.

Vell followed suit, grabbing two jars of her own. "How long will you be gone?"

"About ten days, give or take a few."

Her first few words stung. She'd be gone for longer than Vell had known her.

"Are you sure I can't come with you?"

Aero gave her a look, and Vell sighed, setting two more jars in the box. All she'd do was take up space on the boat—and besides, Yahshi needed her right now.

They went quiet for a while, slowly filling up the wooden box with jarred fish oil. Aero left to grab another wooden box for distribution, and when she returned, they started transferring stacks of paper into it.

"So how did Yahshi do?" Aero asked, finally breaking the silence.

Vell shrugged. "Bad."

"Oh, come on! Emphasize, Vell. Use your big girl words. We've talked about this."

"*Bad* is really the best word to describe his presentation." She quickly changed the subject. "Are you... going up during this trip?"

"Up? No, I wish!" Aero chuckled. "I just collect goods and drop stuff off. Hardly leave the boat. Haven't been up since I was four."

"How much do you remember?" Vell asked.

"A lot more than people think. Well, I wasn't in school yet, so I can't really remember any friends. Or people, really. But I miss the nature, the sky, the changing weather. I used to spend a lot of time outdoors—that I remember."

"I get it. Sometimes, when I couldn't sleep at the Academy, I'd go outside and look for plants in the woods. I used to do that all the time when I was little. Now the closest thing we have to nature is the Waterway, and a very limited amount of plants."

"I'm so sick of those stupid mushrooms."

Vell laughed, and they moved on to transfer canned beans into a box for Aero and Saunti.

"Can you tell me what the moon looks like?" Aero asked. "Sometimes when Saunti would deliver goods, I'd ask him, but he's not the best with words."

"It always looks different," Vell said. "Sometimes it's shadowed by the clouds that hang over the island. Other times, it's bright and clear, presenting itself in different shapes. Even when the night clouds cover it completely, you can still feel its presence, because the clouds carry its light."

"See, that's what I mean by using your big girl words." Aero elbowed her side. "Sounds pretty."

"You'll get to see it again."

"And you'll get to see it too." Aero reached out, wrapping her in a hug. "In the meantime, you've got a life down here. Don't forget that."

She was too stunned to hug Aero back. She couldn't remember the last time she'd hugged anyone but the boys in her graduating class.

When Aero pulled away, Vell grinned. "I'll miss you."

The words came out forced, but Aero seemed to accept their sincerity nonetheless, because she smiled back and said, "I'll miss you too."

CHAPTER 17

BACKSTABBER

Day 9 Underground | Clocks Read 20:14

♫ PRODIGAL - SAINT MESA ♫

According to Rimoso, Yahshi's presentation had flopped as expected, and the Council shared more doubts than ever about the former Nightshade's leadership potential. Eliminating him now, during his period of highest scrutiny, would minimize the Council's grief.

Saunti glanced into the canteen as he passed its multiple entryways.

Aero and Vell shared a late supper together before the trip. *Perfect.*

Dice sat with Varin just a few tables away. *Even more perfect.*

The timing was immaculate. The clocks were ticking. Saunti had one hour to execute his plan.

He left the canteen behind, zooming through the tunnels in search of Dice's lab. He'd been there just once, eight days ago, so he could only recall its general location. Luckily, it was the only chamber in the area with a metal door instead of an open entryway, so he found it easily. The key Rimoso had slipped to him that morning turned in the lock, and a green light struck his eyes upon entering the lab.

Saunti locked the door behind him and tucked the key into his coat pocket, basking in the glow of the bioluminescent fungi reflecting off the room's mirrors. The toad lilies swayed gently as he weaved around their planters, making his way to the smaller connected chamber opposite the door.

He passed the single plant bed of calabar bushes in the center of the room and approached Dice's carved-out desk. While he couldn't open the lockbox containing Vell's belladonna vials, calabar seemed like the better option anyway. Either could kill—but Dice would be less likely to notice one of his own vials going missing than one of hers.

He rifled through the desk shelves, but all he found were old papers—schematics of clockwork parts, journal entries from his time in the Academy program, and senseless scientific calculations.

No vials. He shoved the papers back into place and scanned the room. *He has to keep his calabar serum somewhere.*

The only other place he could think to look through were the two bookshelves chiseled into the opposite wall, one on each side of the entryway he'd come through. From his experience as a courier, Saunti had learned about the different hiding spots collectors above ground stored their supplies in before each delivery, and bookshelves were among the most common. Perhaps Dice would use the same tactic.

Saunti cleared each shelf, one at a time, from top to bottom. Dice kept many nonfiction books that Vakoi had banned, including *The Force's Hidden Agenda*, but the equal number of mystery novels made him raise a brow. The logos on their spines revealed them to be publications of Pandora's Box, an artistic collective based in Vakoi City. It was strange to think that Dice would enjoy the works of a group from the enemy's capital. *Art is art, I suppose.*

Finally, Saunti cleared out the second-highest shelf, and his lips curved into a smile. There they were—a row of ten holes carved near the back of the shelf, seven of them occupied by vials of calabar serum. The liquid glowed with a color difficult to pinpoint, altered by the greenish air, but he was sure it was much lighter than Vell's belladonna serum.

With a gentle hand, Saunti pulled one vial free and put every book from the shelf back in place, covering the hiding spot. Next, he reached into his front coat pocket for a syringe—which he'd snatched from an infirmary earlier that day—and set it on Dice's desk.

His plan had been straightforward so far, but something about opening the vial made his heart race. He remembered the toad lily Dice had destroyed with just one drop of Vell's belladonna serum. Since calabar was just as lethal as belladonna, Saunti couldn't afford to be sloppy and risk spilling the serum on himself.

He wasn't sure if the air could capture its toxins, so he held his breath as he pulled the cork stopper off. The serum inside swayed from the pressure, but thankfully, it didn't overflow.

Saunti nearly sighed in relief but stopped himself, saving his breath. With the vial in one hand and the syringe in the other, he dipped the tip into the serum and, using his thumb, pulled the plunger up to fill it.

There was more poison than the syringe could hold, so he put the cork stopper back on and inhaled a sharp breath. While he didn't want to keep such a dangerous vial, leaving it behind would surely draw Dice's attention. He slipped it into one pocket and capped the syringe before sliding it into the other, careful to keep the needle from piercing through his clothes.

Then he snuck out, a half-empty vial in one pocket and a loaded syringe in the other.

Saunti knocked on a metal door engraved with the name *TONNA*. Exactly thirty seconds passed without an answer—his eyes on the nearest clock—before he decided that his mother was most likely in the apex with the other Council members, discussing Yahshi's presentation. Everything was still going according to plan.

He plucked a note from his coat pocket, his hands shaking despite all his preparation. While he had no intention of getting away with murder—proven by the words on this page—he needed to ensure his mother wouldn't read the truth until *after* he'd finished the job. She could tattle to the Council later, let them deal with him however they saw fit—but for now, he needed to buy himself time to escape with Aero down the Waterway.

He had believed a lie about his father for years, and he would not wish the same upon her. She deserved to hear the truth directly from him.

After a glance left and right, ensuring he was alone, Saunti leaned over, sliding his confession through the crack under Tonna's door.

I'm sorry, Mother. There's no other way.

He straightened and blinked at the door, suddenly aware he couldn't take back the note now. With one simple action, he had sealed his fate.

His expression hardened as he continued down the tunnel, halting at a second door engraved with the name *RUNIX*. He didn't hesitate to pound on the metal, and he continued knocking until the former Nightshade jerked the door open, his hair unkempt, his forehead creased with a frown.

Saunti rubbed his sore knuckles, peering past Yahshi to find wrinkled pages scattered about the floor of his chamber. He had drawn maps of the island, written lists of names with descriptions, and sketched floor plans of buildings in Vakoi City with question marks around the parts he'd forgotten.

By the time Saunti looked back at him, Yahshi's frown had faded. Perhaps he had expected a scolding from a Council member and welcomed a surprise visit from his somewhat-brother instead. Like Rimoso had instructed, Saunti had purposefully kept his distance from him to maintain Yahshi's curiosity and ensure his receptiveness once approached.

"The Prince keeps mentioning you to Tonna and Lira," Rimoso had shared a few days prior. *"He wants a connection with you, wants your approval. We can use that to our advantage."*

Yahshi opened his mouth, but the words escaped him.

"I heard about your presentation," Saunti said, sparing him the trouble of starting the conversation. He shoved his way past Yahshi and looked around. It was a humble chamber, but at least he had his own space instead of a hole in the wall to sleep in. *Why does he deserve this, just because he was born with Atherus blood?*

Saunti shook his thought away. Now wasn't the time for resentment.

Yahshi shut the door and leaned against it, eyes on his boots. "Is *everyone* talking about it?"

"Just the Council. My mother told me everything," Saunti lied, walking circles around Yahshi's notes on the floor. He was a slow reader, but he only needed to finish a few sentences to confirm Rimoso's claim—Yahshi didn't want to hurt anyone on either side. *He's afraid to get his hands dirty.*

Saunti halted and looked up from the notes, staring at the Prince until he met his gaze. "I have an idea that might help you win over the Council."

Yahshi looked away with a chuckle. He seemed suddenly bitter. "A lot of people have ideas, but you don't get it. I don't want to hurt—"

"It's not gonna hurt anyone," Saunti said, which seemed to hold his attention. "I'll tell you everything about it, but we need to go somewhere quiet."

Yahshi frowned and looked around, as if to say, *It's quiet here.*

"I can't risk anyone in the Council eavesdropping." Saunti tucked his hands into his pockets, his fingers meeting the cold glass of the vial and syringe. "So, will you hear me out or not?"

Saunti led him to the most desolate area he knew—the tunnels between the inventory room and the access point. They were about twenty minutes from the center of Headquarters now, which would give him more than enough time for the final part of his plan. He stopped and sat on the ground, pulling two folded pages out of his pocket.

"Can we talk now?" Yahshi asked, sitting beside him. Saunti had ignored every attempt at conversation on the way here.

"Listen. No one knows what I'm about to tell you. Not even my mother." He faced Yahshi with narrowed eyes, fidgeting with the pages in his hands. "Up until eight days ago, I worked at a lumber mill in Atherus City. One of my coworkers, along with an old classmate of mine, was developing an invention for war."

"What kind of invention?"

"They call it a *boombox.* It sets off a massive fire that doesn't grow—it just comes out of nowhere. I've seen it myself." Saunti handed Yahshi his folded pages. "My first note is for you. It contains instructions on how to reach my coworker Podge from the access point. He lives along the coast with his parents. I drew a picture of what his house looks like."

Yahshi unfolded the first paper and chuckled at the sloppy sketch of a generic house.

"The second note is for Podge, where I explain how his boomboxes could help us," Saunti continued. "To put it simply, Vakoi's system is fragile. Most goods from Eastern production points are brought to Saver Stores in the West, and the money earned from them funds the Force. If we boom the production points, the stores won't have supplies to sell anymore. Imagine what would happen if the Nightshades were no longer paid handsomely."

Yahshi stared at the tunnel wall. "That could actually work. It would make the Force scramble and keep us safe by giving them bigger problems than finding us."

"And if we strike the production points at night, none of the workers would get hurt."

With a grin, Yahshi met Saunti's gaze again. "Why are you helping me all of a sudden?"

"I'm *not* helping you," he replied. "I'm helping the Underground."

Yahshi's smile faded a bit—though not completely—as he unfolded the second page and lowered his head to read the message for Podge. That's when Saunti slipped his hand into his coat pocket, his fingers brushing the syringe's cold glass.

"It's done," Saunti said, shutting the door behind him.

Rimoso sat at his desk, dragging a dagger across a whetstone to sharpen it. When he looked back at Saunti, his lips peeled apart to reveal a crooked smirk.

"Where's the body?"

"In the Waterway, like you asked."

"Was my daughter there?"

"No one saw. Her boat was empty."

Saunti gulped as Rimoso stood, sharpened dagger in hand. There was no guarantee that he wouldn't murder the person who had done his dirty work, to fully cover his tracks.

"You did a good thing, Saunti." He tossed his dagger from one hand to the other, scanning the boy from head to toe. "I knew your father well, before he left to raise the Prince in enemy territory. He was a good man, and a good friend. You understand that this thing you've done doesn't change that, right?"

"Of course," Saunti said, though he knew that if his father were watching from the stars, these circumstances would crush him.

Rimoso held his blade up to a wall torch, staring at his reflection in the steel. "I assume you want to know what the next steps are from here."

"I did the job." Saunti stepped toward Rimoso, his tone sharp. "I'm over dish duty."

"Done. You'll get a spot in my Guild, as promised." Rimoso finally set the dagger on his desk. "And since the body's gone, we're going to let this mystery play out. No one is to blame right now. If fingers are ever pointed at you, I'll fix it. You've done me a massive favor, after all."

As Rimoso made his way toward him, Saunti tucked his hands into his pockets. His pulse quickened as he grasped his syringe of calabar.

"But if you tell anyone what we've done," Rimoso whispered, "I'll make you disappear too."

Saunti nodded, his grip on the syringe tightening.

"Now, come on!" Rimoso patted his shoulder, his tone lightening. "Before you hit the water, let me show you—"

Saunti held his breath as the tip of the syringe sunk into the man's back. He jammed his thumb against the plunger, injecting the calabar serum he'd claimed to have killed Yahshi with.

Rimoso turned around, his eyes narrowing. "*You...*"

His poisonous voice proved that he had put the pieces together. Saunti had not killed Yahshi. In fact, he had never intended to. He had known, since the moment he saw Rimoso smother that gecko, that the only way to stop him from murdering Yahshi was to murder him first.

Rimoso reached for the syringe in his back—it was barely out of reach. His face reddened as he stormed after Saunti, whose eyes darted to the only weapon in the room. He stumbled to the desk and snatched Rimoso's dagger, wielding it with shaky hands, but nothing could scare a man who knew he had seconds left to live.

With a shove, he threw Saunti aside, and the dagger slipped from his hands, striking the floor.

The man crouched to pick it up, but Saunti moved faster, darting to kick it out of reach. His heart pounded as it jumped and struck the opposite wall—well out of range.

Rimoso abandoned the dagger and lunged, his hands tightening around the sixteen-year-old's neck. Saunti stepped away to ease the pressure, but soon enough, his back struck the wall, and Rimoso lifted him off the ground, wringing the air out of his lungs.

He grabbed Rimoso's arms and dug his nails into them until they bled, but nothing deterred him. The man squeezed harder and bared his teeth, saliva dripping from the corners of his mouth.

Saunti's eyes widened as the blood left his head, his body weakening. In just moments, Rimoso would steal his life, and his only comfort was the knowledge that this cruel man would die soon after. Rimoso would not stop, just as Vakoi would not stop. They were the same, and there was no place for them on this island.

Yahshi didn't deserve special treatment for his bloodline, nor did he deserve to die—but this wasn't about him. This was about the Underground. Few people—if any but Saunti—would die to kill this corrupt Council member, and that's exactly why it had to be done.

With a few more blinks, Saunti's vision faded, and death inched closer. He stopped fighting the pain—his body relaxing, the world falling still. This was the end. He could feel it. And he chose to make peace with it.

Now it's your turn, Yahshi.

Just minutes ago, Yahshi had promised to seek Podge's help behind the Council's back, knowing Saunti would be gone on his trip and out of reach for a week. Only then had Saunti rushed off, pretending he was late to meet Aero at the Waterway.

He still trusted Yahshi to keep that promise—because nothing about their situation had changed.

Saunti would still be gone. Just in another form.

Before he knew it, he was falling—or flying. He couldn't tell for sure. All he felt was the whipping of air around his face. It seemed to be endless.

He only confirmed that he'd fallen when his head struck the floor, leaving his ears ringing. *That doesn't sound like the quarter-day bell.*

As soon as he opened his eyes, he inhaled a gasp of burning air. His lungs were on fire. Everything was on fire. He swore he could still feel Rimoso gripping his neck, but when he reached to pry the man's hands away, his fingers met his own skin.

Saunti flinched. His neck was tender to his touch.

He lay on the floor of Rimoso's chamber, inhaling rapid breaths over and over, as though each one might be the last. While he knew he was breathing, he couldn't tell if the air was real. Maybe this was all an illusion his mind had made up in the fleeting final seconds of his life. He could still feel death's breath against his cheeks, threatening to take him out.

Even when his vision sharpened to reveal a view of the dagger he had kicked across the room, he didn't believe he was still in Rimoso's chamber. It was only when he craned his sore neck to see the Council member on the floor beside him—his muscles twitching and spasming, his cheek drenched in his own saliva—that he accepted his survival.

Saunti dragged himself across the floor, away from Rimoso, and watched him until he stopped moving. Then he stood slowly, struggling to even his breaths, and crept toward the man. He nudged him with his boot.

No reaction.

Saunti glanced at the dagger. He could stab Rimoso, just to make sure, but he shook the thought away. Even if he was still gripping his life, the poison would end him soon enough.

His eyes darted to the clock on Rimoso's wall, his heartbeats finally slowing down. He and Aero had scheduled to leave in just five minutes, and it would take at least ten to get to the Waterway from here, based on the path Aero had described earlier that day.

Saunti rushed to the door and shuffled to a stop at the sight of his own reflection in Rimoso's mirror. The man's grip had left bruises on his neck from his attempt to drain the air out of his lungs. He couldn't possibly face

Aero looking like this, so he rustled through Rimoso's dresser and grabbed the first scarf he could find—a faded yellow one, which he looped around his neck on his way out.

As Saunti stepped into the empty tunnel outside, he peered back at Rimoso's body. He had killed his own kind. He was no better than a Nightshade.

Don't think like that. He shook his head and left the room. *It had to be done.*

Saunti's eyes widened at the underground river. Its water glowed a greenish hue in the light of its surrounding mushrooms.

So this is the Waterway...

A boat waited along the shore, its cargo hold packed tight with goods, leaving just enough space for Aero and Saunti to ride atop the load.

Aero smiled as Saunti approached her. "You finally get a job that's better than washing dishes, and you show up late?"

"Sorry." Saunti adjusted the scarf around his neck.

"I hope you know how to use this thing."

"Of course. You ready?"

When she nodded, he pushed the boat forward into the river's gentle current, wading a few steps into the water before leaping on deck. He headed for the dashboard and lowered the boat's water wheels with a lever—the wheels would catch the water's flow and convert it into a steady propulsion. He'd learned how to use boats like these in school, as one of the production points in Atherus City involved fishing off the coast.

"Thank the stars..." Aero muttered. She lit a torch and mounted it to a stand on the dashboard, gesturing for Saunti to sit at the steering wheel. "Is that your scarf?"

"Dice lent it to me," he said, his voice stiff.

A few moments after he took a seat, Aero chuckled. "We need to move faster, Cricket. It's always a race against the clocks with the Waterway's changing tides."

The path ahead looked straight for a while, so Saunti didn't need to steer. He detached a pair of paddles from the boat's side and used them to propel the boat even faster. As he rowed and rowed, they drifted farther from the crime scene, but he couldn't out-row the guilt compounding within.

He glanced over his shoulder, and in the flickering torchlight, Aero smiled.

She deserves to know.

CHAPTER 18

GOOD ONE

Beef is back in stock at your local Saver Store!

Evaris gasped, her eyes jolting open as a hand tightened around her shoulder.

"Relax." Pinto released her and smiled. "It's me." He had climbed to her classic spot on a higher bunk to wake her, and as usual, he was already in uniform, his hair damp from a cold shower on a lower floor of the Border Control tower.

She sighed and yanked a quilt over her head. "You wake up too early."

"You sleep too late," he countered, ripping the blanket away.

Evaris curled over and shivered as Pinto climbed down the ladder, taking the quilt with him. She heard him slip his notebooks into his overcoat and knew exactly where each went without looking—his navy-blue notebook in his left interior pocket, and his mysterious scarlet-red one in his right.

"I've given you more than enough time to wake up, Commander." The hint of playfulness in his voice was gone now.

"Fine." She flipped over to peer down at him from the top bunk, a few strands of ash-brown hair flailing over her cheek, obscuring her vision. "Could you just—"

"Already on it," Pinto said, leaving the room with a wave of his hand.

Evaris chuckled, giving her arms a few rubs to warm them up before descending the ladder. On the lower bunk was a fresh set of pants and a white button-up that matched the ones she'd slept in. Pinto had laid them out for her, perhaps to busy himself as he waited for her to shuffle out of bed.

"Mother?" she called out, loudly enough for him to hear from the hall.

"Hurry up!" he yelled back.

Evaris swapped her clothes for the fresh ones, fastened her tie, and strapped her vest with interior armor into place, the clasps clicking shut.

Day five. She grabbed her overcoat from a hook on the wall and slipped it on. *I can't believe it.*

In less than a week, she and Pinto had grown so in-tune with each other's routines that it was strange to realize this trip was ending. It felt as though they'd been living and working together for years, yet at the same time, it had gone by too fast. They only had two more days of investigating before their obligatory return to Vakoi City, when life would go back to the boring normal.

Evaris slung her bow and a quiver of arrows over her back, took a deep breath, and joined Pinto in the hallway.

"Finally!" he exclaimed.

As usual, they burned three hours of the early morning traveling from the border to their next destination near the shore. Today it was Oaken, a grain cultivation town where someone had reported spotting Yahshi toward the end of his journey to Atherus City.

Since they left at dawn, it was only noon when they finished visiting the homes of every recently executed traitor. The new strategy they'd employed yesterday to work in batches—ghost homes first, interrogations second—rather than investigating traitors one at a time, was proving to be a huge time-saver. The only downside was that it required much more careful note-taking, but Pinto specialized in that anyway.

"Oh, great," he muttered, flipping through the last pages of his navy-blue notebook. There were three remaining, and they still had multiple workers left to interrogate at the production point. "We're finally ahead of schedule, and now *this*?"

"Just use your red one," Evaris suggested, though she knew he wouldn't do it. Pinto organized his notes meticulously—everything related to the case went in his blue notebook, and at the end of each night, he would write in his scarlet one. The red book was clearly personal, and she hoped his response to her suggestion would give her a hint as to what he was filling it with.

"No, that one has a different purpose," Pinto said vaguely. His eye widened as he faced her, pointing his finger. "How about your notepad? Could you spare some pages from that?"

"That one has a different purpose too," she replied. It seemed they had put each other in check.

"This is more important than tic tac toe, Commander."

Evaris tapped her fingers against the table, taking a moment to think. There were no Saver Stores in Eastern Territory, and the ration pickup stations only offered necessities—at best, they could snag some loose pieces of paper. For a niche item like a notebook, they'd have to go to a—

"Don't say it." Pinto shut his journal and slipped it back into his overcoat. "We can't go *there*. They're crawling with rebels."

"That's a stereotype," Evaris said.

"Oh, *please*. Our economy has no need for town markets in Eastern Territory. If the sellers were loyal to the Vakoi Empire, they'd work at production points like everyone else, but instead, they're earning money independently and cheating the system."

"Actually, according to our statistics, market vendors make up the poorest segment of the Eastern population. It's not easy to *cheat the system*."

"I bet most of them are with the Underground."

"Then it's even better that we go there to investigate, right?" Evaris stood, heading for the door, and Pinto rushed to catch up to her.

"We *can't*." He lowered his voice as they reentered the main room so the staring workers wouldn't overhear. "It's too dangerous for someone like you. If something were to happen, I'd never forgive myself."

"Someone like me?" Evaris laughed. "I'm two years your senior, Red. I have more experience with the Underground than you."

"No you don't, Commander," he said, his voice stiff.

Evaris looked over at the patch covering his eye, her smile fading. The more time she spent with him, the more invisible his loss became. It was easy to forget that he was a raid victim—the only raid victim in the Force.

"Do you want that notebook or not?" she asked, her voice tight from the lump in her throat.

"I need it."

"Then we're going."

Pinto entered the bustling market with one hand in his overcoat, bluffing to the sellers and customers with a dagger he no longer had. In a matter of seconds, people took notice of his and Evaris's uniforms, and the crowd of shoppers thinned, leaking through the back door. With no excuse to leave, the sellers stayed behind at their stalls, avoiding eye contact.

Pinto leaned over Evaris's shoulder. "Don't make any sudden movements," he whispered, but it was so quiet that she was certain a few sellers must have heard him.

Evaris jerked her head away from him, her cheeks heating up. Pinto seemed to believe the entire East was composed of criminals. Members of the Underground wouldn't work in markets like this, considering the disloyal stereotype it would earn them. These market vendors likely hated the Vakoi Empire, but they were harmless—the silent, brooding type of rebels.

She quickened her pace, forcing Pinto to follow her to a stand offering an assortment of colorful, handcrafted notebooks. The seller grew restless the longer they lingered, surveying the pieces.

"I insist..." The woman behind the stand gestured to the books. "Take whatever you like. Free."

"We're not here to cause trouble." Evaris smiled, hoping to ease the woman's paranoia—but Pinto's glare likely canceled out her kindness. She grabbed another stack of notebooks and flipped through them, searching for a navy-blue replacement. Most were brightly colored with painted patterns and unique stones glued on for decoration. *The Starfalls would love these.*

She paused when she encountered a simple wooden cover that stood out from the rest. The woman had painted it navy blue, but she'd also engraved a symbol Evaris had only seen in textbooks—the Atherus Royal Family's crest.

Pinto gasped, peering up at the woman. "Why would you make that?"

"I didn't know it was in there!" With freakishly large eyes, the woman shook her palms in front of her. "I promise, I'm just a reseller!"

Pinto leaned over the stand, and she stepped back. "Like hell you are."

His voice was so cold that it even sent a chill down Evaris's spine.

The woman struggled to reply, her lips trembling. She took another step back as Evaris reached into her overcoat. "Please don't—"

"How much?" she interrupted, pulling out a velvet pouch of coins.

Pinto's jaw dropped. "Commander!"

"How much?" Evaris repeated, firmer this time.

The woman looked back and forth between them, as though this were some kind of test. Her voice was barely audible as she muttered, "Ten."

She counted fifteen coins and offered them to the woman. It was not what the Force would have wanted her to do, but it would earn her another X in her notebook, so to her, it was worth it.

The woman took the money, her voice even quieter as she whispered, "Thank you." She wouldn't stop shaking, even after Evaris turned to leave, dragging Pinto by his arm before he could intervene. He tensed up in her grip, but thankfully, he didn't argue until they exited the building.

"We should detain her," Pinto said, pacing in front of the market door. "Or at the very least, we should have the officers at Oaken Post deal with her."

Evaris whipped a dagger out of her overcoat and pressed it to the wooden cover, scraping off the engraving of the Atherus Royal Family crest. Her blade took some paint off too, leaving jagged, brown scratch marks among the sea of blue.

"And now you're destroying the evidence?"

"We've got bigger fish to catch." Evaris shoved the notebook into Pinto's hands. "Plus, it was the only blue one available."

Pinto frowned as Evaris tucked her dagger away and pulled out her notepad. She flipped to the latest page and marked another X.

"What the hell are you doing?" Pinto demanded. "And don't even try lying to me again, because I know that isn't tic tac toe."

"It's none of your business." Evaris tucked her notepad away and attempted to step around him, but he blocked her path.

"Quite frankly, it *is* my business, because I made a vow to report suspicious activity within or outside the Force." He waved his new book in her face. "You just purchased something with the enemy's symbol on it and marked another *X*—that's pretty darn suspicious to me."

She scoffed. "Who are you to threaten *me*? I've done nothing but look out for you. No other guardian would have joined you on this crazy trip, and you know it."

Pinto gulped, lowering the book. "I'm not trying to threaten you," he said, his voice softer now. "I'm just trying to understand how you think. It feels like any time I ask you something remotely personal, you brush my curiosity aside—and yet you're always trying to squeeze personal information out of *me*, and trying to understand how *I* think. That's not fair, Commander."

Evaris pursed her lips. It hadn't clicked, until Pinto spelled it out for her, that she *did* want to understand him better. She wanted to know what his little sister was like, how he felt about the trip so far, and what he wrote in that red book of his every night. However, in exchange, she had done nothing but keep him at arm's length.

With a sigh, she pulled her notepad back out and stepped closer to him, allowing him to watch her flip through the filled pages, each line featuring a list of *X*s and *O*s in a seemingly random order. "I've been keeping a log of every good and bad deed I've done."

Pinto's grip tightened on his scratched notebook. "You call it *good* to overpay a rebel?"

"It's a strict black-and-white system." She stopped on the last page and skimmed over the markings, mentally recalling what each recent one represented. "If I kill someone, regardless of my intentions, it's an *O*. If I do something nice for someone, regardless of who they are, it's an *X*. I rate the action in isolation. I keep it simple."

"That's a broken system. Everything has nuance."

"But that's the problem, Red. It's easy to get lost in the gray. This notebook is the only sense of morality I have left in a line of work as complicated as ours."

Pinto's eye narrowed as he studied her markings. "So you consider this purchase a good deed, regardless of the traitorous implications, solely because you tipped?"

"It's that simple."

He met her gaze, his face less red now. He seemed genuinely curious when he asked, "What's the point of that?"

Evaris thought back to her time at the Academy, when she started to feel like the program was turning her into someone else—someone she didn't like. That's when she'd started tracking her deeds.

"I made a promise to myself to be a good one more often than not." Her cheeks warmed as she looked away. Pinto was the first person to pry hard enough for her to say it aloud.

"Well, have you?"

She shrugged, still avoiding his probing eye. "Honestly, I'm too scared to tally my *X*s and *O*s. Maybe someday I'll manage to count."

Pinto's silence made her regret opening up at all. She tucked her notebook away and rushed to untie her white horse from a hitching post, eager to move on from this conversation. His gaze burned through her as she fumbled to get the knot undone.

"Hey," he said, finally drawing her eyes back to him.

Evaris blinked, a weight pressing on her chest. *I feel sick.*

His face held no emotion, but that somehow made his next words feel more genuine.

"Thanks for sharing that."

Without replying, Evaris turned away and finally undid the knot. She was certain that for just a moment, that pressure in her chest turned into something else.

She didn't want to give it a name.

They spent the following day in Erenford, where Evaris's operative unit had intercepted Yahshi during the special operation. With their new system in place, they were doing great on time—it was turning out to be their smoothest day yet—but they still hadn't found any commonalities between the recently deceased traitors.

Evaris tapped her fingers against a desk in yet another cramped production point office, waiting for the next worker in an orange jumpsuit to be sent in for questioning. She could hear Pinto biting his nails, but didn't scold him like usual, because she was worried about the same thing: *What if there isn't a code at all?*

It was strange how invested she'd become in this mystery. After nearly six days on the move, visiting dozens of traitors' homes and speaking with workers who had known them, she'd gone from tagging along to actively waiting for a lead. It was hard to tell whether she'd caught Pinto's obsession like a sickness—or if she simply didn't want to see him let himself down.

"Let's face it, Commander—Erenford is a dead end. I say we end our interrogations here and hit a secondary location. If we move quickly, we can reach Grimward before nightfall."

Evaris yawned for what felt like the hundredth time that hour. "We removed Grimward from our list, remember?" They had made cuts to their schedule a few days prior, allowing them more time at each location.

He folded his hands together, his voice tight. "But what if it's worth the extra stop?"

She met his gaze with a sad smile. He was clearly clinging to what little hope he had left. Tomorrow was their last day before their expected return to Vakoi City. They were running out of time.

"I'm sorry, Red, but we need to finish up here and pack for the night. Let's save our energy for tomorrow, okay?"

"But—"

"If we're going to find a lead anywhere, it's Atherus City."

That night, Evaris shuffled and peered off her top bunk, studying Pinto from across the dim room of the Border Control tower. He sat hunched over on a lower bunk, spilling his thoughts onto the pages of his scarlet journal, as he'd done every night since their second day of traveling.

She frowned, watching his hand zip across the page. "What are you writing about?"

"Nothing really," Pinto replied, as he always did.

"Poetry?"

He chuckled, his pencil pausing for just a moment. "Do I look like I write poetry?"

"About pirates, maybe."

He shook his head and continued writing, his smile gone.

"Fiction or nonfiction?"

"It's nothing," he snapped, his grip on the pencil tightening.

Evaris frowned. *So much for yesterday's lecture about opening up.* It didn't seem like a fair trade—that he could pressure her into telling him about her notepad, but he couldn't offer her at least a hint about what he was writing. However, this was their last night together, and she would rather not spend it bitter, so she changed the subject.

"You know, I really do hope things work out tomorrow," she muttered. "I didn't have much faith in your code theory at first, but I feel like you're onto something."

Pinto didn't reply, which made Evaris wonder if she hadn't spoken loudly enough. Regardless, she figured he wanted to focus on his writing, so she didn't repeat it.

Just a minute later, he closed his red notebook and set it on his folded overcoat, which was on the floor by his bunk. He briefly met Evaris's gaze and smiled.

"Thanks, Commander."

"For what?"

"For that thing you said earlier, about believing in me." He slipped under the sheets and shut his eye. "It makes me feel less guilty about dragging you along."

Evaris smiled, and the room fell quiet again, filled with nothing but the subtle crackling of torches. She tried to come up with a new topic of discussion, but Pinto started snoring first.

"Are you asleep?"

He snored again in response, and that feeling in her chest came back to haunt her. Losing him to sleep this early disappointed her more than she would have liked. This was their last night together, and she surely wouldn't be able to sleep for a while, thanks to the coffee a Border Control officer had offered her less than an hour ago. *I knew I shouldn't have taken that cup.*

Evaris scooted closer to the edge of her bunk, and her eyes naturally wandered to the notebook on Pinto's overcoat. A guilty thought crossed her mind, and she flipped onto her other side, staring at the wall. *No, I couldn't.*

A louder voice in her head said, *This is your last night together. It's the only chance you'll have.*

Her legs moved down the ladder on their own, and she crossed the room as a guardian—without a sound. She crouched by Pinto's bed to pick up his red book, pausing to stare at him for a few seconds. Surely, any moment now, his eye would open, and he'd snatch the book from her in protest.

Go on. Stop me.

But he didn't stop her. He continued snoring, so she retrieved her notepad from her overcoat and added yet another *O* to her list. The letter released her guilt, and now there was nothing keeping her from leaving the room with his journal in hand.

In the hallway just outside, she rolled up the white sleeves of her button-up and rested her arms on a stone windowsill, allowing the chilly night breeze to brush against her cheeks. It was refreshing out here in the woods, without the lights of Vakoi City and the hum of distant parties and award ceremonies. These nights with Pinto had been calming. *Maybe that's why Aunt Cove lives in that cabin.*

Evaris rested Pinto's notebook against the windowsill, took a deep breath, and opened it to read the first page.

Dear Perma,

I haven't written to you since a few days before Vell delivered my last journal. A lot has changed since then, as I'm sure you've read in Capital Weekly. I'll update you as soon as I can.

> Forever your brother,
> Pinto

Another gust of wind rolled by, making the pages flick about. Evaris took that as a sign to turn a few more. She skimmed over Pinto's explanations of everything that had led to this trip, slowing down when she reached an entry about their second day of traveling.

> Dear Perma,
>
> Tonight I'm writing to you from the Border Control tower nearest to Arinoma. And by "nearest," I mean three-and-a-half hours away, because Arinoma lies along the eastern coast, and the Border Control towers are deep inland.
>
> Commander Evaris and I left Arinoma when we were too tired to keep investigating, which proved to be a massive blunder, since it took so long to reach this tower. I need to ensure we leave before I'm tired from now on. Actually, we should leave before Commander Evaris is tired, because she's proven to have a lower work tolerance than me. I've learned she needs frequent breaks for food and conversation or she disengages, and the more brain power I have during this trip, the better.
>
> Forever your brother,
> Pinto

Evaris rolled her eyes and turned the page, reading through every entry he'd written during their trip. While both of his notebooks documented their travels, this red one didn't mention the deceased criminals' homes they visited or the people they interrogated. Instead, it held the mundane, in-between moments that Evaris would never have thought to cherish in words.

He wrote of their water breaks during long travels by horseback, their encounters with local officers, the awful foods they tried at ration pickup stations, and the subtle differences between the handful of Border Control towers they'd slept in. He wrote of his time with Evaris that wasn't spent working—when they were friends disguised as fellow guardians. He wrote of her as a partner with a shared mission, not just a required babysitter while he tackled this challenge alone.

She had read so many books, but none so immersive as this one. It was the first time she had encountered a piece written about her—and she absorbed every word, her fingers trailing along the lines he'd written.

A flame sparked within her as she closed Pinto's red book and leaned through the window, staring up at the stars.

You're a good one, Red. She hugged the book to her chest and smiled. *I can feel it.*

CHAPTER 19

CODE BREAKERS

Our latest shipment of Saver Store firewood
is perfect for cozy nights!

♫ STOP THE STARS · TINY DEATHS ♫

It was hard to feel discouraged in Atherus City, which, in the best of ways, was nothing like the Vakoi Empire capital Evaris had grown up in. Similar to Erenford, it featured a maze of alleyways, but the buildings that formed them towered at least three times taller and were infinitely more beautiful— their architecture unlike anything she had seen before.

As she and Pinto searched the narrow alleyways for the next ghost home on their list, she struggled to believe this place existed. Atherus City wasn't the impoverished destination she'd expected based on her experience in other Eastern towns. The Vakoi Empire had left its mark, proven by the occasional production points and ration pickup stations, but a surprising number of people survived and even thrived without feeding into the system. They passed privately run butcher shops, clothing stores, restaurants with lines out the door, and street vendors offering snacks from rolling carts. She imagined this might be the most untouched part of Eastern Territory since the Vakoi Empire's takeover, despite the Atherus

Palace ruins.

Pinto flipped through his scratched-up blue book as they walked. "I can't believe you haven't been here either."

"The Force only sends experienced guardians to Atherus City," she explained. "It's particularly known for rebel activity—I heard there was a terrorist attack recently that left five officers burned. You can imagine how hard it is to find the culprits here, with so many people around."

Pinto's gaze sharpened as they turned into another residential alleyway, and he tucked his notebook away. "This is where they all disappeared." His eye traced each outdoor staircase up to the doors on higher floors. "The Bayins, Yahshi, Vell, and likely many more. I'd say there's a chance the hideout could be right here, under our noses."

"Maybe." Evaris glanced at the advertisements and *Capital Weekly* articles pasted on the brick wall to their right, her eyes narrowing as a relatively fresh *missing person* notice caught her attention. She skidded to a stop and walked backward, peeling the paper slip free. It contained just a few sentences about a sixteen-year-old named Saunti Suvo.

Pinto appeared next to her. "What is it?"

"Look at the date. He went missing during our special operation."

"Right..." Pinto scanned the other pages pasted to the wall and pointed to another slip. "This one has the same date. A woman named Tonna Suvo. I'm guessing they're mother and son."

"Suvo's a common surname."

"But for them to go missing at the same time? They *have* to be related." Pinto rubbed his chin, then faced Evaris with a smile. "Commander, we could be onto something. If Yahshi had help reaching Atherus City, maybe he had help disappearing from it too. *Someone* had to bring him and Vell to the Underground hideout."

Evaris peered at the paper in her hands, which described Saunti as a production point worker at Atherus City's lumber mill. When she looked back up at Pinto, his smile widened.

"Congratulations, Red. We've got ourselves a lead."

Like usual, Evaris did the talking; Pinto wrote the transcript. They sat in the boss's office at the lumber mill, breathing in dusty air as workers entered one at a time in ascending order, based on the numbers embroidered into their orange jumpsuits.

"Who?" asked worker number six—a man with a matching orange cap.

"Saunti Suvo," Evaris repeated for the third time.

"Yeah, I don't know 'em."

Pinto looked up from his blue book. "Number forty-three," he tried.

The man's face lit up. "Ah, forty-three! Sure, I saw 'em around. We never talked, though. Did you say he's missing?"

"I didn't know he went missing," answered twenty-six.

"Do you know if he's been replaced yet?" thirty-nine inquired. "My nephew needs work."

"He'd always say *morning* to me," shared forty-two. "That's about it."

Since Saunti—number forty-three—was missing, the next worker to enter was forty-four, a sixteen-year-old named Podge. Evaris figured he might know Saunti better than the others, who were mostly men in their twenties and thirties.

"Yeah, I know Saunti," Podge confirmed. He was the first to refer to him by name instead of number.

Evaris propped her elbow on the desk, head on her fist. "He's your friend, isn't he?"

Podge shrugged and looked away. "I went to school with him."

"Did he ever show signs of having traitorous views?"

The corners of his lips curved slightly upward, but with a cough, he forced his grin away. "No, he's always been stiff."

"Stiff?"

"He never hangs out with people. Or makes time for friends."

"So you two *are* friends."

Podge shrugged again, and Evaris spent a few more minutes digging into his past with number forty-three. He had more information about the missing person than the other workers, yet still, he hardly knew him.

"He's a classic Vakoi boy," Podge stated. "I don't know what else to tell you."

"Vakoi boy," Evaris whispered to herself, recognizing the derogatory term used for Easterners loyal to the Vakoi Empire. Ironically, it only heightened her suspicion of Saunti's connection to the Underground—members never drew unnecessary attention to themselves.

Where are you hiding, Saunti Suvo?

Evaris scowled at the pink and orange clouds hanging over Atherus City. She and Pinto had spent the entirety of their seventh day veering off-schedule, interrogating workers at the production points the vanished son and mother worked at—but not a single person hinted at their current whereabouts.

Their only action left was to search Saunti and Tonna's home for clues, but locating it proved more challenging than expected. In the dwindling time before nightfall, they approached residents on the street to ask if they knew of the mother and son. Most said no—apart from a woman who claimed to run a stand at Atherus Market, which Saunti supposedly frequented.

"He showed up every evening to bring scrap wood for the kids to whittle."

"Do you know where he lives?" Pinto asked.

The woman eyed the Research Division badges on his shoulders. "I'm sorry, Professor, but I'm not sure."

Evaris was about to call it quits—until they finally encountered another person who recognized them by the descriptions in their wanted notices.

"Braids and freckles, huh?" said a street vendor selling skewered balls of fish. "Yeah, I've seen a woman like that. Walks through there every day." He pointed to a nearby alleyway, and the guardian duo followed his directions, knocking on the fifth door down.

Greeted with silence, Evaris knocked again.

Nothing. She fidgeted with the handle, but it wouldn't budge.

"I'm on it," Pinto said, pulling Evaris's lock busters out of his overcoat. With a few turns of his fingers, the door creaked open, revealing a dark room with a musky smell. Inside, Evaris found ration slips on the table marked with the surname *Suvo*, which had expired two weeks ago. *We're in the right place.*

Treating this like a normal house search, she unloaded books from shelves to check behind them, removed Emperor Vakoi's mandatory portrait from the wall, and pressed her boots against the floorboards to feel for loose ones. As far as she could tell, the house didn't appear to have any secret compartments.

She took a break to scan the room, considering what a more creative hiding spot might be, and caught Pinto staring at her with a raised brow.

"How do you always know where to look?"

"You keep forgetting—I've been in the Force longer than you." With a smirk, she pointed at the sofa beside him. "Try moving that aside."

Pinto joined in her search efforts, but after thirty minutes passed, he huffed and crossed his arms.

"Forget it. We should start heading back before it gets too late."

Evaris put a hand on her hip, frowning at him. They had spent a week on this mission, and now that they finally had a lead, he was ready to give it all up? This was exactly how Famir wanted their trip to end. She wouldn't stand for it.

"I'm sure their disappearance is unrelated to Yahshi and Vell's," Pinto muttered, eye on his boots.

"No," Evaris snapped. "We technically have all night. Let's finish visiting the ghost homes we were investigating before we got sidetracked."

He raised his head, his lips downturned. "I'm tired, Commander."

Her gaze softened. Normally it was *she* who was tired, not him. He'd even written such a fact in his red book—describing her as having a *lower work tolerance* than him.

"Could we just... rest here for the night?" His voice was barely more than a whisper.

Evaris blinked. Had she heard him correctly? Pinto had made it clear from their first day of traveling that he wouldn't dare break Protocol by sleeping in Eastern Territory. That's why they had made their way back to the border, every night without fail, to rest on their homeland's soil.

"I'm too exhausted for another trip to a tower, and I know you're sick of this too, Commander." He broke eye contact again. "I'm sorry. I wish we had something to show for this trip."

"Hey, it's not wasted. Code breaking or not, I had a good time."

"You did?"

"The *best* time."

Pinto didn't reply, but she knew he had a good time too. He'd written about the moments he enjoyed in the red book she'd flipped through.

Evaris crossed the room, knelt by the Suvos' fireplace, and pulled a matchbox out of her overcoat. Pinto's footsteps left subtle vibrations in the floorboards as he headed for a hallway, returning soon after with a bundle of blankets.

Evaris hunched over as she successfully sparked a flame, and Pinto wrapped a quilt around her shoulders. Taking the other blanket for himself, he sat to her left on the floor, so she couldn't see his good eye.

They stared at the fire together before reaching into their overcoats, almost in sync—Evaris for the novel she'd been reading this week, and Pinto for his blue book. He flipped through sketches, notes, and transcripts to reach the first blank page.

Evaris smiled as she opened her novel to the spread she'd left off on, marked by a feather the wind had tangled into Pinto locks as they rode their horses along the shoreline of Arinoma. Every now and then, she peeked over the pages to watch him sketch the people they'd spoken with today, filling gaps in her memory.

She turned a page. "Do you remember the bookcase on day one, in the first ghost home we broke into?"

"Denya and Luc's place," Pinto muttered. "It was an oak bookcase, with five shelves."

"Could you list off the book titles?"

His pencil paused. He sounded amused when he said, "I can't remember things I don't notice and make a mental note of. But even if I *did* read and process the titles, I'm not sure I could list them a week later. I have limits, you know. I'm not magic."

"Hard to tell." Evaris turned a page, even though she couldn't have read another spread by now. It was her way of signaling that she preferred their conversation to the narrative. "Even if your memory isn't perfect, it's much better than mine."

He chuckled. "It sounds like you're jealous."

"No way. I wouldn't want your memory."

"What?" he snapped back. "W-Why not?"

From his reaction, Evaris assumed herself to be the first person not to envy his ability. It wasn't that she found it useless—it was impressive, in a party-trick kind of way—but she wouldn't want it for herself. With each year, her childhood memories faded a little more, yet even in the haze, they stung. She couldn't imagine how much they would haunt her if she had a mind like his.

"I don't think I'd be able to sleep at night," she admitted.

Pinto stared at the fire. She waited for him to ask a follow-up question about her past, but he didn't—and strangely enough, she wished he would. She couldn't remember the last time she'd *wanted* someone to pry personal information out of her.

What if I just tell him, unprompted?

The thought of being an open book, without someone fishing for the truth, made her sick—but keeping quiet was much easier when she didn't have this gnawing urge to overshare. For some reason, tonight, she yearned to tell Pinto *everything*. She wanted him to hear her voice, and to hear his in return.

Evaris looked at the fire too. "Do you remember your graduation ceremony, when you realized I was from a family of fashion designers and asked how I ended up as a guardian?"

"You told me you liked breaking codes," Pinto recalled.

"Growing up, my mother always ordered me to do the opposite of what she wanted, because I never liked rules. I spent my entire childhood trying to escape my family's pressure to become a fashion designer, and the social codes that came with sharing their name. Their bright clothes and over-enthusiasm exhausted me. I wanted to be someone different..."

She told him the story of when she was ten years old, and her parents had left her to spend a day with her great aunt Cove, hoping it would spark her passion for the needle and thread. She had pricked her finger and thrown a tantrum.

She told him about the day she'd come home from Vakoi City Primary to discover that her father had replaced the dozens of novels in her bedroom with makeup, promising to return the stories once she started acting like a Starfall.

And lastly, she told him about her thirteenth birthday, when she'd spent every gifted coin on dark clothes—not because she wanted to, but because she knew of no other way to retaliate against her parents' pressure. The only piece she could recall clearly was a black turtleneck with a colorful tag on the inside, hidden from sight. It was the only one she actually liked. Simple, plain, with a secret pop of color—it knew it was special but didn't flaunt it.

Pinto listened. He listened in the same way she had read his journal, taking in every word and savoring them. He listened like she told the most interesting stories he'd ever heard.

"...My parents yelled at me for an hour when I came home with all the new clothes. That's when I declared I'd become a guardian someday, just to spite them." She chuckled as she faced him. "It's an odd realization I had, after leaving my little bubble of Vakoi City and seeing more of the island. I always wanted to be different because I thought they were normal, but I was wrong. It's the Starfalls who are unconventional. And look at me now—I follow a whole new set of codes, not so different from before. Sometimes I wonder if I really escaped my family, or if I just traded one cage for another."

Pinto nodded, and it took a moment for him to gather his words. "My parents didn't want me to become a guardian either," he confessed. "They tried to raise my sister and me to ignore the pity that comes with an eye-patch. It worked for my sister, perhaps because she was too young to remember the raid, but it didn't work for me. I couldn't forget what happened. I dedicated my childhood to getting selected so I could work for the Force and put a stop to the Underground.

"Sometimes my mother would say, *Don't let the raid change you more than it already has.* I still think about that sometimes. Maybe if I let go of what happened, like my sister did, I would've pursued something else. I'm not even sure what that would be." Pinto went quiet, staring at his notebook, tapping his pencil tip against the page until the charcoal formed a little pile of dust. "Commander..."

"Call me Evaris," she blurted out. It was about time she insisted that he ditch the honorific.

"Evaris," he said slowly, testing out the name, "I've been wondering something..."

She smiled at the sound of her name in isolation.

"Why did you agree to come out here with me?" He looked up from his notebook and stared into her eyes. "I mean, you didn't *have* to pitch my idea to Professor Famir. No one else would have done it, considering how the entire Force is blaming me for Cal's condition."

Evaris shrugged. "Maybe I like spending time with you."

"Why?"

"Because you're smart, but not the stupid kind of smart."

Pinto chuckled. "I'm not sure what that means."

She set her novel down and leaned back, propping herself up with her hands. "Most guardians in the Force act like they're the best people in the world—like they've got everything figured out. When, really, they're just doing what their unit leader or superior tells them to. They're not actually thinking for themselves. But you do, and... it's kind of refreshing."

Pinto smiled. "Thanks."

She scooted closer to him. He didn't move away.

"I've noticed something." Evaris reached for his journal and pencil, which he surrendered without resistance. She set them aside on the floor, next to her novel.

"Noticed what?" he muttered, his eye darting to the fire again. Maybe he could sense it too—that frightening feeling that they were both tempted to share too much.

"I've noticed that you always position yourself to the left of me, so I can't look into your good eye unless you turn your head."

"Is that so?" he asked, a slight tremor in his voice.

"Can you look at me, please?"

Pinto stiffened, but he still complied, turning his body toward her, his head and eye following.

"Why do you hide?" Evaris asked.

After a tense moment, he smiled a little. "I know it's ridiculous, but sometimes I think about how... *easily* my right eye was taken. So I've developed a habit of shielding my left one, whenever I can."

Evaris chuckled. "I'm not gonna take your eye."

"It's not about you. It just feels safer that way."

She could tell by the look on his face that the rebel who gouged out his eye had marked him more than his patch implied. Yahshi and Vell added to that damage. He needed more than a friend. He needed to know he could trust someone again, that it wasn't hopeless, that he didn't have to turn a blind eye to the people around him who cared.

She reached out and took his hands in hers. "You *do* trust me, right?"

He gulped, his fingers curling to grip her hands back.

"When was the last time you told anyone what happened?"

Pinto shook his head, implying that he hadn't told *anyone*. Not even Yahshi or Vell.

"Well, maybe you should try," Evaris said, her eyes widening. "Maybe it would feel nice."

With a sharp exhale, he shook her hands off. "I can't."

She realized he might be like her—perhaps he also considered it selfish to volunteer information, sharing the truth only when pressed.

"I won't chase you into sharing anything," she said, "but if you *want* to talk about it, I'd be so happy to listen."

They sat in silence for a few minutes, staring at the crackling fire. Pinto's breathing was uneven. Evaris took that as a sign that he was considering her offer.

"I was five when it happened," he finally began. "My little sister was just two."

Evaris slowly craned her neck to look him in the eye again.

"I remember waking up because our neighbors were screaming. My father left to check on them, and my mother stayed in the house to look after my sister and me."

Evaris reached for his hands again, and he let her take them.

"Then this man showed up in the doorway," he continued, voice tight. "He wore a dark, hooded coat, so his face was in the shadows. Plus, it was late, so I could hardly see anything. My mother stood in front of my sister and me, and he just... all he had to do was reach out, and..."

Evaris shook her head, her eyes watering. "You don't have to say it."

"He took our eyes," Pinto choked out. "He took them like they meant nothing."

Evaris noticed that she'd tightened her grip on his hands—so much that it must have hurt him. She loosened her hold, but just a little.

"It took me a while to realize what happened, though," he continued. "I felt the pain, but I was more confused than anything. I heard more people outside screaming. I thought my father might be dying. My mother was wailing. I thought she might be dying too. Maybe we'd all die together." He paused and took a deep breath. "And... I don't know why I remember this, but I felt like the raider was staring at me. And then he—"

The words got caught in his throat, and a few tears fell from his good eye.

Evaris wiped his cheek dry with her thumb, holding her own tears back. This memory wasn't hers to cry over.

"The man looked at me," he muttered, "and how tightly I clutched my little sister, and he said, *You don't need her.*"

Evaris couldn't restrain herself any longer. She wiped the tears from her own cheek, imagining a younger Pinto moving on from such a disaster to face the trials of the Academy. The program had been one of the hardest times of her life, but to Pinto, the filtrations were nothing compared to what he had gone through as a child. He had experienced so much pain yet had grown up to be so strong, and she was proud of him for it. *If I were in his shoes, I wouldn't have turned out like him.*

"I forgot about what he said for a long time. I only remembered on Selection Day, when my little sister begged me not to leave her. It almost felt like I was doing what the raider wanted, by joining the Academy. I still don't understand it, and I don't like it."

She wrapped her arms around him, and he hugged her back even tighter. "I can't imagine."

They hugged for a long time. It was strange how a horrible memory had brought them close like this. Why couldn't the happy moments have this much weight? Why couldn't they share a fun day together and shed tears over how good it had been? Why did such a strong connection happen now, when they had laid out their hearts for each other?

When they finally pulled away, Pinto held her gaze. He looked more relaxed now, his shoulders no longer tense, the creases between his brows gone.

"You're a mystery, you know that?" He cracked a smile. "You trusted me when no one else would, and went on this stupid, pointless trip with me, and you were the only person who ever asked me what happened during the raid. Everyone else is too scared to touch the topic. They don't give me a chance to speak because they think it'll hurt me, but *not* talking about it hurts worse. I've wanted to, Evaris. I've wanted to tell someone so badly."

His tears fell harder now, and Evaris sniffled, catching them all. She couldn't explain it, but she wanted to be here for him. She wanted more moments like these, sitting by a fire, talking late into the night. She didn't want this trip to end. If only they could desert their responsibilities in the Force and stay in this abandoned home forever. They could be happy, right? Far away from the chaos, living in a little house near the beach...

"Sometimes I don't want to be brave," Pinto whispered. "I just want to hide, and let the rest of the Force deal with the Underground."

Evaris's fingers twitched. She fought the urge to grab his arms and propose an impossible idea.

Then let's stay here. Let's live in the enemy's beautiful city and forget about the Underground. Let's forget about all of this, and never go back.

She swallowed the words. Pinto would never agree to such a dangerous plan. He had a stronger head on his shoulders than she did. He was careful, meticulous, meditative. It had taken him an entire week to decide to break the most unimportant rule of sleeping on Western soil.

This was it. This one night in the abandoned house was the only heartfelt moment they would share. Tomorrow morning, they would head back to Vakoi City to return to their ordinary lives, and this feeling brewing in the air between them would fade. Pinto would rejoin Famir's unit, and Evaris would rejoin hers. They would live separate lives again and forget this trip had ever meant something special to them.

And one day, when she'd watch Pinto from afar, feeling just a sliver of what she felt right now, Boa would appear at her side, give her shoulder a pat, and tell her she'd done the right thing.

If she could not stay here forever, she wanted to cherish this fleeting moment in time. She wanted to have something to remember it by, to ensure she would never forget how much it meant, and she could see in Pinto's prolonged stare that he felt the same way. His curls fell in front of his face, the fire glowing in his eye, his cheeks damp from the tears she'd been wiping.

Without thinking, she leaned closer to him, until she could feel his hot breath against her nose. He didn't lean in, but he didn't lean back either. His eye drifted to her mouth, and she closed the remaining gap between them.

His lips were soft, and tasted like the chocolate muffin they'd split for breakfast at the Border Control tower. She could still taste it when she pulled away, her face lingering close to his. For a moment, she wondered if she had kissed him at all, or if it was just an idea that crossed her mind. Maybe she simply tasted the chocolate muffin because she had eaten a chocolate muffin.

"Is this real?" she whispered. "Have I been imagining it?"

Pinto reached out, his warm, shaky hand grazing the side of her face. He didn't say a word, but his eye held the answer, and it was all she needed to hear.

CHAPTER 20

RED RED RED

Our hand-poured Saver Store candles are almost everlasting!

♫ TERRIBLE THING - AG ♫

It was the middle of the night. The cold bit through Pinto's overcoat as he paced the alleyway, but he much preferred his goosebumps to the warmth of the fireplace. He couldn't possibly stay on that sofa any longer, glaring at the flames with the weight of Evaris's head on his shoulder. It stung to feel her resting comfortably while he was losing his mind.

How could she sleep after breaking a Guardian Vow, a crucial code of conduct?

What she had done to him was cruel, deserving of another *O* in her notebook. They were guardians, and she was two years his superior. To keep silent would make him complicit, but he didn't wish to report her either.

Then again, his reputation was already hanging by a thread. Could he afford another mistake? If he didn't confess and someone found out, *he* would be the one sent to correction, not her.

How dare she put me in such an impossible situation?

Pinto stopped, breathless from all his thinking and pacing. He leaned against the brick wall and stared up at the stars in an effort to calm down. But the sky was dark like her eyes, and all he could think of was that moment by the fire when she'd started leaning toward him. So, so very slowly.

I had more than enough time. Pinto buried his face in his hands. *Why didn't I stop her?*

Evaris's voice echoed in the howling wind that grazed his neck. *"Is this real?"*

He shook his head.

"Have I been imagining it?"

He shook his head again. He didn't know. He couldn't answer her now, just as he couldn't answer her then. Yes, he cared for her like any fellow guardian would—but he'd never thought of brushing his fingers against her face. No, not until she kissed him. Not until she started it.

He thought of their conversation by the fire, and how she'd chosen to make a move after he'd shared his most vulnerable story. Even casting the rules aside, why would she choose such a cruel moment to kiss him? Did she *enjoy* watching him break? Seeing him cry?

Despite the cold, his hands started sweating. He dropped them with an exhale and pressed his back to the wall, forcing himself to settle down.

As he focused on steadying his breaths, the flicker of a lantern caught his eye. It hung by a door across the narrow alleyway, its light dancing in the ocean breeze. He fixed his gaze on its wavering glow, wondering if Yahshi's father had a lantern like this in Sitra. Most converts did, bringing just a sliver of their culture to the West. Pinto had never understood the appeal—why cling to the traditions shared by a rebel group that gouged out innocent people's eyes?

He caught himself biting his nails and yanked his hand down. Evaris had told him multiple times how much it grossed her out, and she was right—it was a bad habit. He found that counting the links in the lantern chain offered him a similar therapeutic effect.

One, two, three...

He knew the numbers meant nothing. He always counted them at the ghost homes they visited, sketching them into his blue book. Anything could be the code, no matter how discreet.

His eye narrowed when he counted the upmost link, which connected to a hook on the bottom of a protruding wall post. It was identical in size to the links below it.

That's odd. He reached into his overcoat for his blue book and flipped through the sketches of the ghost homes they'd visited over the last few days. Confirming his memory, he had drawn the highest chain links slightly larger than the rest. He had assumed, throughout this trip, that the highest link was always larger so it could attach to the hook easier—but the home ahead of him had equivalently sized chains from bottom to top. It looked less intentional.

Perhaps it's an anomaly, Pinto considered, tucking his book away. He sidestepped to the adjacent home, which had an identical post by the door. Once again, its lantern hung from a chain with equivalently sized links.

He rushed to the next door over. Equal.

And the next. Equal.

Every single lantern by every home in this alleyway hung from chains of equal sizes—all except one lantern that didn't glow, which hung by the Suvos' door.

Pinto's jaw dropped at the sight of its slightly larger chain link. He had been so fixated on studying the deceased criminals' homes for commonalities that he hadn't observed the homes of those who *weren't* affiliated with the Underground. He had been conducting a study without a control group. All it took was focusing on one normal house for him to identify the key detail that set the Underground affiliates' homes apart.

Pinto burst into the abandoned Suvo household. "Evaris!"

She sat right where he'd left her on the sofa, fast asleep, her head drooping toward her shoulder.

He pursed his lips as he approached. *I shouldn't speak so casually, even if she wants me to.*

"Commander," he corrected, hesitating to shake her shoulder like he normally would. Instead, he snapped his fingers in front of her face.

Evaris clenched her eyes and shuffled, slowly stirring from sleep. "Red?" she grumbled.

Pinto snapped a few more times until she fully woke, her gaze sharpening as she looked up at him.

"Don't tell me it's morning already..."

He smiled, his cheeks warming up. He had always liked her raspy, drawn-out morning voice, and it was hard to stay mad at her when she looked him right in the eye like this.

"I—I think I broke the code."

Long before sunrise, they retrieved their horses from the local officer post and made their way toward the next town south. It didn't take long for them to reach the ruins of Atherus Palace, where they slowed their horses to dodge the broken walls and mounds of rubble.

"How did you figure it out?" Evaris asked.

"Believe it or not, we've been staring at the code all week, but I didn't notice because I never saw what a normal lantern chain looked like. So when I was standing outside tonight and saw one for the first time, I finally put the pieces together. I essentially broke the code backward."

There was a pause before Evaris spoke again. "What were you doing outside?"

His smile faded. He could feel her gaze but refused to meet it. "Just getting some fresh air."

"Were you feeling... bad about what happened?"

Pinto's grip on the reins tightened. Here they were, on the brink of a breakthrough, and she wanted to talk about *that*? Did she even care about his goal in the first place, or had she joined him with ulterior motives? How long had she felt this way?

"Red?"

He shook his head at the tired nickname. "It doesn't matter how I feel."

"Of course it does."

He sharply met her gaze, his brows furrowed. "No it doesn't. We're guardians—simple as that. We can't just... I mean, it's not right. It's against the rules. You're my superior."

"I'm your friend."

"A friend would *never* do what you did."

"You didn't stop me."

Pinto scoffed, looking away. "That doesn't make it okay. I confided in you, Commander. I told you something deeply personal, that I've never told *anyone*, and you respond by kissing me? By putting me in an impossible situation? You know guardians can't be involved like that!"

"I wasn't trying to start a relationship," she said. "I wanted to... to capture the moment."

"So you were being selfish."

"Fine. Be bitter about it." Her voice was colder now. "We can pretend it never happened. I don't care, so long as you keep it to yourself."

He stared ahead with a tight expression. "Maybe I won't."

"*Excuse me*?" She chuckled bitterly and raised her voice. "You know, for someone with a memory like yours, I find it *fascinating* that you forget everything I've done for you. I was the only person who didn't blame you for what happened to Cal. You wouldn't have cracked the code if I hadn't gotten you this opportunity first. I put up with your early mornings and skipped meals, and your insane insistence on always sticking to *The Guardian Handbook*, and your snoring and—"

"Oh, so I owe it to you?"

"Yeah, Pinto, maybe you do."

He didn't say another word, and that was the end of it. The burden of the Vow they'd broken outweighed his excitement of cracking the code as they spent another ten minutes traveling to the next town over. He couldn't stop thinking about his interrogation, when he'd snitched on Keiyo. If he were to do the same to Evaris, he would have no one in the Force left who cared for him. Did he really want to lose her over this?

It was horrible—how much he resented yet treasured her at the same time.

When they finally reached the next town, they nodded in unison, refocusing on the mission at hand. There was only one task left to fully confirm Pinto's theory.

They rode their horses down road after road, scanning the glowing lanterns to their left and right until they found one with a slightly larger upmost chain link.

Pinto pounded on the door, Evaris at his side. It took several minutes for a man to answer, his eyes widening at the sight of their uniforms.

"We're here for a quick search," Evaris announced.

The man stepped aside, allowing them in. Pinto guarded the doorway to ensure he wouldn't run as Evaris sifted through bookshelves, removed Emperor Vakoi's portrait from the wall, and checked for loose floorboards. It took less than five minutes for her to find the man's hiding spot—a false base to a ceramic stove, which she tugged open to reveal a compartment filled with neatly packaged dried fruits.

The code was real. The Force finally had a way to identify members of the Underground without relying on suspicious activity reports.

This is how we win.

Evaris didn't waste another moment. Unlike Famir, who would have probed the man for more information, she simply unslung her bow, plucked a single arrow from her quiver, and shot him down before he could utter a plea.

Then she pulled out her notebook to add two *O*s to her list. Pinto didn't ask what the second one was for.

"Please, have a seat, Professor." Ogga gestured to the chair across from him in his private office. "I've heard all about yesterday's big discovery."

Pinto's heart pounded as he sat at Ogga's desk. He had known from the moment Embre had sent him to the Investigation Office that this meeting would be serious, and despite various guardians celebrating him for cracking the code, he couldn't shake the feeling that Ogga would know about the kiss—that he'd magically see a mark on his lips.

The old guardian leaned back in his chair, his dyed red hair disheveled, the upper buttons of his shirt undone. No one would dare shame Ogga for his uniform, but Pinto knew that if he were to dress the same way, the Force would put him in his place within the hour.

"Do you know why you're here, Professor?"

Pinto shook his head.

"Guess."

He broke eye contact. "You... wanna know how it happened?"

"I don't care how it happened. I care *who* did it."

Pinto looked back at him, and Ogga narrowed his eyes.

"Some guardians believe you and Commander Evaris broke the code together. Others claim *she* did it, *you* took the credit, and vice versa. There are a lot of theories floating around, but for some reason, neither of you wants to clear the air by talking about it—or, it seems, even talk to each other. It's an odd look, I'll admit."

Pinto gulped.

"So, I'm going to ask you directly." Ogga pressed his hands together in anticipation. "Who did the code-breaking?"

He thought of his argument with Evaris as they'd passed through the Atherus Palace ruins.

"You didn't stop me."

As much as he wanted to condemn Evaris for what happened by the fire, pinning the blame on others had turned Quax and Keiyo against him. Maybe Quax was right about his accountability problem, and he was partly to blame for Evaris's kiss, just as he was partly to blame for Cal's condition.

"I have a confession to make, Professor." Pinto inhaled a deep breath, bracing himself. "The night before breaking the code, Commander Ev—"

"Shh!" He held his palm up. "Since I like you, Professor, I'm gonna let you in on a little secret."

Pinto frowned as Ogga leaned over the desk, lowering his voice.

"When something happens," he whispered, "and no one's around to see it, did it *really* happen in the first place? Why ruin your career? But more importantly, why ruin a good thing?"

Pinto studied Ogga's fiery eyes, wondering if he was testing him. Was one of the oldest guardians in service truly advising him to keep quiet?

Ogga sat normally again, raising his voice. "Now, I want you to stop thinking about whatever it is you're feeling guilty about and answer my question again: Who broke the code?"

This time, Pinto thought of himself, alone in the alleyway, studying the lantern chains. "I did, Professor."

Ogga smirked. "I thought so." He reached into a drawer and pulled out a golden slip, but he didn't offer it to him just yet. "Considering your discovery, the Research Division took the day to think through our next move from here, and decided that we want you involved as a unit leader."

Pinto froze. It was everything he'd ever wanted, handed to him on a silver platter, but he couldn't forget the crime that overshadowed the biggest achievement of his life. He and Evaris had broken a Guardian Vow. He deserved a punishment, not a promotion. Even if he were to take Ogga's advice and keep what had happened a secret, he couldn't possibly accept the position.

"I'm honored, Professor, but—"

"Good." Ogga handed him the golden paper, which contained a list of three names. "Tomorrow night is your promotion ceremony at Vakoi Palace, and the following day, you'll be responsible for leading the members of our first multi-divisional unit. It's something we've wanted to try for a while, and considering how you worked so well with Commander Evaris, a member of the Defense Division, we believe you're the perfect guardian to pull it off."

Pinto read the names on his slip. Two guardians were in the Defense Division, and one was from no division at all.

He smiled as he looked up at Ogga. Surely this was some kind of joke.

The professor chuckled. "I realize the last name is a bit of a wildcard, but remember that we only have ninety-seven guardians in active service. It'll take time to replace Commander Cal, Yahshi, and Vell, but your third unit member is a good starting point."

"What about the Academy? Does our work to become guardians mean nothing now?"

"No, not at all. This is only a *temporary* lowering of our standards. Right now, recruiting a perfect guardian isn't necessary. We just need one that shows up for the job, because clearly, that alone is a big ask these days." Ogga's eyes widened. "So, is this something we can trust you with?"

Part of him still wanted to decline the offer. He didn't deserve this opportunity. It belonged to someone who had done no wrong.

"This is your chance, Professor," he urged. "The Underground took something from you, and now you can finally strike back."

The image of the hooded man in his doorway flashed through his mind. His right eye socket burned at the memory of what the raider had taken. He could never get his eye back, but this was his chance to play a larger role in dismantling the Underground. Forfeiting the job over a personal moral quandary would be selfish—he had broken a code the Force didn't even know existed, so clearly, they needed his help now more than ever.

Pinto sat up straighter and nodded. "I'll do my best."

"And to that, I congratulate you, Professor, for becoming the youngest unit leader in guardian history." He turned to the closed door and yelled, "Boa!"

Just a second later, it opened, and Pinto's ex-unit member peered into the room. "Yes, Professor?"

"Contact Doctor Blimmery right away. We need the news transcribed for *Capital Weekly* first thing in the morning."

Boa shot Pinto a disappointed look and ran off. It seemed he already knew that the *news* regarded the recent graduate's promotion.

Ogga turned his attention back to Pinto, and held out his hand. "Welcome to the inner circle."

Pinto reached out and took it. His fingers were cold.

"You're officially a key player."

The following night, the entire Force and a few hundred privileged guests gathered in the Vakoi Palace ballroom for Pinto's promotion ceremony. He watched Ogga from behind the stage's bunched curtains, waiting for his cue to step forward. The last time he'd seen Ogga in his formal wear was over a month ago during his graduation ceremony—and just like back then, the old man had buttoned his dress shirt in misalignment. However, he had at least lined up his stubble cleanly, and freshly dyed his hair a bright shade of red.

"We are here today to celebrate the promotion of Professor Pinto

Dempsey of Frontal." Applause filled the ballroom as Ogga referred to a crinkled page. He recounted the story of how Pinto had cracked the lantern code—and with more claps came the sound of a ringing gong.

Cheers joined the mix as Pinto emerged from behind the curtains.

He spotted Keiyo in the crowd, dressed in a modest brown suit that fit him tightly now. He clapped slowly with a frown. His cheek was bruised.

Leaning against the wall was Quax, dressed in white, his face expressionless. He nodded once.

Roz smiled but didn't clap; Blimmery clapped but didn't smile.

Of course, it was Evaris who caught his attention the most. She stood out among the sea of subtle colors in her leather jacket and striking red dress—like a thorny rose among cherry blossoms. Her eyes widened as they saw each other.

"We now call Professor Famir to bid farewell to his former unit member!"

Famir left the crowd, joining Pinto and Ogga onstage. "It was a pleasure to have you," he muttered, offering a hand, "though our time was short."

Pinto smiled and accepted the gesture. "Thank you for everything, Professor."

As Famir rejoined the crowd, Ogga turned to Pinto and whispered, "The stage is yours, my friend."

He took a deep breath and faced the crowd, recalling the words he'd prepared the night before.

"Thank you, everyone, for welcoming me into the Force." Pinto nearly shouted, projecting his voice to fill the ballroom. "It hasn't been easy, but I'm finally ready to embrace my role in defeating the Underground. With the code broken, we now have the upper hand."

A few guardians clapped, but most watched him solemnly. He caught Embre wiping a tear, and her pride made his heart swell.

"Commander Evaris," Pinto called.

She froze in her tracks as guardians and guests faced her.

"Thank you for helping me break the code," he finished. "I couldn't have done it without you."

The crowd cheered again—this time for her.

Evaris grinned at the guardians that hugged her before returning her gaze to Pinto, her lips pressing into a straight line. The questions were written clearly across her face. *Have you told anyone our secret? Are we okay now, or is acknowledging me part of a bigger plan?*

He waited until the band began to play, and music filled the air, to approach her. She crossed her arms and gulped, expecting him to break the silence first.

As people around them spun to the beat, he offered his hand. "I like your formal wear."

Evaris blinked a few times, but then she seemed to make the connection. He stole the first words she'd spoken to him at his graduation ceremony.

Her shoulders dropped, the tension leaving them. She looked down at her dress, then at Pinto's crimson red suit.

"Because it matches yours?" she asked, stealing his first line too.

He sharpened his gaze and held it. "Maybe I like red."

Her lips twitched upward, just barely, but he noticed. After a moment, she unfolded her arms and took his hand.

Pinto led her through the crowd, cutting between dancers to reach a back door. Thankfully, it was unlocked and led into an unknown hallway of Vakoi Palace. He shut the door behind them, blocking out most of the noise from the ballroom.

It was silent in the hallway, and oh, so dark.

"When something happens, and no one's around to see it, did it really happen in the first place?"

Evaris shook her head. "I'm so sorry, Professor. I never should have guilted you into keeping quiet. I know I put you in a tough situation, and..." She trailed off as Pinto leaned toward her, but she didn't stop him. Their faces were so close.

"Why ruin a good thing?"

Evaris tightened her grip on his hand, their fingers interlocking as she leaned in, pressing herself against him.

Their lips met. She didn't taste like the chocolate muffin anymore.

She tasted like the color red.

Pinto ran his hand along her hair. *It's definitely my color.*

PART 3
COLLIDE

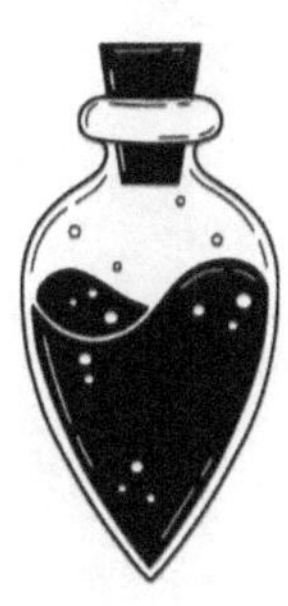

CHAPTER 21

IT WAS FOR YOU

Ten months after returning home…

♫ THE NIGHT BEFORE THE FUNERAL - THE MARY ONETTES ♫

A cut of steak sizzled on the frying pan, setting off a cloud of steam. To air out the kitchen, the young man opened a window and paused, smiling at the view. Though he'd never admit it aloud, he had always appreciated the vast flower meadow that bordered his family's home in Nominner. There was something serene about the bluebells waving in the breeze, the sparrows cutting through the morning sunlight, and the—

"Eyes on the pan, boy," scolded an old man from a bed where the dining table used to be. "You're gonna burn my steak."

"Hey, *watch it*." The young man whipped his head from the window, pointing his spatula at the old man. "If it weren't for me, you'd be eating lettuce for breakfast, and your bed would still be in that stuffy room of yours."

His grandfather grinned. "Oh, what would I do without you?"

He smiled back and flipped the steak. "How are your legs? Do you need a hot pack?"

"*I* should be the one concerned about *you*. When's it happening?"

He rolled his eyes. "Soon, Grandfather, but not yet. I haven't even finished the ring."

"How is that possible? You've been working on it for the past month."

"It needs to be perfect."

"Well, I'm not getting any younger, and I'd like to see you seal the deal before I hit the meadow." The old man raised his voice. "Can you add some salt to that?"

"Definitely not. You heard the medics."

"The same medics who said no to red meat? If we're breaking one rule, we might as well break them all."

The young man laughed. "As convincing as you are, old man, I prefer to break rules in moderation." He plated the steak, grabbed a fork and knife, and carried the meal to his grandfather's bed, which the family had moved into this room a few months earlier. He liked being in the middle of the action—and he deserved it, especially now that moving around took so much energy.

"Do you want me to feed you?"

The old man snatched the plate and utensils. "Oh, you think you're *so* funny." His hands shook as he cut the steak, but he managed. They both knew he didn't like being coddled.

"Is that *steak* I smell?" A middle-aged woman entered from the hallway, sharp creases marking her brow. Her eyes narrowed on the plate, and she put a hand on her hip, glaring at them.

"Quick, hide it!" The young man snatched one of the blankets, as though he was about to cover the plate with it.

His grandfather snatched his wrist, stopping him. "No, it's too late," he whispered, eyes on his daughter. "She already saw. I'll need to eat it quickly." He flung his utensils aside, and they clamored against the floor as he grabbed the steak with his bare hands.

The woman's jaw dropped as he raised the hunk of meat to his lips.

"Father!" she exclaimed.

He snickered as he took a greasy, drippy bite.

Her eyes darted from the old man to the young one. "You are *such* a bad influence on him." She headed for the stove. "Now be a good grandson and cut his steak. I'll prepare a hot pack for his legs."

The young man smiled and slid a fur coat on. "Sorry, Mother, but as much as I'd absolutely love to cut his steak, I need to get going."

"Today's the day he does the thing," his grandfather mumbled with his mouth full.

The woman looked back at them, her face lighting up. "Really?" She darted back and attacked her son with a suffocating hug before he could say no. "I can't believe it!"

"Calm down. He's just messing with you." The young man wiggled free from her grip, smiling at the sight of her necklace. It was a simple silver chain with a metal pendant melded into the shape of a sun. He had crafted it nearly a year ago, soon after returning to Nominner, and she hadn't taken it off since. *How incredible it is that a simple gift could change the entire course of my life...*

"Well, everyone's waiting." His mother ruffled his hair. "Don't be such a worrybug."

"He's just a scared little boy," the old man teased.

"What is *wrong* with you people?" He started backing up to the front door. "You should be telling me *not* to do this. I'm eighteen. Aren't I too young?"

His mother laughed. "I'd have married you off at twelve, if I had the power."

"*Gross.* Don't tell anyone you said that." He opened the door and shivered as a winter breeze rushed into the house. "I'm escaping now. Love you."

"Love you too," they echoed back.

As he made his way to the shop, he pondered their urgency. Perhaps they were right to criticize his hesitation. He knew, without a doubt, that he wanted this. He had known since the day he returned home, and that feeling hadn't faded since. Maybe he really was being a scared little boy—a worrybug—and he'd been ready all this time.

Without thinking, he slowed to a stop by Nominner Market, his gaze drawn to the *Capital Weekly* article by the door. For the past two weeks, he had made a habit of revisiting it each day on his way to work. The paper was beginning to tear, its edges worn and ink fading, holding a solemn story he had promised to honor until the wind or someone's hand finally peeled it away. How else could he pay his respects?

His eyes watered as he reread the story. Why would Yahshi let his Underground allies kill Vell, one of his closest friends—along with Cal, the older sister of another dear friend?

It was cruel and unfair, but such was life.

He shook his head and continued walking. *They were too young.*

The story weighed on him more that morning than it had before. Unlike Vell and Quax's older sister, he was still here, still breathing. What was he waiting for? Was he really going to let his fears hold him back? No, there was a better way to honor their deaths than to read their tattered article every day. He would live, because they couldn't. This evening, he would finally propose to Shaye.

He swung the door to his workshop open.

"Is that my boy?" his father called, not looking up from his desk. His hands were busy shaping the leather of a worn boot, tools laid out beside him as he meticulously restitched the seams for a client.

"It's your grown, adult son," he corrected, hanging his coat on a hook.

"Oh, what a big boy you are," his father said in a sing-song voice. Laughing, he stood from his desk and dusted off his pants. "I'm glad you're here. I've got to pick up some thread and dye from the Saver Store. You'll hold up shop?"

"Of course." He caught the keys his father tossed him.

"I'll be back soon. Love you."

"I love you too."

As soon as his father left, he headed to his own desk on the opposite side of the room, tucking the keys into the front pocket of his cargo pants. His father had converted half of his cobbler shop into a jewelry store after admiring the sun pendant he'd made for his mother. In just a few months, they gained so much popularity that some clients even made trips from Vakoi City—which was practically unheard of. With their current numbers, they could even move to the capital, if they so pleased, but they'd never leave their town. Their family was here, and their ancestors were buried in the flower meadow. Their hearts belonged to Nominner.

He slipped a pair of gloves on and secured his crafting glasses over his eyes, reaching into his desk drawer for the piece he'd been working on for the past month. *I need to finish it today.*

It was a beautiful diamond ring, likely his best work, but no amount of beauty could express his admiration for Shaye. Reuniting with her upon his return to Nominner had erased the bitterness he carried from those pointlessly wasted months away. He had lost one battle, but had won the war.

"You're not gonna say hi?"

He jumped in his seat, the ring flying out of his hands and toppling onto the wooden floor. In the corner of the room, Shaye sat perched on a stool, sketching. She'd been so quiet that he hadn't even noticed her.

"Why so spooked?" She looked up from her sketchbook with a raised brow. "Am I not allowed to visit my boyfriend on the way to work?"

"Sorry," he muttered, his eyes darting to the ring he'd dropped. He knelt to pick it up and hoped she wouldn't notice. *It's too early. I still need to make my finishing touches.*

"Is that a new piece?" Shaye left her sketchbook on the stool and walked over.

He considered hiding the ring, but that would only look more suspicious, so he opened his hand.

Shaye plucked the ring from his gloves and spun it between her fingers, right in front of her eyes. "Looks like it's finished."

"Almost," he replied, his cheeks warming up.

"Who is it for?" She returned the ring. "Another big client from Vakoi City?"

"A woman here in Nominner, actually." He broke eye contact. *She already saw the ring. Have I lost the element of surprise? Should I just do it now?*

"You're being a worrybug, aren't you?" Shaye set a hand on his shoulder and waited until he met her gaze again. "Relax, okay? She'll love the ring. I know it."

He knew this was his chance—but his knees buckled, betraying him, and he couldn't stop imagining the millions of different ways she might say no.

She blinked at him, awaiting a response.

The ring is done. He removed his crafting glasses and gloves as quickly as he'd put them on. His fear of her rejection would never fade—but he chose, in this moment, to ignore it. *I've been planning this for weeks. I'm ready.*

He fetched a wooden jewelry box—decorated with floral carvings—from the bottom drawer of his desk. As he placed the ring into its holder, his mind raced with memories of all the years he and Shaye had gone to school together, secretly concealing their feelings, their families teasing them for their inevitable marriage. He had lost her once, when he foolishly left to chase dreams beyond Nominner, and now that he was back, he would never leave her again.

"Wow..." She peered down at the box. "Did you make that too?"

"Shaye," he said, his voice firm.

She looked back up at him, her smile fading.

He took a deep breath. "Will you—"

The door jingled a bell as it opened, interrupting him. He sighed and looked over, expecting to greet a client, but his blood ran cold at the sight of a familiar face.

"Long time no see," said a guardian with a leather patch over his right eye. He crossed the room and offered the jeweler a paper—its header sunk his heart.

MANDATORY SERVICE CALL

"Sunna Rickabee of Nominner," Pinto addressed, "the Force invested in you, and now calls upon that investment for the greater good."

Sunna took the ticket from Pinto's hand, reminding himself to stay calm. He couldn't afford to let his worries paralyze him. He would need to stand his ground.

"What does he mean?" Shaye whispered in Sunna's ear.

"We have three open spots in the Force," Pinto said, answering Shaye's question and drawing Sunna's eyes back to him. "Since you made the final six, you're first in line to get called back. Luckily, you won't be expected to finish the second half of the program, so you can get started right away."

Sunna took a step toward Pinto. He wasn't as tall, but he stood up straight to make a statement. He would not be bullied back into a life he didn't want.

"Look, Pinto. It's wonderful to see you again, and I'm honored that the Force wants me back, but I have a life here. I'm not interested in guardianship anymore—that's why I filtered myself, remember?"

Pinto looked around at the homely shop, then at Shaye, and a look of realization crossed his face. He sighed as he returned his gaze to Sunna.

"I'm sorry, but it's a mandatory service call, which you agreed to in your contract. There's nothing I can do to get you out of this."

"You agreed to this?" Shaye gripped Sunna's arm, fishing for his gaze, but he couldn't bring himself to face her. His thoughts drifted back to Selection Day, when he had followed a commander named Galler into Nominner Secondary's main office. Stuttering through every clause, he had explained the rules of the contract.

Pinto pulled out that very contract and cleared his throat. "*Should you be filtered from the program,*" he read, "*yet the Force later encounters a situation that demands an augmented guardian presence, your acquired training, albeit partial, may obligate you to a mandatory service call.*"

Sunna stiffened. How had his sixteen-year-old self been so careless to assume that such a situation would never occur?

"Aren't there other people you could call instead?" he pleaded, his voice quickening. "Like—oh—what was his name? Ceylon, right? That twin from Vakoi City? He made it pretty far, and I'm sure he'd be much more enthusiastic to join the Force than I am."

"That's not up to me," Pinto said.

"Please, don't do this." Shaye stepped toward the guardian, repeating the same words she'd said to Sunna over a year ago on Selection Day, when she had tried to stop him from leaving.

Pinto still wouldn't look at her.

"I won't let you take him from me," she pressed.

"Shaye," Sunna warned.

"He's happy here. He has an amazing job that he loves, his family needs him, and I... I'm *so glad* that he's back."

Sunna's eyes watered. "Stop."

She closed her mouth but gripped his arm tighter. He still couldn't bring himself to look at her as memories of the program came flooding back. He thought he'd finally broken free of the pain, but with a snap of the Force's fingers, they could bring it all back—just like that.

"Pinto..." Sunna's eyes drifted to his shoes. "Could you give us a minute?"

"Of course." His boots struck the floor softly as he headed for the door. "You have one minute."

The door bell jingled again as he left, and before Sunna could blink, Shaye had turned him to face her, lifting his chin so his eyes met hers. "You can't go with him."

"I'm afraid I don't have a choice."

"Then let's run," she said in a low, raspy voice. "Let's slip through the back door, and go somewhere they'll never find us."

Sunna gulped, wishing he could agree to such a ridiculous plan. However, no matter how much he wanted to stay with her, he couldn't disobey the Force. There was no knowing how they would retaliate—if there was even a chance they'd come after his family, it wasn't a risk worth taking. Plus, it was too dangerous to do what Yahshi had done, especially without connections to the Underground. To run would be a death wish for them both, at the minimum.

Sunna reached out, and wiped her tears away. "I need to go now," he said, his voice breaking.

Shaye shook her head. "No. You can't leave me. Not again."

"I'll talk to Pinto's superiors. I'll do what I can to get back."

"No," she repeated, still shaking her head.

He pulled his arm free from her grip and backed away. She tried to close the distance, but as soon as he held the wooden jewelry box out, she froze.

He sniffled, his eyes on the door. "It was for you."

Shaye choked on a breath as she took the ring, and he turned his back on her for the second time.

That evening, after a tense trip by horseback and a tour of Vakoi City, Sunna sat across from Pinto at a round table on the top floor of Pandora's Hall. The restaurant servers, in their suede suits, had ushered them into a private room, where the muffled chatter from the bustling main dining area seeped through the walls.

Pinto tapped his boot and checked his pocket watch—*again*. "They should be here by now."

Sunna fiddled with his fork, watching it catch the chandelier light. He couldn't muster interest in who *they* were, or why he and Pinto had been waiting for them for the past ten minutes. His thoughts were with his family and Shaye.

This can't be the end. I'm getting back home, no matter what.

The door opened, letting in a short burst of noise from the main room. He didn't look up as a pair of black boots approached him.

"Sunna?" The guardian came to a halt. "What the hell are you doing here?"

His eyes widened, and he finally raised his head to see Quax, in uniform, take one of two empty seats at their table. His brows crept toward each other as he awaited a reply.

The words clotted Sunna's throat as he recalled the *Capital Weekly* article announcing the deaths of Vell and Cal. Once, at the Academy, Quax had confided in Sunna, sharing his hope of becoming a guardian so he could reunite with his sister and spend more time with her. He couldn't imagine how tragic it must have been for Quax to join the Force only to lose her within a month.

"I'm so sorry about your sister," Sunna choked out.

Quax's face hardened, and he faced Pinto with narrowed eyes. "Is this some kind of joke?"

Pinto waved his palms in front of him. "Of course not. Sunna's a fellow member of our unit."

"*Him?*" Quax abruptly pointed to Sunna, making him flinch. "He's no guardian, Pinto."

Sunna concealed a smile. He could see in Quax's eyes that he didn't want him as a unit member—not because he didn't respect him, but because he cared for him. During the program, he had seen Sunna at his worst points. If anyone understood how unfit for the Force he was, it was Quax and Keiyo, his old roommates.

My old friends.

The door opened again, and Keiyo entered, messing with the pieces of his tight uniform as though searching for a way to escape them.

"I need a refitting." He plopped onto the last chair.

Sunna squinted at the bruise on his cheek and his tangled, shoulder-length hair.

"Don't worry about it," Pinto said. "You'll drop weight now that you're back in service."

He bore his teeth. "Shut it."

Pinto smirked—the fact that Keiyo hadn't noticed Sunna yet seemed to amuse him. "You can stay mad at me if you like, but at least say hello to our newest member."

Keiyo looked over, his face draining of color as he locked eyes with Sunna. He whipped his head to face Pinto again, his voice seeped in rage. "What the hell did you do?"

"It wasn't my decision."

Quax scoffed and shook his head.

"Look, I understand that you're upset. The three of you each have your own grudges against me, but look on the bright side—you're finally back together!" Pinto gestured around the table. "You three were inseparable at the Academy, remember? Before the final filtration split you up?"

Sunna's blood simmered. "I *chose* to split us up by filtering myself. I freaked out when I saw you, Pinto, beaten up on the grass—possibly dead— and knew I wanted nothing to do with guardianship."

Pinto shrugged. "I don't get it. Ten months later, and you want nothing to do with each other?"

"Real friends don't hold each other hostage," Keiyo muttered.

Pinto's eye shot to Keiyo, and he looked away, shuffling in his chair and rubbing his upper arm. He couldn't keep still, a sharp contrast to Sunna's memories of him during the program. Keiyo had always made himself comfortable as though he owned every room he entered. The weight gain, the bruise, the messy hair, the restlessness—what happened to him?

A server arrived with their starters, and Pinto inhaled as their plates met the table, folding his hands together, formulating a strategy. He waited until the server left before his eye drifted from Quax to Sunna to Keiyo.

"I hate to be a bad guy here, but this situation is bigger than your individual problems." He turned to Quax. "Now that Ca—"

Sunna raised his brow, and after a glance in his direction, Pinto started again.

"Now that you're blacklisted from... that hospital room, you've finally been getting back to service and *living* again. Your love was a crutch. You weren't even wearing your uniform."

Blacklisted? Sunna wondered. *Hospital room? What is he talking about?*

Whatever he meant, it struck a chord with Quax, who dropped his head, offering no rebuttal.

"And let's be honest, Keiyo," Pinto continued, facing him next, "if I didn't convince the Force to take you on as a unit member instead of Galler, you'd still be in correction."

Correction. Sunna remembered the term being part of a Guardian Vow, but there was always a sense of vagueness around it.

"I got you out of that situation," Pinto finished.

"You also got me *into* that situation," Keiyo replied.

"So now we're even."

Keiyo tried to cross his arms, which made him wince. He reached to massage his shoulder again, meeting Sunna's gaze before looking away, lips pursed.

"And Sunna," Pinto addressed, stealing his attention. "I know it's almost been a year since you left the Academy, and you've come to embrace your life in Nominner, but this is your chance to be a hero, and protect the family and... *girl*... you love."

"Girl?" Keiyo questioned, dishing a few helpings of potatoes onto his plate.

"As guardians, it's our responsibility to put aside personal desires for the greater good." Pinto scanned their private room—as if someone could possibly be listening—lowered his voice, and leaned forward. "The Underground doesn't know that I've broken their code. We're going to use that to our advantage in four days, during the Incursion."

"What code?" Sunna asked.

"Every Underground traitor has a distinct detail about their lanterns that sets them apart. It's a code for their allies to seek refuge while on the run—traitors like Yahshi and the Bayins. It's how they survived with the entire Force tracing them, and we're going to use it to identify and eliminate members of the Underground all in one night. Without a smuggling network to rely on, Yahshi and the rest of the hiders will run out of supplies and be forced out of hiding."

Keiyo dropped his fork, and it clattered against his plate. "All in one night?"

"It's a brilliant idea," Quax said, his voice raspy. By the tight grip on his fork, it seemed that he didn't like agreeing with Pinto.

Sunna couldn't even think about touching his food. "What if someone's lantern just happens to match the code?"

"It's too specific for that to happen," Pinto said. "But even if it did, I'd consider it a sacrifice for the greater good."

Keiyo swallowed a bite of potatoes and opened his mouth, possibly to support Sunna, but he hesitated and then resumed eating.

Sunna frowned at Pinto. In the nine months he'd spent with him in the program, he'd always considered him overly serious and, at times, overconfident—but never cruel. For the glory of Vakoi, he was a raid victim! If anyone should care about potentially hurting innocent people, it was him.

"How is this any different from the Eastern raids?" Sunna asked. "You're acting just like the rebels who took your eye."

"No," Pinto snapped. "This is different. Those were random attacks on the innocent."

"If your code is wrong, it could very well be the same."

"It's *not* wrong. I broke the code. I'd know."

"Sunna," Quax butted in, drawing his gaze. "If it were *my* choice, I'd never bring you back, because I know you couldn't handle it. But the reality is that *someone* needs to do this kind of work. The Underground is dangerous. If it weren't for Yahshi, my sister..."

Pinto shot Quax a look.

"My sister would still be in the Force," he said, his words selected carefully. "It's our job to eliminate the Underground, and we're doing that in the most humane way possible."

Sunna shook his head. Quax spoke coldly now. He spoke like a true guardian, like someone he'd never met before, and it was starting to freak him out.

"I want no part of this," he declared, raising his voice at Pinto. "I need to go home *tonight*."

Keiyo looked sick. He rubbed his shoulder again.

"I really didn't want to say this, Sunna," Pinto replied, "but do you seriously think you're ready to get married?"

"You don't know our history."

"I can make an educated guess." Pinto lowered his voice. "You gave up your spot in the program for her. How could she say no to a grand gesture like that?"

"I didn't leave the Academy for her. I left for *me*."

"And don't even get me started on your career," he continued. "The only reason you know how to make jewelry is because of the program's tool crafting classes, and the only reason you get clients is because of your reputation boost of being a selectee. Even without making the final five, you never left the Academy behind. It made a permanent mark on your life, and you need to respect that."

"He's right," Quax murmured. "We all have to make personal sacrifices to be here."

"You need to remember your love for the Force," Pinto said.

"Love?" Sunna's eyes darted back to him. "You know, Pinto, I'm starting to think you know nothing about love at all. I thought Vell was one of your best friends, but you're not even grieving her!"

"Hey," Keiyo snapped, meeting Sunna's gaze. It was like he was warning him.

"You have no right to take your anger out on me—or the Force, for that matter," Pinto said. "On Selection Day, you signed the contract with your own free will, and that's the end of it. From now on, you need to accept that your life is here, under my leadership."

Sunna clenched his fists under the table. It was Pinto's first day as a unit leader, and the power was already going to his head.

"The Incursion will ensure that our people are finally safe, and that includes your girlfriend. You need to decide if you care more *about* her, or being *with* her."

"I don't see why I can't care about both."

"Because you're a guardian." Pinto looked away, his thoughts drifting elsewhere for a moment before he looked back at his unit members, waking himself up. "Tomorrow, we start preparing for the Incursion, and I expect the four of us to be united. Can you handle that, or not?"

Quax nodded, Keiyo stuffed another bite into his mouth, and Sunna looked away.

It was nearly midnight when Sunna stepped out of the Guardian Complex for some fresh air, still dressed in the clothes he'd put on that morning—the last he had of Nominner. He wasn't sure when the Force planned to fit him for his uniform, but he would cherish the little piece of home that remained.

"It's nice out here, isn't it?"

Sunna's eyes shot to his right, and there in the shadows was Keiyo, glowing cigarette in hand. He puffed out a gray cloud.

Sunna smiled and sat next to him on the step. "Can't sleep?"

"You know how it is."

"Just like old times," Sunna said, recalling their late nights at the Academy. They'd often sit on the balcony while Quax slept inside, chatting about the events of the day. Keiyo was always nicer alone than in groups—he had a calmness about him that he normally cloaked with brash confidence.

"So you're a smoker now?"

Keiyo shrugged. "Just when I'm stressed. It's one of the few things that calms me down." He turned his attention back to the road. "I feel awful about you being here, you know."

Sunna had nothing to say. He felt awful too.

"It's scary how fast life can change." Keiyo took a long drag from his cigarette. He looked so tired up close. "Just a month ago, I was sitting out here with Pinto, hoping Commander Cal's unit would bring Yahshi home. I was starting to think he and I were becoming friends, but look at us now—Pinto's my unit leader, and he wants Yahshi and Vell dead."

Sunna leaned toward him. "*What?*"

"Yeah, that's right. Vell's alive. She injured Commander Cal to help Yahshi escape, and I tackled Pinto to buy them time to flee. Then he snitched on me, and the Force sent me to correction. Now Commander Cal is paralyzed from the waist down, and she blacklisted her own brother from visiting her at Vakoi Hospital to force him back into service, to do what she can't. So that's what you missed. That's the story."

Sunna's eyes watered.

"I know I shouldn't have helped them get away, but when Vell turned sides, it finally clicked to me that she wasn't happy here." Keiyo leaned back, shaking his head as he looked up at the moon. "I just had to do something, you know? Because if you care about someone, how could you trap them in a life they hate?"

"You did the right thing," Sunna said.

He bit his trembling lip. "You really think so?"

"Of course."

Keiyo smiled a bit, shaking his head. "You know, it's stupid, but I've never had a friend like her before—someone who actually entertained my enthusiasm instead of tuning me out. She always seemed excited when I told her about my latest tool crafting ideas." He reached into his overcoat and pulled out a steel throwing star. "I made her a set of these a few months after you left, for her seventeenth birthday."

Sunna took the throwing star and flipped it around in his hand. Keiyo had welded each protruding blade with perfect balance, and the edges were exceptionally sharp.

"Amazing," he muttered.

"I stole them from her flat before the Force cleared it out. I couldn't help myself. And now they're all I have left of her."

Sunna handed his star back. "Maybe you'll see her again."

"I hope not." Keiyo sniffled as he tucked the star away. "If I see her again, I'll have to detain her."

He wished he could tell Keiyo that it wasn't true—that he always had a choice—but to do so would be hypocritical considering the events of the day. Sunna had joined Pinto, despite it being the last thing he wanted to do. The Force had a way of bending people's wills.

So instead, Sunna set a gentle hand on Keiyo's shoulder. "I'm sorry."

He shrugged off his touch, wincing slightly. That was when it dawned on Sunna.

"You're hurt, aren't you?"

"No," Keiyo said.

He tried to make eye contact. "Can I see?"

"There's nothing to see."

Sunna reached for his shoulder again, gripping it harder this time. Keiyo winced and gritted his teeth, in far too much pain to even pry himself free. The cigarette fell from his hand, and his face contorted as he fought off tears.

Sunna pulled his hand away and covered his mouth, watching his old friend writhe in pain. *How could the Force punish him for caring about his friends?*

Keiyo took a few rapid breaths, staring at the glow of his cigarette a few steps down. He was trying to bottle it all up again.

"How long has this been happening?" Sunna asked.

"It doesn't matter. It's over now."

"How long, Keiyo?"

He didn't have an answer until his breathing settled. "A little over two weeks," he said, his voice bold like usual. "It wasn't this bad at the start, though."

"What happened?"

"Professor Ogga's convinced that I'm aligned with Yahshi and Vell. I kept telling him the truth—that I only helped them out of instinct—but he didn't buy it."

"No," Sunna said, responding to a question that hadn't been asked. "He can't do that to you."

"Who's to stop him? And it doesn't matter anymore. It's done."

"Keiyo, you *need* to tell a superior."

"Tell them what? That *their* superior beat me? I think most guardians already know, and what have they done about it?"

As Sunna struggled to find a reply, Keiyo lit another cigarette.

"You know, whenever I wasn't in correction," he continued, "I'd lock myself up in my flat with bags of candy from the convenience store, because sugar was the one thing that took my mind off the pain. And now I'm back to where I was in primary school, where nobody likes me, and nobody cares."

"*I* care." Sunna shook his head. "I'm really sorry."

"Oh, stop being a baby about it."

"I know it's been a long time since we've seen each other, but you're still my friend, Keiyo. If I had been there during the special operation, and you switched sides like Vell did, I would have done the same. I would have helped you get away."

Keiyo hesitated to bring the cigarette to his lips. "You really mean that?"

Sunna nodded.

"I always thought you were secretly afraid of me."

"Only sometimes," he said with a chuckle.

Keiyo finally cracked a full grin. "I know it's absolutely wrong to say this, but I'm kind of glad you're here. Misery likes company, you know?"

Sunna laughed.

Keiyo's smile faded a bit as he continued. "So, can you tell me about the unlucky girl?"

"Are you calling her unlucky because she's my girlfriend, or because I had to leave her?"

He shrugged. "Bit of both."

"Well, either way, I don't think it's a good idea to talk about her. It's not like I'm going home anytime soon—it'll take a while to find a way out."

"Oh, just humor me, Sunna. I miss talking about stupid stuff like this."

He hesitated, but it occurred to him that most guardians wouldn't care about his life in Nominner. It would be nice to talk about it, even if just for tonight.

"Her name is Shaye. We grew up as family friends. Our parents teased us all the time. *You'll get married one day.* And then we'd say, *Ew, gross! You know how kids are.*"

"Kids, or guardians?" Keiyo asked, which made Sunna laugh again.

"She was *so* mad at me on Selection Day. Told me that if I left, I'd regret it forever. That I wasn't fit for the Force. I didn't believe her, but she turned out to be right. As soon as I was back, she told me, *I'm so glad you failed.*"

Keiyo opened his mouth. There seemed to be so much he wanted to say, but something held him back again. He looked away, moving his shoulder uncomfortably. With a gulp, he said, "Is she pretty?"

"Gorgeous."

"Ah, an answer." Keiyo managed a smile as he leaned back. With a wince, he propped himself up with his arms. "Usually that's when people tell me to *shut it.*"

Sunna sat sideways, facing him. "Did you ever like anyone back home?"

"No one liked me back there."

"That wasn't my question."

Keiyo tossed his head back and forth. "I had crushes now and then. Sure."

"So you'd get married, if you were allowed?"

"Hey..." He leaned toward Sunna. "If I weren't a guardian, and someone could tolerate me enough to marry me, I'd sign right up."

Sunna frowned. He'd always thought it was a given that guardians weren't interested in romance. Even he, back when he'd signed the contract, hadn't found the idea of a traditional life appealing. That changed when he returned to Nominner, and he wondered if that was the case for others in the Force. If someone were to fall in love as a guardian, what would they do? Would they just suppress their feelings for the rest of their lives?

"It sounds like you were living a dream in Nominner," Keiyo said after a moment of silence. "I hate that the Force ripped it from you. I hate it so bad. You were supposed to be the smart one who got out unscathed, you know? So I'm going to do what I can to look after you, and help you find your way out. Okay?"

Sunna nodded. To have someone on the inside willing to assist him was priceless. He wished he could express his gratitude with words, but all he could manage to choke out was, "Thanks."

Keiyo turned his gaze back to the sky, and a moment later, Sunna looked up at the same stars. He had a feeling Shaye was looking at them too.

CHAPTER 22

FIT FOR THE FORCE

Keep the dust at bay with a new Saver Store broom!

♫ SILHOUETTES OF YOU · ISAAC GRACIE ♫

Pinto led Sunna into a fitting room on the first floor of the Guardian Complex. Cobwebs marked the corners, the air reeked of food wafting in from the nearby cafeteria, and somehow—despite the cold weather—it was humid inside.

"As you can tell, uniform refittings don't happen often." Pinto shut the door behind them, conjuring a cloud of dust. With a few coughs, he gestured to Evaris, who stood waiting for them across the closet-sized room. "Sunna, meet Commander Evaris. She'll be taking your measurements."

Evaris waved, measuring tape in hand, and Sunna backed up as though she were holding a dagger.

"Relax." She laughed. "I won't bite."

Pinto leaned against the dusty wall, smiling as Evaris wrapped the measuring tape around Sunna's chest. Despite leaving her life among fashion designers, she still had a Starfall elegance about her. She measured like she'd done it a million times. Perhaps she had. He hadn't asked her about her childhood too much, and he made a mental note to do so more.

"What are you staring at?" Evaris smirked as she wrapped the tape around Sunna's waist.

"I'm just grateful that you volunteered to help," Pinto replied. It was strange to go from following the same schedule for a week, spending every moment with her, to living separate lives as guardians in different divisions. They had both made an unspoken vow to use any excuse to see each other, and this uniform fitting was just one of them.

"Well, you're welcome, but you're free to leave," she teased. "I'm sure you have much more important tasks to attend to, *Professor.*"

"My work can wait. I'd rather stick around to supervise."

"Oh? And why is that?"

He went quiet, struggling to think of a clever reply—but dropped his efforts when Sunna furrowed his brow, staring at Evaris through the corner of his eye.

"Were you two unit members before?"

She shot Pinto a look that said, *I'll let you answer him.*

Pinto chuckled. It was strangely flattering that Sunna had noticed how close he and Evaris were. Perhaps that was subconsciously his goal—to prove Sunna's claim during last night's supper wrong. He *did* know something about love.

"We weren't exactly unit members," Pinto said. It was hard to explain what his relationship to Evaris was, even professionally. She had once been his babysitter. His superior. And now she was his... lover? Would it be absurd to call her such a word?

"All done." Evaris unwrapped her measuring tape. "Welcome to the Force, Sunna."

"We'll meet in a few hours." Pinto opened the door for him. "In the meantime, get breakfast with Keiyo or something—make sure he doesn't eat too much."

As soon as Sunna left, he shut the door and leaned against it.

"Wow, look at you." Evaris crossed her arms with a grin. "Your very own unit."

"It sounds like you're jealous—again."

"I've never been jealous of you, and certainly not now. I prefer doing the bare minimum." She shrugged and took a step toward him. "Plus, you were the one who cracked the code. You deserve it... You deserve a lot."

"What else do I deserve?"

She stepped even closer, her gaze flicking to his mouth. Pinto leaned in, their lips almost meeting—until he gasped, his hands brushing something strange on her back. Not her slung bow, not her quiver of arrows. It was something... *stringy.*

She frowned. "What's wrong?"

He looped around her and wiped the cobwebs from the back of her overcoat.

She laughed. "Should I shower first? Disinfect myself?"

"It's not funny. There could be spiders, and I *hate* spiders."

"Oh, but you *love* me, don't you?"

His cheeks warmed up, and he found himself at a loss for words as he dusted the rest of her cobwebs off.

"Get mine too, will you?" he asked, turning his back to her.

She crept toward him, her voice unusually firm. "Hold still."

"Is there a spider?" Pinto clenched his eye shut. "Is it on me?"

She clamped her arms around him from behind, pinning his hands against his sides.

"Hey," he snapped, struggling to wiggle free. "I'm serious. I—"

"It's crawling up," she whispered. "It's making its way toward your neck."

"Stop that." A tingling sensation crept up his spine, but he couldn't tell if it was real. "Seriously, Evaris—that's not funny!"

She spun him around and pulled him by his tie, bringing his lips down to hers. That crawling sensation vanished as he leaned in, closing his eye. He didn't even care if there *was* a spider anymore. The last time they'd kissed was at his promotion ceremony two days ago, and that already felt like too long of a gap. Ogga had eased his doubts about pursuing a relationship—as long as it stayed a secret—and so far, keeping quiet had been easy. The real challenge, the one Ogga hadn't addressed, was finding the time. Pinto needed Evaris around more than their schedules allowed.

When she stepped away, her smile faded, as though she were thinking the same thing. "What are we gonna do about this, Red?"

A knock turned their heads to the door.

"Hello?" It was Keiyo's voice. "Is Commander Evaris still there? I need a refitting."

They held still, pretending the room was empty.

Keiyo knocked once more before his footsteps trailed away, and as soon as they could no longer hear him, they faced each other and broke into laughter.

Pinto's palms found her shoulders, and as they shared the moment, he pulled her into a tight embrace. It was overwhelming—the joy he felt with her—and he wished he didn't have to hide it in such a dreary fitting room like this.

"Do it," Pinto ordered.

"I don't know *how*," Sunna exclaimed, shakily gripping the reins.

"I don't believe you."

"I swear it!"

Pinto scoffed and marched a few steps away. This was Sunna's third full day in the Force, and it was clear he was feigning incompetence so Pinto would grow impatient and send him home. The worst part about his infuriating plan was that it was working. Regardless of whether or not he remembered how to ride a horse, Pinto couldn't make him do it. Co-operation was the bare minimum to ask of a unit member, and Sunna had none.

After taking a breath, Pinto turned and looked up at Sunna, who sat stiffly on his high horse. He was wasting precious time before the Incursion, one of the most crucial operations in guardian history, and that needed to be fixed.

"We both know what you're doing, okay?" His voice was softer now. "Let's drop the act."

Sunna raised his brows. "Act?"

His face heated up again. "How could you possibly forget the dual sword sequences you learned at the Academy?"

"That was months ago," Sunna replied.

"And how could you get lost in the Complex?"

"All the floors look the same."

"And why is it that yesterday, you kept dropping your dagger and blaming it on your muscles?"

"The repetitive motions of jewelry crafting has worn down my—"

"No, Sunna. You're eighteen. Your muscles are fine, including your brain. You should have no problem riding this horse. We've drilled this at the Academy field class after field class. Forgetting how to ride a horse would be like forgetting how to walk."

Sunna pursed his lips, and for the first time, he didn't have a clever response.

"You're not special." Pinto narrowed his eye. "You're one of us now, and tomorrow night, you'll be expected to aid the Incursion. You'll need to kill, and this time, you won't be able to gather the bodies and make cute little graves for them like you did for those rabbits at the Academy. You'll need to be ruthless. We're dealing with the most dangerous criminals on the island—the same ones that took my eye. If you don't kill them, they'll kill *you*. That's your fate now, and there's no getting out of it, no matter what tricks you pull. So if I were you, I'd start cooperating—not for the Force's benefit, but for your own."

Sunna gripped the reins tighter and scowled at him. That's how Pinto knew his words had finally reached him—he hadn't seen Sunna display such a hateful look since his first supper in Vakoi City.

"I'll be back in five minutes, and I expect you to be riding that horse." Pinto swiftly headed for the Detainment Facility just across the grass clearing.

"What happened to you, Pinto?"

He stopped in his tracks, listening.

"I never thought you'd turn your back on your own people."

Pinto peered over his shoulder. "I'm doing no such thing."

"You're threatening me, you want Yahshi dead, and you don't even care about Vell, even though she's still alive."

"You're not supposed to know about that."

"You're doing the wrong thing. I'm not your enemy here."

Pinto glared at Sunna, his blood boiling. While he knew he should correct his unit member for disrespecting him, he couldn't bring himself to argue. Memories of his time with Yahshi and Vell invaded his head and took his voice away. It felt like they were just kids at the Academy, but in reality, that was only a matter of weeks ago. How could so much have changed in such little time?

He shook himself from his daze. "You have five minutes," he repeated.

It took Pinto less than a minute to cross the clearing and round the corner to the front of the building. Evaris stood by the door, smiling at him, amused by his predicament—he'd caught her peeking around the corner to watch him and Sunna a few times in the past hour.

"You chose a good spot for a horseback riding lesson." Evaris gestured at the grass ahead. "Lots of empty space. Plenty of shade. Not many people around."

"And I heard you'd be working here today, so that's a big plus." Pinto leaned against the stone wall next to her, the creases between his brows loosening—and when he looked over, he couldn't help but smile back. It was hard to stay in a bad mood around her, which made a few minutes in her company the perfect break from his nightmare of a unit member.

"I'm sorry you're having a hard time with Sunna. The Force really wants your hands full, don't they?"

He sighed. "I've just about exhausted my patience."

"I get it." An oddly serious look crossed her face, and she seemed hesitant to say her next words. "But maybe you should cut him a little slack."

Pinto offered a questioning look, and she sighed.

"Consider it from *his* perspective, Red. You just ripped him away from the love of his life. How would you feel if I were to suddenly leave the Force?"

"First of all, that would never happen. And second"—he leaned toward her—"are you implying that you're the—"

"I'm gonna stop you right there," Evaris said, raising her palm.

Pinto laughed, but joke aside, she really did have a point. No one else cared about him in the way Evaris did. If she were to vanish, he'd be completely alone. Perhaps that's how Sunna felt—and if so, of course he'd do everything in his power to get himself booted and sent home.

Evaris flinched and pressed her ear to the front door. With a nod, she turned back to Pinto, whispering, "Meet me at Vakoi Square tonight. I have important news."

He frowned. *Vakoi Square?*

As they heard a commander unlatch the door from inside, Evaris slipped into her usual position, standing tall by the door, and Pinto fled before the exiting guardian could spot them together.

He shuffled to a halt as he concealed himself around the corner.

Across the grassy field, Sunna rode his horse in a perfect figure-eight formation—one they'd learned at the Academy.

The sight brought a smile to Pinto's face.

A few blocks from the Complex, Pinto strolled down the north wing of Vakoi Square. Unlike the time he'd walked here with Vell, the lively array of restaurants, bars, and live music didn't invite the urge for him to cover his ears with his palms, nor did he mind being the center of attention.

He stared out at the bustling crowds of people in both directions, meeting pair after pair of eyes, but it was a certain pair he was searching for. A fiery kind, with just the faintest hint of red.

Finally, he found her—Evaris sipped on a glass of red wine in the same bar he'd entered with Vell about a month ago.

Pinto waved at the violin player—a man in a clown outfit—as he entered, approaching Evaris in the dim light. He pulled out the chair next to her, and while she didn't look at him, her smile said she knew he was there.

Evaris offered her glass with a jerk of her arm, making the liquid inside swish from side to side.

"Want a sip?" she shouted over the music, finally meeting his gaze.

Pinto glared at the wine. He had never tried alcohol, but Evaris didn't know that.

Evaris laughed and pulled the glass away. "It's not poison, see?" She took another sip. "I'd never poison you."

Pinto smiled at the terminology, remembering how he'd always call belladonna-laced beet juice *poison* at the Academy. Perhaps Evaris did too.

Finally, he reached for the glass, and Evaris passed it along with a crooked grin. It was chilly against his fingers as he raised it to his lips. He was immune to belladonna—he took his maintenance vials every morning without fail. How could a lighter toxin like alcohol do any harm?

A stream of wine slipped along his tongue. It was bitter, with just enough sweetness to make it bearable.

"What do you think?" Evaris asked.

His cheeks warmed up—clearly, she knew it was his first time tasting it.

"I hate it," he admitted.

"But it's better than beet juice, right?"

He slid the glass closer to her. "It's all yours."

Evaris took a final, hasty sip, grabbed a bag, and slung it over her shoulder.

"Where are you going?" Pinto asked. "I just got here."

"This was just our meeting spot, Red." She darted for the door. "Pay for me, will you?"

Before Pinto could ask another question, she was gone, and the bartender was holding out a palm, announcing the price. He shook his head with a smile and reached into his overcoat for a velvet pouch of coins.

As he counted the gold pieces, a shadow appeared to his left. This was the first time he'd met with Evaris publicly during their shared time off, and a pit formed in his stomach at the idea that someone was onto him. He handed the coins to the bartender and turned to leave, but the shadow spoke first, making him freeze.

"Professor."

Recognizing the voice, Pinto closed his eye with an exhale. "What do you want?"

"I know w-what you're doing."

He finally faced Galler, shaking his head. "I'm not sure what you mean."

"P-People are talking," Galler said, glaring in the direction Evaris had walked in.

"Well, they're *wrong*," Pinto stated firmly. He had not been deaf to the rumors. The fact that he and Evaris had gone from not talking to being close friends had confused their fellow guardians, but the buzz would eventually fade. People hardly talked about Yahshi anymore, now that Pinto had broken the code. All news, at some point, would become old news—and in turn, irrelevant.

With his arms crossed, Galler peered around before leaning in, lowering his voice. "They gave me d-drugs, okay? It w-was an accident."

"What the hell are you talking about?"

"My st-stutter."

Pinto frowned. The twenty-five-year-old tended to speak in short bursts—perhaps his stutter made him choose his words carefully and only say the essentials. It took a moment for him to realize Galler was admitting to breaking *that* Vow too, and his face ran hot. He was not careless, nor did he have little influence in the Force. He was a unit leader now. Even Ogga, one of the oldest members in active service, respected him as a colleague. He would not get caught, and even if he did, the Force would not send him to correction. They couldn't waste him—he cracked the code!

"I'm sorry for your experience, Galler," Pinto said, purposefully using his first name, "but frankly, I find your accusation offensive."

Galler flared his nostrils. Without another word, he turned and stomped to a corner of the room where twenty-year-old Boa and a few other young guardians sat staring at him. They must have seen him take a sip from Evaris's glass, but that proved nothing.

Pinto scowled at the gossiping guardians, and they shriveled under his gaze, breaking eye contact.

With a nod, he left the bar, where Evaris stood waiting outside, reading a mystery novel.

"What took so long?" she asked, tucking the book away.

"I just had to take care of something." He grinned. "So, what's the big news?"

Evaris had secured her horse a few blocks away from Vakoi Square, in a narrow alleyway where they could still hear the hustle and bustle but couldn't see it. She mounted her horse and held out her hand, offering Pinto a ride. He had no choice, without his horse around, and he trusted that Evaris would be smart enough not to lead them through any parts of the City where they could be recognized, so he placed his hand in hers and joined her on the horse.

With a whip of the reins, they traveled through the darkest streets of Vakoi City, toward a destination she still wouldn't speak of. The news, supposedly, needed to be broken somewhere special.

Soon enough, they were no longer near the center of the City, but in the surrounding woods that bordered it from the western coast. They passed various cabins—vacation homes for the wealthy. Pinto assumed Evaris likely knew of this area because the Starfalls owned a few cabins. What she didn't know was that he had been here before, when he had snuck off with Vell to burn the Meridian book.

I should have turned her in. Maybe then she would have been forced to stay during the special operation, and she wouldn't have—

He shook his head, cutting himself off. His time of thinking about Yahshi and Vell was over.

Finally, Evaris brought her horse to a stop along a secluded beach. The moon hung low that night, as though trying to touch the water. They dismounted the horse, and as soon as Pinto's boots hit the sand, she thrust her bag into his arms.

He pulled out a pair of dress pants and a shirt he couldn't quite make out the color of. It was too dark out here.

"What's all this?" he asked, holding up a wad of clothes.

"What do *you* think, Red?" She held up another set of fabric—pants and a bright blouse that he imagined would suit her nicely.

She unslung her bow and quiver of arrows, but it only occurred to him that she was planning to change when she removed her overcoat next.

"Wait," he said, holding out his palm.

Evaris paused, her brows raised with amusement. He knew exactly what she was thinking. They were already breaking the most taboo Guardian Vow. Surely it wouldn't hurt to also break the rule about only wearing their uniforms. Plus, it wasn't like anyone was around to catch them.

"Never mind," he muttered, dropping his arm.

She plopped her overcoat onto the sand and opened her mouth, but after all the time they had spent traveling together, he already knew what she was going to ask.

"Already on it." He turned around and listened to the rustling of fabric as she changed.

"Now it's your turn," she said once she'd finished. "I'm not looking."

"I don't care if you do," he said, but she kept her back turned.

Pinto removed his bow and quiver, followed by his heavy overcoat. The clothes from Evaris were soft, like butter against his skin. He couldn't imagine how luxurious it would feel to wear such smooth fabrics every day.

He turned around. "Wow."

"Right?" She sensed his movement and faced him with a smile. "I figured it'd be nice, just for a night, to not play heroes for a change."

He smiled at her outfit. She looked like a normal Vakoi City girl. And funnily enough, she *had* been a normal Vakoi City girl once. Becoming a guardian wasn't an upgrade for her, as it was for most. She had everything she needed as a Starfall. Money. Status. Connections. And she left it all behind. It was admirable, really.

They walked toward the shoreline, the wind blowing through their hair.

"Are you finally ready to tell me the news?" he asked. "Red wine, fancy clothes, the beach... surely you're up to something."

"What I've been up to is already finished." Evaris handed him a quarter-folded, golden page, and cautiously, he unraveled it to reveal a grant for a visitation right to Frontal.

"You're kidding." Pinto's jaw dropped. "How did you get this?"

"I know the right guardians to ask."

His eye watered as he thought of Perma. He had been working so much that he hadn't even thought about when he could ask for a visitation right—but Evaris had done the work on his behalf.

"Thank you." He wrapped his arms around her, which seemed to catch her by surprise, because she took a moment to hug him back. "You didn't have to do this."

"Obviously, but I wanted to." She chuckled into his neck. "So when do you plan to see Perma?"

Pinto frowned and pulled away. He couldn't recall telling Evaris his little sister's name. Had he really forgotten? Had that sip of wine thrown his memory off?

"Is something wrong?" she asked.

"Nothing." Pinto's expression softened. *It must be the wine.*

He studied the visitation right and nodded, solidifying his decision.

"I'll leave right after the Incursion. Maybe just a few days from now."

"That sounds great," Evaris said.

"And I want you there with me. I want you to meet my family."

She tilted her head, and he dropped his smile, realizing he might have misread the situation.

"Unless, of course, you'd be uncomfortable with—"

"No, I'd love to meet your family, Pinto, it's just..." She trailed off and sighed. "We both know there are limits to what we can get away with. I could have a shift—"

"Then I'll plan it for your first day off after the Incursion."

"If people see us leaving together, then—"

"We'll leave at different times. You'll travel in another direction, and then switch ways and meet me in Frontal. I promise, my family won't say a word."

Evaris considered his idea for a moment longer, a smile meeting her lips. "You've made your case."

"You'll join me?"

She shook her head, eyes watering as she took his hand in hers. It was like she couldn't believe what she was agreeing to. "I can't wait to meet them. We'll make this work."

Pinto's heart struck his chest as he soaked in her words under the moonlight. How could it be that he deserved her?

As he tightened his grip on her hand, they shuffled on the sand, holding each other and staring out at the horizon. It was the first time, Pinto realized, that he had something to live for that was more meaningful than taking down the Underground. He even felt, strangely, that if he were to never avenge the group that had stolen his eye, it wouldn't even matter, so long as he had her.

Despite being to her left—offering her a clear view of his bad eye—Pinto took his patch off and tucked it into his pocket.

Evaris looked at his face, and he couldn't shake the feeling that she hated what she saw.

"Sometimes it itches when I keep it on for too long." He reached for his pocket. "But you know, I can just—"

"Leave it off, Red," Evaris muttered, stopping him. She reached for his face, and her fingers barely grazed his eyelid. "You look better without it."

CHAPTER 23

WATERWAY

Day 21 Underground | Clocks Read 09:43

♫ CRATER ON THE MOON · OK MOON ♫

"Aero. Aero. Aero…"

The tunnel multiplied the unseen boy's voice and carried it to the boat. It was impossible to shout on the Waterway without ten ghosts with the same voice echoing every word.

"Fenn!" Aero sprang to her feet so quickly that she rocked the boat.

"Fenn. Fenn. Fenn…"

She smiled into the darkness as the Waterway echoed her call.

"Can you cut that out?" Saunti snapped, his grip on the steering wheel tightening. Aero and some sister base dweller named Fenn had been yelling back and forth for the past ten minutes.

Aero laughed and sat back down on the cargo box next to him. "Don't be such a grump, Cricket. It's part of our ritual…"

She kept blabbering, likely sharing a humorous biography about Fenn—just like she'd done for every other handler they'd encountered during the trip. Saunti tuned her out, focusing on his steering. It was their twelfth—and most likely *last*—day on the water, but he still hadn't broken the news to her. He had spent hours spinning different words together in his head, but no combination seemed to lighten the blow.

Maybe there's no right way to say it.

Aero nudged his arm. "Isn't that crazy?"

"Uh-huh." Saunti nodded. "Crazy."

She went quiet for a second, then laughed and yanked his ponytail. His head jerked back, and the yellow scarf around his neck drooped, letting cold air brush against his skin.

Saunti's eyes widened. He removed a hand from the wheel and tugged the scarf back into place, concealing the bruises that may or may not have faded—their sister bases hardly had mirrors to check.

Aero's laughter fell as he grabbed the wheel again, returning his attention to the water.

The tunnel delivered another call from Fenn.

"Aero. Aero. Aero..."

"Is something wrong?" she asked, finally ignoring the echoing voice.

"I'm just tired," Saunti muttered, which was a partial truth. For the last twelve days, one of them had to remain awake at all times to monitor the current, waiting for it to come to a stop. These lulls, which lasted about ten minutes, provided a brief window to either paddle to the dock of their nearest sister base—if lucky—or secure the boat with ropes to a rock protruding from the tunnel walls. And from there, they would wait at least a few more hours for the tides to turn back in their favor.

"I'm tired too," Aero replied. "Just a few more hours, and we'll be home, okay?"

A few more hours. Saunti swore they were already close enough to hear the thousands of clocks in Headquarters taunting him. *I'm running out of time.*

He had planned to tell her on the first day of their trip, which he'd postponed to their second, then their third. Even when they reached the southernmost tip of the Waterway and turned back north, he still didn't tell her. He knew that every day he waited would only add to the betrayal, but he still sabotaged himself and put it off. He could no longer do so. If he didn't tell her in the next few hours, she would hear the truth upon their return to Headquarters, and she didn't deserve that. She needed to hear the truth from *him*.

"Aero. Aero. Aero..."

"Fenn!" she yelled, springing to her feet once more.

Saunti rolled his eyes as the Waterway carried her voice.

"Fenn. Fenn. Fenn..."

Just a few seconds later, a dock of stacked rocks materialized from the darkness ahead, bioluminescent moss highlighting its posts. At the end stood a smiling boy around the same age as them—roughly sixteen or seventeen. Beside him were three stacks of cargo boxes prepared for the exchange.

Our last stop. Saunti turned the wheel, leading their boat toward the dock.

Fenn waved with one hand, a fishing rod in the other, as he yelled, "Aero!"

"Fenn!" she yelled back.

This time, the Waterway carried more than their echoing voices. Saunti frowned as a chilly breeze met his cheeks, pulling a few strands of hair free from his ponytail. He had never felt wind in the Waterway before.

"That's strange," Aero noted, peering southward into the darkness.

Saunti flinched when a rope looped itself around the boat's gunwale right in front of him. From the dock, Fenn grunted and pulled the other end, his grip tightening until his knuckles turned white.

"Cricket, the wheels," Aero scolded, nudging his arm again.

"Right." Saunti yanked the lever, bringing the water wheels back up.

The boat slowed, no longer catching the current's flow.

Fenn relaxed his grip a little, and with a heave, he pulled the boat until it thudded against the stone dock. A few loose cargo boxes behind Saunti and Aero slid around as Fenn let out a sharp sigh, kneeling to secure the boat to a post.

"Hi, Ponytail." Fenn looked up at Saunti as he tied a knot. "You the new boat guy?"

"Something like that." Saunti frowned at Fenn's fishing rod lying on the dock. At the end of his hook was a piece of canned meat that had seen better days. His gaze drifted to the dark, bluish-green water, which reflected his confused expression. "Are there even fish in there?"

"Hardly. That's what makes fishing such a good way to kill time." Fenn smirked as he finished securing the knot. "I'm guessing you're the old courier from Atherus City?"

Saunti nodded. It seemed his question about fish in the Waterway had given away the fact that he wasn't from *down here*. Even after three weeks underground, there was still so much to learn.

With a huff, Aero lifted two stacked cargo boxes for distribution, swaying under their weight. Saunti stood to take them from her, then stepped off the boat to set them on the dock. Their labels read *GRIMWARD*, the shared name of Fenn's sister base and the town located directly above it.

Aero passed another pair of boxes to Saunti, and in exchange, Fenn began transferring his own boxes into the boat, narrating their contents.

"Extra canned goods," he said, plopping one down.

Saunti took another pair of boxes, wondering how much food sister dwellers like Fenn kept for themselves. According to Aero, only about a dozen people lived at every base, and they only used the smuggled supplies they needed to survive—saving the rest for Headquarters to collect during trips like this. Some goods were common, like canned food, while others were goods that Atherus City couldn't offer alone.

"Salt," Fenn said next, lifting another box. It hissed as he walked over and set it in the boat.

Saunti thought of the canteen's bland food. "I've never tasted salt down here."

"Not for seasoning." Aero handed Saunti two more boxes. "The one thing Grimward has that Atherus City doesn't is a production point that evaporates sea water. We use their salt bags for chambers with less ventilation, to prevent mold."

"We've lost good people to mold down here," Fenn chimed in, setting another box down.

"Almost lost Lira. That's how she got that cough." Aero ran out of boxes to transfer, so she started organizing the Atherus City boxes into the cargo area. Saunti hopped back in to help her as Fenn set his last box labeled *HEADQUARTERS* down in the boat.

The sound of waves and splashes echoed in their direction, halting their exchange. All three of them turned their eyes southward, into the darkness of the tunnel where the river faded off into a black void. It was like nothing Saunti had heard before—and once the sound faded, the dashboard's torchlight wavered in another breeze.

"Sounds like a storm," Fenn muttered. "You should camp at our base until it passes."

Aero chuckled. "We'll be fine, Fenn. We're almost home."

"Plus, the tides just turned north twenty minutes ago," Saunti said, nodding in agreement. He couldn't put off his confession any longer. "We have plenty of time left until the next lull."

Fenn sighed. "Alright, but be careful." He knelt to untie their boat from the post, and as soon as he finished, Saunti pushed the lever down. The water wheels caught the current, and they continued north toward Headquarters.

Saunti and Aero looked back at Fenn, who waved goodbye from the dock of Grimward. It didn't take long for the darkness to swallow him.

The two were alone again, traveling downstream. Aero moved to her usual spot on the wooden box to Saunti's left and replaced the torch on their dashboard with a new one from the storage compartment, sparking a flame with a match. The renewed torchlight illuminated the water ahead in a brighter shade of green.

Saunti took a deep breath. "Do you mind taking over the wheel? I'm a bit tired."

"Yeah, of course." Aero waved her hand, urging him to move. "No problem."

He gave Aero his seat and walked to the back of the boat, staring over the railing at his reflection in the water. What if he told her the truth and she threw him offboard? Could she handle the rest of the trip alone? If the tides shifted early, would she be in danger? In the worst-case scenario, did she know how to swim?

Excuses, excuses, excuses, he told himself.

Saunti flinched when a wave disrupted his reflection, cutting through the still water and leaving behind thousands of fizzing bubbles. He raised his chin and looked southward—waves clashed against each other in the wake they left behind. The storm chased their boat, threatening to catch up.

"Oh, great," Aero muttered, her hands tightening around the steering wheel. Grimward was their closest sister base, but they couldn't possibly travel back against such feisty tides to reach Fenn's dock and wait out the storm.

Saunti couldn't shake the feeling that the Waterway was warning him to confess—and while there was no logic behind it, he felt confident that telling her the truth would make the storm subside.

"The scarf wasn't from Dice." He turned around and stared at the back of Aero's head. With a few steps toward her, he reached for the yellow fabric coiled around his neck. "It was your father's. I took it from his room to hide the marks on my neck after he tried to strangle me."

Aero looked over her shoulder at him with a smile. "Strangle you?" She clearly didn't believe his story, and for the first time, Saunti's eyes watered at the memory of stabbing Rimoso's back. While he didn't regret murdering him, he had every reason to regret robbing Aero of her father.

"Because I poisoned him," he blurted out, unraveling the scarf and allowing her to see his neck for the first time in twelve days. "Look at the bruises he left."

A wave struck the side of the boat, knocking Aero's grip off the steering wheel, but she was too focused on their discussion to worry about the storm. She turned around in her seat and squinted, scanning his neck. He could tell by her expression that she didn't see the marks from her father's hands. Had they faded by now, or was she simply too far away?

"See?" Saunti took another step toward her, trailing his finger along the spots where he recalled seeing bruises before.

She let out a short, bitter laugh. "Don't joke about something like that."

"I'm *not* joking. Rimoso's dead. He's been dead this whole time." Saunti scowled and tossed the scarf to the deck. If the bruises had faded, how else could he convince her of the truth? He desperately spouted out facts, in hopes that one of them would click with her and confirm that his story wasn't a twisted prank.

"He wanted me to kill Yahshi." Saunti raised his voice. "I knew that if I didn't do the job, he would have found someone else. I wanted to tell someone, but everyone looked up to him, and I wasn't even sure my own mother would believe me."

Aero stared at him with a neutral expression, her eyes suddenly cold. The boat rocked as the storm caught up to them, and she gripped the edges of her seat to steady herself.

"I'm so sorry, Aero. I didn't want to kill him—I swear. I've been trying to tell you what happened this entire trip, but I... I was scared."

Aero stood and stepped toward him, swaying slightly on the unsteady boat. Her lips curled downward as she lunged, shoving Saunti back into a cargo box right as another wave slammed the boat, knocking him sideways. He caught himself on the railing before the river could snatch him.

His breath quickened as he pushed himself back up and faced Aero, expecting a final shove.

But instead, her dark eyes drilled into him. She reached through the collar of her shirt, pulling out a necklace concealed beneath the fabric. It was the piece Saunti had purchased for her at Atherus City market three weeks ago, before joining Headquarters. She had been wearing it all this time.

"I thought you were different," Aero said, her voice breaking as she unlatched the necklace. "You were so curious about Headquarters, so eager to help in any way you could. But it turns out you're just like everyone else down here. Paranoid... and *violent*."

She clutched the necklace tightly in her fist, shaking her head.

"I know it was wrong, Aero. That's why I left my mother a letter to confess. That's why I'm telling you the truth right now. I'm sure everyone in Headquarters already knows, but I wanted you to be the one to hear it from me."

"Oh, *congratulations*." Her words were like venom to his ears. "That makes everything better."

He inhaled a shaky breath as a cold breeze swept past the boat, chilling him to the bone. His honesty meant nothing to her. He hadn't expected it to fix this—but he'd hoped it might count for *something*. That it might ease the guilt, not deepen it.

Before he could utter another word, Aero chucked his necklace into the water, and the waves swallowed it in a greedy gulp.

She looked back at him, her hands rolling into fists at her sides.

"I'm sorry," he repeated, backing up as she stepped toward him. A rampant wave jumped from the river, eating the torch on the dashboard and putting out the flames.

It was darker now. Her eyes shimmered with a glint of green as she closed the gap between them, shoving him back again.

He winced as his back struck the railing, but he didn't fight her.

"Do it," he said, his voice raspy and breathless.

Her hands tightened around his shoulders.

"Throw me off. I deserve it!"

The Waterway carried his statement. *"I deserve it. I deserve it. I deserve it..."*

Aero gritted her teeth and hesitated, her hands shaking. She looked at the raging water, then back at Saunti. The waves were so violent that they splashed water at them, like rain from all directions.

The storm could kill him, and they both knew it.

Her face reddened as she gripped him tighter and leaned in. "You want me to be like you?" She choked on a breath, tears slipping down her cheeks. "You want to see blood on my hands?"

Saunti's pulse quickened as Aero shook her head, stepping back and letting him go.

"You never should have joined me on this trip!" she screamed. "I should have been there! I should have stayed!"

More tears fell, and she turned away, storming back to her seat at the wheel.

Saunti took a step toward her.

"*Stop,*" she snapped without looking back. "Don't you *dare* move."

He gulped and lowered himself to the deck. The waves continued to splash, water occasionally hitting his face—but her paranoid glances every few minutes struck him even harder. He watched her sob at the front of the boat. Alone. Terrified. Defenseless. If only he could say something or comfort her—but he couldn't, because *he* had done this to her.

There was no knowing how the Council would punish him for this, but he hoped their choice would give her peace.

Not a soul awaited them at the riverbank.

Saunti had imagined his return to Headquarters a dozen times. In every iteration, the Guild—with janky weapons drawn—prepared to rescue Aero from the sixteen-year-old monster who had killed their leader. It was the endings he imagined that varied. Sometimes they'd lock him up, exile him, or kill him on the spot. But in no iteration had he imagined a peaceful return like this.

The storm had passed. It was quiet, dim, and green.

As soon as the boat met the shore, Aero stumbled out and darted down the tunnel to the main part of Headquarters. He figured she wanted confirmation that he hadn't lied—that he truly *had* killed Rimoso. Perhaps she hoped for the rare scenario that he had pulled a sick prank on her after all, that her father was still breathing, still here.

Saunti stepped out of the boat and sighed. His heart pounded, even though his mind had already accepted his fate. People would soon notice Aero's return—which marked *Saunti's* return—and the Guild would rush his way.

In the meantime, he secured the boat to its post and busied himself with unloading the cargo. He couldn't carry the boxes to the inventory room without Aero's key, but he could at least stack them along the cave wall for someone else to transport later.

He'd nearly emptied most of the boat when footsteps echoed from the tunnel. As he carried another box to stack along the wall, he shuffled to a stop and stared at Yahshi. It had been twelve days since he'd last seen the person he had killed for.

"I saw Aero running," Yahshi said. "I figured you were back."

Saunti set the cargo box down and dusted off his hands, struggling to read Yahshi's expression.

"Rimoso was the life of this place." He shook his head, his lips parted in disbelief. "The Council was horrified to lose him, and after they announced the news publicly, most people didn't show up to work. The carventers paused the tunnel project, and half the Guild isn't training in protest of their new leader. They're losing hope."

"They would have lost *more* hope," Saunti muttered, "had it been you who died instead."

"No one had to die. You should have told me what was happening, so I could take care of it."

Saunti scoffed. "Rimoso wanted me to kill you, and if I didn't do it, he would have found another way. He made that clear."

"We're talking about *my* life, Saunti. Killing him wasn't your choice to make."

"You would have made the *wrong* choice." Saunti had assumed such before, but he knew it for certain now. If Yahshi had tried to compromise, Rimoso would have laughed at his kindness and killed him anyway.

Yahshi was about to argue back when more footsteps echoed from the tunnel, interrupting them. From behind Yahshi entered Tonna, her brows furrowed, her gaze sharp. She locked eyes with her son, and the weight of her stare made him gulp. He had almost forgotten that he'd returned to face whatever the Council had in store for him.

"What now?" Saunti asked, his voice breaking.

Tonna glanced at Yahshi, then back at her son.

"No one knows."

Saunti frowned. "No one knows *what*?"

"As soon as I found your letter," she explained, "I rushed to Rimoso's chamber and removed the syringe from his back. When the other Council members found him, they ruled it a heart attack. Apparently, he had one a few years ago —they figured he wasn't as lucky this time."

Saunti's eyes widened. Why would she cover for him?

Tonna smiled at Yahshi, who crossed his arms, as though he wasn't fully on board with what she was about to say.

"Prince Runix told me about your plan," Tonna said. "We've been waiting for your return so we could help you execute it."

"What?" Saunti fished for Yahshi's gaze, but he wouldn't look at him. "I gave you all the information you needed to take over."

"It's too risky for anyone else to take on but you," Tonna said. "We don't know for certain how this Podge character will react to learning about the Underground. But you know him personally, so you can handle him best."

His expression lightened. "The Council's on board with this?"

"The Council knows nothing, and they don't need to. Not yet."

Saunti pursed his lips, shaking his head. This was the first time his mother had ever opened up to one of his ideas, but he couldn't get involved. Aero knew everything, and she would tell the Council any moment now, disrupting the cover story Tonna had allowed to spread. That was how it should be. He didn't deserve protection.

"I can't, Mother. You'll have to send someone else to recruit Podge, and accept the added risks."

"Why?"

"Aero knows everything," Saunti revealed. "She deserved to hear it from me."

His mother gasped and shook her head. There was no way Aero *wouldn't* tell the Council. For all they knew, she might have already done so! Saunti could leave Headquarters now to get Podge on board—to complete the mission before the Council could come after him—but it was still light out. Someone could see him leave the access point.

"Vell." Yahshi's face lit up. "She's friends with Aero. Maybe she could quiet her."

Saunti frowned at the thought of pressuring her into silence. "Oh, I don't think—"

"Find her," Tonna ordered, and Yahshi darted off.

It was only Saunti and his mother now, alone, as the river came to a complete lull, the tides preparing to shift southward. He and Aero had made it back just in time.

There were so many questions he wanted to ask his mother, but one in particular fought its way to his mouth.

"Why did you cover for me?"

Tonna walked forward, finally closing the gap between them. "I wish you felt that you could have told me. I've kept you in the dark for so long, and as a result, you had to deal with Rimoso alone. You must have been terrified."

He looked away. "I handled it."

She laughed to herself. "Oh, Saunti." Her arms encased him, catching him by surprise. "I'm so proud of you."

His eyes watered as he melted into her embrace. He had expected to return to weapons drawn, not open arms.

"But he was your friend."

"He was, once," she muttered. "But had your father been in your shoes, I'm certain he would have done the same. That's how I know you made the right choice, as much as it hurts."

Saunti held her back, fending off tears. At least one person believed he'd done the right thing.

CHAPTER 24

TELL HIM

Day 21 Underground | Clocks Read 13:07

♫ ALMOST TO THE MOON - DAISY GRAY ♫

The Council took two weeks, just to choose him?

Vell leaned against the wall of the arena, studying Rimoso's replacement as he explained how to wield a sword to Flaire and Mont. His smile certainly made him more likable than his predecessor, but he took the job even less seriously. The older majority of the Guild mainly stretched or lingered about the room chatting instead of training.

Varin appeared at her side, arms crossed. "We're doomed, aren't we?"

Vell briefly glanced at him. It seemed that losing Rimoso had started to chip away at Varin's confidence in the Guild. She would like to say she was pleased that his eyes were open, but part of her was starting to understand how important their sense of pride was. It united them. Now the portion of Guild members who even bothered to show up for training were scattered across the arena in groups, unsure of what to do or who to turn to for guidance.

"I'm not sure if he even remembers how to fight," Varin continued. "You know, he used to be a palace guard like Rimoso, but for the past fourteen years, he wasn't even part of the Guild. He's only served the Underground as a math instructor. I'm starting to think the Council doesn't know what they're doing anymore."

Vell nodded in agreement as she watched Flaire struggle to raise a rusty sword the math instructor had given her. Mont made fun of her shaky arms, and the three of them laughed together.

"The Council *never* knew what they were doing," Vell replied. They didn't even have the experience to recognize that Rimoso had clearly not died of natural causes. Every sign of his body pointed to poison—which Saunti had injected to protect Yahshi, according to Tonna's recount of his confession letter. How had he planned such a murder in secret? Where did he get the poison? What kind of poison was it? How did he administer it?

Vell wondered all of these things, while the rest of the Guild didn't even question his death.

"If it were *my* call, I would have chosen someone who actually gives a damn," Varin said.

"Someone who's grieving Rimoso." She nodded. "Someone who understands the stakes."

"Exactly." His gaze softened as he faced her again. While he didn't say a word, she sensed his guilt for how he'd treated her when she'd first arrived at Headquarters. They thought more similarly than either of them would have admitted back then.

"I'm sorry about your brother," Vell muttered. She worried the apology would come across as superficial, but she meant it. According to Aero, Varin's older brother had stayed above ground to smuggle goods, only to die at the hands of a Nightshade who discovered the surplus of canned sardines in his closet. While Vell had not killed his brother, as a guardian, she would have, and that left her with a sense of responsibility.

"Thanks," Varin said, offering the slightest of smiles. He seemed to know that she meant it.

"Vell!" a familiar voice called from across the arena. It was Yahshi, waving her down. Moments like this still caught her by surprise—seeing him in public spaces without a Council member glued to his side. They were too busy handling the aftermath of Rimoso's death to shape their perfect Prince, but neither Vell nor Yahshi was complaining about *that* change in particular.

She offered Varin a parting glance before rushing to join Yahshi, who led her into the connected tunnel. From afar, she hadn't noticed the hard lines creasing his brow, and seeing such a worried expression left her face hardening in anticipation of news she didn't want to hear. What else could Yahshi be this stressed about other than Saunti and Aero's return to Headquarters, the very event she'd been dreading for the past twelve days?

"They're finally back," Yahshi said, confirming her fear. "And you were right—he confessed."

She wasn't surprised. If Saunti had left a confession letter for his mother, why else would he flee with Aero down the Waterway? The only explanation was that he intended to tell Aero the truth, before she could hear it from anyone else.

Now it was up to Vell, as expected, to deal with the aftermath and walk the tightrope between comfort and manipulation. She needed to somehow console a girl who was the last to know of her father's death—while also convincing her to keep quiet and protect her father's murderer. It was an impossible mission, and of course, it landed in her hands, because Aero was her friend.

"We really don't *need* Saunti's help," Vell argued. "He gave you instructions."

"Please, Vell," Yahshi urged. "We're lucky to have Tonna on our side. As a member of the Council, she could ensure the others don't come after us once Podge gets here. We need to play by her rules for now."

She rolled her eyes, but he had a point. "Fine. Where's Aero?"

"I asked around on the way here, but no one seems to know."

"Let's check the Waterway," Vell suggested, turning down a different tunnel.

Yahshi caught up to her. "But she just *came* from the Waterway."

When he met her gaze, his eyes widened as he realized her point—if Aero wanted to be alone, the river was the last place anyone would look.

They made a beeline for the Waterway, where Vell spotted stacks of cargo boxes along the tunnel wall. The boxes were back, but the boat was gone.

She squinted down the tunnel and spotted a flicker of light in the distance.

A torch, perhaps? It took a moment for her eyes to adjust to the darkness, but once they did, she confirmed the silhouette of a boat heading south. She glanced at Yahshi, and in unison, they faced the water and shouted Aero's name.

"Aero. Aero. Aero..."

The Waterway carried their voices down the tunnel, but the boat continued to glide away, deeper into the darkness.

"Aero. Aero. Aero..."

Vell stopped shouting and looked around—there were no other boats, but it wasn't like she knew how to use one, anyway. Her gaze sharpened on the dark water next. There was so little light that she didn't know what could possibly be inside. She had once seen a rare fish in the Waterway, but were there other creatures too? More dangerous ones? Sharks? She had never swum in open water before—apart from a lake in Miranda when she was a young child and went through a phase of investigating aquatic plants with medicinal qualities.

Yahshi stopped shouting too. "She's leaving Headquarters. Maybe that's okay. She'll come back when she's ready, and in the meantime, no one will find out."

Vell shook her head, taking a few steps back. Convincing Aero to keep quiet was only one of her responsibilities. She needed to be there for her.

Yahshi gave her a look, realizing what she was about to do. "Vell, don't—"

She leaped forward, pointing her hands to dive into the Waterway. It was chilly, numbing her body. The water that sprinkled into her mouth when she popped her head up to breathe was salty and stung her eyes—exactly how she imagined the ocean to feel like.

"Vell!" Yahshi called from the riverbank.

She threw her arms forward and kicked her legs, pushing into the coldness, but it felt that no matter how fast she swam, the boat remained the same distance away. She treaded water to catch her breath, shivering as she stared at the silhouette by the steering wheel.

"Aero!" Vell yelled.

"Aero. Aero. Aero..." echoed the Waterway.

The silhouette shifted. *She heard me.*

Vell inhaled a deep breath before submerging herself into the water again. Exhaustion gnawed at her muscles, but she kept swimming—there was no turning back. Aero was closer than the riverbank.

Gasping for air, she resurfaced just a few strokes from the boat.

Aero leaned over the gunwale, offering her hands. "Vell!"

"Vell. Vell. Vell…"

With her arms reaching out, Vell kicked her legs, propelling herself just high enough for her wet fingers to meet Aero's dry ones. She swung a knee over the railing and tumbled inside, splatting onto the deck, her back to the wood. It took her a moment to catch her breath—and for the first time, she noticed that mushrooms grew upside-down on the tunnel roof.

Aero leaned over, popping into Vell's field of vision with a hand on her hip. "What were you *thinking*? No one swims in the Waterway."

Vell rolled onto her side and tried to push herself up, but her arms collapsed under her, fatigued from the swim. She chuckled at the absurdity of what she'd done, and Aero laughed too, pulling Vell by her shoulders into a seated position.

Now they faced each other in the rocking vessel, heading south on an underground river that most people didn't know existed.

Vell's smile faded as she remembered the reason why she'd swam here.

"Where are you going, Aero?"

She shrugged. "South."

"But we need you in Headquarters." Vell couldn't stop trembling, even as she rubbed her arms repeatedly. "You're our handler."

Aero's eyes watered, and she turned her head away, shielding her face. "Dice can take my job permanently. I don't care."

"*I* care."

"I can't go back. Not to such a pathetic Council. They covered up the real cause of my father's death. It was *Saunti* who killed him."

"The Council didn't cover for him," Vell said, drawing Aero's eyes back to her. "It was just Tonna, and Yahshi, and… me."

Her eyes sharpened. "*What*?"

Vell looked down. While she hadn't killed Rimoso, what she was about to reveal made her feel complicit. "Saunti has friends above ground that could benefit the Guild." The guilt lodged in her throat like a pebble, and she swallowed hard before continuing. "That's why Tonna hid the truth and awaited your return. She wants to send Saunti and me up tonight, so we can propose joining forces."

"Then go." Aero's voice was a low rasp. "I don't care."

"Aero..." Vell set a hand on her shoulder, but she brushed it aside. "I'm not asking you to forgive him. I'm asking if you'll forgive me, if I help him with this."

"You want me to keep quiet and protect my father's murderer?"

"If that was my only goal, I would have let you leave quietly," Vell said, her voice softer now. "I want you to come home."

"I don't feel safe there."

"When have you ever?" A sharp question, but it had to be said. "I know it's unfair, but this is a matter of survival. If we don't act soon, we're *all* dead—not just your father."

Aero gulped. "You really think Saunti's friends could help?"

Vell nodded. "I'm sure of it."

"When do you leave?"

"Tonight."

"And what about your allies on the other side?" she said, still skeptical. "Last time I checked, you cared about them more than us."

"This plan could protect everyone, including them."

Aero's face twisted as she looked away, her shoulders shaking. It was quiet for a moment.

"Do you remember the woman I told you about? The one my father killed because she tried to leave Headquarters?"

She nodded. "The woman in bunker forty-three."

Aero's face paled as she whispered, "She was my mother."

Vell bit her lip.

"I know he wasn't a good man, Vell." Her voice trembled and frayed, barely her own. "But I... I didn't want to lose him too."

As Aero hunched over, tears spilling from her eyes, Vell scooted closer and wrapped an arm around her. She likely soaked her clothes with saltwater, but Aero didn't seem to care. She pressed her face to Vell's shoulder, no longer fighting her tears.

Vell rested her chin atop Aero's head and closed her eyes.

"It's okay," she muttered.

A lie. Nothing was okay about this. But it was all she could think to say.

Once Aero gathered herself, she and Vell spent an hour paddling back to the riverbank. The water wheels would have worked against them, so they could only rely on brute force to fight the southbound current.

Yahshi waited by the shore, waist-deep in the river. As Vell turned the steering wheel, he helped guide the boat toward its mooring post and secured it with the untied rope hanging in the water.

Aero jumped off the dock first, her boots sinking in the mud, eyes lost in the tunnel leading to the main part of Headquarters. She hesitated to walk toward it, but Vell didn't judge. That tunnel led to the home of her father's murderer—and thousands who believed he was innocent. Aero had a strong head, but not a heart of steel.

Yahshi stepped out of the water, cargo pants dripping, boots sloshing in the dirt as he approached Aero.

Vell watched from the boat, which lulled softly beneath her. She had never seen them interact, though she'd spoken to both about each other.

Yahshi's first words for the girl, practically a stranger, were, "I'm sorry."

Vell gulped, her grip on the side of the boat tightening. The guilt had bitten at Yahshi for the past twelve days. He had blamed himself, as he had a tendency to do, believing the blood on Saunti's hands might as well have been on his own. After all, had he not joined the Underground, Rimoso would still be alive.

"It's not your fault." Aero set a hand on his shoulder, and though she still didn't look at him, her gesture and tone of voice lightened his expression.

Vell smiled, loosening her grip on the gunwale. Even while grieving, Aero still comforted Yahshi when she could have lashed out and pinned the blame on him.

"Would you like to speak with Tonna?" Yahshi offered. Perhaps confronting the woman who had chosen to cover for Saunti would provide Aero with a sense of closure.

"No," she said, her hand leaving his shoulder. She stepped forward into the tunnel alone.

Yahshi watched her go, the tension leaving his shoulders as he exhaled a long sigh.

Finally, Vell propped a boot onto the railing and jumped forward, landing into the mud. Her clothes were still soaked from the swim, despite how long she had spent paddling to the dock, and the water dripped from her in a patterned song.

"I know that was hard," Yahshi said, wrapping her in a hug. Like Aero, he didn't seem to mind the water.

Vell hugged him back, closing her eyes. While she respected Saunti's choice to confess, she could only hope that the truth wouldn't burden Aero. Would she have been happier believing her father had died of a heart attack, instead of knowing the truth but being pressured into hiding it?

They pulled away from each other and sat on the dry dirt they often lingered on during breaks. It was astonishing how much free time Yahshi spent with her, now that he actually had some. She wondered if he felt a need to make up for all his disappearances, but she didn't question his intentions. She simply appreciated the extra time.

A quiet rested between them as they stared at the Waterway. She knew the conversation was about to happen—Yahshi would speak the words he'd been holding back ever since Vell volunteered to go up with Saunti. He had not mentioned his opinion yet, though she could read it on his face every time the topic came up.

"Do you really have to go with him?" Yahshi asked, facing her with a shake of his head. "Saunti has lived in Atherus City all his life. He can do this alone."

"I need to, Yahshi." She wouldn't look at him. "You were the one who said it wasn't fair—that the Council should appreciate me more. Finally, Tonna's giving me a chance to help."

"You should be helping the Guild, especially now that Rimoso's gone.

You could show them how the Force fights so they could better defend themselves."

"So they could hurt our friends more efficiently?" She finally looked at him. "I like Saunti's plan for the same reason you do. It keeps everyone safe, including Pinto, Quax, and Keiyo. *This* is the only plan I want to help with."

Vell knew the Council member only accepted her help because she feared Saunti might run into trouble on his way to Podge's house. If he encountered Nightshades, he'd need backup who could handle them. Still, Vell appreciated her trust. Tonna could have easily claimed that involving her was riskier than sending Saunti alone. It seemed Vell's quiet submission—working as an apprentice timekeeper and cowering under the Council's glares—had earned her just enough credibility for Tonna to take a chance on her.

"If there's no convincing you out of this," Yahshi decided, "then I'm going too."

She bit back a chuckle. "You're too recognizable, and three people sneaking around would draw too much attention. Plus, you're the one who wants to play by Tonna's rules, remember?"

"But—"

"If something bad happens, losing you would destroy the Underground's morale even more. It's bad enough with Rimoso gone."

Yahshi froze, his eyes widening, and Vell looked away, regretting her choice to even mention such a scenario. She should have known better than to plant such an idea in his head.

"I can't lose you," he muttered. "While I was on the run, I couldn't stop wondering if you were okay, and... I hated not having an answer."

Vell's eyes watered, because she had felt the same way. She wished to tell him that she had worried endlessly about him, wondering if he was even alive—but this situation was not the same. She was not running from the Nightshades. She was just going up, for a few hours, to assist Saunti with his plan.

"Nothing bad will happen." She reached for his hand and squeezed it. "I'll be up and down before you know it. I promise."

In that moment, as they looked into each other's eyes, Vell was certain that he felt the same way about her. Why else did he cling to her now in the same way she had clung to him for the past three weeks? This was her moment to finally say it, to speak the words they both knew were there, tucked away in their throats.

Tell him, ordered the clocks.

Vell leaned her head on his shoulder. The truth was like a pebble in her boot she couldn't ignore no matter how hard she tried.

Tell him, urged the Waterway, splashing against the shore. A gentle mist of seawater sprinkled against their cheeks.

"Yahshi?" Vell muttered.

"Yeah?"

"Do you like Headquarters?"

"I do," he said, "because you're here."

It was the same answer she'd given him over a month ago, when he'd asked if she liked Vakoi City.

Her heart pounded against her chest, yelling, *Tell him!*

She closed her eyes, blocking out the noise. It was not the time. Not yet.

Up. The word weighed heavily on Vell as she made her way to the access point in the middle of the night, swerving through Headquarters into tunnels without clocks ticking, voices mumbling, and footsteps echoing. It was barren and quiet. The space between the main part of Headquarters and the access point was like a waiting room for the afterlife's ladder.

She had a feeling she was running late, and with no clocks around, she could only check her watch—a gift from Dice, which, she realized now, no longer worked thanks to her swim in the Waterway. *I'll have to fix it later.*

She only confirmed she was last to arrive when she spotted four people down the tunnel, waiting for her by the access point.

The first was Dice, who Vell had convinced Yahshi and Tonna to involve in their plan a few days prior. As Aero's replacement over the last twelve days, he had been covering the late-night and early morning shifts guarding the access point. Thankfully, it hadn't taken much to convince Dice to unlock it behind the Council's back. He no longer trusted its members after learning that Rimoso had planned to kill the beloved *Prince Runix*. A true royalist, Dice was.

"What a *timekeeper*," he mocked, tapping his watch. "We were supposed to meet at 02:00. It's already 02:04."

Vell smirked at him, then faced the second person waiting at the access point. It was Yahshi, of course, brows raised, his face twisted into that classic, anxious look of his. He took a few steps toward her, his voice quiet.

"Did you get the tools?"

She parted her coat, revealing inner pockets stuffed with tools from the Guild. They were just the right size to serve either as daggers or throwing blades.

"Varin lent me these. He didn't even ask what they were for."

Saunti, the third person, chuckled to himself. "No kidding." He stood by the access point door beside the fourth—Tonna, who distracted him from Vell's appearance by offering him a hug, anticipating that it was almost time to part.

Vell closed her coat. While Yahshi didn't know it, Dice had insisted she lace the blades from Varin, handing her the vial of half-used calabar serum that Saunti had returned to him earlier that day.

"I won't tell the Prince," Dice had said, watching Vell prepare her blades in his lab of mushrooms. *"I know how much he hates this kind of thing."*

When Tonna pulled away from Saunti, her hands lingered on her son's shoulders, her face marked with pride. A moment passed before her gaze drifted to Vell, and though her expression lightened a little, it was the same look.

"Thank you for doing this," Tonna said.

"Thank you for trusting me," Vell replied.

Yahshi took her hand by surprise. His fingers were warm. "Please be careful," he said, his gaze darting back and forth between her and Saunti. "Both of you."

"I'm always careful," they said in unison.

Vell and Saunti smiled at each other before facing the metal door to the access point.

Yahshi released her hand. "We'll be right here, waiting."

Dice looked at Tonna. "All three of us."

"Me too," another voice chimed in, and from around a corner emerged Aero, her eyes red. Vell hadn't heard her footsteps, and she wondered how long she had been lurking there.

Saunti's eyes widened at the sight of her. Vell couldn't quite read his expression, though she could imagine how he felt—surprised that Aero hadn't fallen into a pit of despair. He had heard about her attempt to flee down the Waterway, and yet here she was, just hours later, confronting him.

Their group split as Aero rushed after Vell and wrapped her in a suffocating hug. Vell hugged her back, and it was clear then that she and Saunti had it wrong—this was not a confrontation. In fact, this had nothing to do with him. Aero simply wanted to await her friend's safe return.

As they hugged, Vell recalled her first day in Headquarters, when Aero had been the one person to make her feel welcome. She had done nothing but support her, and even after her father's death, she still dusted her pants off and stood on her own two feet. Perhaps Vell had been wrong. She had a strong head *and* a strong heart. Not one of steel, but of something hard and alive. Like a tree—scarred and splintered but always grounded, clinging to life.

When they pulled away from each other, Aero muttered, "I can't lose you."

Vell shook her head, clutching her friend's arms. "I'll be right back. Up and down."

Aero nodded and backed away, placing herself next to Yahshi. That's when she and Saunti finally made eye contact. He opened his mouth, perhaps to apologize again, but her sudden glare forced his words away.

He gulped and turned from Aero, as though he just remembered the brutal fact that he was the last person she would ever seek comfort from.

Vell locked eyes with him. It was time to go.

With a nod, Saunti opened the door and led Vell into the manhole. The faces of Yahshi, Aero, Dice, and Tonna vanished as she closed the door between them, sealing their two groups in different worlds.

The air turned black.

In sync with the *click* of someone locking the door from the other side, Saunti lit a match and pinched it between his fingers. His face glowed ominously in the dull orange light as he peered up at the ladder leading into Atherus City.

"And up we go," he muttered, hoisting himself onto the first step.

As Vell climbed, it felt as though she were about to enter a foreign world rather than the one she'd come from. Over the course of three weeks, she had been an unwelcome Nightshade, a girl without purpose, and an apprentice timekeeper. Now, after so much confusion, she had finally found her place in Headquarters—a group of people who cared for her so much that they would anxiously await her return tonight. The Underground, while not perfect, had become more of a home to her than the Force had ever been.

When they reached the top, Saunti put his match out. It was completely dark before he pushed the manhole cover up, just a crack, letting in a sliver of light. He peered out to ensure the alleyway was empty before sliding the cover aside completely and climbing out into the world above.

Vell joined him soon after, and together they slid the cover back into place, hiding their tracks.

Spinning around, she soaked in the alleyway, her eyes widening at normal buildings lit under the moonlight. Somehow, it felt *high* in Atherus City. If not for common sense, she would have believed that she and Saunti had scaled a mountain.

A gentle breeze glided past them, and Saunti closed his eyes. "Do you feel that?"

Vell closed her eyes too. The chilly air tickled her cheeks and neck.

"Wind," she whispered.

"And do you hear that?"

"Crickets."

"Waves."

"Trees," Vell finished, tuning into the sound of rustling leaves in the distance. She swore she could smell them—a faint scent of plants in the air that didn't exist underground. *It's so much easier to breathe up here.*

With a smile, Vell opened her eyes, and she was surprised to find Saunti grinning back at her. For the first time, it felt like they'd come from the same place. There was no Vakoi Empire and Eastern Territory. Just one beautiful island, and it was theirs to protect.

"I would have done the same thing," Vell admitted, now that Aero couldn't overhear them.

"I know." Saunti's smile faded, and she couldn't tell if the bitterness in his voice was directed at her, or at himself. "It's what a Nightshade would have done."

"I've felt guilty too, about killing," Vell said. "Not the way Yahshi feels guilty—the way *you* do. More sorry for the people that grieve than for the victim."

His voice was soft again. "Do you think she'll ever forgive me?"

"I don't know. Maybe she *shouldn't*."

He lifted his gaze to the crescent moon, and a moment passed before he said, "I just hope she can enjoy the real world someday."

Vell thought of all the times Aero had asked her about the sky, the ocean, the plants above land...

"Me too," she whispered.

If Saunti was right about these so-called Boomers being the key to ending this War, she would do anything to ensure they'd return to Headquarters with them tonight. The Underground hiders deserved to return above and live free from Emperor Vakoi's rule.

"How far are we going?" she asked, redirecting her focus to the mission at hand.

Saunti gestured for her to follow him down the alleyway. His steps were so quiet that if she were listening from afar, she might mistake him for a guardian.

"My friend Podge lives along the outskirts of Atherus City, close to the ocean," he whispered. "Give it twenty minutes or so. We'll have to move slowly."

The ocean. Vell hadn't seen it since the night she and Pinto had burned *The Force's Hidden Agenda* at the beach. The Waterway carried only a fragment of the sea's beauty, along with just a fragment of its life, and she found herself eager to see its mother again.

Saunti made turns down different alleyways—avoiding areas where they'd be more likely to run into officers. According to his occasional whispers, they were heading to the home of his ex-classmate and ex-coworker. Apparently, Podge was the true owner of the Meridian book Saunti had thrown.

Vell flinched when Saunti skidded to a stop in the middle of an alleyway, his eyes darting to a door. It was slightly ajar, and he frowned, creeping toward it.

A few seconds passed before Vell made the connection—she had been here before. The very home Saunti approached was the first one she and Yahshi had stopped at during their search for Tonna in Atherus City. A round man had answered them and given directions on where they could find her.

"Noris always locks his door." Saunti pressed a weak palm against it, hesitating to push.

Vell scanned the alleyway, ensuring no one was around as Saunti finally entered Noris's home, disappearing into the darkness. She retrieved a blade from her coat and stood guard, expecting him to call her in at any moment, but nothing happened. Moment after moment passed without a sound. It was like the house had devoured him alive.

She scanned the alleyway a final time before pushing the door open, a chill running down her spine. Blade in hand, she entered the darkness, just enough moonlight following her in to illuminate Saunti, who knelt on the floorboards with his back to the door, his head shaking.

Vell inched forward, joining Saunti's side and following his gaze to a body by his boots.

A deep puncture wound marked Noris's chest, blood dripping through the cracks between the floorboards around him.

Her chest tightened, the air thinning as she inhaled a sharp breath. From what Aero and Dice had told her, Noris was not just a collector—he was Tonna's carefully selected replacement, the Underground's only courier in Atherus City.

Saunti was still frozen, his breaths narrow, his hands shaking as he hesitated to reach for the dead man. She gave him a moment to regain composure and knelt beside the body, studying Noris. His wound was clean and slightly curved—clearly the work of a guardian's sword.

Vell stood to her feet with a gasp, her eyes widening. "We need to go back," she said, tugging Saunti's arm. "There are guardians nearby."

Saunti yanked his arm free, refusing to stand. "He was the most careful person I've ever met," he said firmly, his eyes glued to Noris. "If the guardians got him, they must have gotten others too."

While Vell understood his paranoia, even careful people could make mistakes. Unless the Force had somehow broken the lantern code, the collectors in Atherus City were surely okay. Right now, their priority was to head straight to Headquarters and alert Tonna of Noris's death so she could select someone else in the area to fill his shoes.

"We need to check on the collectors," Saunti said. "To make sure they're okay."

"Just a few," Vell compromised, knowing it would likely calm his nerves.

"Just a few," he echoed in agreement, finally standing. He turned his back to the man's body and swallowed hard, lingering for a moment longer. It was his own way of saying goodbye.

Finally, Saunti tucked his shaky hands into his coat pockets and led the way out of Noris's home.

Vell left the door open a crack, like they had found it, and followed Saunti down the alleyway. He took a few more turns before stopping at another house with a lantern matching the code Yahshi had told Vell about. Like Noris's home, the front door was slightly ajar.

Vell and Saunti made eye contact before bursting inside, finding two dead bodies on the floorboards. Their puncture wounds were even fresher, marked with arrows of a different guardian's primary tool.

They rushed to a third house, which contained yet another man spilling with blood.

Vell listened for signs of movement, but Atherus City was eerily still. They had already found four bodies of Underground members, which meant there were likely more. Had the guardians caught Noris, and tortured him into snitching on his allies?

No, it couldn't be. The wound in Noris's chest did not speak of torture. It was clean, as though a guardian had simply walked in and sliced into him without a word.

The guardians are on a silent killing spree.

"We need to get back." Vell's voice hardened. "*Now.*"

Saunti nodded, leading the way back at a slow walking pace. His arms were tense as he fought every effort not to run, despite the many slightly open doors they passed on their way.

Vell stopped at the sound of footsteps that weren't theirs. She wished it was a figment of her imagination, but when she closed her eyes, honing into the noise, it became even clearer.

Saunti halted a few paces ahead, looking back at her with a questioning look. "What's wrong?"

Vell's eyes snapped open. If Saunti didn't hear the footsteps, the approachers *had* to be guardians—and based on the sound, they were closing in on them.

"Run," she whispered.

Saunti's gaze sharpened. He faced ahead again, darting for the end of the alleyway, Vell following in his trail. She heard the guardians following them, and from the patterns in their steps, she identified two people—not a full unit. There was at least one other guardian in the area.

Finally, Saunti stopped in the alleyway where the access point was located, dropping to his knees to pull the manhole cover open.

Vell knelt to help him, their hands shaking as they dragged it aside, cueing a loud scraping noise of stone against stone. The approaching guardians were even closer now, and she was certain that even Saunti heard them, because his face paled as he lowered himself down to the ladder.

There were just seconds left—not enough time for both her and Saunti to climb into the access point and drag the manhole cover back into place. The guardians would follow them down to capture them, and they would surely discover Headquarters.

Noris was dead, the collectors in Atherus City were dead, and the ones in other parts of Eastern Territory could possibly be dead too. She couldn't allow the Force to find Yahshi, Aero, Dice, Tonna, and so many more people who didn't deserve such a fate. So long as the hideout went undiscovered, they would be safe.

Vell rose to her feet, wielding a dull, calabar-laced blade. If she could hold off the guardians, she could buy Saunti time to return to Headquarters and alert the Council of the assassinations. They could figure out a plan to survive before supplies would run out.

"Vell!" Saunti whispered fiercely, as though he knew what she was planning.

She sent him a look of farewell before running off toward the approaching guardians.

CHAPTER 25

QUICKLY BUT QUIETLY

Stay clean with lye soap and vinegar—
now bundled at your local Saver Store!

♫ HUNTING THE WREN · FINNEGAL TUI ♫

"Here's another one." Pinto pointed to the lantern by a door in Atherus City, which hung from a chain with a slightly larger upmost link. He raised a fist but paused before knocking, looking over his shoulder to cue his unit members to draw their primary tools. While having so many shiny, pretty blades wasn't necessary, it helped quiet their targets—a crucial factor for a smooth Incursion.

Quax already held his swords.

Keiyo plucked a star from his bandolier the moment Pinto met his gaze.

Sunna unsheathed his dual swords with a soft metallic hiss—last, like always.

"We'll strike at night, dispersing our units throughout Eastern Territory," Pinto had explained during a Force-wide meeting in the Complex that morning. *"Once we're in, the smugglers will start disappearing, quickly but quietly, and we'll leave as though we were never there."*

Finally, Pinto knocked on the door. It was past 2:00 in the morning, so while he waited for the traitor—or *traitors*—inside to stir, he raised his dagger and tilted it, glimpsing Sunna in the blade's reflection. He and Keiyo were exchanging glances again. It was clear they had made a pact of some kind, because whenever Pinto didn't kill their target immediately, Keiyo would take the initiative to do so without an order. The only explanation for his super-cooperation was that he wished to spare his friend from dirtying his hands.

Pinto lowered his secondary tool, his eye darting to the window. A curtain shifted as an eye peeked out, vanishing just as quickly and leaving the fabric swaying.

Next came footsteps—there were always footsteps. Everyone knew that if a guardian wasn't allowed inside, they would force their way in, lock busters in hand.

"Sunna," Pinto called.

"Yes, Professor?"

"This one's for you," he said, as though it were a gift. He gripped his dagger tighter as the door opened, revealing a woman in her thirties with wide eyes.

Great. A woman.

He had hoped for a man—ideally a dangerous-looking one—to make Sunna's first kill easier. But taking the order back would make him seem less confident, so he could only double down on it.

Pinto shoved himself through the doorway, pressing the tip of his dagger to the woman's throat. In close encounters like this, he found his secondary tool far more practical than his bow.

"Not a sound. If you wake your neighbors, we'll kill them too."

It was a bluff, of course—the same bluff every unit leader in the Force was making during this special operation. They wouldn't kill the innocent, but threatening was yet another effort to keep the Incursion as quiet as possible. If their targets screamed and caused a ruckus, other members of the Underground might have time to flee. A few strays would be manageable, but they couldn't let the numbers spiral out of hand.

The target backed up to lessen the tension of the blade against her neck, palms raised. Her familiar, oblivious expression made Pinto's blood boil.

His targets always looked as though they were victims, when in reality, they simply didn't understand why they had gotten caught.

"We know about the lanterns," Pinto said as his unit members entered the house from behind him.

The confusion dripped from her face, leaving behind pure fear. This was his favorite part—when they realized they could no longer fool him. He applied more pressure to his dagger, and she clenched her eyes shut.

Then he stilled, waiting for Sunna to step in, but he didn't move.

"Please," the woman whispered, clearly just as uncomfortable with the stillness.

"Quiet," Pinto said. He looked back at Sunna, who stood a few strides behind him, his swords at the ready. He wouldn't even need to pierce her deeply—even a shallow slice would get the job started, allowing the belladonna on his blades to handle the rest. She would be dead in seconds, regardless. It was such an easy kill.

This time, Keiyo nudged Sunna, urging him to follow Pinto's order. He could only protect him for so long.

Sunna's face drained of color, and Pinto nearly scolded—but the sound of footsteps in the distance distracted him. The Force had instructed local officers to stay out of the way, which meant it could only be ordinary residents of Atherus City roaming the alleyways. Perhaps they were members of the Underground who discovered a dead smuggler and were making their way to the hideout.

If we secretly follow them, they might lead us right to it.

Pinto turned back to the trembling woman, and with a sharp jerk of his wrist, he slashed his blade through her throat. A bubbly, croaking noise left her lips as she dropped to her knees, clutching her neck. Thankfully, the belladonna took care of the noise before *he'd* have to. It was much cleaner when the extra stab wasn't necessary.

I'll deal with Sunna's behavior later, he decided as he watched the woman die. Her muscles twitched as blood dripped from her neck.

Cringing, Pinto turned his back to her, wiping the blood from his dagger with a red handkerchief.

"Let's split up," he announced in a hushed voice. "Sunna, you're with me."

He couldn't trust that he wouldn't run off tonight—which should have been the least of a unit leader's worries—but he had bigger problems to deal with. The only option was to keep him close.

Sunna gulped, eyeing the smuggler as she fell still, finally dead. He sheathed his dual swords.

Pinto turned to Keiyo next. He couldn't fully trust him either, but at least Quax had been dependable so far. He waved his fingers between the pair. "You two stick together."

"Yes, Professor," Quax and Keiyo said in unison. They left the house and turned right.

"I'm sorry," Sunna muttered. At least he admitted he was wrong—that alone was an improvement.

"Then start showing up." Pinto led him through the door, leaving it open just a crack to avoid making more noise than necessary. Then he gestured for Sunna to follow him left, down the opposite end of the alleyway Quax and Keiyo had traveled.

They moved through the night like ghosts, following the sound of distant footsteps and whispers, struggling to place exactly where they were coming from. It took several minutes to spot the source of the noise—a silhouette in the distance, zooming past the open end of the alleyway. They rushed to the other side and turned right, following the figure.

There, in the distance, turning out of sight into yet another alleyway was a girl with long, black hair whipping behind her.

I thought I heard two people. Pinto raced after her, Sunna at his tail. *Did they split?*

He could only hope that Quax and Keiyo were onto the other one.

Pinto quickened his pace, gaining on the figure with every turn. He couldn't afford to lose her, especially if she had ties to the hideout Yahshi and Vell had vanished to.

She made a swift turn into a narrow alleyway, and Pinto ran slightly past it before skidding to a stop. He turned and looped back into the same one, only to find her standing at the end of it—her back to him, her face to a dead end.

Pinto and Sunna crept into the alleyway, closing in as she scanned the walls for an escape. But this was not a residential alleyway, and there were no stairways leading up to higher floors—just flat stones, slick with moss, and windows spaced too far apart to reach between. She had nowhere to go.

Pinto stopped and looked at Sunna, urging him to wield his swords. He complied faster this time.

"Turn around," Pinto ordered, taking another step toward the girl. "We have you cornered."

Finally, she faced him, her brows furrowed, her hand gripping the handle of a dull blade.

Pinto shuffled back, his eye widening. *Could it really be?*

The shocked expression on his unit member's face confirmed he wasn't hallucinating. While her clothes were brown and shaggy, unlike anything he'd seen her wear before, there was no denying that face.

Their target was none other than Vell Patura.

She took one step away from the dead end, landing in a blade-throwing form. The half-dart, half-dagger she threatened him with looked rusty and jagged—far from the beautiful pieces she had wielded as a guardian in the Force. Pinto wondered if it would be psychologically harder to kill with such an ugly, dull thing. Something about it seemed barbaric.

He wielded his dagger, preparing to deflect. There was no need to threaten her with an arrow yet.

Vell narrowed her cold blue eyes, as though Pinto were the enemy and not herself.

"Was it you?" she asked, her voice hoarse. "Did you kill these people?"

"Drop the tool," Pinto ordered.

"Was it you?" she asked again, readjusting her grip on the handle of her blade.

Pinto thought of the fifteen houses they had entered so far, and the people he and Keiyo had collectively eliminated. The only way Vell could know about them was if she had been around during the Incursion, lurking in the City. Why had she been out here, instead of the hideout? Or, was the hideout in plain sight? Perhaps if he played his cards right, Vell would answer some of his questions.

"And what is *he* doing here?" Vell continued to glare at Pinto, her eyes briefly shooting to Sunna. "Why is he wearing a uniform?"

Pinto shook his head. Once again, a fellow graduate treated him as though *he* was at fault for Sunna's mandatory service call. If it had been *his* choice, he wouldn't have wanted him either. There were plenty of filtered trainees who could have served with gusto if called back—but now wasn't the time to complain.

"Say something." Vell's hand paled from the pressure of her tight grip.

Pinto stepped toward her, and she backed into the light of a nearby hanging lantern. It was hard to tell in the dark, but it seemed like her tan complexion had dulled.

"Where have you been?" His voice came out smoother than expected, and his own restraint impressed him. "Somewhere dark, away from the sun?"

He took another step forward, and Vell looked at the brick walls on either side, as though they were closing in on her too.

Wherever she had vanished to for the past three weeks had weakened her. If she were a guardian fighting a member of the Underground, she would have thrown that blade a long time ago.

"Stay back," she said, more of a plea than a warning.

"Why?" Pinto asked, recalling her words at the bar in Vakoi Square. "I thought we were friends. I thought you'd do anything for me."

She threw her blade, but it struck Pinto's vest with interior armor, clattering against the cobblestone ground by his boots. He kicked it behind him, and Vell wielded another knife from her coat. He wondered if she had missed on purpose, or if she was getting rusty, forgetting the components of a uniform she no longer wore.

"If I were you, I'd be careful. You haven't been taking your maintenance vials. One little cut, and you won't be able to fight anymore." He slashed his dagger toward her, and she raised her arm, gritting her teeth as she blocked his pretty, shiny blade with her dull one.

He noticed her free hand slipping into her coat for yet another knife, like he was stupid. He pressed his dagger in deeper, forcing her to grip her current one with both hands.

Pinto scoffed at the hatred in her eyes as she struggled to fend off his blade.

A few weeks ago, if he'd encountered her in an alleyway like this, he might have trusted her and tried to help her. Now he could see that she despised him, just like the Force claimed. In Vell's eyes, he found proof that Evaris had been right to encourage him to move on.

"Pinto," Sunna said, rejecting his honorific. "Cut it out!"

Pinto pulled his dagger back, and Vell inhaled a few sharp breaths, regathering herself. He watched her calmly, his breaths even. She needed to know that she wouldn't win in combat against him. She was no guardian anymore.

"You shouldn't have killed them," Vell said, a few silent tears falling down her cheeks. "They're not your enemies."

He chuckled bitterly at her misplaced empathy. How could she say such a thing, knowing the Underground had gouged out his eye? *Of course* they were the enemy.

"What happened to you?" Pinto asked.

"What happened to *me*?" Vell scoffed. "Can't you see that what you're doing is worse than the raids? At least they left victims like you alive. You're killing them!"

"You've killed them too."

"And I regret it," she said. "I thought I didn't have a choice, but Yahshi proved that there's always another way." She looked past Pinto, locking eyes with Sunna, smiling just barely.

Pinto gritted his teeth. The words that left her mouth weren't like anything she'd said before. When had she ever been such an idealist? The Underground had brainwashed her, just as they'd done to Yahshi.

I need to bring her back to Vakoi City for questioning. He took another step toward her, and she backed into the wall. *We can force her to tell us where the hiders are.*

A cold tool slid against Pinto's neck, and he froze. It wasn't Vell's blade.

"Step back." Sunna applied more pressure to the sword. He had crept up behind Pinto, soundless on his feet, quickly but quietly—the mark of a true guardian.

Pinto had no choice but to back away to avoid a puncture wound. Even a perfect tolerance to belladonna wouldn't protect him from a blade sawing through his neck.

The chilling sword vanished, but before he could move, Sunna shoved his face against the mossy wall, and the impact knocked the dagger out of Pinto's grip.

"Run!" Sunna yelled.

Pinto struggled to free himself as Vell's footsteps raced behind him. He reached over his shoulder for an arrow in his quiver, only for Sunna's blade to slice through the fabric of his overcoat sleeve, biting into his arm.

He winced, dropping his hand, writhing with his face against the bricks. His arm throbbed too much to reach for another arrow, and trying again might entice Sunna to cut his limb off completely.

I won't die at the hands of a coward.

"You've made a huge mistake," Pinto choked out. "Once the Force hears about this, they'll realize how much of a liability you are."

"Then they can send me home."

He kicked his boot back, jabbing Sunna's shin. His grip eased, allowing an opening for Pinto to sweep around, unsling his bow, and draw an arrow in one fluid motion.

"Home was never an option, Sunna." His arm shook and strained the puncture wound, but he bit his lip to fight through the pain. "Move, even a little, and I'll shoot."

Sunna froze, his breaths heavy, his eyes wide as Pinto aimed at his heart. He wondered what he was thinking about at that moment—he could only hope it was Vell, and how much he regretted saving her life, because it would surely ruin his.

"Professor!" Quax called from the end of the alleyway.

Pinto didn't turn his eye away from Sunna as he replied, "What?"

"We have her."

Her?

He took a few steps back before turning in Quax's direction. He and Keiyo clutched Vell's arms from both sides as she wriggled in their grips, kicking to get free. By the way her coat hung, it was clear they'd confiscated her awful tools.

"What do we do?" Keiyo asked, his voice hoarse.

They had covered most of Atherus City already—there couldn't be many Underground members with the lantern code left, if any.

Pinto faced Sunna and slowly lowered his bow. "Let's take the *prisoners* home."

It was quiet in the passenger box.

Pinto tuned into the sound of the vault's rumbling wheels as Quax drove them west, toward Vakoi City. He couldn't place why he didn't feel victorious. The Incursion was over, Sunna had acted up enough to give Pinto a valid reason to remove him from his unit, and they had captured Vell—who likely had information on Yahshi's whereabouts that could speed up their progress even more.

Perhaps it was the realization that everyone always seemed to treat him like the bad guy. He thought of how Keiyo had tackled him in the woods, and how Sunna had pinned him to the wall—both for Vell. Why was everyone holding him back, and protecting *her*? It was *he* who fought for the right cause!

An hour passed in near-silence, Pinto's arm wound stinging more with each passing minute. When the vault hit a rocky patch, Sunna's confiscated dual swords slid from their hiding spot beneath the bench, nudging the back of Pinto's boot as though mocking him. Guilty blood marked their blades, and he so badly wanted to wipe them for the sake of his eye. But he didn't dare—they were evidence for the Force.

His arm continued bleeding, soaking the sleeve of his overcoat and dripping onto his pants. It would be smart to inspect the wound, but treating it would be more painful than sitting still—and he didn't want to look weak in front of Keiyo and the two prisoners.

"Let me help," Vell said, breaking the silence. She looked dead serious, and it made him scoff. Surely it was a ploy to buy her freedom, or a sick way to mock him. Why else would she offer?

"It could get infected," she added.

"No." Pinto looked from Vell to Keiyo, who sat opposite him on the other bench. He had placed both himself and Keiyo next to the door to deter Vell and Sunna from rallying together to break out. But if they were to attempt an escape, could he trust Keiyo as backup? After all, he had pinned him down to let Vell flee during their last special operation. Why wouldn't he do the same during this one? Pinto would've preferred Quax here instead, but that would leave Keiyo to drive—and he didn't trust him not to steer their vault straight into the ocean.

I can rest after reaching Vakoi City. He winced as he reached for a pocket watch in his overcoat. *We should arrive in—*

A burst of movement drew his eye upward, and he forgot about checking the time.

As Vell darted for the aluminum door, he sprung to his feet and gripped her shoulder, yanking her back with his good arm.

With Pinto occupied, Sunna rushed past Keiyo next. He managed to unlock the door, and it swayed in the wind, giving him a perfect opportunity to jump.

But he didn't—was he waiting for Vell?

"Keiyo," Pinto called, still holding her off. "Close the door."

"Sunna!" Vell shouted, as though it were her turn to protect him. "Run!"

In the corner of his eye, Pinto glimpsed Sunna leaping from the vault. He couldn't possibly get far. From the driver's seat outside, Quax would hear his landing, stop the horses, and pursue him on foot. But still, it would be an inconvenience. *I can't seem to catch a break tonight.*

Thankfully, Keiyo reached out at lightning speed, snatching the back of Sunna's overcoat. He reeled him in by the heavy fabric and slammed the door shut, trapping the four of them in the darkness again. Vell settled in Pinto's grasp, and Sunna's breathing softened as he retook his seat in the corner.

They were back to where they were before, with Vell and Sunna at the end of the benches, sitting as far from Pinto and Keiyo as possible.

Pinto winced as he rested his arm in his lap, trying to keep it still to minimize bleeding.

"Thanks," he choked out, meeting eyes with Keiyo. "You did the right thing."

"Like hell I did," he said under his breath.

Pinto raised a brow. If he didn't want to stop Vell and Sunna, then why had he? Perhaps, thanks to his time with Ogga, there were lines he would no longer cross, even if he wanted to.

"Keiyo," Vell called from the corner, her voice quiet. "Did they send you to correction?"

He nodded, and Vell brought a hand to her mouth, fighting a sob as tears fell down her cheeks.

Sunna leaned over, his head in his hands, shaking.

"Cut it out!" Pinto snapped in their direction.

Sunna broke, unable to contain himself, but Vell wiped her face dry.

CHAPTER 26

THE BOOMERS

Day 1 Without Vell | Clocks Read 02:48

♫ DEEP BREATHS · COLD WEATHER COMPANY ♫

Saunti jumped and locked his hands on the roof overhang of a short building. The chasing footsteps quieted as he swung his legs forward, lodging his boots onto a window frame—but he knew better than to associate silence with victory. Nightshades were inhumanly quiet. He had not lost them. They were still in the alleyways nearby, listening for him like predators.

His foot lost hold of the window frame, and he gritted his teeth, swinging his legs forward again to catch it. Another slip of his boot. And a third. He had climbed onto this roof during every delivery night as a courier—always effortlessly. But this time, his boots felt heavier than normal, his movements sloppier, his arms wearying.

The thought of Vell made him pause for a moment. She had run toward the Nightshades to buy him time to conceal himself in the access point, but he had slid the manhole cover back into place, unable to abandon her. If he were to get captured now, her bravery would have been in vain. He needed to escape these Nightshades and regroup with her so they could return together.

With restored resolve, Saunti's boots gripped the window frame again. His hold on the overhang tightened as he pulled, dragging himself onto the roof. Once his upper body latched over the edge, he slid the rest of himself up and stilled, breathing narrowly against the bricks and listening for the men that were surely listening for him too.

He had spent the past few minutes running from a pair of Nightshades—one with wavy hair just past his shoulders and the other who he recognized as Quax from the lumber mill *inspection* over a month ago. They were faster than him, but he knew these alleyways like the back of his hand, which bought him barely enough time to climb onto this rooftop.

Saunti closed his eyes, hearing breaths in the alleyway he'd vanished from—or was it the wind? He held his breath anyway, just in case, knowing he was trapped here now. He couldn't risk the noise of climbing down the other side, and if one of the Nightshades were to scale the building, he couldn't escape without the other waiting below to capture him.

It felt like an eternity passed. His lungs cried for help—a familiar feeling. He could have sworn the tightness around his neck was Rimoso's hands, and the thought made his heart beat louder in his head. It was all he could hear anymore, disrupting his sense of whether the Nightshades were closing in on him.

Shut it, Saunti told his heart.

He fought the urge to reach for his neck and gasp for air.

You're not dying, he told himself.

"Run!" yelled a distant voice, disrupting his quiet panic.

He heard footsteps next—a pair of them, much closer, coming from the alleyway he'd left. It was not the wind, after all.

The pair of Nightshades ran toward the man who had yelled, their boots slapping against the cobblestone.

Saunti finally breathed normally, the air filling his lungs.

Next came a scuffle and a variety of voices. He pushed himself up and crept to the end of the roof, peering in the direction of the noise.

There, in the distance, a one-eyed Nightshade dragged Vell into a shiny aluminum vault. Behind them were the pair who had chased Saunti earlier, and a third who struggled in their grip, as though he were trying to *help* Vell. An old friend from the Force, perhaps?

Clearly, the Nightshade with the eyepatch was the one in charge, their unit leader, and that choking sensation returned as Saunti watched him disappear into the passenger box, following in after Vell. *He* was the Nightshade behind the killings in Atherus City, wasn't he?

Saunti clenched his fists, fighting the urge to race after them. Vell deserved to be free, and the unit leader deserved a brutal death—but he couldn't possibly deliver such fates. He had no tools, no combat skills, no allies alongside him. It would be a death sentence.

Quax looped around the passenger box to drive the vault, the wavy-haired Nightshade urged the last of their group inside, and the door shut with a slam that echoed through Atherus City.

Saunti's eyes watered as he watched the horses trot, carrying them away. He had let Aero down first—and now Vell. He owed it to her to finish their mission alone.

I'll make it up to you, Vell.

As soon as he lost sight of the vault, he climbed down the building and headed for the ocean.

We'll get you back, but until then, stay strong.

Saunti leaned on a tree as waves crashed against the rocky shore ahead. His thoughts of Vell had morphed into thoughts of an even greater problem— potentially all fifteen collectors in Atherus City were dead. The only explanation? The Nightshades broke the lantern code and sent units to every Eastern town for a silent overnight slaughtering.

With the Underground's entire smuggling network—their supply line—*dead*, they couldn't rely on old tactics anymore. To beat the Nightshades, they needed a bold move to turn the tide.

Saunti took a deep breath to brace himself, stepping forward to approach a door to a modest home on the beach. He had been to Podge's house once before, years ago, behind Tonna's back. It was the first time he had confirmed the rebel beliefs of his classmate's family—because behind *his* parent's backs, Podge had shown Saunti their secret compartment of banned books.

He knocked on the door, over and over, progressively louder, until Podge opened it, his eyes half open. In a daze, he reached out to shake Saunti's shoulder, as though it were a dream.

When his fingers grazed Saunti's shirt, he pulled his arms back, his eyes suddenly awake.

"Saunti?" His lips parted in a gasp. "What the *hell*, man? Where have you been?"

Saunti stepped past him, entering the main room. It was just as he remembered it—cluttered but cozy, with so many decorative distractions that if a Nightshade searched their house, they'd grow bored before finding the stash of incriminating books.

"Saunti Suvo?" In the light of a single lantern, Podge's mom peered through the open door of her bedroom. "Is that really you?"

"Yeah, Mother, it's him," Podge said, as though it were obvious. "I'll handle this, okay?"

His mother chuckled to herself, not at all concerned that her son's missing coworker was visiting in the early hours of the morning.

"Let me know if you need anything," she said, closing the door.

Saunti managed a soft grin, and Podge waved a hand in his face. "Hello? Are you hearing me?"

"Did you say something?"

"I asked why you're sweating so much. You look like you just showered."

Saunti sat on the sofa.

"And now you're soiling our cushions."

"Just sit down, Podge. It's a long story."

Skeptically, Podge complied, and without a second thought, Saunti broke the most crucial rule of the Underground's smuggling network.

He told an outsider everything.

Saunti shared about his and his mother's role as couriers, the deliveries he used to do, and how he'd lived in the hideout for the last three weeks with the secretly alive Prince Runix—also known as the Belladonna Traitor. He told him about the ex-Nightshade Vell, whom the Force had captured after slaughtering their collectors and couriers within the past few hours.

"You've met Noris, right? He worked at the paper plant."

"The guy with the big ears?" Podge asked.

Saunti nodded. "He replaced my mother and me as Atherus City's courier three weeks ago, and now he's dead."

Podge took in the news solemnly—at first—but once Saunti began to lay out the details of how he could help, his face lit up.

"Oh, please tell me you're not kidding!" Podge sat up straighter, his eyes sparkling. "You *actually* need my help?"

"We could really use your BS, or BP, or whatever you—"

"BPBs." Podge grinned from ear to ear. "If you need Black Powder Boomboxes, my friend, you've come to the right place."

"This isn't funny. You'll have to disappear like I did. It'll be more dangerous than anything you've done before. And if you're caught, you'll have to keep quiet, no matter what the Nightshades do to you. Thousands of lives depend on it."

"Yeah, I hear ya. How many boomboxes do you need?"

"Thirty-nine."

His smile faded. "You're kidding, right?"

"Can you do it or not?"

Podge looked away. "Well, yeah, but we'll need to get Kwinnie on board." For a moment, he just stared off—but then a spark lit behind his eyes, and he leaped from the sofa. "Mother!"

"Yeah?" she yelled through the walls.

"I'm going on a trip, okay? A long one. Saunti has a plan for our BPBs."

"Oh, wonderful! Be safe!"

"Bring some dried fruit from the pantry!" his father chimed in.

Saunti shook his head in disbelief at the whole family as Podge rifled through a kitchen cabinet, gathering a bag of dried fruits for the road.

A couple of hours later, the sky lightened to a paler purple, signaling the oncoming sunrise. Saunti lifted the manhole cover and gestured for Podge and Kwinn to descend.

Podge lugged a bag of boombox supplies over his shoulder, Kwinn tightened the ropes holding scrap lumber to her back, and down they went.

Saunti followed last, sliding the cover back into place before striking a match. Podge and Kwinn pinched their noses, not used to the sewer smell, as he climbed to the bottom and knocked on the secret door. Thrice. Twice. Thrice again.

A *click* sounded from the other side, and Yahshi pulled the door open, his face twisted in concern. Behind him stood Tonna, Aero, and Dice, who stepped forward in unison, eager to hear why his return had taken so long.

"These are the Boomers?" Yahshi asked, his eyes darting between the newcomers.

Podge grinned and nudged Kwinn's side. "See? Our name's catching."

Kwinn rolled her eyes, still holding her nose—but she was smiling too.

Saunti ushered them into the tunnel and closed the door, turning the rectangular block to lock it.

That's when it finally clicked to everyone waiting that something horrible had gone wrong. Yahshi tried to step toward the door, but Saunti blocked his way, pressing his back against it.

"Where's Vell?" Yahshi raised his voice. "Where is she?"

Saunti couldn't bring himself to answer, and the color drained from Yahshi's face.

"Why didn't you help her?" Aero yelled, her eyes eerily wide—more white than pupils.

"I couldn't have won against the Nightshades," Saunti said.

Her voice shook with rage. "You could have *tried*!"

"And *died*?"

"I hope she doesn't talk," Tonna muttered to herself, earning a glare from Yahshi. He turned back to Saunti and gripped him by the shoulders.

"Who did this?" His words were raspy and slurred together. "Who? What did they look like?"

"The only one I recognized was the Belladonna Prodigy's little brother." Saunti winced as Yahshi's nails dug into him. "Their unit leader had curly hair, an eyepatch, and—"

"Pinto..." He pushed Saunti aside, leaving him stumbling. "I need to get her—"

"It's too dangerous." Dice lurched forward and snatched Yahshi's arm right before his fingers met the lock, yanking him back.

Yahshi shook his arm free, but by the time he darted for the door again, Saunti looped his arms around him, lugging him away—and Dice joined to help. Yahshi was too impulsive right now. If he were to leave Headquarters, the Nightshades would capture him too.

"All of you, stop this!" ordered Tonna, but they didn't listen.

"Enough!" Yahshi's voice was like fire, scorching Saunti and Dice's hands off of him. He glared at them both and lowered his voice, which sounded calmer now—but Saunti didn't buy it. "There's still time. I can steal a horse from the local officer post and stop them before they get back to the City."

Yahshi turned and finally unlocked the door.

When Saunti tried to stop him from opening it, Yahshi pivoted, landing a stiff boot to his shin.

Saunti grimaced and stepped back as Podge, despite his lack of context, shoved Yahshi away from the unlocked door—right into Dice's arms.

"Stop!" Tonna demanded, but her shout only pushed Aero into the mix.

"Let him go!" She attempted to pry Dice off of Yahshi. "Let him help her!"

From the sidelines, Kwinn chuckled and muttered, "I'm so lost."

Yahshi jabbed his elbow into Dice's jaw, sending him staggering off. Then he dodged Podge's attempt to shove him a second time and jammed a fist to his side.

Podge tumbled sideward.

Dice stood still, rubbing his sore face.

Yahshi opened the door. He was an ex-Nightshade, and right now, no amount of force would stop him from leaving this tunnel.

While his shin throbbed, Saunti tried to reason with words instead.

"They won't kill her."

Yahshi peered back, one hand around the door. "You don't know that."

"The Nightshades know how much she means to you. They'll keep her around as bait to lure you out. By leaving, you're giving them exactly what they want."

"I don't care what they want."

"They're *dead*, Yahshi!"

"*Who?*"

"Who?" Aero and Tonna echoed.

"Our entire network," Saunti said. "The Nightshades broke the lantern code."

"Unit leader..." Yahshi's eyes widened as he turned away from the door, piecing a story together. "Pinto broke the code. That's how he got a promotion. And now he took..." He closed his eyes, unable to finish the sentence.

"Listen, we need to get to the Waterway quickly, before Headquarters begins to wake." Saunti faced Podge and Kwinn. "While we execute our plan, we can think of a way to get Vell back."

Kwinn tilted her head. "What's the Waterway?"

"It's an underground river," Dice answered.

Saunti frowned at how easily he'd given it away.

Yahshi nodded, making up his mind, and turned to Tonna. "I'm going with them. I need to get her back."

Tonna opened her mouth as though to protest, but something stopped her. Perhaps she finally realized how much she and the Council had been holding Yahshi back, instilling their own wills upon him.

Vell had saved his life. Who was she to demand that he couldn't return the favor?

"Be safe," she muttered. "I'll do my best to keep the Council off your tail. They need to focus on restoring the Guild anyway."

"I'm going too," Aero said, and her choice caught Saunti by surprise. How could she so easily choose to travel alongside her father's killer?

Aero met Saunti's gaze. "For Vell," she clarified, like she'd read his mind.

Finally, all eyes turned to Dice, and he tightened the bandana around his head.

"I'm staying here." He chuckled. "It sounds like I need to make a lot more calabar serum."

Saunti looked around at their strange group of five. Podge and Kwinn.

Aero. Yahshi. He never would have imagined that his role in the Underground would turn into something like this.

Tonna stunned him with a hug. "It's not your fault," she whispered.

"I'll be back, Mother," he said, though he knew there was a chance of never seeing her again.

Yahshi sat hunched over near the tail end of the boat. By the way he dragged his fingers across the deck, muttering words under his breath, he seemed to be envisioning a map of the island and brainstorming ways to steal Vell back. Aero, next to him, set a hand on his shoulder, tears marking her cheeks.

Sitting at the wheel, Saunti turned his attention back to the river. To his left and right, Podge and Kwinn gawked at the glowing mushrooms that lined the Waterway.

A few minutes passed as the boat sailed smoothly, riding the southbound current.

Kwinn cleared her throat. "So we're booming Saver Stores?"

"Not Saver Stores. The production points, which will cut the supply line *to* Saver Stores," Saunti explained. "There's a total of fifty-five across Eastern Territory, and thirty-nine of them are located along this river—those are the ones we're targeting first. We'll stop at our sister bases, pop up, boom, come down, and hit the water again."

"Brilliant," Kwinn muttered. "Those stores fund the Force."

"And the Nightshades will fall apart without pay," Podge concluded.

Saunti smiled. "Exactly."

"How many days will this take?" Yahshi called out, drawing Saunti's eyes to the back of the boat again. All he cared about was getting to Vakoi City as soon as possible.

"Less than two weeks, if we move quickly."

"*Weeks*? That's too long!"

"*Too long. Too long. Too long...*" the Waterway echoed.

"But that's what it has to be. It gives you and Aero time to come up with a plan." Saunti looked at the water again, his grip on the wheel tightening. "Vell's a fighter. She can wait."

His eyes narrowed at the darkness ahead.

CHAPTER 27

ONE OF US

Your local Saver Store now offers affordable burial cloths.
Our deepest condolences!

♫ FANGS · LITTLE RED LUNG ♫

It was nearly daybreak when Quax pulled his unit's vault up to the Detainment Facility. He hopped from the driver's seat, shouting, "Open the door!"

Evaris complied, frowning at the urgency in his voice. The only reason Pinto's unit would return to the Facility rather than the Complex was if they'd brought back a prisoner.

Quax looped around the vault to open the passenger box, and Evaris's heart skipped a beat when Pinto jumped out, his overcoat sleeve soaked in blood. She stepped forward to help him, but the sight of Sunna leaving the vault next stopped her. His dual swords were no longer strapped to his back, meaning they must have been confiscated.

Her blood ran cold. *Oh, Sunna, what did you do?*

Quax snagged Sunna by his shoulder and dragged him toward the door. His expression hardened, his eyes widening, as though he didn't want to lock up a young man who had once been a roommate at the Academy. A friend.

Evaris took a deep breath, calming her nerves. If Sunna had acted impulsively, Protocol demanded his prompt detainment, but the Force would punish him too harshly. After all, he was an experimental case—joining with just half as much training as the ordinary guardian, and against his will too. What did the Force expect? A perfect integration?

She sensed movement from the vault and turned back to see a girl with baggy beige clothes and silky black hair jump out. Her blue eyes swept over the grass clearing surrounding the Facility, as though scanning for an escape route—but Pinto gripped her arm before she could run, pulling her toward the windowless stone building.

"You're making a mistake!" she yelled, struggling against his grip.

The second detainee's voice snapped a final puzzle piece into place for Evaris—though she had only spoken to her once, she recognized her. Vell Patura, the most recent deserter of the Force, the real cause of Cal's condition. How had Pinto managed to find her during the Incursion? Had she and Yahshi been hiding in Atherus City the entire time?

Pinto gritted his teeth as he struggled to retain his hold on Vell. His jaw was tense, and Evaris could tell he was fighting not to show his arm's pain. He vanished with Vell into the building before Evaris could utter a word.

She shut the door behind them, as was Protocol, and found herself alone with Keiyo in front of the building. He leaned against the aluminum passenger box and crossed his arms, dark bags under his eyes from a night awake—a night of slaughtering—but despite his exhaustion, he looked directly at her, inviting conversation.

"What happened?" she asked.

"Sunna tried to protect her. He's the one who injured Pinto's arm." Keiyo's voice was sharp, but a softer, shameful look crossed his face. He seemed embarrassed that it hadn't been *he* who tried to protect her.

Evaris blinked, tilting her head. From the brief interactions she'd observed between Pinto and Sunna, the newest member of the Force wasn't guardian material. She had even heard rumors circulating that during his time in the program, he had sobbed over dead rabbits. If such a heartfelt young man could inflict an injury on his own unit leader, what did that say about the situation the Force had put him in? They had backed him into a corner, pushing him to do too much too soon. Sunna wasn't ready for the Incursion.

"Commander..." Keiyo spoke slowly, intently, as though any word could be his last. "I don't know what Pinto is to you, exactly, but you clearly have an influence on him. So I just want to say that... I don't think Sunna should die because of this."

Evaris shook her head repeatedly. She didn't need to convince Pinto of *anything*. The Force wouldn't execute Sunna for this.

Keiyo seemed to sense her skepticism. "Professor Ogga beat me," he said, as though it were the simplest statement in the world. "He beat me for tackling Pinto and allowing Vell to flee. What do you think he'll do when he finds out that Sunna *spilled Pinto's blood* to protect her? The only person who can vouch for Sunna's safety is Pinto, and the only person who can talk him into that is you."

Evaris said nothing. While she didn't want to validate his delusion, she wouldn't berate him for it either. In fact, she admired the effort he put into keeping his friend safe, even if it wasn't necessary. That was one of their Guardian Vows, after all—to protect each other. *For we are one.*

The door swung open, turning their heads to Pinto and Quax as they left the Facility without their prisoners.

Pinto sighed and finally met Evaris's gaze.

I'm relieved to see you too, Red. She offered him a smile, but it faded when she remembered his bloody sleeve.

"Quax, Keiyo," Pinto called. "Report to Ogga at the Complex. He'll know what to do."

Quax took the driver's seat again, and Keiyo gave Evaris a heavy, lingering look before entering the passenger box alone, slamming the door behind him.

Evaris's eyes tracked the vault as it disappeared into the trees surrounding the clearing, heading to the Complex to report the news of their detainees. The field stood empty for a minute before she and Pinto faced each other. With his unit gone, that cold shell of his fell off, and he flung himself into her arms, his breaths racing.

She held him, his blood marking her overcoat, but she didn't care. "You're okay now."

Pinto clutched her tighter, and her eyes watered as she imagined the weight on his shoulders. He had just spent a night killing not one, not two, but likely over a dozen traitors. That alone would leave anyone shaken—and in addition, he had fought off his old friend and one of his own unit members.

"Why does everyone hate me?" he asked, his voice cold in her ears.

"I don't hate you," she said.

"Just you." His voice shook. "It's always just you, Evaris."

She gently pulled away, lips parted, eyes narrowed as she fished for his gaze. "You're a good one, Red. It was just a heavy night. That's all."

He stared at his boots and nodded, his breaths a little calmer now.

Evaris noted the traces of Pinto's blood on her hands. "Watch my post, will you? I'll fetch some medical supplies."

She entered the chilly, dark Facility and barred it from inside. Her unit members' footsteps padded lightly in the distance as she headed down a corridor for the nearest medical closet, reaching into her overcoat for a ring of keys to unlock it.

Before her fingers even grazed the brass, the sound of clinking steel caught her attention. She had heard that sound during her week in Eastern Territory every time Pinto reached into his overcoat for her lock busters.

Her pulse quickened as she closed her eyes and listened. As she feared, the noise came from the direction of one of their holding cell corridors.

Did Pinto fully strip Sunna's overcoat of tools? Her eyes fluttered open, and she crept toward the noise, her hands reaching for her dagger instead of her keys. *What if he still has his lock busters? He and Vell could easily flee, and slip out the back door.*

Her unit members were patrolling too far. By the time she'd get to them, Vell and Sunna might already be on their way out, and in Pinto's exhausted, injured state, she was certain he couldn't stop both of them outside.

She neared the sound of clinking steel, and voices joined the mix.

"It's not working," Sunna said, his words strained.

"Try again," Vell pressed.

They spoke quietly to avoid drawing attention from Evaris's unit, but from the connected corridor, she heard them loud and clear. She peered around the corner to see Vell and Sunna locked in adjacent cells, unable to see each other, but close enough to interact. Sunna stuck his hands through the barred door of his cell and slid his lock busters in the direction of Vell's.

"You try," he whispered. "You were always the best with locks."

With a deep breath, Vell reached out of her barred cell, snatching the lock busters and attempting to unlock her own door.

Evaris gripped her dagger tighter, about ready to intervene, but the stunned look on Vell's face stopped her. The tools didn't work on her cell as they should have.

Evaris had always thought that a guardian's lock busters could work on anything, but it seemed like the Facility cells had even accounted for foul play *within* the Force.

"Dammit," Vell muttered under her breath, moving the tools more frantically.

"It's okay," Sunna said.

"No, it's not." Vell stopped messing with the tools and faced the stone wall that separated her from Sunna. While she didn't know it, he was looking directly at her too. "If we could just get out of here, I could take us to the hideout."

"Where is it?"

She seemed to hesitate before saying, "I can't tell you. Not here."

Smart, Evaris noted. *She knows anyone could be listening.*

Vell sighed at the lock busters in her hands. "I'm sorry, Sunna. I got you into this." She sat on the cell floor and set the lock busters down.

"It's not your fault," he replied. "It's Pinto's. He's the one who broke the code."

She held her head in her hands, her voice unsteady. "What happened to him?"

"I don't know," Sunna said. "Something bad."

Evaris released her dagger and pulled her head back, concealing herself around the corner. She couldn't help but note that the only thing that had changed in Pinto's life was *her*.

She shook her head and slipped away, heading for the medical closet again. The words of a traitor and a struggling guardian shouldn't change how she viewed her relationship with Pinto. At the end of the day, it was simple—they made each other happy. How could that be anything but good?

Sunna's sword had inflicted serious damage to Pinto's arm. Not the kind that would deem it unusable, but the kind that would leave a deep scar. With time, it would fade, but never completely. His own unit member had marked him like the raider had marked his sight, like the Force had marked his forehead.

As she mended his arm in silence, Evaris found herself wondering the same thing as him. What made Pinto such a magnet for betrayal? He was ambitious, thoughtful, curious, a pinch romantic—and at times a little brash, of course, but who wasn't? She had met bad people before. He wasn't one of them.

Half an hour passed before Quax returned on horseback, without Keiyo and the vault. From across the clearing, Evaris and Pinto watched him secure his horse in the Facility stable. She had finished wrapping Pinto's arm, and she sat beside him on the grass, their backs to the Facility wall.

"Commander Quax is back," Evaris told him.

Pinto nodded, eyes on his boots, shivering in the cold. He had slung his bow and quiver over his bloodied, white button-up, unable to put his overcoat back on first—the fabric weighed too heavily on his arm.

For the first time since he'd sat down, he attempted to move and winced. Evaris rushed to wrap a hand around his waist, stabilizing him as he stood. The pain was settling in harder now.

"We should get you to the Hospital."

"You wrapped my arm perfectly," he countered.

"But they have medicine for the pain. I could have a unit member fill in for me, so I could take you there."

Pinto stood up straighter, wiping the pained expression from his face as his unit member neared them.

"We'll leave soon," he decided.

Satisfied, Evaris turned her attention to Quax, whose face was pale, his steps brisk. He stopped a few paces away and looked back and forth between them, struggling to get the words out.

"Where's Doctor Keiyo?" Evaris asked.

Quax blinked, confused for a moment. "I—uhh—Ogga didn't want him here. He thinks he'd get in the way."

"Get in the way of what?" Pinto asked, his voice strained.

Quax choked on another breath, struggling to speak once again.

"What's going on?" Pinto asked.

His unit member looked away, gray eyes lost in the woods, as though he wished he were *there*, not here. "Professor Ogga ordered Sunna's execution," he muttered, his voice hardly more than a whisper.

Execution? Evaris's eyes widened. Surely she had misheard him. The Force *wouldn't* kill Sunna. They *couldn't*. He wasn't a traitor or a member of the Underground. He was just a young man who wanted his old life back.

"When?" asked Pinto.

"Now," answered Quax. "I tried to convince him to reconsider, but he wouldn't hear it."

Pinto stared at him for a moment longer before meeting Evaris's gaze. He was still shaking, and she couldn't tell if it was from the cold, the pain, or from what was about to happen.

"Will you join us?" he asked, his hand twitching as though he wanted to reach for her but couldn't.

Evaris struggled to breathe, remembering what Keiyo had said less than an hour ago.

"The only person who can vouch for Sunna's safety is Pinto, and the only person who can talk him into that is you."

This was her chance to convince Pinto to dispute Ogga's decision. If she said the right words, perhaps he'd rush to the Complex on horseback and convince the old guardian to change his mind—to give Sunna a second chance. Ogga had not listened to Quax, but he'd respect Pinto more, right?

"Evaris?" he called.

She wanted to believe Keiyo's claim that she could talk sense into him. She really did. But if there was one code she knew Pinto wouldn't break, it was respecting Ogga's orders. He looked up to him—how could he not? He had been the guardian to promote him to unit leader.

So instead of doing what Keiyo wanted, Evaris nodded and croaked, "Of course."

She opened the front door for Pinto and Quax, followed them inside, and slid the bar into place behind them. Pinto struggled to navigate the Facility corridors, and though she wanted to help him, she didn't—she'd picked up on his effort not to look weak in Quax's eyes.

When they finally reached the adjacent cells where Vell and Sunna were held, the prisoners stood in unison, unsure of which they'd shown up for. Her heart tightened in her chest as she met eyes with Sunna, an eighteen-year-old who—if things had turned out a little differently—might have been married right now.

Vell must have noticed that their eyes weren't on her. "Pinto," she warned, "you can't hurt him. He's one of us."

"*One of us?*" Pinto scoffed. "You're not a guardian, Vell. You made that clear."

"Quax!" Sunna called, gripping the bars of his cell. "We're friends, aren't we?"

Quax wouldn't look at him. He turned to Pinto and muttered, "Professor Ogga demanded death by arrow, to avoid the risk of removing him from his cell."

"You can't!" Vell argued.

"Please, Quax!" Sunna pleaded. "Don't let them do this. My grandfather doesn't have much time left. My family's waiting for me, and..." His voice cracked. "And I'm supposed to get married!"

Evaris's eyes watered, and so did Quax's—though he still wouldn't look at his friend.

"Pinto, this isn't you," Vell said.

"You don't know me, and I don't know you." Pinto reached back to unsling his bow, but his face tightened in pain, and he dropped his arm with a gasp. His wound kept him from using his primary tool, so he turned to the only other guardian among them with a bow.

Evaris froze under the weight of their stares—Vell and Sunna's pleading ones, Quax's guilty one, and Pinto's demanding one. The prisoners directed their pleas at *her* now, but she tuned them out as she reached for her bow. Ogga's order had passed from Quax to Pinto to her. If word of her hesitation were to get back to Ogga, there was no knowing how he'd respond. The last thing she wanted was to end up in correction like Keiyo had, so she plucked an arrow from her quiver.

Sunna's face paled as Evaris aimed between the bars at him, still blocking out the sound of the prisoners' begging, just as she had whenever Cal ordered her to kill a traitor on their expeditions.

Vell screamed louder as Evaris released her arrow.

It whipped through the air and struck Sunna right in the heart.

He fell, and without even seeing him, Vell heard the impact and dropped to her knees, sobbing.

Evaris didn't look at Pinto and Quax again. She simply slung her bow over her back and left the corridor, quickening her pace until she reached the front of the building. Her hands shook as she unbarred the door and stepped out into the light of the rising sun, struggling to catch her breaths.

Pinto ran after her just moments later, which must have hurt, considering his arm.

"Evaris!" he yelled.

She wasn't sure why, but she felt the urge to flee, so she kept walking without looking back.

"Evaris!" He rushed forward and grabbed her arm, urging her to stop.

She finally looked at him, her eyes burning. "Why me?" The words spilled out before she could stop them. "Why did *I* have to shoot him? I'm not even in your unit!"

Pinto frowned, leaning his head back a little. He seemed confused about why this kill had affected her, blind to how glaringly different this was from her other murders.

Sunna had once been a trainee just like them. He had shared an Academy experience that most people on the island could never relate to. He might not have been a perfect guardian, but the fact that the Force had selected him for the program proved they had more in common than not.

Vell was right. He was one of us.

"I would have done it myself," Pinto said, lowering his voice. "But my arm..."

He looked down at his wound and described the pain he'd felt when he'd attempted to unsling his bow, but Evaris refused to listen. She wrenched the notepad out of her overcoat and scribbled another *O* to her list, and a second, and a third.

"Hey, hey..." Pinto grabbed her hands, keeping her from writing more. "Don't do that."

Evaris looked up at him, tears marking her cheeks. "Who's to say how many *O*s he's worth?"

His gaze softened as he took the notepad and pen from her, scribbling out the three *O*s she had marked. She knew he was trying to make her feel better, but in doing so, he had called Sunna worthless, and more tears spilled from her eyes. She couldn't quite place the emotions whirling through her chest, but she knew that she couldn't be around him right now. She couldn't stand it.

"You did the right thing," Pinto assured her, offering a smile.

"So if the Force ordered you to kill me, you wouldn't care either?" She snatched her notebook and pen back. "You'd react just like this?"

He dropped his smile, shaking his head. "Of course I'd care."

"Then why didn't you care about Sunna?" She ducked her head, adding back every *O* that Pinto had crossed out.

"I *do* care. I didn't want this either, but... he broke the rules."

Evaris shoved her notepad and pen away, her lips curling in disgust as she stepped away from him. "For the glory of Vakoi, Pinto, *we've* been breaking the rules!"

She turned and ran, and ran, and ran. It didn't even matter where she was going, so long as Pinto wasn't there.

"Don't you see what the Force has done to you?" Evaris sat at Cal's bedside in Vakoi City Hospital, peering down at her ex-unit leader, her ex-friend. "How could they lie about your death? Why would you let them erase you like that?"

Cal scribbled on a notepad and turned it around.

THE FORCE SAVED MY LIFE

"But they also *took* your life." Evaris gestured at Cal's hospital bed and the piles of books scattered about the room—her only way to pass the time. "I mean, just look at yourself!"

Cal stared, her gray eyes cold like her brother's, but somehow less distant than Evaris remembered. She set her notepad down and reached for her old roommate's hand, squeezing it gently.

"Do you miss Quax?" Evaris asked, her voice softer now.

Cal nodded.

"Then why blacklist him? Why not let him visit you?" She thought back to how easily Quax had given up on protecting Sunna. "He needs something else to live for—something *besides* his role as a guardian."

Cal took one hand away to write, but the other lingered on Evaris's fingers.

I WAS HOLDING HIM BACK

HE NEEDS TO WORK

TO DO WHAT I CAN'T

"So you're letting the Force take him away too? When they've already taken everything else?" Evaris raised her voice. "The guardians set you up—swooped in as heroes by pardoning your crime, just so you'd devote your life to them!"

THE FORCE SAVED ME

Evaris shook her head, standing from the chair at Cal's bedside. This was pointless. There was no changing her mind, and she should have known that from the start. She should have ignored the urge to rush here from the

Facility, but without Pinto, she knew of no one else to vent to.

"It's a lie, Cal. The Force convinced you that you're nothing but their Belladonna Prodigy. You don't have to believe that without your uniform, you're as good as dead. You could choose another story, but if you want to stick to the *worthless* narrative, go right ahead. I won't stop you." Evaris turned and marched for the door, shaking her head.

I shouldn't have come here.

Cal clapped her hands, as though calling, *Wait!*

Evaris stopped, her lips pursed as she looked back at her old roommate, her old unit leader, her old friend.

I LIKE YOUR BOOKS

"*What?*" Evaris snapped.

Cal looked around at the novels stacked in her hospital room, and upon closer examination, Evaris realized that she knew these books. She had read them before—some at the Academy, and some in the Force, but always in Cal's presence.

"You remembered?"

Cal held up her notepad, her grip shaky.

WILL YOU VISIT AGAIN?

Evaris gulped, the heat leaving her cheeks. She had spent so long despising Cal for leveraging their friendship for her own benefit, but she had never considered that she didn't *know* how to have a friend. Perhaps only her brother knew that if you looked closely, you could see it—how hard she *tried* to connect, even though she didn't know how.

Her eyes watered, and she nodded, again and again.

"Of course, Cal. Of course I'll visit you."

Sunna Rickabee's burial took place that same evening, coordinated by the service that managed every death in the Force. Men in black suits carried his casket across the guardian graveyard, where generations of heroes lay to rest.

The dark clouds looming overhead rained even harder, blurring the sorrow on Evaris's face and soaking her red dress.

She heard weeds squishing to her right and turned to find Keiyo approaching. Like her, he had dressed in his formal wear—a modest brown suit—as was customary for guardian funerals. Attending Sunna's wasn't mandatory, and it seemed they were the only two to show up.

I wonder if more guardians would have come, had it not been raining.

She wasn't sure. Perhaps no one cared about Sunna because only a handful of guardians knew him. Perhaps Quax wasn't here because he couldn't handle the pain of losing a friend he had turned his back on.

Keiyo didn't meet Evaris's gaze, even as he planted himself next to her. Perhaps he blamed her for this—it was *her* arrow that killed his friend.

"I'm sorry," she muttered. "You were right."

He shook his head, eyes on the casket as the men lowered it into Sunna's grave, out of view. "I was the one who promised too much, Commander. I let him down, and that's on me, not you."

Evaris stepped closer to him, and as soon as her hand met his shoulder, he choked.

"It's okay," she said as he lowered his gaze, struggling to fight off tears. That's when the sound of more squishing plants interrupted them, and a third guardian arrived to pay his respects.

They turned to their left, where Blimmery emerged from the trees. His gaze lingered on the men in the distance, as though saying goodbye, before gesturing for Evaris and Keiyo to follow him.

The rain poured in spiky bursts as he led the way to the gravestone of Maelin Vandros. Beneath her name was an engraving that read, *A noble soul taken too young.*

The gravestones to her left and right belonged to Taig Bitterview and Wick Saratoga. Evaris had never heard of them before, but their names sounded so brutally *real.*

"See that out there?" Blimmery pointed to a fence in the distance, beyond which were endless rows of guardian graves. "Those are the guardians who passed after retirement."

He gestured back to the area they stood in, which contained the graves of Maelin, Taig, Wick—and as of this evening, Sunna. "And this side is for guardians who lost their lives in active service."

A moment of silence passed as they paid their respects.

"I've lost many friends to the Force," Blimmery continued. "And I'd hate to lose another."

Evaris frowned at the old guardian, and he raised his head with a strong look, one she'd never seen him foster before—not during the eighteen months she had spent at the Academy with him as an instructor, or during the nearly two years she had spent in active service with him as a fellow guardian.

He looked... *angry*.

And it struck her, in that moment, that Blimmery was thinking about Vell.

"Wouldn't you hate that too?" he asked.

Evaris thought of the ex-guardian prisoner trapped in the Detainment Facility. She had escaped, just as Yahshi had, only for the Force to capture her and bring her back. She was not too different from Sunna—but unlike him, she still had a chance to survive.

"Of course I would hate it," Keiyo replied.

Blimmery faced Evaris next, and for the first time, she understood why her distant relative hadn't wanted her to join the Force—why he'd pressured her to grow up as a normal Starfall. He had known, for much longer than she had, that this organization wasn't good, and he didn't want her to be part of it too.

Evaris stared out at the graves of guardians who had died young. Sunna had not been the first, but perhaps he could be the last.

She turned to Keiyo, who nodded. It seemed he was also on the same page, and had realized the same thing.

They faced Blimmery in unison, eyes narrowed.

"How can we help?" Evaris asked.

CHAPTER 28

BURROW

Day 13 in Captivity | No Clocks to Read

♫ SHORE · HOLLY ABRAHAM ♫

Unlike in Headquarters, there was no sure way to tell time in the Detainment Facility. No clocks. No windows to note the rise and fall of the sun. All Vell could rely on for a sense of how many days had passed was the number of times she'd slept—twelve, so far—yet the Force still hadn't brought her in for questioning.

Isolation was surely part of their game. They wanted to exhaust her before her interrogation by barely bringing her food and water and ordering guardians on patrol never to glance her way. The Force was sending a message that they didn't care about her or what she knew. They planned to make her so sick of her monotonous life as a prisoner that once her interrogation came around, she'd beg for a chance to tell them everything.

That won't work on me, Vell thought as she crawled under her metal bed, feeling for the patch in the stone floor of her cell. She smiled when her fingers brushed the familiar groove. The chipped circle marked the entrance to her burrow—a hidden escape she'd been working on since day two of captivity. She had used a spoon to chip at the stone to access the dirt beneath her cell, and in the days since then, she'd dug a hole large enough to climb into.

She wiggled into her burrow, gripping the edges to keep from dropping straight down. Gravity stopped fighting her when her palms met the flat bottom, and from there, the tunnel bent into a flat segment leading under the wall of her cell. She knew—thanks to her memory of the Facility's floor plans—that the outside world lay just beyond.

At the end of the flat segment, the burrow arched one last time, leading up toward the surface. She had almost broken through.

Vell closed her eyes to keep dirt out of them as she dug into the dent above, dragging her hands to free dry clumps with every scrape. Once she had gathered a handful, she climbed backward to her cell and dumped the excavated dirt onto the stone slab near her burrow, starting a little pile.

And down she went again, reaching the far end of the hole and scraping the dirt above her to form another handful, which she brought back out before climbing down again.

Her stomach grumbled, and her dry throat ached for water, but she worked through the discomfort. Relief would come soon enough.

Just one more session, and I'll be gone.

Sweat dripped down her face as she dug, savoring the scent of fresh dirt. It smelled like *freedom*, and with it came thoughts of Yahshi. It was strange how often that happened, especially while she worked on her burrow.

Lying in bed, she usually thought of her family. Pacing her cell, she thought of Aero, Saunti, and Dice. Hearing the guardians pass her by, she thought of Pinto, Quax, and Keiyo.

But while she dug, it was only ever Yahshi Konya.

Vell plopped another handful of dirt under her bed. She knew better than to believe he would show up at her cell one day to break her out. The Council wouldn't even let him near a tool in fear that he might hurt himself. Ever since she'd landed in this cell, she'd accepted that to survive, she would need to do it on her own. No one was coming to rescue her.

Still, it was comforting to imagine him breaking her out. She enjoyed playing the scene in her head, vividly, over and over. *I just miss him,* she'd tell herself.

But today, that scene didn't come to mind. She imagined a new one entirely—the image of her breaking free from this burrow alone and returning to Headquarters to reunite with him. She thought of how tightly she and Yahshi would hug, and then she realized that she didn't just miss him. She was surviving *for him*.

Vell paused to catch her breath at the end of her burrow, and in the quiet, she tuned into the sound of footsteps. Her eyes widened as she climbed backward, shuffling out into the space under her bed as the guardian neared.

No, not now!

She crawled out from under her bed and scooped some excavated dirt into her palms. Quietly, she crossed the room and dropped it into the toilet, rushing back to grab another handful.

The footsteps grew louder.

I don't have time.

She ditched her usual protocol to destroy evidence and focused on pushing the dirt pile deeper beneath her bed. Next, she flushed the toilet, using the noise to cloak the sound of her dusting off her pants, shirt, and face. The dirt that clung to her fell off, forming another pile on the floor, and she kicked it to scatter its pieces around.

Vell grabbed her coat and used it to wipe the sweat from her face before slipping it on. As usual, whenever a guardian patrolled down her corridor, she curled up on her bed and stared at the wall, her back to the open area of her cell so they couldn't see her face. They would pass without a word, and in a few minutes, she would climb back down to continue digging.

The pair of footsteps grew closer, right by her door, but this time, the guardian halted. She forced herself to breathe evenly to cloak her windedness.

Seconds passed. She could hear her own heartbeat. The guardian still hadn't left.

Had she been too sloppy this time? Was there too much dirt on the floor? Was the pile of dirt she hadn't flushed visible from the door?

A voice echoed through her cell. "I know you're awake."

Vell's eyes sharpened, glaring at the stone wall ahead. She knew that voice all too well.

"It's time," Pinto said. "Will you walk with me, or do I need to call for help?"

Calm down. She closed her eyes and exhaled a deep breath. *They won't execute you this soon. They're just here to question you.*

Finally, Vell turned over to get up. The last thing she needed was for a group of guardians to drag her out of this cell. Both she and Pinto knew that if she were to run, the Defense unit on patrol would capture her before she'd reach an exit.

As she approached him, she tucked her hands into her coat pockets to conceal the dirt she hadn't picked out from under her nails. Her gaze fell to the floor, spotting a clump of dirt on her boots, which she shook off with a quick step.

Pinto reached into his overcoat for a ring of keys to unlock the cell. For the first time in twelve days, it opened, and he gestured for her to step out.

Vell crept behind him as Pinto made turn after turn, leading her through the stone building without looking back. He didn't fear that she'd attack him from behind—he believed the Facility was brutally secure.

Just wait, Pinto. Inside her pockets, she picked at her nails, ensuring they'd be as clean as possible before the interrogation. *Wait until I'm long gone, and you find my burrow.*

A few minutes later, Pinto stopped at the metal door of Interrogation Room 3, unlocked it, and gestured for her to enter first. His eye was cold and soulless as she passed him, stepping inside. The room only contained a metal table—a single chair on one side, and two on the other.

Pinto entered next, locking the door behind them as Vell approached her interrogator, a guardian who appeared to be around Blimmery's age. It took a moment for her to recognize him by his fiery red hair—he was Ogga, the professor who led the meeting in the Complex prior to the special operation to present Yahshi's pardon.

I won't say a word. Vell stared back with a blank expression, sitting calmly across from him as though meeting someone for tea.

"Hungry?" Ogga slid a plate from his side of the table to hers. It was a blueberry muffin.

Her stomach rumbled.

"Go on." He smiled. "It won't hurt you."

Vell looked at him, then back at the muffin. She carefully took it into her sore hands and brought it to her lips. Her eyes met his as she took a bite, proving she wasn't afraid. The Force wouldn't use a fatal dose of poison on her—not when she was their key to the Underground hideout.

"What are you doing over there?" Ogga turned to Pinto, who was still standing by the door. "Come join us."

Pinto nodded and took the empty seat next to the old professor. He pulled out a notebook to write an interrogation transcript, but Ogga held his hand out, stopping him.

"No notes this time. It's just us and your dear fellow graduate."

Vell raised the muffin and took another bite. Did he think her to be so gullible that she would reveal the truth, just because he had called her Pinto's *fellow graduate*? She knew they had no plans to pardon her. If she were to tell Ogga what he needed to know, he would drop that smile of his and kill her on the spot.

"We both know why you're here, so let's not beat around the bush." Ogga reached into his overcoat for something but frowned when his fingers grazed the wrong items. He parted the fabric wider to search with his eyes.

From across the table, Vell caught a glimpse of messy, disorganized pockets—tools in the wrong places. He didn't even seem to carry *The Guardian Handbook* as required.

"Ah, there you are." Ogga pulled out a syringe containing a pale amber fluid. "I'm sure you know what this is, Commander Vell."

Commander. I haven't heard that word in a while.

She swallowed a dry bite of blueberry muffin and squinted at the fluid. Based on its color, it was likely diluted calabar serum. She had heard rumors of guardians using it during interrogations, as microdoses could act as a truth serum, though she didn't believe in such a power. Drugs could only influence the mind—not control it.

Ogga held out a gentle hand. "Your arm, please."

As Vell set her blueberry muffin down, she glanced at Pinto. He eyed the wall, fidgeting with his ring of keys. Repeatedly, he pressed his thumbnail against a ridge in her cell key until his nail slipped with a *click* sound.

His nails weren't as bitten down as they once were. Had he replaced one tic with another?

Ogga emphasized his outstretched hand, regaining Vell's attention. She held her arm out, resting it on his palm, and his grip tightened around it. With his thumb, he pressed around, feeling for a vein in her inner elbow.

"You know, there's a theory that the Underground's hiding place is near Atherus City. Maybe even *in* Atherus City." Ogga found a vein and inserted the needle with his right hand. "That seems to track, considering where Professor Pinto found you."

Vell held her breath, struggling not to react as the fluid sharply entered her arm. *The calabar can't make you talk*, she assured herself. It could encourage her to think her deepest thoughts, but nothing could make her speak against her will. She would fight its effects—just as many interrogated members of the Underground once had, before the Force started killing them on the spot, knowing they wouldn't talk. If the microdoses truly worked as a truth serum, they would have found Headquarters a long time ago.

Vell pulled her arm back after Ogga finished the injection and picked up her muffin again. She took another bite as though nothing had happened.

He reopened his overcoat, pulled out a second syringe, and set it on the table as a warning.

"Are we correct to assume the hideout is in, or near, Atherus City?"

Yes, Vell thought as she chewed. The muffin shook in her grip, but she didn't care. They both knew it was from the calabar and didn't indicate her fear.

Pinto cleared his throat. "Vell."

She recoiled a bit. Her name sounded poisonous now, coming from his lips.

"How many people are in the hideout?" he asked.

Vell swallowed, pressing her lips together to ensure she wouldn't accidentally mouth the words in her head. *A few thousand.*

When she looked back at Ogga, his face turned blurry. She had moved her head too swiftly. It seemed her vision was lagging, so she set her muffin down and stilled. So long as she kept quiet, they would give up and send her back to her cell, where her burrow was.

It's waiting for me.

Ogga frowned. "*What's* waiting for you?"

Vell's blood ran cold. *Did I say that aloud?*

When Ogga nodded, she took another bite, knowing that at the very least, chewing would keep her from talking. She couldn't do both at once—but the muffin wouldn't last forever.

"Don't worry." The redhead opened a drawer and pulled out a plate. "I have another muffin for you right here. I figured you might be hungry. But first..." He grabbed the syringe on the table and held his hand out again.

Vell froze. If the first dose had already blurred the lines between her thoughts and speech, how could she trust herself not to accidentally reveal everything she knew?

Don't think about the access point, she ordered.

For a second, she feared that she'd said *access point* aloud, but based on Ogga's face, it seemed she was in the clear.

"Your arm, Commander," he reminded her.

Vell offered her trembling arm to him again. Without warning, he injected the dose right where he'd put the last one. She swore she could feel the poison course through her veins, and no matter how hard she willed herself not to move, her body shook. Were her lips shaking too? Was she talking?

She tried to focus on Pinto and Ogga, but their silhouettes merged.

Is Ogga on the left or right? She glanced back and forth. *Is that Pinto, or Ogga?*

"That's more like it." The old man's voice echoed in the air, and Vell couldn't tell where it had come from. The interrogation room turned into a blur of colors and movements. She couldn't feel the cold, metal chair she was sitting on—or hear the flickering of torches mounted to the walls.

Vell pursed her lips, and thankfully, she still felt them. If she forced them shut, she could keep the Underground safe. She could keep *Yahshi* safe.

"You're thinking about Yahshi Konya, aren't you?"

Vell scanned the room for Ogga, but she still couldn't find him. There was too much motion, so much that it dizzied her. She closed her eyes to quiet her thoughts, but they raced back to the memories she and Yahshi had shared. Turning against her operative unit to save him, their brief stop at Atherus Palace, the toad lily he had offered her at the Waterway, the many late nights they'd spent brainstorming a plan to propose to the Council...

She had given up everything in exchange for time with him, but she wished she had told him why. Back in Headquarters, she had countless opportunities to put into words how much he meant to her, instead of assuming he could read between the lines, but she hadn't.

"Where is he?" Now it was Pinto questioning her. "Where is he hiding, Vell?"

She interlocked her fingers, fighting the burning sensation in her empty stomach, gritting her teeth as the poison shook her core. It was like she wasn't even conscious. She could feel the sensations of her own body, but everything else was a blur.

A needle pricked her arm again, and she cried out into the mess of motion and colors. She could have sworn she'd been gripping her hands under the table, but now she could feel the sensation of the table beneath them. Had she moved? Was she even sitting anymore? Was she running? There was so much movement. Surely she was running!

"Professor," Ogga said, his voice muffled as he gave Pinto an order. The next thing Vell knew, a coarse rope looped around her wrists, and her sensations sharpened just enough to realize that Pinto was tying them to the legs of her chair.

With focus, Vell managed to regain a little more vision too. She saw Ogga, smiling, another syringe in hand. He knew she understood his voiceless threat—one more injection could cause *permanent* side effects.

Vell focused on his face, trying to hold the image, but her vision disintegrated again, and soon enough, everything turned black. The ropes that restrained her bit into her wrists.

"You're brave to be willing to stay in that cell forever, keeping quiet like this."

While she couldn't see him, she knew Ogga had leaned in closer. His voice was thicker now, right in front of her—she could feel it against her face.

"But I wonder if you'd show the same courage... if your mother were in danger?"

Vell clenched her eyes shut, her mind racing with memories of her mother, sick in bed. It was a miracle she'd survived. She couldn't lose her over something like this.

"Or perhaps the girl Sunna left behind?"

She bit her lip until it bled.

Snap out of it!

The Force *wouldn't* hurt innocent people like her mother and Sunna's girlfriend—not for a while, at least. So long as they could threaten people she cared about, they had leverage. They wouldn't kill anyone before sending her back to her burrow today, and once she escaped, they would have no reason to follow through with their bluffs.

"Where's Yahshi?" Ogga asked. "Where's the Underground hideout?"

She leaned forward, her brows pressed together as she fought against her thoughts. The darkness grew stronger, their questions a blur, and the next time she opened her eyes, she was lying on her metal bed, staring at the ceiling of her cell.

With a gasp, Vell shot up into a seated position, gripping her head as everything whirled around her. The injection points in her left arm and the red marks around her wrists proved that it hadn't been a nightmare. The serum had likely pushed her out of consciousness, stalling their interrogation.

Vell held her trembling hands over her face and let out a long sigh of relief.

When she slid her legs off the bed, a tremor ran down her spine, making every part of her body shake. In order to stand, she gripped the metal platform to steady herself. It would take a few days for the calabar to leave her system, and while escaping in this state wouldn't be easy, it was better than staying behind to face whatever Ogga was planning next.

Before her last digging session, she closed her eyes, tuning into the distant noises to ensure there were no guardians nearby. Despite her best efforts, she couldn't make out any sounds. Her senses were still murky, and when she opened her eyes, she half-expected to find herself back in the interrogation room.

I better not lose my sense of time.

Vell gripped her bed harder, opening her eyes and willing herself to focus. Her vision cleared, and though her heart pounded so hard she feared it might explode, she lowered herself to her knees and climbed under her metal bed. She felt for her burrow, her fingertips grazing the rough edges of the stone she had chipped through—but instead of finding a recess beyond it, her fingers met a patch of dirt flush with the floor.

She whimpered, and in the darkness, continued to feel around, dragging her hands along the stone and dirt. Stone and dirt. All even. No hole. Her burrow was so tightly packed that only specks of dust came out with her desperate scratches.

At the sound of muffled footsteps, Vell shuffled out from under her bed. The quick movements left her reeling, and she pressed her hands against the floor to catch herself.

The footsteps stopped, and when she looked up, Pinto stared at her through the bars.

Her stomach sunk to the floor, her face running hot. How long had he known? Why would he allow her to dig her burrow almost completely, just to fill it up at the end? Who would do such a thing?

Vell stumbled to her feet, gripping her bed again to balance herself. Pinto wasn't just a Nightshade. He was a monster. And with this realization, she spoke to him for the first time in nearly two weeks.

"I hate you," she said through gritted teeth.

Pinto stared a moment longer before walking off, disappearing from view.

The dizziness kicked back in, knocking Vell off her feet. She collapsed onto her bed as hot tears stung her eyes and spilled down her cheeks. The last thing she wanted was for Pinto to hear her, so she clutched herself and bit into her coat, sobbing into the fabric.

This is just the start. They'll be back tomorrow, and the day after, and the next, and the next...

CHAPTER 29

THE STARFALL QUALITY

Needles and threads are now restocked
at your local Saver Store!

♫ THEN AGAIN · BROOKE ANNIBALE ♫

Evaris stood guard by the Facility's front door, staring at the trees across the grass clearing. Just two weeks ago, she would have been anticipating a visit from Pinto any time now. Part of her longed for his old interruptions— back when they'd use any opportunity to squeeze time together during shifts and shared time off service.

But whenever she found herself missing him like this, all she had to do was remember how cold he looked after Sunna's death, when he crossed off the *Os* in her notebook.

She yawned and checked her pocket watch. It was nearly 6:00 in the evening. Within the next ten minutes, another Defense unit would arrive to swap places with her and her unit members inside.

Finally. This shift had been so boring that she could hardly stay awake despite the early hour and a couple of good novels to read.

She raised her brows and turned when the front door opened beside her. Exiting the Facility was Pinto, his eye wide, his breaths heavy. She hadn't even known that he'd been inside. *He must have entered before my shift.*

Pinto noticed her and froze, his lips forming a shaky smile. "Hi."

She huffed and looked away. *Hi?* They hadn't spoken in nearly two weeks, and *that* was the best he could come up with?

When he shut the door behind him, she noticed that his nails weren't as short as they used to be. Even stranger, though, was the dirt on his hands. *Why did you stop biting your nails? What were you doing in the Facility? How is your arm healing?*

There were so many questions she wanted to ask him, but instead, she glued her lips shut and mentally willed him to leave.

"I—" Pinto's voice broke, so he started again. "I visited his grave yesterday."

She felt him looking at her but didn't meet his gaze.

"Sunna's," he clarified. "I really didn't *want* him dead. You know that, Evaris. I was just trying to make you feel better, because you mean a lot to me, and I've... I've really missed you lately. You were the only person who didn't hate me—who saw good in me—and now that you hate me too, I don't even know what to think of myself anymore."

Evaris's eyes watered. *I don't hate you, Red.*

As she watched him cross the clearing, making his way to the Facility stable, a knot formed in her throat. She had been telling herself that Pinto didn't see the difference between killing Sunna versus a member of the Underground. But maybe that wasn't true. Maybe she was only taking her anger out on him because she wished *he* had fulfilled Ogga's wish instead— that his wounded arm hadn't stopped him, so she wouldn't have killed one of her own.

How do we save the Saver Stores? That was the question the Force pondered as Evaris entered the Complex after her shift that day. About thirty off-duty guardians filled the common room, discussing the Underground rebels who were terrorizing Eastern production points. This group—a count of five, according to sightings—had already destroyed over thirty of fifty-five production points across Eastern Territory in the twelve nights since the Incursion.

As she looked for Blimmery, Evaris swerved around groups of guardians, each discussing a different aspect of the Saver Store conflict.

Roz and his fellow middle-aged graduates were brainstorming new ways to generate funds for the Force. Without many supplies being imported from Eastern Territory, humble residents of the Vakoi Empire were raising their brows at the empty shelves of their local Saver Stores. Less stock meant fewer sales, and fewer sales meant reduced Imperial revenue. Emperor Vakoi had already announced a twenty percent cut to their next bills of exchange.

She passed Embre next, who sent accusing stares around the common room, muttering her *worst-case scenario* to a few other female guardians as though it were a secret. She feared the Force's pay cut would result in otherwise loyal people turning into Yahshi and Vell types—in other words, *guardian deserters*. The group of women discussed ideas for how to rally the current guardians to *stay* in active service, even if they eventually ran out of pay.

Evaris paused her search for Blimmery to study the map in Galler's hands. The rebels were destroying production points in a near-perfect line from north to south.

"They're efficient," stated Quax.

"They're running out of locations," worried Boa, anxious as ever. "What comes next? Will they destroy our towns? Our capital?"

"One problem at a time," Evaris chimed in before turning away.

Finally, she spotted him. Blimmery stood with his fellow graduate Kanter and a third editorial member of *Capital Weekly*. She approached as they devised a cover story to explain the low-stocked Saver Stores—one that wouldn't result in widespread panic.

Evaris stopped just a few steps away from them. *I know you see me, Doctor.*

He pretended not to notice her, even after she lingered nearby for a minute.

Shaking her head, she marched for the staircase, giving up on him. It felt like an eternity had passed since she and Keiyo had agreed to help Vell, but Blimmery still hadn't approached them with a plan as promised. Was he backing out of their deal? If so, she would like to know, but he had done nothing but ignore her since their discussion at the graveyard—she didn't even have a safe opportunity to ask, *Are we still doing this?*

She cut through the buzzing room and made her way up the staircase, leaving the chaos behind.

Just seconds passed before a faster pair of footsteps echoed below. Before she knew it, Blimmery was walking beside her at a matched pace.

"I told you to keep your distance," he scolded.

"I'm losing patience, Doctor. I don't even know if we're still working together."

"*Of course* we are. I made you two a promise, and it's time to fulfill it." He spoke urgently, a pinch of fear in his tone.

"Did it finally happen?" she asked. The Force had been isolating Vell, hoping it'd pressure her to break during her eventual interrogation. Unfortunately, no one knew when that would happen, or who would be leading it.

Blimmery nodded, confirming her fear. "Ogga and Pinto interrogated her today."

Evaris sighed, disappointed, though she wasn't surprised. His news explained why Pinto had been at the Facility without Quax and Keiyo earlier—Ogga wanted Pinto's assistance. They were handling Vell together. No wonder he had looked so shaken upon leaving.

"You have a plan, right?"

"Meet me tomorrow morning at Cove's cabin. Eight o'clock. Bring Keiyo with you. And in the meantime..." He looked up and down the staircase, ensuring they were still alone, before pulling a book out of his overcoat.

As soon as Evaris took it, he pivoted, exiting into the hallway containing his flat.

She tucked the book into her overcoat, knowing better than to study its cover until she was somewhere private. Up the staircase, she continued until she reached the floor leading to Keiyo's flat.

He opened his door as soon as she knocked, ushering her in.

"Any news from Doctor Blim?" he asked in a hushed voice, closing the door behind them.

"We're finally meeting with him tomorrow morning." Evaris pulled the book out of her overcoat. Its cover featured an illustrated portrait of a girl in a trainee uniform, and its title—*Maelin*—matched the name on the gravestone Blimmery had pointed out during Sunna's burial. Maelin Vandros had been a friend to him once, and somehow, her death was relevant to saving Vell.

She held the book up for Keiyo to see, pointing to the author's name. "Doctor Blimmery wrote this himself. He slipped it to me in the staircase just now, after hearing word about Vell. I think he wants us to read it tonight."

Keiyo took a step toward her, his tone almost accusatory. "What *word about Vell*?"

"Pinto and Professor Ogga interrogated her earlier."

"Ogga?" Keiyo's face drained of color as he paced the room. "No, not *him*. He's the worst!"

Evaris tilted her head. "Why do you say that?"

Keiyo stopped abruptly, staring her dead in the eye. "He was my corrector."

She gulped, recalling the bruises on Keiyo's face that every guardian had pretended not to see.

"Oh," she muttered, unsure of what else to say. "Sorry."

He shook his head, continuing to pace. Part of her wanted to ask what exactly Ogga had done during the correctional meetings, but to do so would likely make Keiyo more nervous about Vell, so instead, she sat on his bed and gestured for him to join.

"Come read his book with me."

He waved a finger at its cover. "When did Doctor Blim even have time to write that thing? Over the past two weeks, as we've been twiddling our thumbs, waiting for him to come up with a plan? Now Vell's suffering because we waited too long to—"

"She won't be there much longer," she assured him. "Now please, can we read this? I'm sure Doctor Blimmery will explain everything tomorrow."

Keiyo slowed to a stop, his head held low. His fingers reached for his cheek as though recalling a memory, and with a sigh, he nodded.

"Fine. But you're reading it aloud."

Evaris chuckled as he sat next to her. "Luckily for you, I happen to love books." She flipped to the first page and looked up with a smile.

"How long will it take?" Keiyo asked.

Based on the spine width and the size of Blimmery's handwriting, she estimated, "Three or four hours, probably."

He groaned. "*Four hours?*"

"Do you want to help Vell, or not?"

He dropped the act quickly and faced the pages.

Evaris cleared her throat, reading the first chapter in a hushed tone, just in case anyone could hear from the hallway.

"*Two months into the program at Belladonna Guardian Academy, a field class exercise sent us into the woods to extract willow bark, a medicinal pain reliever. While I scanned the trees for—*"

"It's about Doctor Blimmery's time as a trainee," Keiyo concluded, as if it weren't obvious.

Evaris paused, deciding whether to reply, before ultimately continuing. She turned page after page, occasionally interrupted—but with time, Keiyo grew quieter, invested in the story of Blimmery's key encounters with Maelin over the course of about five or six years—everything from their time as trainees to their first few years of service in the Force.

About halfway through the book, Blimmery and Maelin obtained a copy of *The Force's Hidden Agenda* by Meridian Owding, a banned book written by Blimmery's own uncle. Together with his cousin, Cove Starfall, he and Maelin read the Meridian book and learned the truth about the Force.

Through their narrative, that same truth unraveled for Evaris and Keiyo.

While she had already known about corruption within the Force, she had never known it was *this* bad. If a handful of guardians had committed crimes and blamed them on the Underground, could they have initiated the raids too? Had Yahshi told the truth after rejecting the pardon? Was Pinto really working for the same organization that gouged out his eye?

Once she finished reading, she looked over at Keiyo, who stared at the wall, thinking. Clutched in his hands was an empty package of dried mangoes that he'd grabbed earlier, insisting he needed a snack while he listened. She frowned at it now—it was the exact same brand as the one Kia had tossed to Pinto at Vakoi Palace.

"*Dried mangoes?*" he had asked.

"*You look hungry, Professor,*" Kia had said.

"Oh, stop judging," Keiyo whined. "At least I'm taking a break from candy, okay?"

She pointed to the package. "Where did you buy that?"

"The convenience store, south of the Facility."

Evaris recalled how a clerk at that store had seen Yahshi with a girl the night before his desertion. He had traded five hundred coins for nonperishable goods, including dried mangoes like the one Keiyo held now. However, the Force didn't find those goods in his getaway bag, meaning the girl retained them. A Research unit had opened a case to find Yahshi's accomplice, but they hadn't made progress in weeks—and most simply assumed that the girl was Vell.

How did Kia get snacks from a convenience store? For their own safety, the Royal Family doesn't eat anything prepared outside the Palace.

She recalled the rumors she'd heard about Defense guardians who had once worked as Kia's bodyguards. All of them had ended up in correction as a result of her compulsive lies. A few said she had a secret way past the Wall that Emperor Vakoi himself didn't know about. Even more claimed she hated her own family—hated the Force.

Just like Yahshi.

Though his time as Kia's bodyguard had been short, he had shared plenty of alone time with her. They could have easily devised a plan to leave together, and thanks to her secret way past the Wall, she could have met him at the convenience store that night.

Of course. It was never Vell. The Princess was Yahshi's accomplice!

Over a month later, Evaris finally understood that Kia had dropped a clue that day. She didn't know *why*, or what she'd do with the information, but it was fascinating nonetheless. The idea that the Princess had almost run off with a guardian left her chuckling.

Keiyo poked her arm. "Are you okay?"

Evaris shook her smile away. "I was just blanking out."

Her pocket watch read 10:56. They both needed rest before their meeting with Blimmery in the morning, so she stood, tucking *Maelin* into her overcoat.

"Meet me at the stable around 7:30, okay?"

Keiyo nodded, and she left his flat as another guardian entered the hallway from the staircase.

It was Pinto. His flat was still located on Keiyo's high floor—unusual, given his promotion. It was likely the Force's busyness with the Incursion, and now the Saver Store dilemma, that delayed his upgrade to a lower floor.

Evaris shut the door, her cheeks hot. She had just left Keiyo's flat, and Pinto had caught her in the act.

He slowed to a stop, his face stern, no longer marked with the remorse she'd seen earlier at the Facility. She had spent the days since Sunna's execution hating him, blaming him—but after what he'd said earlier, her old feelings were creeping back.

She scrambled for an explanation, but every lie she tested in her head fell short. Could she tell him the truth instead? Would he believe her, or call her brainwashed like Yahshi? Would he offer to help, even if it meant turning against Ogga and freeing the prisoner in his custody?

Pinto nodded and walked on, accepting her silence, and that's when she pondered a bigger question—even if she *didn't* come clean to him about her plan, could she bear to leave him behind? Deserting the Force was easy, but the thought of leaving Pinto burned a hole in her heart. If she left him, she would forever bear the burden of not knowing what could have been, had she trusted him rather than deceived him.

While his footsteps echoed behind her, she walked to the staircase, pausing at the landing to glance over her shoulder.

Pinto stood by his door, fidgeting with his ring of keys, his eye catching her gaze. He continued to flick his thumbnail against a brass key, filling the hallway with a *tick, tock, tick* noise.

Tell him, urged her heart.

Lie, ordered her mind.

Evaris couldn't choose. She peeled her eyes away and made her descent.

At 7:30 sharp the next morning, Keiyo waited for Evaris in the stable, his horse already tacked up with its lead rope attached. They traveled to a one-story cabin along the outskirts of Vakoi City that belonged to her great aunt, Cove Starfall.

It was just as Evaris remembered—surrounded by trees that blocked most of the daylight, with neon lanterns of different shapes and sizes swaying from the roof overhang. A pole boasted a handmade flag embroidered with the image of an open box overflowing with stars—the logo of Pandora's Box. Cove had always been a fan of the artistic collective, as well as a major sponsor.

"Doctor Blim mentioned this place in the book, right?" Keiyo asked as they secured their horses in Cove's stable. "It's his cousin's place, the home of that fashion designer."

"She's also my great aunt."

Keiyo frowned. "Wait, so is Blimmery your grandfather or something?"

"No. Aunt Cove is my grandfather's sister, a Starfall like me. Blimmery's from the Owding side of the family. We're not closely related."

He looked away, as though trying to solve a mental math equation. "So he's like a really old uncle, or—"

"Doesn't matter." Evaris laughed as they left the stable. Guardians always got confused about her familial connection to Blimmery. "Oh, and by the way, I heard Aunt Cove's not doing well, so don't be surprised if she's not as peppy as she was in the book."

"When was the last time you saw her?"

"Probably about five years ago."

"*Five years*? You would have been, what? Twenty?"

"Shut it. I'm not *that* old."

"You graduated before me. You're ancient."

They dodged the hanging lanterns on their way to the front door. It was Blimmery who answered Evaris's knock, and he scanned the surrounding area before allowing them in.

The living room, like always, was a disorganized mess in a cozy kind of way—drawers overflowing with fabrics, dress clothes lying about, and lanterns hanging from the ceiling in the order of a rainbow. Evaris looked around for Cove, but she wasn't here.

"Cousin Cove is resting," Blimmery told her, gesturing to a round table. "Come sit."

Evaris set *Maelin* down as she took a seat, and Blimmery swiped the book, hiding it back in his overcoat. His eyes hopped back and forth between them. "Did you read it?"

They nodded.

"Good. That'll make this next part faster." Blimmery spread a map of the island across the table, and Evaris found comfort in his confidence.

When he pointed to the town of Nominner, the three of them stilled, sharing a brief silence. They all knew Sunna had grown up in that town. His body belonged to the flower meadow, not the guardian graveyard, and Evaris grieved the cruel misplacement.

"There are two Saver Stores in Nominner," Blimmery continued. "One's on the west side of the flower meadow, and the other's on the east." He pointed to both stars, which marked the buildings, his index finger lingering on the second. "I've made contact with a trader who transports goods from Eastern production points to this specific store. He can get you past Border Control into Eastern Territory, and from there, Vell should know the route to the Underground hideout."

"What do you mean *you*?" Keiyo questioned. "You're coming with us, aren't you?"

Blimmery smiled, his voice soft, as though he believed this was goodbye. "I'm afraid you'll have to make this trip without me, kids. Cousin Cove and I have work of our own to take care of, related to the book you read."

Evaris and Keiyo met each other's gazes, reality sinking in. What they were planning was crazy. Could they really break Vell out and leave the Force? Even if they were to reach the Underground hideout, how much longer could they survive? The smuggling network was gone, and while the hiders were striking back against production points, they could only survive for so much longer without additional supplies.

Are we joining the losing side? Goosebumps sprang over Evaris's arms. *Are we breaking Vell out, just for us all to die?*

"Of course, the first step is to handle Vell," Blimmery said, his voice bold again. "Don't even bother with your lock busters—they won't work on cells in the Facility. You need to get the key from someone in charge of her custody. Right now, there are just two guardians with access to her cell."

"Pinto and Ogga," Keiyo whispered. He turned to Evaris. Blimmery did the same.

Her jaw dropped, and she waved her hands in front of her. "No. No way."

"I've seen the way he looks at you, Commander," Keiyo said. "You two obviously had something special going on, and while I'd rather not think about what that was, exactly, you can use that to our advantage here." He pretended to gag, and Evaris scoffed, elbowing him in the side.

She faced Blimmery, hoping *he* would have some sense. "You're not seriously suggesting that I steal his key, are you?"

"It's the only way," Blimmery said. "Taking it from Ogga would be too dangerous, but Pinto is already primed to trust you."

Evaris thought of that night in the Investigation Office when she'd supervised Pinto after the special operation. He had opened the door with a spare ring of keys, which he'd duplicated without the Force's knowledge. She later learned that he had done so out of paranoia, because Yahshi had stolen a key of his to rob documents from the archives before.

"I'm not saying it'll be easy," Blimmery replied, "but to save Vell, it needs to happen."

She stared back at him, blinking, waiting for him to take it back and propose a better alternative. But with time, she realized that there wasn't one. He was right. Who could fool Pinto better than the girl who knew him best?

Blimmery cleared his throat with a grin, as though he knew she'd accepted her fate. "Through my connections, I've confirmed that Pinto has a meeting with Ogga at the Facility around five o'clock this evening for a second interrogation with Vell. We can't be certain how long he'll be there, but I'm going to guess, conservatively, that he won't leave any later than 8:00. And your night shift starts when?"

"Around 11:00," answered Evaris.

"So that leaves about three hours for you to get that key." Blimmery pulled a small object out of his overcoat and slid it across the map toward Evaris.

She stopped it with her finger and picked it up. A brass key.

"To keep him from getting suspicious later," Blimmery explained. "It looks almost identical to Vell's except it won't work. It weighs the same. He shouldn't notice the difference. You'll have to take the real key off his ring, and replace it with this one."

Evaris raised the key and narrowed her eyes, studying it. The Force had once assigned a prisoner in her joint custody and had provided her a key just like this. Everything Blimmery said should work in theory, but how could she possibly distract Pinto for long enough to perform the swap?

"Good luck," Keiyo teased, but by the way he tapped his fingers against the map, she could tell he was worried about this too.

"I'll try my best, Doctor," Evaris told Blimmery, tucking the dummy key into her overcoat.

Keiyo stopped tapping the table, the map stealing his attention. "Are you sure no one will stop us on our way out of Vakoi City? It's not a short ride to Nominner."

"It'll be dark already, so that plays in your favor. I recommend traveling along the outskirts. If you can, stay by the water, right through here." He trailed his finger along the western coast. They could travel southward down the beach for most of the journey before making an eventual turn toward Nominner.

As Blimmery broke down their route in more detail, Evaris couldn't stop thinking about the key in her overcoat. She had seen how much Yahshi's betrayal had scarred Pinto, and she couldn't imagine hurting him in the same way—even down to stealing a key. What if she didn't need to mark another *O* in her notepad? Maybe they could *trust* Pinto, instead of viewing him as the enemy.

When Blimmery finished recapping the plan, he left Keiyo alone to study the map, and took Evaris to Cove's bedroom, where she was resting.

"Oh, Cousin, come in! Come in!"

Blimmery entered first, Evaris trailing behind him. She caught sight of Cove in bed, syringes and medicine bottles lined up on her nightstand. She looked frailer now, and her gray hair had thinned.

"I know, I'm a sight for sore eyes these days." Cove laughed, and

Blimmery patted Evaris's shoulder before leaving to give them time alone.

Evaris stood an odd distance away from her great aunt's bedside, finding it challenging to step closer. She understood now, after reading the book Blimmery had written, that Cove had known the truth about the Force since she was in her twenties. It was no wonder she had been so vocal against Evaris's choice to become a guardian.

While she knew that berating a sick old woman would earn her another *O*, she couldn't help herself. Her eyes burned as she thought of all the times Cove had spoken out against her choice to become a guardian. Her words had even turned Evaris's own parents against her.

"Why didn't you just tell me the truth?" she asked, her voice raspy. "If I knew what the Force was really about, I wouldn't have tried so hard to get selected."

"I couldn't just *tell you*," Cove said, maintaining her smile. "You were so young, Ev, and kids can be talkative. I figured it was best to hope you wouldn't get selected, but you were always too stubborn for your own good. You caught the Force's eye, graduated, wore the uniform and everything."

Evaris peered down at her boots, pants, armored vest, and overcoat. Then she looked around at the frilly, half-sewn garments slung over the edge of Cove's bed. What shocked her wasn't that her great aunt still found joy in her passion despite her condition—it was that she could do it despite knowing the truth about the Force. How could she carry on like everything was fine?

"I haven't been doing nothing," Cove said, reading the judgment on Evaris's face. "I've been a long-time sponsor of Pandora's Box. Not just because I'm a fan—which I am, of course—but also because they're spreading the truth subtly, through the messaging of their plays and publications, and they've been hosting secret banned book sales during masquerade balls for years. I've been convincing them, with money and lots of charm, to publish Blimmery's book. He wrote it decades ago, and we've been waiting for the right time to release it. Obviously, given my condition, I'd like to see it happen in my lifetime, and it seems he's finally ready to face the consequences."

Evaris gulped, the weight of Cove's reveal striking her like an arrow. Publishing *Maelin* would get Blimmery killed, just like *The Force's Hidden Agenda* got his uncle killed. In his effort to spread the truth, he would die before knowing whether his plan would make a dent.

"The Force will come after him, and me, and potentially our friends at Pandora's Box—though I hope not. Copies will circulate for at least a few hours before the Force catches wind of it and starts rounding them up. By then, we can only hope that enough people will have read the story, and that it will be too late for them to cover up the truth. But we cannot know for sure." Cove paused, her eyes beginning to water. "I know you love your books, Ev. So tell me, is this one worth dying for?"

Evaris thought of last night in Keiyo's flat, and how she had lost herself in Blimmery's words. He told his story with a passion that could reach even the most closed-off to the truth.

"It's a brilliant book." She walked up to Cove's bedside, her eyes watering too. "It's worth it."

Cove's smile returned. "Then I'm happy to say that, soon enough, the Starfalls won't just be known for dresses anymore."

Evaris took the old woman's hand in hers, squeezing it gently. "I'm sorry for leaving the family."

Cove squeezed her hand back, her grip weak but steady. "You never left us. You're a Starfall, and if there's one thing a Starfall is, it's *unshakable*."

Evaris smiled back.

"I'm so proud to hear what you're doing to save this young girl's life. I've been grieving you, feeling like the Force took you away. I should have known that you were too strong for them. You have found your way back, and it is such a gift to witness before I go."

"Thank you, Aunt Cove."

Evaris stood at her bedside for a few minutes longer, exchanging occasional glances and grins, but the conversation stopped there. By the time she left the room and closed the door, she realized that she'd likely never see Cove again. Strangely, it wasn't a sickening feeling—more of a bittersweet relief. How nice it was to learn that Cove was a good one.

At around 9:00, it was time to go. Blimmery ushered Evaris and Keiyo out the door, wishing them luck. His job in their mission was done.

"Good luck to you too, Doctor," said Evaris.

"You were the best instructor," said Keiyo.

"Thank you," Blimmery whispered, and closed the door.

When Evaris and Keiyo reached the stable, she looked over to find his face pale, his eyes somewhere else.

"What's wrong?"

Keiyo's voice deepened. "This plan means nothing if the Underground fails. Cutting off the production points won't be enough. They're running out of supplies, and if we're gonna join them, we're taking on their odds. I just... I wish there was something we could do to give them leverage."

He shared the same worry she did, though she hadn't considered his solution before. What if they *could* do more than bring Vell back? There had to be *something* they could offer to give the Underground a better chance of winning.

Her eyes widened, remembering the package of dried mangoes. If Kia had been willing to leave with Yahshi before, perhaps she would be willing to leave again.

She exhaled sharply, her pulse quickening. "I have an idea, but Doctor Blimmery wouldn't like it."

CHAPTER 30

LANDLOCKED

Day 14 Without Vell | Clocks Read 17:33

♫ RIGHT PLACE · NATHAN BELL ♫

The brazier's fire reflected off the chamber walls, illuminating Yahshi's face with a soft glow. He sat across the flames from Saunti, picking meat out of the bowl of supper their sister base had kindly offered. Saunti would have scolded him for wasting already scarce supplies, but he knew better than to be too hard on him, given the Vell situation.

This was their fourteenth night without her, and in that time, they had destroyed thirty-eight production points, each located along the Waterway's path. Their last target was in the seaside town of Arinoma directly above, and after booming it, they wouldn't return underground as usual.

Instead, they would split.

Saunti, Yahshi, and Aero would head west to rescue Vell. Podge and Kwinn would stay in Eastern Territory to destroy the sixteen remaining production points located off the Waterway's path. Neither of their groups would be close to the safety of an access point and a sister base. After tonight, they would be landlocked—trapped in the same world as the Nightshades.

It'll be a miracle if all five of us survive.

Saunti took another bite of canned meat and vegetables, turning his attention to Podge and Kwinn. His appetite vanished at the realization that he might never see them again. They had once been fellow classmates of his at Atherus City Primary, and now he had led them into the most dangerous mission of their lives. By the cheerful, indestructible look on their faces, he couldn't tell whether they realized how grim their odds were. They knelt on the ground, laughing as they showed the only child in this sister base how to make a boombox.

The ten adults were packing in the other chambers, preparing for their move to Headquarters now that Saunti's group no longer needed the boat. There was no point in staying here, given the death of their collectors and couriers. All they would leave behind were two canoes tied to the dock—for whoever managed to make it back.

"You know, I never thanked you," Yahshi muttered, drawing Saunti's attention back to him. "I still don't like what happened with Rimoso, but the fact stands that you saved my life. Just like Vell."

Saunti frowned. Yahshi's words sounded grateful, but his tone of voice didn't reflect that.

"And now I'm..." His breath hitched. "I'm starting to worry that it's a pattern. That *I'm* always the one being saved."

Of course—it was about Vell. Saunti should have known from the start. Whenever he spoke, it *always* tied back to her.

"You and Aero came up with the perfect distraction," he assured him.

"No matter what the distraction is, the Force won't leave the Facility unattended."

"That's why we had weapons made in Grimward." Saunti kicked his boot against a bag on the floor. "You still remember how to fight, don't you?"

"I'm not immune to belladonna anymore. One cut, and I'll drop dead."

"Then don't get cut," Saunti ordered, his words sharpening. "Aero and I will be right behind you. No matter what gets in our way, we'll break into the Facility and free Vell with the lock busters you crafted."

Yahshi stared back, his expression cold. "She could be dead by now."

Saunti cringed, the words grating his ears. "Look, I know the past two weeks have been hard on you, and surely hard on her, but it all ends tonight, and I need you to be here with us. We don't have time for doubts."

He looked away, his gaze softening. "I know. Sorry."

"Are you with us?"

Yahshi nodded. "I'm with you."

Saunti sighed, sending Podge and Kwinn another glance while his own doubts crept up on him. Back in Atherus City, before they'd boomed the pile of Vakoi's portraits, they had told him about a mysterious third person in their group—a trader named Runner who supplied them with saltpeter and sulfur for their BPBs. About a week ago, they also claimed to know Runner's trade route by heart and insisted he'd be at Arinoma Market tonight with his carriage.

"Oh, I'm a hundred percent positive he'll be there," Podge had said.

"A thousand percent," Kwinn had confirmed.

Vell's rescue plan completely hinged on Runner's ability to get them past Border Control. Saunti could only hope that Podge and Kwinn were as correct as they were confident.

As he and Yahshi fell quiet, the Waterway's rushing, Podge and Kwinn's laughter, and the brazier's crackling merged into one unified noise. The sound of safety. He relished it. The five of them wouldn't have it for much longer.

Saunti's eyes drifted back to Yahshi, who was back to picking meat out of his bowl. He had been curious, of course, but the perfect opportunity to ask had never come around until now.

"Can you tell me about the Nightshade who killed him?" Saunti asked.

Yahshi looked up from his bowl, his eyes darkening. He seemed to know that Saunti was asking about the man known as Martu Konya.

"Roz." He said his name in a low rasp, like it was a secret. "He was one of my instructors at the Academy. I trusted him, only for him to murder my father right in front of me."

"Just to spite you?"

"To *save* me, I think. He thought killing the rebel in my life would bring me back *home*."

"This Roz guy doesn't sound very smart. If you want someone's trust, you shouldn't kill their father. I learned that the hard way."

It was a dark joke, but Yahshi laughed.

Saunti's smile faded when he realized that his own motive wasn't too different from Roz's. He had killed Rimoso for the believed benefit of the Underground, just as Roz had killed Martu for the believed benefit of the Force.

"Do you think you could ever forgive him?"

"No," Yahshi said without hesitation. "But I've moved on from wanting him dead."

Saunti nodded. Maybe that was the best he could do—get to where Aero could stand to be in the same room as him. Even after two weeks of working together, she was sitting on Arinoma's dock, watching the Waterway alone.

"I almost tried to kill him once, after I hitched a ride with a trader," Yahshi continued. "He was riding a horse just behind a carriage I was hiding in, but he didn't see me. I thought about jumping out and killing him. Almost did. But I stopped myself when I realized that it would make me exactly what he wanted me to be—a heartless killer, a Nightshade. So I chose to be like Father instead."

Saunti managed a weak smile. "What was he like?"

Tonna had told him all kinds of stories, but in hindsight, they might have been lies too.

"Well, he was a good fighter, for one. His style was different from what the guardians taught us in the program—more defensive, less aggressive." Yahshi paused and smiled to himself, as though recalling a distant memory. "And he was kind to everyone. My classmates loved the bread he sold at Sitra Market. I have a feeling the only person he viewed as the enemy was Vakoi himself, because even after I became a guardian—the last thing he wanted—he forgave me so easily."

It was an odd feeling—connecting with his late father through the Underground's Prince—but there was something therapeutic about it. No wonder Tonna spent so much time with Yahshi, clinging to him as though he was her biological son. He was the best mark her husband had left on the island.

"I'm sure he'd be proud of you."

"He'd be even more proud of you," Yahshi replied. "You know, you share a lot of his features."

"Well, he's *my* father," Saunti teased, "so, you know…"

"Not just looks." Yahshi set his bowl down. "You make up your mind and stick to it, no matter what—just like him. You killed Rimoso. You told Aero. You never back out of anything you plan. That's why Podge and Kwinn agreed to help, and why Aero's here even though she can't stand you."

Without thinking, Saunti rose from his chair and reached out.

"Brothers?" he asked, his hand lingering above the fire.

Yahshi stood even faster, his eyes catching the flames as he took his hand.

"I've always wanted a brother."

Saunti peered around a tree. For the fifth night in a row, a handful of officers stood guard at their targeted production point. Word of the boomings had spread, and the Force was taking measures to predict and intercept their next attacks.

He exchanged a glance with Podge, who hid behind another tree, then at Kwinn, who crouched with Yahshi and Aero in the shrubbery behind.

Our final boom together.

He turned back to the building and squinted. The five officers leaned against the exterior wall, chatting and laughing to kill time. He could sneak up from behind the building and plant a boombox without them noticing, but Yahshi wouldn't support murdering the officers—he had made that clear, and Saunti respected it, considering he'd lost his birth parents to flames.

"Can we take them out?" Podge asked.

"No," Yahshi and Saunti said in unison.

Kwinn sighed. "So boring…"

"Let's split up now. Yahshi, Aero, and I will handle the decoy," Saunti decided. "Once they run off, the two of you can go in for the production point. Then, my group will head straight to Arinoma Market, and you two can head toward your first location off the Waterway."

"So, this is goodbye?" Podge's face paled. There was a confidence that came with their team of five, and that faded with splitting up. Leaving the safety of the Waterway didn't help either. They'd all be staying above ground this time—and there was no knowing for how long.

"We're not regrouping after the boom?" Kwinn asked.

Saunti shook his head.

"Good luck," Aero said, setting a hand on Kwinn's shoulder.

"Could you try to limit the bloodshed?" Yahshi adjusted his hat, which concealed the mark on his forehead. "For me?"

"I was just playing, Yahshi," Kwinn assured him. "We'll do our best, okay?" She met eyes with Saunti and nodded, a subtle goodbye.

"What you're planning to do to help that girl is crazy," Podge said, drawing Saunti's attention back to him. "And that's coming from *me*."

"It's my fault they have her. It's my responsibility to get her back."

"And this is the only way," Yahshi added.

A silence grew between the five, their eyes meeting each other and falling away. It was hard to believe that any shared glance could be their last.

Eventually, Kwinn broke the silence.

"Time for a boom." She slung a bag off her shoulder, shuffling through it for a boombox, which she passed to Yahshi.

He crept away with it, lugging a bag of weaponry over his shoulder.

For a separate mission, Kwinn handed two more boomboxes to Aero, who tucked them into her own bag. She met eyes with Saunti, and in unison, they followed in Yahshi's tracks. Together, the three of them snuck through the woods until they could no longer see Podge and Kwinn in the distance. That's when Yahshi stopped and set the boombox on the ground.

With the flick of a match, Aero leaned over, lighting the rope that protruded from the wooden box. As soon as the fuse caught the flame, they raced off toward the center of town.

The ground rumbled beneath their boots, nearly tripping Saunti, but he regained balance and covered his ears in anticipation.

A violent *boom* filled the air, and the instant fire warmed the backs of their coats as they continued running.

As they stumbled back into the heart of town, the residents of Arinoma woke, doors slamming and children screaming. Some ran toward the water, anticipating a second attack on their homes.

Saunti, Yahshi, and Aero navigated the crowds, heading straight for Arinoma Market in the center of the coastal town. It didn't take more than a few minutes to reach it, and they arrived to find a carriage parked near the building. According to Podge and Kwinn, this was Runner's stop.

Please be right about this...

By the carriage stood a bearded man in his thirties, staring at the distant trees as a second boom set off in the distance—Podge and Kwinn taking out the production point. He smiled, pleased with the destruction.

Saunti cleared his throat, approaching the trader with Yahshi and Aero at his sides.

"Runner?"

The man met eyes with him, responding to the name. "Do I know you?"

Saunti let out a sigh of relief. *It's really him.*

"Wait a minute..." The man's eyes widened. "I *do* know you."

Saunti frowned, tilting his head, but then he realized that Runner wasn't looking at him, but at Yahshi.

"You were that kid with the bandana who hitched a ride with me." Runner pointed at him. "The one who turned out to be a Nightshade."

"You saved me that night." With a smile, Yahshi removed his hat and shook the hair out of his face, revealing the four-petaled flower on his forehead.

Runner eyed his mark. "*Wow.*"

Aero nudged Saunti's side, giving him a look. He got the message—they didn't have time for a reunion right now. For all they knew, there might even be Nightshades in town.

"For the past two weeks," Saunti interrupted, "we've been working with Podge and Kwinn to destroy the production points."

"Ah, I just *knew* they were behind these attacks!" Runner exclaimed.

"They told us you'd be heading to the Vakoi Empire tonight."

"*Tomorrow* night."

"No..." Yahshi whispered.

"Oh, *great*," Aero muttered.

Saunti took a step toward him. "We need to get past Border Control as soon as possible. Is there any chance you could cross early?"

"Well, that depends. What's your offer?"

He shared a look of concern with Yahshi and Aero. They didn't have any money.

"I kid!" the trader yelled, bursting into laughter. "Any friends of Podge and Kwinnie are friends of mine." He gestured for them to follow, leading them to the back of his carriage.

Saunti sighed in relief.

"Nice kids, those two." Runner shuffled the Saver Stores bags and boxes around, making space for them to hide behind the goods. "I was their parents' apprentice before the War. Used to source items for them all the time, and Vakoi's takeover didn't stop me. Actually, it made my job easier. I get my hands on all kinds of stuff as a trader."

Saunti and Aero climbed into Runner's carriage, but Yahshi seemed to hesitate. He stared back at the ruckus in Arinoma and the smoke rising in the distance, his grip tightening on his bag of weapons.

"Get in before anyone sees you," Runner said with an odd tone.

Perhaps he had spoken those words to Yahshi before, because he grinned at the man and finally hopped into the carriage.

Three hours later, they approached the nearest Border Control tower. Yahshi peered over the stack of supplies, studying the familiar structures of the town they had just passed through.

"Vori," he said to himself. "We're heading toward the same tower I snuck through."

Saunti stood, setting up another layer of boxes and bags to conceal the three of them better. Considering how much the Saver Stores had to be suffering by now, Border Control might not even inspect the carriage. *But it's better safe than sorry.*

While Aero joined to help, Yahshi tucked himself in a corner, reaching into his bag to wield a dagger. It was darker now, the bags and boxes blocking out even more moonlight.

Saunti lit a match as he and Aero sat on either side of Yahshi.

"The guardian who took her used to be a friend of ours," said the former Nightshade, his eyes lost in the darkness. "Back at the Academy, the three of us went through everything together, but even with all our history, I can't shake the feeling that he's lost his way, and that he's even hurt Vell."

Saunti wished he could say something encouraging, but the reality was that Pinto likely *had* hurt Vell.

The carriage jolted to a sudden stop, interrupting their conversation. *Runner must have reached Border Control.*

He waved his hand, putting out the match he'd been pinching. It was hard to hear with so many goods stacked in the way, but with enough focus, he managed to make out words from outside.

"Yeah, I get that, but I'm not seeing you on my list," said a Border Control officer.

"I'm just doing what the officers in Arinoma told me," Runner replied. "There was another boom, and they told me to get my stuff to the Saver Store as quickly as possible."

"Let me have a look."

Dammit. Saunti glanced at Yahshi and Aero, but it was too dark to meet their eyes.

The officer's footsteps approached the back of the carriage, stopping right at the opening. Light from his lantern streamed into their hiding place—slipping through the cracks between the items that blocked them.

"Is that saltpeter?" the officer questioned.

"Yeah!" Runner called from the front.

"I've never seen this much imported at once."

Saunti gulped. Traders usually transported saltpeter to other production points—not across the border to Saver Stores.

"Like I said, my route was cut short! But I guess I could head back, and get the saltpeter to—"

"No need," the officer interrupted. His lantern light vanished from inside the carriage as he walked back to Runner.

Saunti relaxed and slumped over, releasing a slow breath. *Thank the stars...*

"You're all clear," the officer said, and at his cue, the carriage rocked back into motion.

Saunti waited a few more seconds before striking a new match.

Yahshi and Aero smiled back at him in the orange glow. They had made it safely to the Vakoi Empire, and in a matter of hours, they would reach their target in Vakoi City.

It was almost time for their biggest boom yet.

CHAPTER 31

KEY PLAYER

Saver Store lanterns are brighter than ever!
Don't get caught in the dark!

♫ CORPSES · SAINT SISTER ♫

Evaris waited on the front steps of the Complex that evening. Blimmery had anticipated that Pinto would leave the Facility before 8:00—after Vell's second interrogation—but it was already 9:47, and he still hadn't returned.

She gulped, tucking her pocket watch away. *What if he doesn't come back in time?*

As though on cue, a horse finally pulled up to the stable. She walked down a step in anticipation, but it was Keiyo returning from his shift at Vakoi City Hospital—not Pinto.

After securing his horse, Keiyo scaled the steps, his face twisted with anxiety. He stopped beside her and whispered, "You're still here?"

Evaris nodded, her eyes on the road. "Pinto's not back yet."

"We're tight on time," he continued. "Since you're handling Pinto, at least let me take over the Palace tonight."

"No way. The Princess would freak out even more if a guy confronts her."

"Oh, but I'm harmless."

"She doesn't know that," Evaris snapped, finally meeting his gaze. A worrying session with him wouldn't fix anything. "Let's just stick to our original plan, okay?"

Before he could reply, the sound of another approaching horse redirected their attention to the road, where Pinto slowed to a stop. He looked over at them, and Evaris lowered her head.

"*Great*," she muttered. "He saw us together again."

"*I'm* not embarrassed," he whispered. "You're a catch."

"Not the time, Keiyo."

"Oh! So there *is* a time?"

"Get out of here."

"Fine. If you need me, I'll be in my flat, lacing my tools."

Evaris nodded, watching him vanish into the common room.

As Pinto crossed the emptiness between the Complex and the front steps, a memory flashed through her head. She had been guarding the Facility once as Pinto walked across the grassy clearing to reach her, his eye darting around suspiciously. This time, she didn't find the awkward distance charming—every step reminded her that she was one second closer to pulling off an impossible swap.

Run, her heart whispered.

Pinto stopped a few steps before reaching her, frowning as they made eye contact.

She forced herself to smile and take two steps down, closing the distance between them.

"Do you need something?" he asked, his voice dry.

Her smile faded. "Could we speak privately, Professor?"

He stared for a few seconds, testing whether or not she was being serious. Then, carefully, he continued up the steps past her, whispering, "Be at my flat in five."

Evaris stood in the chilly air, goosebumps on her arms as Pinto slammed the front door behind him. She checked her pocket watch. To time it right, she'd have to enter in a few minutes from now.

As she waited, she brainstormed an excuse as to why Pinto had seen her leave Keiyo's flat the night before, and why she'd been speaking to him a moment ago.

With a deep breath, she checked her pocket watch again.

Her pulse quickened.

It's time.

She barely noticed the few guardians in the common room until Boa smiled and waved. He'd been awfully chipper since hearing the gossip that she wasn't on speaking terms with Pinto anymore. Their falling out eased his anxiety, but he'd surely go crazy if he knew what she was about to do.

Evaris smiled and waved back as though nothing were wrong. For Keiyo and her to save Vell, every part of their plan from here on out needed to go perfectly, and it all relied on this very task. She reached into her overcoat while scaling the steps to Pinto's flat, ensuring the faux key was still there. Her fingers wrapped around the cold brass.

Is it really necessary to fool him?

She shook her head, releasing the key. *I already made up my mind.*

As much as she wished she could tell Pinto the truth, she knew her recount of *Maelin* wouldn't be enough evidence. He would demand extra sources, extra proof—which she wouldn't have.

Her eyes watered as she stepped off the staircase into his hallway. *It's time to say goodbye...*

She stopped at the door to his flat, but before she could raise her hand to knock, Pinto opened it, pocket watch in hand. He'd been timing her too.

Quickly, he stepped aside, and she entered his flat for the first time. It looked just like hers, but there was an element of order to it. His bed was perfectly made—not a single crease in the blankets—and unlike her desk, Pinto's wasn't covered in novels and unwashed mugs. It was like he'd never fully moved in.

He sat on his bed and shrugged. "Well?"

Evaris gulped, struggling to gauge what he expected to hear. An apology? A declaration of love? An explanation for why he'd seen her with Keiyo, alone, twice?

She decided to address all three at once.

"Pinto," she said, ignoring the piece of her that almost called him *Red*. "I never should have shut you out."

He stared coldly, lips pursed, as she took a seat next to him.

"I've missed you." The line was part of her scheme, but she really did mean it. "I hate not spending time with you. I hate that I never got to meet your family after the Incursion like we planned."

His gaze softened, just a little.

"But let's be honest," she continued. "This thing between us was never going to work. At some point, we'd get caught, and we'd get sent to correction, and Keiyo's been warning me about how horrible that is."

Pinto tilted his head, piecing together her imaginary story.

"You were right from the start. I was cruel when I kissed you in Atherus City. I never should have started something destined to burn."

"No." He finally broke, turning to grab her hands. "No, don't say that. I'm glad you did it. I'm glad you kissed me."

Her heart skipped a beat. With his hands on hers, she remembered the guardian she had fallen for—the kindhearted man who would do anything for his loved ones.

The key in her overcoat called to her, and again, she second-guessed her decision. Pinto's friends had turned against the Force, and he'd taken that as a personal betrayal. If she were to leave the Force too, he would hate her in the same way he hated Yahshi and Vell. Could she bear to live knowing he despised her?

On the other hand, if she *didn't* steal Pinto's key—if she told him the truth—he might not oppose Ogga to help her. She and Keiyo would be trapped.

No matter how much she loved Pinto, staying in a life she hated wasn't worth staying with him.

So she squeezed his hands back. "You really mean that? You're glad that I kissed you?"

"Of course I am." He smiled. "If the last two weeks have taught me anything, it's that I can't live without you."

She let his hands go, raising them to meet his face instead.

You can do this. You're a Starfall. You can do anything.

She leaned toward him, and her lips met his without another word.

He kissed her back, and her eyes watered, dampening her lashes. She should have known this wouldn't work. Pinto was serious, practical, and adored the confines of authority. It didn't matter whether he followed the rules or not—he lived for the thrill of navigating the Force's structure.

Meanwhile, Evaris crumbled within it.

He was made for guardianship. She was made to leave it behind.

Pinto tried to hold her waist, but his fingers bumped against the components of her bow. She pulled back to remove it, and he did the same with his own.

Then he removed his overcoat too, tossing it aside.

Evaris watched it land on the floor, knowing that somewhere in that fabric was the key to Vell's cell.

She pretended to remove her overcoat, gripping the fabric at both sides. Her finger slid against the concealed dagger within—and she pressed against it harder, slicing her skin.

With a wince, she released her overcoat, keeping it on.

"Oh, great..." A trail of blood spilled down her palm. "I snagged my dagger."

Pinto cringed and headed for the exit. "I'll be back," he said—likely on his way to grab medical supplies from the common room cabinet.

Evaris waited until he closed the door behind him before staring at the overcoat he'd left behind, examining the placement of the fabric. Considering his sharp memory, she wouldn't be surprised if he'd notice a different set of creases.

After forming a mental image, she dropped to her knees and rummaged through the overcoat with her non-bloodied hand, searching for his key ring. It wasn't hard to find, as she remembered where he'd kept his duplicates.

She removed the ring from his inner pocket, ignoring the sting in her index finger as she flipped through its keys for the one to Vell's cell. Careful not to mark the others with blood, she removed it, then reached into her own overcoat for Blimmery's dummy key. She slipped it onto the ring as a replacement.

With the real key safely stored in her overcoat, she returned Pinto's ring to his inner pocket and adjusted the fabric to match how he'd left it earlier.

Evaris glanced at the clock on the wall and nodded. The swap had taken less than a minute, so she used the extra time to search for his ring of duplicates in case he'd made one for Vell's cell. It wouldn't hurt to have a second key tonight—one for Keiyo, and one for herself as a backup. There was no telling who would reach the cell first.

She rustled through Pinto's nightstand drawers, which he'd filled with notebooks of various colors, including the ones from their trip together. With a smile, she pushed his scratched-up blue book aside to find his personal red one.

Evaris peered back at the door. The hallway was quiet, so in the spur of the moment, she flipped to the last used page.

Dear Perma,

I think I love her.

Her heart swelled, and she slammed the notebook shut, returning it to its rightful place. She knew that as soon as she left, she would need to add another *O* to her notepad.

The nightstand only seemed to contain notebooks, so she moved on to his desk drawers. The first was labeled *FINANCES* and contained crinkled receipts, loose paperwork, and bills of exchange.

As footsteps echoed from the staircase, she closed the first drawer and opened the second, which was labeled *ORGANIZE LATER*. No keys.

The footsteps were closer now. She closed the second drawer and opened the third. Pinto had labeled this one *MISC*.

Her eyes widened at another ring of keys identical to the last. She rustled through them and found one that looked exactly like Vell's, though far less worn.

She winced, a pain zapping her cut finger as she removed the duplicate. If she had thought this far ahead, she would have asked Keiyo to make another dummy key earlier, but she'd been too focused on *how* she'd perform the swap in the first place.

She closed the drawer and crossed the room, concealing the backup right as Pinto reentered with a white briefcase of medical supplies.

"Here," he said, holding out his palm.

Evaris placed her hand in his, and Pinto surveyed the cut with a level of care she would only expect of a doctor. Sometimes she forgot they had studied the skills of all three divisions during their time at the Academy, and Pinto had a sharper memory than most.

"You're lucky we're guardians." He set the briefcase on his bed and opened it, retrieving a bottle of alcohol and a piece of gauze. "If you weren't tolerant to belladonna, you'd be dead by now."

Evaris flinched as the alcohol dripped over her dagger wound. It took a moment for the stinging to subside, and only then did she manage to speak.

"If we weren't guardians, I wouldn't have this cut in the first place."

Surprisingly, Pinto laughed, and her cheeks ran hot. She hated how much she missed that sound.

"If we weren't guardians," he said, leaning toward her, "I'd never leave your side."

Evaris turned her face away, and despite the bitter taste of betrayal on her tongue, a smile escaped her.

He laughed again as he wiped her hand with a red handkerchief, removing the bloodied alcohol. She hoped that when he looked back on this moment someday, he would remember how he felt right now, and realize that she could betray him and love him at the same time.

Evaris didn't linger for long. It was past 10:30 when Pinto finished mending her finger, and by then, she had the convenient excuse of a very real night shift awaiting her.

Pinto hugged her goodbye, assuming they'd have much more alone time together like this. He didn't know that their story ended here.

She lingered in the warmth of his arms before parting ways for the last time.

As she passed the door to Keiyo's flat, she crouched to slide one of Vell's keys beneath it. If the next part of their plan were to fail, at the very least, he could finish the rest alone.

Her pocket watch read 10:38 when she left the Complex that night, but instead of heading straight to the Detainment Facility, she turned and headed for Vakoi Palace. It took a few minutes for her to reach the Wall, stopping her horse right next to Galler's post at the gate.

"E-Evaris?" he called.

"You were right, Galler." She dismounted her horse, her voice intentionally shaky. "I-I made a mistake. I never should have involved myself with him."

"W-What happened?"

Evaris secured her horse to the nearest hitching post, her hands shaking, her lips sealed in feigned fear of speaking out.

"Your f-finger," he said, pointing to the gauze Pinto had wrapped around her cut.

"It's nothing. I just—I need to get away from him tonight, okay? Could I take over your shift?"

He hesitated. "You don't have one to-tonight?"

"No," she lied. "It's my day off and Pinto knows all my days off and—"

"Y-Yeah, of course," Galler cut in, nodding repeatedly. "Not a question."

"Thanks." She took his spot by the gate, letting out a genuine sigh of relief. *I lucked out tonight.* If the Palace guard had been anyone else, it would have taken far more convincing.

He lingered nearby. "Do you wa-want me to stay here with you, or..."

"Actually, I'd rather be alone right now."

"Sure." He set a gentle palm on her shoulder before turning to leave. She hoped his kindness wouldn't land him in trouble later.

As soon as Galler left on horseback, she opened the Palace gate and left the Wall unguarded. No one else could interfere now, apart from the Royal Family themselves. Security was relatively minor at the Palace, considering the building's location right by Complex in the safest, most secure part of the City. If there was trouble, the entire Force could arrive in a matter of minutes.

Evaris crossed the garden, which, while beautiful during the day, sent a chill down her spine at night. Branches reached toward her like lonely skeletons, and tall, pruned bushes resembled the silhouettes of people. A gust of wind washed her in a shower of cherry blossoms, and she dusted off the stray flowers as she scaled the front steps.

The door was open, and she slipped inside like a ghost. Her murky memory of the Palace floor plans she'd studied at the Academy told her that Kia was likely on the second floor.

Evaris lit a single match and pinched it between her fingers. It did little to light the vast room, but it was enough for her to see directly ahead. She walked in the darkness until a staircase materialized. It led up to a narrow hallway with an endless string of doors on either side.

Oh, great...

She grabbed the handle of the closest one and pushed it open. The room was almost empty, nothing but a single easel in the center. Its canvas featured an abstract painting of a man with two faces.

She shuddered and closed the door, moving on to the second one. The room's curtains were drawn, blocking all moonlight out, and the match between her fingers illuminated nothing from the doorway. She entered to explore, piecing together different parts of the room with her little ball of light. A desk. A sofa. A bed.

A teenage *boy* in bed.

She froze in her tracks. This was definitely a bedroom, but not the right one.

Prince Kodo shuffled, and in a panic, Evaris shook her hand, putting out her match.

Everything went black.

"Kia?" the Prince whispered, shuffling again. "Is that you?"

Evaris held her breath, fighting every urge to run as the blankets rustled again. Two feet padded against the floor, and she stepped sideways, feeling the air shift as he passed her.

Don't light a lantern, Prince Kodo. Don't do it.

He stopped at the door, feeling around to find it open.

"Weird," he whispered to himself, closing it again.

Evaris took another step back as he passed her a second time and crawled into bed. She gave herself a rule to count to a hundred, giving him time to fall asleep again. Only then did she cross the room and crack the door open.

Prince Kodo didn't shuffle.

She swiftly returned to the hallway and struck a new match, continuing to the third door.

I hate this game, she thought to herself, pushing it open. The hinges creaked louder than the Prince's had, a sign of wear.

Thankfully, the curtains weren't fully drawn in this room, allowing a bit more light inside. From the doorway, she could tell this was another bedroom, and after a step inside, she saw Kia, deep asleep.

As Evaris approached, her mind raced with the thought of how quickly this plan could spiral out of control. If Kia were to scream, any of the Royal Family members could ring an emergency bell, and the Force would swarm through the gate before Evaris could even think of escaping.

She leaned over Kia's bedside and blew out her match. The moonlight from the window was just enough for her to make out the fifteen-year-old's features.

She forced her hand down against Kia's mouth.

The Princess's eyes jolted open, and after a moment of silent panic, she thrashed against the guardian's grip.

"Shh..." Evaris held her down, muffling her shouts with her palm.

The Princess fought harder.

"I'm not here to hurt you," she whispered fiercely. "I'm here to break you out."

That seemed to catch her attention. Kia calmed a little, her pupils darting, scanning Evaris's face.

"Do you recognize me?"

The girl nodded, her gaze locking and sharpening as though saying, *Let me go!*

Evaris removed her hand.

Instead of screaming, the Princess grinned. "I knew the dried mangoes would work, but not on *you*. I was dropping a hint for the smart one."

Evaris glossed over the insult. "You were Yahshi's accomplice."

"Oh, congratulations, Commander," she said with condescending enthusiasm. "You finally figured it out..."

On a normal day, Evaris would mock the girl back, but tonight, the stakes were too high, so she sucked up her pride and took another jab.

"I'm breaking Vell out tonight," she explained. "She's the one who—"

"I know who Vell is. I'm not stupid."

"She knows where the hideout—"

"Again, I'm not stupid."

Evaris's face ran hot.

"You want me as a hostage for the Underground," Kia concluded, reading between the lines. "That's quite a big ask, Commander. What's your sales pitch?"

"You'll have a new life."

"On the losing side?"

"If you join us, it won't *be* a losing side. Just imagine —Saver Stores completely out of stock, guardians underpaid, Vell no longer in their custody, and... *the Princess held hostage.*"

A pause. "Sounds like fun."

"Loads," Evaris said, taking a step back. "That's my pitch, Princess. Take it or leave it."

She sighed and slid her legs out of bed, looking around at her lavish room as though saying a mental goodbye. Her eyes lingered on a portrait of her brother on the wall, which she had embellished with a painted unibrow and blushing cheeks.

Evaris cleared her throat. "I'm in a hurry here, so this is your final—"

"I'm joining you," she snapped, her eyes darting back to the guardian. "Rush me one more time, Commander, and I'll scream my lungs out."

CHAPTER 32

RIDGE

Reliable padlocks are now available at your local Saver Store!

♫ SINKHOLE · OLD SEA BRIGADE ♫

Pinto hunched over in a common room sofa, pen in hand, spinning words across the pages of the red notebook on his lap. He hadn't written about Evaris in two weeks—every time he tried, the words ran dry. But now, their reconciliation had broken his dam, and the words flowed endlessly. His hand moved faster than his thoughts, finishing sentences for him like a mind-reader.

The pocket watch in his lap ticked, faster and faster, attempting to fool him. In reality, he knew it was hardly past 11:00. Evaris had only just begun her shift at the Facility, meaning he had four more hours to wait for her return. The gap felt brutal, but with his red notebook and a pen, he would write to fill the time. And if he lost patience, he could always ride down to the Facility for a chat—though he'd try to avoid doing that to appear less desperate. He was lucky to have her back at all, and the last thing he wanted was to scare her away.

A guardian entered the common room, and though he knew it wasn't her, he stopped writing and looked up anyway.

Galler made eye contact and slammed the door behind him, his lips curving downward. He had never seemed to like Pinto, especially after their discussion at that bar in Vakoi Square—but the pure hostility written on his face tonight was like nothing he'd shown him before.

"What are you d-doing down here, Professor?" The sharpness of Galler's tone overpowered his stutter, and for the first time, he actually made Pinto recoil.

"It's the common room." He closed his red book with a frown. "I can be here if I please."

Galler's arms tensed up, as though fighting the urge to reach for his dual swords. "You better not be w-waiting for E-Evaris."

"So what if I am?"

He scanned the common room, ensuring no one else was here, before creeping toward Pinto. "Look. I-I don't know what ha-ha-happened between you two tonight, but y-you need to back off, and take a hint."

Pinto resisted the urge to stand—which would prove that Galler had raised his guard—but luckily, the commander stopped, glared as a final warning, and marched off to the staircase.

As Galler's raging footsteps echoed behind, Pinto furrowed his brow. *Take a hint?*

He tucked his red book and pen into his overcoat, sitting alone in the silence, mulling over Galler's words. Why would Galler assume that something had happened, good *or* bad, between him and Evaris tonight? She had met him in his flat five minutes after he'd entered it, a precaution he'd planned to ensure no one would see them in the Complex together.

Pinto shook his head. *No, she wouldn't talk about me.* Evaris was too smart for that. She wouldn't tell Galler about their relationship, and even if she did, she would have nothing bad to say. They had kissed and rekindled their feelings. Informing Galler of such would alarm him, surely. He might still react by telling Pinto to *back off*—but to *take a hint*? Such a phrase implied a sense of predatory ignorance, and that didn't describe him, did it? Had he not taken a hint?

He shook his head, casting the doubts away. Evaris had made it clear, verbally and physically, that she *wanted* him. He had not been predatory nor ignorant. Of course not! That wasn't him.

Puzzled, Pinto raised his fingers to bite his nails but stopped himself, remembering how much Evaris hated that habit—the same habit he'd broken recently in a futile attempt to catch her attention. If she would not listen to his apology, maybe she would see it in his hands.

Instead of biting, he reached for his keys and flipped through them, one at a time, as he debated whether he should knock on Galler's door and ask him directly. It wasn't like Evaris to lie about him, so someone else must have spread the rumor. Perhaps someone jealous, who wanted to ruin his career? Who might that be? Boa? He and Galler were friends. It wasn't too far of a stretch.

Without even looking, his fingers identified Vell's key based on its weight. He turned it sideways and slipped his thumbnail against the side, feeling for the chip.

His nail slid smoothly. There was no *click* or *tick* this time.

Pinto's thoughts stopped racing in an instant. He flipped the key over, studying all of its sides.

The ridge is gone.

His chest tightened, replaying his encounter with Evaris in his flat. He had been so thrilled about her willingness to talk to him that he hadn't considered how strange her shift in demeanor was. Even recently, at every opportunity she had to speak to him, she either said something negative or nothing at all. Why had she been so quick to change her mind and declare that she missed him? He had been too caught in the moment, at the time, to inquire about her change in heart.

Pinto clutched the key, feeling every part of it, trying to convince himself that it couldn't be a fake. He imagined various scenarios throughout the day in which another guardian could have reached into his overcoat, replaced his key, and slipped it back into his possession—but the scenarios were all ridiculously implausible. The reality was that no one could have performed a swap like this unless he had left his overcoat unattended.

Which he had done, just once, when he fetched medical supplies for Evaris's wound.

He stopped feeling the key. *Would she really lie to me about her feelings, kiss me when she didn't want to, and go so far as to cut herself in order to steal my key?*

No, it was too cruel. It was impossible. It didn't matter if it was the only explanation that made sense right now—he needed to prove it wrong.

Pinto rushed upstairs and knocked on Galler's door.

He opened it with a sneer. "W-What?"

"Who told you all that? About me not taking a hint?"

Galler scoffed and shook his head, as though it were obvious. "Go to s-sleep, Professor," he hissed, slamming his door.

He rushed farther upstairs and knocked on Keiyo's door next. Evaris claimed he'd been telling her about his time in correction, and Pinto needed to verify that—to prove she didn't lie.

No response.

Pinto knocked again. "Keiyo!"

Silence.

It didn't make sense. Keiyo was his own unit member now, and he knew his schedule inside and out. He didn't have any responsibilities tonight.

Maybe he's just a deep sleeper. He traveled a few doors down, his hands shaking as he unlocked his own flat. *Or maybe he's staying out late at Vakoi Square.*

Pinto's door swung open, and his heart pounded harder, his eye locking on the lowest drawer of his desk. If Evaris had stolen his main key, could she have taken his backup too? She was the only person who knew about his key paranoia, so finding his duplicate gone would prove that it was *she* who had tricked him.

On the other hand, if the backup remained, she could still be guilty of taking his *main* key.

He hated how unfair the odds were. In a moment, she would either be guilty or *maybe* guilty. No matter what state his duplicates were in, he would not gain confidence in her innocence.

But he *would* get one step closer to the truth.

Pinto raced to his desk and opened his junk drawer. He snatched the ring of duplicates and flipped through them, one by one.

The keys fell from his trembling grip as he gasped.

It's gone.

Evaris wasn't standing guard at the Facility's front door like she should have been. An hour ago, she had left Pinto's flat, claiming she couldn't be late. He had hugged her, and she had leaned into his arms as though she needed it. That wasn't something a person could fake.

Pinto's eye widened as he dismounted his horse. *Of course!*

It all made sense now. Keiyo blamed Pinto for Sunna's death and wanted to ruin his career by framing him for Vell's escape. He knew Evaris was the only person who could steal his key, so he had blackmailed her into it. That explained why he had seen her leaving Keiyo's flat the other night—and why Evaris felt that she couldn't be honest with him.

Pinto led his horse into the stable and counted four others—one more than there should have been.

Keiyo's here too.

He secured his horse in a stall, whipped out his dagger, and rushed back out.

Don't worry, Evaris. I'll handle this.

As soon as he turned for the Facility, the sound of a wince stopped him.

To his right, a girl sat in the shadow of a tree, folded over, clutching her ankle. Her black hair fell to shield her face.

Pinto's grip on his dagger tightened. He glanced at the unguarded Facility, then back at the girl.

"Vell?"

She looked over at him. It wasn't Vell.

"Your Highness!" He tucked his dagger away and hurried over, kneeling at her side. "What are you doing out here?"

Kia tried to push herself up and winced again.

He gripped her arm to stabilize her. "How did you get here?"

"I don't know." She spoke quickly, her eyes darting between him, the Facility, and the surrounding trees. "I-I think they took the prisoner. I saw them running, but... but then I tripped, and then..."

Pinto frowned as she continued babbling, still stuck on the same question. Nothing about her presence at the Facility made sense, but if Keiyo and

Evaris had already freed Vell, leaving their horses behind, then he needed to focus on finding *them*—not answers.

"Listen, Your Highness," he said, interrupting her story. "I'm gonna get you into that stable over there, okay? I'll take you back home, but first, I need to find them."

She sniffled and nodded, her eyes glistening in the moonlight.

"Which way did they go?" he asked.

"I don't know. I think..." She pointed between the trees in the same direction Pinto had come from. "I think that way?"

East.

He shifted positions to lift Kia, freezing as a realization crossed his mind.

I thought she was Vell.

Their faces were far from similar, but the basic features matched—black hair, bangs, blue eyes. The same description that matched the girl at the convenience store, Yahshi's accomplice. The Research Division assumed she was Vell, and that she had thrown out the nonperishables to avoid getting caught, but Pinto realized now that they were wrong.

Kia had tossed him a package of dried mangoes, but the Royal Family didn't eat food from outside the Force, so she must have obtained the snacks in secret—with the Belladonna Traitor.

He narrowed his eye at Kia, and the pain in her eyes faded, replaced with the realization that he'd pieced together her clue at the most inconvenient time. He would not let anyone play him for a fool again, especially not someone on Yahshi's side. Kia had somehow involved herself with Keiyo, and was faking helplessness to cover his tracks.

Pinto rose and raced for the Facility.

"Professor!" she called, standing without a wince.

He skidded to a stop in front of the door. It was slightly ajar.

Gulping, Pinto pushed it open to find a member of Evaris's unit on the floor, his hand stretched out, a metal bar in his limp grip.

He was dead.

A throwing star had punctured his face, leaving a shallow cut. How could such a small wound end his life? Where were his other injuries? Where was the pool of blood?

Bile rose in Pinto's throat at the sight of such a cruel, senseless death. He yanked the four-bladed star out of the man's head and recognized the design.

This is Keiyo's tool.

Tossing the star to the grass behind him, Pinto stepped over the guardian's body. The sound of shuffling boots and voices echoed in the distance.

I'm not too late.

He quickened his pace, heading toward the noise—until he spotted moving shadows in a connected corridor. He peered around the corner with his good eye.

Closest to him, Evaris's unit leader stood petrified in a defensive stance, one used for deflecting long-range attacks with his dual swords.

Pinto peered farther around the corner, expecting to see Keiyo wielding a throwing star, but it was Evaris who threatened the Defense guardian, her bow drawn. Keiyo stood beside her as backup, ready to draw a star only if needed.

"Evaris," her unit leader pleaded, "think about what you're doing."

Pinto recalled how Evaris had shouted at him in the clearing after Sunna's execution. She had broken down after killing *one of her own*, and yet here she was, threatening a fellow member of the Force who had done nothing wrong—unlike Sunna, who had left Pinto with a wound that still hadn't fully healed. How could she be so hypocritical?

Pinto unslung his bow, preparing an arrow. While he didn't understand the full story, there was one thing he knew for certain—he wouldn't allow another innocent guardian to die tonight.

"Evaris," her unit leader pleaded again. "Lower your bow. Please."

Pinto's eye widened at the sound of shuffling boots—was she preparing to shoot? With no other choice, he jumped out from around the corner, offering Evaris's unit leader long-range support.

Keiyo gasped, plucking a star from his bandolier.

"Drop your tools." Pinto aimed his arrow back and forth between Evaris and Keiyo, gritting his teeth to combat the pain of his pulsing arm. He hadn't drawn a bow since the Incursion, and clearly, it was still too soon.

Keiyo's hand shifted back, a sign that he was preparing to throw his star.

In defense, Pinto lowered his bow, aiming for his unit member's leg to avoid any serious injuries—but his bad arm shifted with a grimace, and the arrow shot off higher, heading straight for Keiyo's head.

Before Keiyo could throw his star, Evaris pivoted, shoving him aside. His cheek crashed into the corridor wall just as Pinto's arrow grazed the side of his neck.

Leaving a minor slash behind, it zipped onward and struck the wall behind him.

Thank the stars, Pinto thought, hesitating to reach for another arrow. If Evaris hadn't pushed Keiyo out of the way, that shot could have killed him.

Sighing in shared relief, Evaris's unit leader looked over his shoulder at Pinto—and in that moment, an arrow pierced his head, sending him to the floor. He thrashed and wailed in pain, clutching his temple.

In a fluid motion, Pinto stepped back and aimed another arrow—this time at Evaris. She mirrored him with her own bow, threatening to shoot, glaring as though she believed he had *tried* to murder Keiyo. But even if she believed that, why would it justify killing her own unit leader, an innocent bystander?

Keiyo rubbed his cheek, regathering himself from Evaris's shove into the wall. He plucked another star from his bandolier to replace the one he'd dropped, his breaths racing as he aimed.

"Keiyo," Evaris said firmly. "I'll handle him."

With his star still raised, he sent her a final glance, hesitating.

"Go," she snapped.

Finally, Keiyo bolted off, disappearing around the corner.

Now Evaris and Pinto were alone, targeting each other from opposite sides of the dim corridor.

"I'm sorry," she said, her voice breaking. "I've been bad for you."

Pinto's mouth twitched. He struggled to place what she meant.

"You were loyal to your friends, and I turned you bitter. My *love* turned you bitter." She stepped closer, her eyes watering, but she still didn't lower her bow. "Let me fix this, Red."

Red.

Pinto gulped, his mind racing back to every time she'd called him by that cursed nickname. He had started associating *Red* with the scent of charcoal and the warmth of a late-night fire—but now it felt cold, like a dose of scarlet belladonna serum injected into his arm, its temperature lower than his body's. This wasn't the same Evaris who had called him *Red* before.

"I know it's a lot to ask," she continued, "but I need you to trust me one more time. Just once is enough. As soon as we get to safety, I'll explain *everything*."

We? Did that include Keiyo and Vell? By getting to safety, was she referring to the Underground hideout? Why would she possibly join the same group that gouged out his eye? And even if she did, how could she propose that he join too, after hearing his Eastern raid story—the story he'd never trusted with anyone else before?

Most of all, how could she say this while aiming an arrow at his heart?

Keiyo's distant footsteps grew quieter. He was almost to Vell's cell. If Pinto didn't put a stop to their escape, the Force would blame him for it. He would deserve it too, for being careless with his keys for a second time. He would lose his promotion, get sent to correction...

He grimaced, his hand slipping from the bowstring.

The arrow whipped across the corridor and struck Evaris in the face.

He blinked. She fell.

His pulse weakened as though the arrow had pierced something within him too.

"No," he whispered. "No, no, no. I couldn't have..."

His bow fell from his grip and clattered against the floor as he watched Evaris yelp and curl and push, struggling to get back to her feet.

In his effort to stop Keiyo from breaking Vell out, his brain had shut down, and his body had taken over, and now it was done. He had shot her, betrayed her in a way far worse than deceit.

"Wait!" he yelled, as though she could *choose* not to suffer. He sprinted over and tried to help her stand, but by the time his hands met her back, she fell limp to the ground again and stayed there. It was like his touch had granted her permission to give up.

"Evar—"

Her name died in his throat. To say it would confirm the fading life beside him as hers. It *couldn't* be hers. He wouldn't accept it.

The distant sound of Keiyo's footsteps caught his attention once more.

Pinto clutched her arm, feeling her pulse in his tight grip, wishing to stay by her side, but it wouldn't be fair. She was slipping away because he had so badly wanted to shut Keiyo's plan down. He needed to follow through with it—for Evaris's sake. He wouldn't let her pain amount to nothing.

"Stay with me," he said, tightening his grip. "I'll be right back, okay?"

Evaris didn't answer him.

He wielded his dagger and raced for Vell's cell.

CHAPTER 33

OLD STARS

Day 14 in Captivity | No Clocks to Read

♫ ALL IS LOST - KATIE GARFIELD ♫

Vell winced and shuffled on her metal bed. Unfamiliar voices echoed in the distance, speaking words she couldn't quite place. It had been this way for minutes, or hours, or days—she couldn't tell—but surely it was another hallucination, like the time she swore she could hear Grandfather Clock ticking from the other side of the island.

Now there were footsteps too, each one louder than the last. Her eyes fluttered open, her blurred vision barely clearing in the middle. It was enough to see shadows cast on the stone wall opposite her bars, soon followed by its shadow-maker, Keiyo Pickett.

She rubbed her eyes, certain he wasn't real. She hadn't seen him in days, or weeks, or months...

How long have I been here?

"Hey," Keiyo called, his voice crisp in her ears. That's when she knew he was real—and that he'd finally come to visit her.

She swung her legs off the bed, eager to greet him at the bars, but a wave of pain shot up her spine when her feet made contact with the floor.

She yelped and pulled her feet back, breaths falling out of rhythm as she struggled to recall what kind of injury she'd obtained or what had caused it. All she remembered from her interrogations was a blur of needles, drugs, and muffins—along with flashes of Pinto's locks and Ogga's fiery hair.

"Just breathe," Keiyo muttered. "I've got you."

He pulled a brass key out of his overcoat, and her pulse quickened. He wasn't here to visit. He was here to break her out.

Another pair of footsteps approached, and Keiyo glanced over at someone Vell couldn't see from her cell. His face twisted, his eyes sharpening as he jammed the key into the lock. He nearly turned it when a guardian dove out from the darkness, tackling him to the ground.

The key fell from the lock, clattering against the floor as Keiyo's back landed with a heavy blow, the other guardian pinning him down.

Vell gasped, forcing her feet down and gritting her teeth to fight through another wave of pain shooting up her spine. She couldn't watch another friend die thanks to a failed effort to protect her—not after Sunna.

"Stop!" she yelled.

Ignoring her plea, the attacking guardian swung his dagger down, and Keiyo jerked his head aside just in time to dodge it. The steel clashed against the stone with a sound that grated Vell's ears, and before she could even think of how to react, the guardian scoffed, jerking his dagger back up.

Then he brought it down again—aiming much lower this time. His blade landed into Keiyo's thigh, making him thrash like a fish out of water and scream at the top of his lungs.

"No!" Vell stepped forward faster than her body could handle, and her tunnel vision faded into a full black. It hurt even more to only *hear* Keiyo's pain.

The middle of her vision returned in time to see the guardian yank the dagger out of Keiyo's thigh, resulting in another surge of screams. He calmed himself faster, staring down at his wounded leg, blood spreading outward, staining his pants.

His face reddened as he looked back up at the guardian who had stabbed him, and with a grunt, he brought a tight fist up, knocking him right under his jaw.

The guardian straightened up on his knees, reeling back from Keiyo's blow—and that's when Vell saw his face clearly for the first time since he'd arrived.

She stood frozen, panting, her aching body trying to pull her to the floor. Of course it was Pinto! Who else would hold Keiyo down and stab him in the leg as though it were personal, instead of shooting him from afar? If there was one thing Vell had learned about Pinto, it was that he didn't shy away from vengeance—even if he called it justice.

As Pinto gathered himself, Keiyo turned his head toward Vell's cell, still curling in pain as he met her gaze between the bars. He reached for his bandolier with a shaky hand, plucking a throwing star free and sliding it into her cell.

Vell crouched swiftly, snatching Keiyo's star from the floor just as Pinto regained composure, rising to his feet.

Her fingers wrapped around the tool, concealing most of it from view, and its familiar feel made her eyes water. She remembered this star. It was *her* star—one from a set Keiyo had gifted her for her seventeenth birthday at the Academy, not long before graduation. The only way he could have kept it was if he'd stolen it from her flat.

As Pinto stared down at Keiyo with sharp, heavy breaths, his grip on the dagger tightened. He stepped forward, preparing to deliver a final blow.

Keiyo lay trembling on the floor, gripping his tender leg, completely defenseless.

Vell stepped back into a throwing form, exhaling a slow breath.

This is all I have.

One throwing star. She couldn't kill him with a blade this small, considering his tolerance to belladonna, so at most, she would need to put him out of commission.

She tried to aim for his good eye, but she didn't have the heart.

So instead, she aimed for his neck, and right before he crouched to stab Keiyo a second time, she flung the bladed star forward.

It spun, whirling between the cell bars and stabbing Pinto in the side of his neck. He dropped his dagger, his hands reaching for the star and yanking it free. With a shout, he gripped the open wound—it wasn't deep enough to take him down, but it caused enough pain to buy Vell and Keiyo a few more seconds to act.

She knelt by the bars, holding her hand out, urging Keiyo to pass her another star, a dart—anything she could use to keep them both alive.

A guilty look crossed Keiyo's face. He groaned and shuffled on the floor, reaching for the dropped key instead of his bandolier.

Vell frowned. Opening her cell wasn't their priority. They needed to focus on landing more hits to Pinto to slow him down and—

She froze at the sound of a body hitting the ground, and when she looked over, Pinto lay on the floor, convulsing, wailing as though a sword had sawed off a limb. She knew that reaction. It wasn't from the pain of her throwing star. It was from the *poison* on her throwing star.

Even in his current state, Pinto reached for the dagger he'd dropped, and Keiyo swerved on the ground, kicking it out of reach. Only then did he grip the bars of Vell's cell and drag himself to his feet, the key in his control again.

Vell stared past Keiyo as he swung her door open.

Pinto's mouth produced foam as he stopped crawling toward his dagger. It couldn't be belladonna that entered his system. He never forgot to take his maintenance vials.

Keiyo limped into Vell's cell, reaching out for her, but she stepped back like a wounded dog.

"What did you do?" she yelled, her eyes locked on Pinto's body.

"We need to go." Keiyo gripped her shoulders and tried to guide her toward the corridor, but tears fell down her face, and she fought against his grip.

She knew it wasn't fair. Keiyo had risked his life for her, yet she was repaying him with rage.

He's dead. Vell shook herself free from Keiyo and stumbled out alone, falling to Pinto's side.

"What kind of poison?" she demanded. *I might be able to save him.*

"He tortured you, Vell. He's not worth it."

The tears wouldn't stop as the calabar in her system loosened its grip. Her clarity returned, her sense of time striking back. She knew for certain now that two weeks had passed, and for the first time since her capture, she wasn't thinking about Pinto's silent massacre, his involvement with Ogga in her interrogations, or the time he had filled her burrow. She thought only of their shared experiences at the Academy, working to help each other graduate. She knew who he was, isolated from the Force. She *liked* who he was without the uniform.

The real Pinto didn't deserve such a tragic story.

"I'm sorry," Keiyo said, his voice softer now. He took Vell's arm with a gentle hand, and she didn't fight him anymore. She allowed her fellow graduate to help her up, crying harder as she turned her back on someone who had once been a best friend.

They traveled down the corridor, arms around each other, both struggling to stay upright. Vell looked over her shoulder at Pinto until they made their first turn, losing sight of him.

"Please," Keiyo said, urging her to move faster.

She tried to keep up with him, but she was getting dizzy again, the black edges of her vision fading in deeper, narrowing her field of view.

Keiyo shuffled to a stop, his urgency vanishing at the sight of a body.

Vell held a shaky hand over her mouth. It was Evaris, her hair draped over her face, her skin lifeless and pale. A single arrow was lodged in her head—resulting in a fate even a guardian's tolerance to belladonna couldn't escape.

Keiyo struggled to squat beside her, given his bleeding thigh, but he did so anyway, pushing through the pain. He lowered himself to Evaris's level like it was the last thing he'd ever do, gingerly pushing her hair out of her eyes.

Vell gulped as he pressed two fingers to her neck.

They waited a few seconds, then a few more.

With a sniffle, he shook his head, and Vell helped him straighten up. She could only assume, based on his reaction, that they had worked together to break her out. Another kind soul had died for her, and when she looked down at Evaris again, she saw the face of Sunna Rickabee.

Finally, closure. She saw him in death—and said goodbye.

They stepped over Evaris's body and continued, eventually reaching the foyer, where another dead guardian lay by the door. Creeping past him, they entered the cold night air.

Vell's eyes reached for the stars, which were plentiful.

Keiyo tightened his grip around her shoulder. "It's over, okay?"

She lowered her head, sobbing, and he turned to hug her, nestling his face into her neck. A moment later, he cried too. She had never seen him do that before.

They pulled away from each other when a pair of footsteps and a set of horse hooves approached.

Vell's heart skipped a beat, but Keiyo managed a chuckle as he wiped his cheeks dry.

"Relax, Vell. She's with us."

Vell frowned at the sight of the Princess bringing a white horse toward them by its lead rope. She stopped a few paces away and looked around. "Where's Commander Evaris?"

"Gone," Keiyo said dryly, springing forward into the next phase of their escape. Vell wanted to argue that he couldn't ride a horse, given his leg, but it wasn't smart for her to take over with tunnel vision and dizziness either.

Once Keiyo mounted the saddle, he held his arm out, and Vell took it, crying out as he pulled, straining her aching arms.

Kia sensed something wrong and stepped in, trying to push Vell up. It did little to help, but she appreciated the gesture nonetheless. They invited her up last, and she clung to Vell's shoulders from the back of the horse. Riding with three people would slow them down, but it was their only option.

Keiyo whipped the reins, and as they sped off into the woods, toward the western coast, Vell couldn't stop shaking. This wouldn't work. The horse would tire before reaching Eastern Territory, and Keiyo's injury needed to be treated with time they didn't have. She was finally free, but realistically, this could only be a short-lived success.

A dark, rich noise erupted in the air, shaking the ground beneath them and scaring the wildlife out of the trees. Their horse whinnied and jumped on his hind legs, nearly shoving them off the saddle.

The Princess screamed, and Keiyo yanked the reins, managing to regain control and steady their horse to a complete stop.

"What's happening?" Kia shouted over the lingering *boom*. It was still winter, but with the noise came a warm breeze.

"Sounds like a production point attack," Keiyo said, his voice dripping with worry. "But... that's never happened on our side of the island before."

"A production point attack?" Vell broke a smile, finally confirming that Saunti had managed to get his friends on board.

"The Palace?" Kia gasped. "My brother..."

Vell's eyes widened. She knew Yahshi wouldn't allow Saunti's group to kill people with their invention. There was only one building in Vakoi City they could destroy without casualties, while still leaving an impact.

"The Academy," Vell said, her voice breaking. "Keiyo, go to the Academy!"

He didn't hesitate to whip the reins, racing toward the outskirts of Vakoi City, the air growing warmer the closer they traveled, carrying soot and ash.

It didn't take long to see a rising cloud of smoke in the distance.

"You're right," Keiyo said. "It *is* the Academy."

Finally, their horse galloped onto the grass clearing, slowing to stop. Vell and Keiyo turned their heads to watch the building they'd lived in for eighteen months *burn*.

Kia chuckled. "So much for the most prestigious school in the Empire."

"Is that..." Keiyo trailed off, squinting at three silhouettes in the distance. He whipped the reins, crossing the field to reach them.

"Vell?" a familiar voice called.

Keiyo stopped their horse, and Vell peered down as Yahshi rushed up to her. He stretched his arms out, and she struggled to dismount the horse, but she had no intention of waiting. She practically fell sideways, sliding off from between Keiyo and Kia.

Yahshi caught her upright and stabilized her, wrapping her in a hug.

Her eyes watered as she burrowed into him.

"I wanted to help sooner," he choked out, resting his chin on her head.

"Happy birthday," she replied, recalling the date he'd told her by the Waterway. If she was right about how many nights had passed, he should have turned sixteen today.

"You remembered?" he whispered.

"Of course. I'm a timekeeper."

He laughed softly, though she hadn't meant to be funny, and she smiled, relishing the sound. If only she could stay in his arms longer—much longer—but there were other reunions to be made.

As they pulled away, Keiyo slumped in the saddle, wincing, and Yahshi rushed over to help him down.

"Your leg!"

"Oh, it's *fine*," Keiyo replied, his voice tight with pain. "I'll get a cool scar and everything."

"I need to mend it."

"Not *now*!" He hovered his hands over his thigh like a shield.

Saunti approached Vell next, catching her attention with a smirk. "I don't know what you did to break out, but I'm glad we didn't have to get involved."

She frowned, and it took a moment to connect the dots. Booming the Academy was not just a political move. It was their distraction to sneak into the Facility.

Vell dove in for a hug. "Thank you."

Saunti chuckled and returned the gesture, but they didn't embrace for long before Aero stole Vell away, lifting and spinning her around.

"You're okay!"

"Careful," Keiyo warned. "She's still drugged up."

"Oh." Aero stopped, leaving Vell's vision whirling. "Well, drugged is okay. Better than dead."

"Much better than dead," Keiyo agreed.

Finally, the Princess cleared her throat, drawing everyone's gazes—but her eyes were only on Yahshi.

"Hi, Commander."

In the chaos of their reunion, Yahshi hadn't even noticed her until now. He chuckled at the old honorific, and Kia smiled back.

"What are you doing here?" he asked.

She tucked her hands into her coat pockets. "I'm your hostage, of course."

"*What?*"

"Well, your *willing* hostage."

An aftershock interrupted all six of them, the ground beneath their shoes rumbling as the Academy's roof began to collapse. Vell watched, her smile fading as she recalled the memories she had made in that building. They turned bitter in retrospect, tainted by the presence of Pinto, a cruel *Nightshade*—and she didn't use that term lightly.

"Pinto's dead," she blurted out as Yahshi appeared next to her. "I didn't know Keiyo's blades were poisoned. Potentially calabar, and I used one to—"

"Good," he interrupted with a nod.

Vell's eyes widened as she faced him. It wasn't the saddened reaction she'd expected.

"He hurt you, Vell." Yahshi's fingers found hers and interlaced with them. "That's where I draw the line."

Her heart fluttered, and she stared at him for a moment longer before turning back to the Academy. A four-petaled flower emblem, matching the marks on their foreheads, fell from the gable and struck the stairs, setting off another bloom of flames.

Vell stepped closer to Yahshi and leaned her head on his shoulder. Despite the fire, a gust of hot wind carried an untarnished cherry blossom right past her eyes, and with it came a sense of clarity. There was no knowing how the next few months would play out. The Force had already captured her once, and she had spent her entire time as a prisoner regretting everything she hadn't said.

It was likely the traces of calabar in her system that urged her to speak— but she didn't care, because the words were true.

"Yahshi," she muttered, squeezing his hand tighter. "I love you."

She had said it before, but never like this.

CHAPTER 34

FINAL COUNT

Buy two boxes of Saver Store matches
and get a third for half off!

♫ PAST LIFE - COVENHOVEN ♫

A *boom* shook the ground, and Pinto gasped, his eye opening. He found himself on the floor of the Detainment Facility, his body trembling beyond control, his overcoat drenched in sweat. The cell in front of him, though blurry, was clearly void of its prisoner.

His heart raced when he realized that he couldn't recall falling asleep. The last thing he remembered was his muscles spasming as he fought against his own body, Vell and Keiyo leaving him for dead. If the poison had taken him under once, he couldn't trust that it wouldn't do so again—and the next time, he might not be lucky enough to wake up.

I don't have much time.

He shakily reached into his overcoat for his emergency neutralizer. Made of calabar, every guardian carried one in case their belladonna levels spiked beyond their tolerance. His fingers brushed against the contents of his overcoat, searching for the cold glass syringe, but his thoughts were foggy, and he couldn't quite link his touch to his knowledge of *what* he was touching.

Something cold, something cold, something cold...

He repeated the phrase like a mantra in his head, continuing to touch the items in his coat before, finally, his fingers grazed something cold.

He pulled out the syringe of calabar and held it over his leg, gritting his teeth and bracing himself to stab it through the fabric of his pants. He swung it down, but his hand fought against him, keeping the needle at a distance. His thoughts were still murky, hazy, corrupted by pain—but he knew better than to fight an instinct this close to death.

Something's wrong.

His fingers crawled to the side of his neck, feeling the wound he'd plucked the star out of. It wasn't deep, and it was his only injury—the same as the one on the dead guardian he'd seen in the foyer. A single star couldn't hold enough belladonna to overload his tolerance.

Calabar.

The realization came to him slowly, in the fading echo of the *boom*, like a whisper in his ear. Perhaps Keiyo had laced his tools with the Force's own antidote, meaning the syringe in his hand would kill him instantly.

This was a life or death decision. He wanted to mull it over, make some calculations, but he didn't have time. He could feel his body weakening again, his vision growing more blurry and fading, ever so slightly.

It took all his strength to press his finger against the plunger, releasing a stream of amber-colored emergency neutralizer onto the floor next to him. Once he'd emptied it, he reached into his overcoat again, fumbling for a vial of belladonna serum and popping off its cork stopper. It took three different attempts for him to finally get the tip of his now-empty syringe into the vial, and once he did, it took an additional few tries for him to lift the stopper back up, filling the syringe with red fluid that would either kill him or save him.

Without thinking, he stabbed the tip of the syringe into his thigh and yelped. With a few deep breaths, he pressed the plunger down halfway, injecting the belladonna serum. Over a year had passed since he'd practiced this neutralizing technique on a rabbit at the Academy, and he remembered how easily so many of them had died. If he injected too much belladonna, he would overcorrect and die.

Pinto closed his eye, tuning into the effects of his body. It took several minutes, but he could feel the shakiness in his muscles loosen. Under normal circumstances, he knew he should wait fifteen minutes to measure the effects and decide whether to inject more, but he didn't have the time. The noise that had woken him had come from somewhere nearby, here in Vakoi City.

The Force needs me.

He pressed the plunger down a little more, injecting some extra belladonna, before removing the needle from his leg. His breaths began to stabilize, the tightness in his chest subsiding. He tucked the belladonna-filled syringe into his overcoat, rose to his feet, and pressed his palm against the walls to steady his dizzy self. The corridor seemed to rock back and forth as he made his way down, his boot splashing in the pool of amber neutralizer.

Pinto crept forward, one hand pressed against the wall as he took one step after the other, wondering what the noise could have been. Had the Underground attacked Vakoi Palace and killed Emperor Vakoi? He hoped not, but whatever it was, he needed to put a stop to it. He had already failed at keeping Vell as a prisoner, and he could not afford to give the Force any more reason to punish him.

He had nearly reached the foyer when he encountered a body.

Evaris.

Pinto's eye widened, and he pushed himself from the wall, nearly tripping as he took a few steps toward her. Nevertheless, he continued, slowly gaining confidence on his feet again.

"Evaris," he muttered, kneeling beside her and touching her limp arm. His own arrow had pierced her head, and though he knew it could have killed her by now, he clung to the hope that he could pull her out of the darkness, like the booming noise had done to him.

"Please, don't go." Pinto clutched her arm tighter, his hands shaking at the realization that her body was colder than it should have been. "Don't leave me. I didn't mean to."

Evaris lay in the cold, her lips parted, unmoving. He reached for her neck.

A pulse.

Beat. Beat. Beat.

His eye watered as a dull sign of life pressed against his fingers.

"Don't worry. I'm getting you out of here." He pulled his hand away to lift her, freezing at the realization that the pulse against his fingers remained.

"Is this real?" He felt her neck again, then pulled away a second time.

Her pulse lingered like a ghostly joke.

"Have I been imagining it?"

Evaris didn't reply, and Pinto leaned over, holding her, shaking as the tears fell. The coldness of her neck proved that the pulse *wasn't* real. He *had* imagined it.

"I'm sorry," he choked out between breaths. "I wasn't thinking. I need you..."

He forgot about the noise outside and his duty as a guardian. It was just him and Evaris now, and all he could think of were their moments together—the good and the bad.

He thought of the day they'd visited the Paturas, when she'd nudged him with her boot under the table, urging him to stop tapping his foot.

He thought of those first few days traveling through Eastern Territory, when they both resisted each other—and themselves—for a chance to get closer.

He thought of their first kiss in Atherus City, when he'd felt, for a fleeting moment, that if they were to leave the Force together and never turn back, they could be happy.

We could have been happy.

Pinto sobbed, embracing her, his grip unrestrained. He would have feared squeezing her too tightly, but he didn't, because he knew she was already gone. If only it had been Keiyo or Vell who had killed her, and not himself. If only she had died by some fatal accident that was not his own arrow. It couldn't have been *he* who had done this—not after all they'd been through.

He recalled Sunna's uniform fitting in that dusty room, and how Evaris had wiped the cobwebs from Pinto's back, playfully asking if he loved her. He wished he could return to that moment and tell her that he did. Of course he loved her. He loved her more than anything in this world.

When they had changed out of their uniforms into normal clothes, he should have told her, *Let's run away from this place. Let's escape, just like Yahshi did, and live our lives together. Our love isn't fit for the Force.*

He took a few deep breaths, fighting against another stream of tears. There was no denying now that she had stolen his keys, but he knew, as he looked back on their shared time in his flat, that she hadn't wanted to betray him. He remembered her shimmering eyes, right before they had kissed, and in them, he found an apology.

If only I could give her the same.

Pinto gulped hard to clear the clot in his throat, reaching into Evaris's overcoat for her notepad. He flipped to the first page, a few tears spotting the *X*s and *O*s as he did what she had never been brave enough to do.

"Honestly, I'm too scared to tally my Xs and Os," she had told him. *"Maybe someday I'll manage to count."*

So he did. He sat there in the darkness, hunched over her body, flipping through page after page. He counted every mark she had made, keeping a careful count of each good and bad deed.

When he reached the part of the book when Sunna died—recognizing it by the multiple shaky *O*s in a row that he'd crossed out for her—he counted them anyway, even though she rewrote them afterward. He counted the extras because he knew she would have been careful like that, to ensure that her answer was true, without a doubt.

Pinto turned a few more pages before reaching the end and tucking the notepad into his overcoat. He would keep this little piece of her with him. He would never let it go.

A faint smile was all he could manage as he grazed his hand against her cheek, just as he had in the Suvo house in Atherus City.

"You're a good one, Evaris." He bit his trembling lip. "You're the greatest."

Another stream of tears fell as he rose to his feet, staring down at her dead body. He couldn't hold back his tears anymore, nor did he want to. He needed to remember this. He deserved to pay the price for what he'd done. He deserved a million *O*s in a notepad of his own, and he would spend the rest of his life futilely tallying up *X*s that would never amount to enough.

It was likely the traces of calabar in his system that urged him to speak—but he didn't care, because the words were true.

"I love you."

He wished he had said it before, exactly like this.

Pinto stopped his horse at what remained of Belladonna Guardian Academy. Nearly a hundred guardians huddled in groups on the clearing, embracing each other as the building that shaped them crumbled to ashes under the moonlight.

The Academy—their most treasured place, their second home—melted in flames that roared and hissed with a fury.

Galler and Boa stared at the destruction, stone-faced.

Famir rubbed Embre's back as she sobbed.

Roz cursed and drew a dagger as though he could fight it.

The dark bags under everyone's eyes proved that the booming noise had woken them. They had rushed to save what they loved but were too late.

I know how that feels, Pinto thought as Evaris's notepad pressed against his heart.

He dismounted his horse and stumbled as his boots met the grass. The remaining calabar in his bloodstream still clung to him with a deathly grip, and it took Quax's steady hands on his shoulders to stop him from falling.

"Where is he?" Quax yelled.

Pinto stared over his unit member's shoulder at the fire, his stomach twisting into a knot as the hot wind blew soot into his face.

"Where's Keiyo?" His grip on Pinto's shoulders tightened. "He wasn't in his flat when the bells rang, and then I realized you were gone too, and I thought you might be together, or…"

Pinto ignored his babbling, shaking free from his hold and limping toward the fire alone. His head raced with every memory he had made in that building. Five hundred and forty-six days, each as clear as crystal. They turned bitter in retrospect, tainted by the presence of Yahshi and Vell, traitors who had burned his life to the ground.

"Pinto!" Quax called from behind, his voice an urgent plea.

A hand gripped Pinto's arm, stopping him. At first, he assumed it was Quax, but when he turned, a pair of fiery eyes scorched him.

"Where the hell have you been?" Ogga demanded. His hair was red like the flames.

Pinto's breaths quickened, his vision darkening as he remembered the consequences he'd face. Demotion. Correction. Potentially *execution*. Perhaps he deserved it. He had lost the Force's most valuable prisoner, had killed a fellow guardian, and had woken too late to catch the terrorists behind the Academy's attack. He had failed in every possible way. If only he had allowed the poison to kill him instead—it would surely be a kinder fate than whatever the Force had in store for him.

He gasped for air, struggling to hold his gaze on Ogga. One moment, he was staring into the old man's hair, and the next, he was looking at the flames again. Ogga. Academy. Ogga. Academy. He couldn't keep still, and the jolting of his head left his vision blurry until all he could see was red.

Red.

Two hands gripped his shoulders again, shaking him. "Get a hold of yourself!"

"I-I was trying to stop them," Pinto muttered, his vision whirling. "But Keiyo got away with Vell, and Evaris—"

He choked. He couldn't say it.

Ogga's voice hardened. "And Evaris?"

Slowly, Pinto's vision returned, and he found himself staring up at the old man, his mouth curling into a pout he couldn't hide.

"I killed her, Professor." A few more tears fell down his face, but the other guardians didn't care. For all they knew, he was crying about the Academy.

Ogga stared back at him, his face expressionless.

"I didn't mean to. Really, I wish I could take it back. I wish I could—"

"Stop." Ogga broke and held up his palm, a disgusted look spreading across his face. "Enough with the tears. You don't need her."

Pinto stiffened, his blood running cold.

Suddenly, he was five years old, trembling in his childhood home, clutching his little sister. The neighbors outside were screaming—his mother, inside, wailing.

Ahead of him lurked a man in a dark, hooded coat, and the shadows of the night no longer cloaked his face.

"You don't need her," said a younger Ogga, a flash of red peeking out from under his hood.

It was him. It had *always* been him.

Pinto turned away from the hooded man, finding himself back on the field, staring at the blazing Academy. He was eighteen again, dressed in the uniform of the organization that had taken his eye.

He fell to his knees, and the heat caressed his face. It was the only source of warmth he had left.

POISONOUS
REMEDY

BELLADONNA, BOOK 3

While the Force scrambles to restore order and loyalty,
the Underground fights to maintain their lead
despite dwindling supplies.

ACKNOWLEDGMENTS

Thank you to my editors, Katie Flanagan and Eesha Prakruthi "Nyx" Kavattur, for helping me improve *Underground Royalty*—and for catching every time I accidentally referred to Pinto as having eyes instead of a singular eye (sometimes my fingers forget).

Thank you to Aleksandra at MAD Book Covers, once again, for the beautiful cover design.

Thank you to Dad, Mom, John, Aunt Robin, and Uncle Tom for your encouragement and support.

Thank you to Sebastian Delgado for listening to my insufferable rants about this book and the songs on its playlist over and over and over...

As always, this story wouldn't be what it is without the advice of my incredible beta readers:

Luke Veldkamp, Laurel O'Brien, Germaine Han, S. J. Robert, Jamie Pitman, Martine Alexandra Hassel Baardseth, Jaclyn B, Ishana Balan, Victoria Nunweiller, Víctor Cantelar Sagrado, Hessa S, Anaïs L, Abigail Lavery, Concha Alvarez

Thank you to Grayson Taylor for the accountability check-ins. Our impending calls pushed me to finish this book on time.

Shoutout to my fellow authors at Lost Island Press—Shira Behore, Amanda Michelle Brown, Sowon Kim, and Julia Rosemary Turk.

Thank you to Angie, Joy, Liza, Non, Ploy, and Kayla. Even though we rarely see each other, your friendship means the world to me.

Last but not least, thank *you* (yes, you) for reading this. It means a lot to me that you picked up the second book in this series. I hope you'll join me for the next one.

MAELIN

A BELLADONNA NOVELLA

Uncover the shocking truth behind Maelin's death through the eyes of a young Blimmery, long before his time as *Nightshade Academy*'s beloved instructor.

CAPSULE

When a menacing app called Capsule auto-installs onto Jackie's phone, she enters a game interlaced with reality —a game threatening to kill.

LEAVING WISHVILLE

Ten years after his father's disappearance, Benji plans to escape from his self-isolated coastal town—but leaving Wishville may cost him his life.

ABOUT THE AUTHOR

MEL TORREFRANCA is a full-time author and founder of Lost Island Press. Her books feature morally gray characters, bold endings, and a pinch of awkward humor. Mel discovered her passion for writing at the age of seven and published her debut novel, *Leaving Wishville*, during high school. She also drinks way too many lattes.

MELTORREFRANCA.COM

ABOUT THE PUBLISHER

LOST ISLAND PRESS publishes dystopian, sci-fi, and fantasy books. Unlike mainstream presses, we don't publish everything for everyone. We publish for *you*. Our catalog offers grounded, character-driven stories that linger long after the last page. The kind you get lost in, that keep you up at night. And because our books have the same vibe, if you enjoy one, you'll enjoy them all.

LOSTISLANDPRESS.COM

Join our newsletter to claim a free ebook

9 781962 876087